TURQUOISE SEAS

A Tale of the Old Bahamas

ROSEMARY MINNS

Media Enterprises
Nassau, Bahama
2020

Minns, Rosemary.
Turquoise Seas: a tale of the old Bahamas / Rosemary Minns.
pages cm.
ISBN 978-976-8231-92-5
1.Bahamain literature. 2. Pirates—Bahamas—Fiction.
PR9220.9 .M56 T87 2020

Cover design and photography Tamara Knowles
Schooner image - https://commons.wikimedia.org/wiki/File:La_Recouvrance.JPG

Media Enterprises Ltd
31 Shirley Park Avenue, P.O. Box N-9240, Nassau, Bahamas
Tel: 242-325-8210   Fax: 242-325-8065
E-mail: bahamasmedia@gmail.com   www.bahamasmedia.com

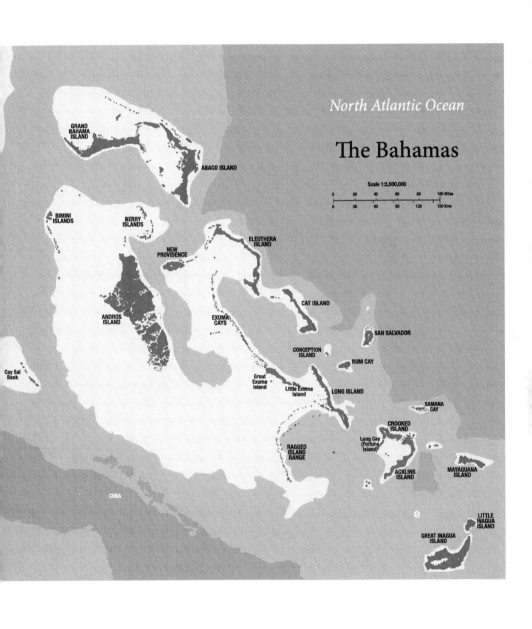

North Atlantic Ocean

The Bahamas

GRAND
BAHAMA
ISLAND

ABACO ISLAND

BIMINI
ISLANDS

BERRY
ISLANDS

NEW
PROVIDENCE

ELEUTHERA
ISLAND

CAT ISLAND

ANDROS
ISLAND

EXUMA
CAYS

SAN SALVADOR

CONCEPTION
ISLAND

RUM CAY

Cay Sal
Bank

Great
Exuma
Island

Little Exuma
Island

LONG ISLAND

SAMANA
CAY

CROOKED
ISLAND

Long Cay
(Fortune
Island)

RAGGED
ISLAND
RANGE

ACKLINS
ISLAND

MAYAGUANA
ISLAND

CUBA

LITTLE
INAGUA
ISLAND

GREAT INAGUA
ISLAND

Scale 1:3,500,000

0   20   40   60   80   100 Miles
0   30   60   90   120   150 Kms

1

The clatter of hooves brought Kath O'Brien running to her cottage door early in the morning. She leaned out the top half of her door just in time to see Sheriff Hugh Twynam and two men ride through the open gate to their property, which was surrounded by a dry stone wall.

Morning sun drenched the world and a lark was singing off in the meadow, its joyful melody cascading through the warm air in celebration of the glorious day. For the rest of her life, this moment would remain fixed in Kath's mind as the point when her life changed forever.

The riders were leading a horse with a man tied across its saddle.

Holy Mary, could it be Duncan or Kevin? One of her boys? No, the riders passed her door and stopped two hundred feet further along, in front of her sister-in-law Maggie's cottage. Blessed Mother of God, it was her nephew Evan, then!

"Untie him and get him down," the Sheriff said. "We've got to push on to Ballyvale House."

The men dismounted and untied their prisoner, who slipped from the horse and fell to the stony path with a thump. One of the men moved to help the lad up.

"Oh, leave him!" the Sheriff commanded, wheeling his horse. He started for the gate as his men scrambled to remount.

Kath ran over to join Maggie as she and her three littlest ones boiled out of their cottage.

"Evan!" Maggie wailed, as she bent over the crumpled form of her eldest son. The little children started crying when they saw their brother's face, which was purple, swollen and crusted with blood, while the two women lifted Evan to his feet.

"What happened?" Maggie demanded.

"Oh Mam!" Evan groaned out. "Sheriff took us...beat us..." He gasped, then yelped as his mother touched his left shoulder.

"What's the matter?" Maggie asked sharply.

"My shoulder..." Evan replied with another groan, and started shivering.

Maggie pulled his shirt collar aside. "Your collar bone's broken," she said, and put her palm on his forehead. "And you're feverish!"

Maggie turned to her seven-year-old. "Cullen, run and ask Mrs. Ryan to come quickly! And you Evan, lean on me!" She put an arm around his waist. "Kath, go throw the mattress in front of the fire. We'll lay him there."

Kath rushed into the cottage, her heart pounding. Inside, a peat fire smoldered, its pungent odor mingling with the ripe scent from the byre at the end of the room where the animals were kept at night. She hurried to the sack of straw hanging from a nail on the wall. She shook it and laid it on one side of the fireplace, just as Maggie and Evan came staggering in with the wailing children.

The women laid Evan down and covered him with a blanket.

Maggie took a bowl from the shelf by the fireplace and ladled hot water from the cauldron hanging over the fire.

"Pass me that rag on the table, Kath. Let's clean him up. And you children stop that racket! Evan's all right! Go outside and play now!" Maggie pointed towards the door. "Go on, get out of the way!" Maggie dabbed at Evan's face. His breath came whistling softly through his swollen lips.

"Why did they beat you?" Kath asked Evan. "What happened?"

"Sheriff's men came to Sumner's Farm looking for us O'Briens. Said we'd killed Lord Roxbury's lamb. Duncan said he had done it, and to leave Kevin and me alone, we were innocent. Sheriff took us anyway."

Maggie and Kath exchanged puzzled looks. "Killed a lamb! But why?" Kath asked. "Where are my Duncan and Kevin now?"

"Don't know," Evan replied. "Twas dark when we got there, a big empty room is all I know. They beat me first, made Duncan and Kevin watch, then they beat Kevin. To teach us a lesson Sheriff said."

Maggie put dried herbs into a jug and added boiling water. In a few minutes she poured the tea into a wooden cup and held it to Evan's lips. "Drink some of this, son," she coaxed. "It'll help you feel better." The tea ran from the corners of his mouth as he tried to swallow.

Kath paced back and forth, wringing her hands. Duncan and Kevin! Her rash, headstrong boys...what had they got up to now? Yes, they poached the occasional pheasant or rabbit, but kill a lamb? Lord Roxbury's lamb? "Do you know anything about this Evan?" she asked.

"No, but Duncan said he did it. And Kevin said he helped him."

"I don't doubt they would be in it together, whatever they did. Those two are thick as thieves!" Kath replied.

Maggie continued cleaning Evan's face. "And those English have no pity!" she exclaimed. "I hate them! To beat a lad of fifteen like this...really it's better to be one of their horses than Irish! Their horses have oats and warm stables. We starve and struggle for food, while they thrive on land they stole from us!"

Kath stood by the door, frowning, looking down the lane. She was too worried to berate the English. She hated the English Protestants too, but her two sons were lying somewhere now, probably in a worse state than Evan. She walked over to the table, sat down and put her head in her hands. "Oh Maggie, what am I to do? If only I knew where my boys are. If only John were here!"

Kath had struggled to raise Duncan and Kevin alone, since John had been hanged as a Rebel nine years before. She had done her best to be father and mother. She had worked long hours sewing for a few shillings, and working in their vegetable garden, to keep them clothed and fed. She had tried to teach them good manners, to read and write, to be good Catholics by learning their catechism. She had constantly preached at them to stay away from bad company.

Her boys were exuberant as all boys were, rough and tumble, scraping knees, getting into fights. She was constantly mending their clothes, trying to keep them decent. It had been exhausting, although the pressure on her had eased now that they were out of the house, and had gone to work on the Sumner Farm. She felt overwhelmed with this new trouble, unable to cope.

"John should have thought of his family before getting mixed up with the Rebels," Maggie said sharply, as she spooned tea into Evan. "But no, he was always too canny to be caught by the English."

"Well, his brother, your own Patrick, was in with them too!" Kath replied hotly. "Patrick was lucky to escape when John was taken. We all knew the risks; but our men had to fight for Ireland. Though I'm glad Patrick has seen sense and stopped going with the rebels now."

"I can't tell you how relieved I am about that," Maggie said. "But your John was too devil-may-care. He never backed down from anything. And your Duncan's just like him! It's a wonder he's not been in trouble before now." Maggie looked up. Kath's delicate, heart-shaped face was strained and white; her generous mouth, always smiling, was now pinched with anxiety. "Pour us a cup of tea, Kath dear," Maggie's tone was gentler. "It'll help calm our nerves."

"Duncan and Kevin were only seven and five years old," Kath mused as she poured tea into two wooden cups on the table. "I'd have died of a broken heart, if I hadn't had them to live for." Kath turned to Maggie, her green eyes glittering with unshed tears. "They just can't take them from me now. They're all I have!"

Maggie sighed. "I wish Cullen and Mrs. Ryan would come." Taking the bowl of bloody water to the door, she threw it out onto the grass and looked down the lane. "Oh, here's Mrs. Ryan coming now!"

Kath sat and took a gulp of tea, and gazed out the open door.

Finally she put her cup down with a rap. "I can't just sit here, drinking tea and doing nothing!" She got up and strode to the door. "You take care of Evan. Mrs. Ryan will know what to do. I'm going up to Ballyvale House to see if I can find out anything. That's where the Sheriff said he was going." Her eyes narrowed. "I've nearly finished that set of table linens Mrs. Doherty bespoke for Lady Roxbury. I can take them over now. If she notices that two napkins aren't embroidered, I'll pretend I overlooked it."

She sighed. "We'll be needing money; and Mrs. Doherty still owes me for all that bed linen I embroidered last year. I've been waiting nine months! The English have no conscience! Why won't they pay what they owe? If Mrs. Doherty hasn't the money by her, I'll demand to see Lady Roxbury herself!" She looked down at her fingers, thinking. "Or, she can keep the money, in payment for the sheep. Maybe that'll put it right. And maybe I can find out where they're holding the boys. They might even be right there at Ballyvale House."

"At least you'll feel you're doing something," Maggie sympathized.

Kath opened the door, said a terse good morning to Mrs. Ryan, and hurried over to her own cottage. Suddenly her stomach was in knots, with blood rushing in her ears. She collapsed on a bench just inside her door and doubled over. Acid foamed in her mouth. She spat through the open door.

When the nausea receded, Kath lurched over to a bucket standing on the rough plank table, splashed water on her face, and then drank from her cupped hands. "I must clear my head and decide exactly how to go about this," she mumbled to herself. "Ach, I want to get going! I'll think about it on the way over there."

She moved to the fireplace and put more turf on the fire. On the mantle shelf was a small picture of the Virgin Mary, a wooden crucifix and her rosary. She took down the rosary and lovingly fingered its amber beads. It was the only thing of value she owned, and had been passed down through generations of women in her family. She would take it with her, to pray as she walked. Then, kneeling before the picture and crucifix, she made the sign of the cross.

"Blessed Virgin Mother," she prayed aloud "...remember what it was like when your Son was beaten, and put to death. Please pray for us now. Have mercy on me and my sons, I beg you. Please keep them safe!"

Kath got up, combed her long dark hair, put on her best dress, cap and shawl, and then threw on her old cloak. She put her shoes, stockings and gloves in a basket with the parcel of needlework on top and headed out, kicking the door shut as she left.

2

Ballyvale House lay six miles from the O'Brien family property, over hilly country. Kath set out hoping that someone would pass by and give her a lift. No one did.

As she climbed, the countryside spread out beneath her. The meadows were full of wild flowers and made a patchwork of green, with golden gorse growing along the dry stone walls separating the fields. Far off in the distance, past the peat bogs, beyond the silver-glinting lakes, the purple hills brooded.

Kath thought about meeting Lady Roxbury; she must curtsy and call her "My Lady." She practiced saying it aloud, and made a few trial curtsies as she walked, holding her skirt out and bending her knees. She had never met Lady Roxbury, but she had seen her once, cantering along their lane on her little gray mare, following the hunt.

Kath had been sitting under a tree with Maggie at the time, shelling peas. Suddenly Maggie had grabbed her arm and pointed. "See there! Quick!" Maggie had said. "That's Lady Roxbury!" Kath had turned to follow Maggie's pointing finger. For one brief moment she had glimpsed a neat figure in scarlet and black, blonde hair beneath a feather-plumed riding hat, sitting sidesaddle on a horse. For weeks after that Kath had thought of Lady Roxbury. She could not help wondering what it would be like to live in a manor house with servants and have all the food and firewood you could ever need. Not have to think about it even. *Like her own family used to have just twenty-five years ago.* She could barely remember it now, she'd only been a little girl of seven when they'd lost everything.

Kath knew Lady Roxbury would probably never speak to the likes of her, a despised Irish Catholic. Scum of the earth to the English Protestants! Kath spat at the hedgerow. In truth, she wondered if she'd even find the nerve to demand to see Lady Roxbury if Mrs. Doherty, the housekeeper, wouldn't pay. Mrs. Doherty herself was intimidating enough.

*

Just inside the gates of Ballyvale House, Kath stopped to change. She put on her shoes, stockings, and gloves, combed her hair, and dusted herself down. Leaving her cloak and everyday things behind a shrub, she squared her shoulders and set off up the drive to the house. Tall chestnut trees lined the way, covered in spikes of waxy blossom, standing like candles against the rustling leaves. What a chestnut harvest they must give in autumn! Kath's stomach rumbled, thinking of roasting chestnuts at Christmas. Her feet began to hurt.

The chestnut avenue ended and Kath emerged onto the green lawns surrounding Ballyvale House. Kath hadn't seen the house since she'd delivered the bed linen all those months ago, and now it took her breath away.

Set in acres of tended gardens and built of massive stone blocks, Ballyvale House stood three stories high. There were six wide steps leading up to the columned front door, with three French windows on either side. More windows gleamed from the upper stories. On the left was a terrace with stone railings and steps leading to the lawns. A path wound through formal gardens and down to the lake, where a large willow dripped its branches into the water. There was a small jetty, with a little boat tied up. A gazebo stood on the far side of the lake, with morning glories twining through its latticed walls.

Kath sat down to rest, and to drink in the sight for a moment before facing Mrs. Doherty. At thirty-two, she was not as energetic as she'd been in her young years, and it felt good to sit and rub her sore feet. But only a few minutes had passed before Kath heard dogs barking, the sound moving towards her. She scrambled to stand, her heart leaping into her throat as two Irish wolfhounds rushed towards her.

"Remus! Bruce!" a voice shouted. "To me!" Like magic, the dogs loped over to a stooped old man who came from the back of the house. It was Mr. McFadden, the Scottish gardener. Kath exhaled with relief, hands over her heart, breathing again.

"Sit and stay!" McFadden commanded, and the dogs dropped to the ground, long pink tongues lolling from their mouths. "Oh, it's you, Missus O'Brien," McFadden said, his piercing blue eyes peering from beneath bushy white eyebrows. "These two hairy beasts must have given you quite a fright. What brings you here today?"

"I've brought some table linens for Lady Roxbury," Kath answered, clutching her basket to her chest. "Mrs. Doherty bespoke them several months ago. Would Lady Roxbury be at home?"

"No, I believe Lady Roxbury is in Belfast visiting her sister." McFadden replied. "But Mrs. Doherty is here. Come along with me. You look all done in! Don't worry about Remus and Bruce, they won't hurt you. They're awful big, but they're daft soft things."

Kath followed McFadden, making sure she kept him between herself and the frolicking dogs. Around the back of the house, Kath saw the large kitchen garden and an orchard, with a stream running through it into the lake. McFadden opened the kitchen door and delicious, savory odors wafted out. Kath's mouth watered; she had eaten nothing since early morning.

"Mrs. Nugent, is Mrs. Doherty about?" McFadden asked the cook, who was making pastry at a large wooden table in the center of the room. A young girl sat by the hearth peeling apples. "Mrs. O'Brien has brought some linens for her."

"I believe she's above stairs," the cook replied. "Sheila, go and tell Mrs. Doherty that Mrs. O'Brien is here."

Kath stood just inside the kitchen door and leaned against the wall. The kitchen was large, with cupboards and work areas down one side. The hearth took up half the other side, and a cauldron above the fire gave off the fragrant aroma of stewing meat. Hooks with shining pots and pans covered the wall to the right of the hearth, while larger pans were stacked on an iron rack to the left.

On a shelf near Kath was an exquisite small silver mug, engraved with "Charles Roxbury". Its soft gleam beckoned Kath. She sidled over so she could look at it properly, could touch it. She traced the delicate chasing with her index finger, marveling at its smooth coolness. The only sounds were the bubble of stew, the click of Mrs. Nugent's rolling pin and the tick of a large clock on the end wall, showing ten minutes to eleven.

Mrs. Doherty burst through the door at the far end of the kitchen, her black dress rustling. Kath jumped; she whipped her hand back, plunging it into her skirt pocket.

"Yes, Mrs. O'Brien," Mrs. Doherty said crisply. "What can I do for you?" She wore her red hair in a severe bun at the nape of her neck. She had a ruddy complexion, with a nose that seemed to smell something unpleasant.

Kath proffered her crumpled parcel, wrapped in an old piece of coarse linen. "I've brought the table linen you bespoke."

"Well, let's have a look at it," Mrs. Doherty answered, taking the package over to one end of the table, untying the string. She unfolded the tablecloth and closely examined the finely woven embroidered linen. "I must say, Mrs. O'Brien, you do a grand job. There's no finer work this side of Londonderry," her voice warmed a degree or two to deliver this grudging praise.

Finished with the tablecloth, Mrs. Doherty began inspecting each napkin. "Look at this work, Mrs. Nugent! Mrs. O'Brien is a nonpareil...." Then she saw the two unfinished napkins. "What is this?" Mrs. Doherty's voice plunged back into frost. "Two napkins are not embroidered! What do you mean by bringing me unfinished work, Mrs. O'Brien?"

"Unfinished?" Kath quavered. "Let me see... Oh, Mrs. Doherty, I am sorry, I've made a mistake. I thought everything was finished!"

"Mistake? How could you make such a mistake?"

"And am I not human, Mrs. Doherty? All humans make mistakes."

"But not a mistake like this, Mrs. O'Brien. Not you, at any rate."

"Well, Mrs. Doherty, I confess that I brought the work in a great hurry. I'm in desperate need for the money just now." Kath wiped her forehead with the back of her hand. "If you could see your way to paying me what's owed for the bed linen and most of the money for this work so far, I'd be ever so grateful. I have been working for nine months now, with no pay at all."

"Indeed!" Mrs. Doherty's eye brows shot up. "D'you think you can come here with unfinished work and demand immediate payment?"

"Mrs. Doherty, this is a large order, full of embroidery and lace!" Kath's face grew pink. "I've worked on it all these months, every day and far into the nights. And Lady Roxbury still owes me for the bed linens I delivered last December. All my time has gone into working for her since last year September. That's nine months of my time I've not been paid for."

"And what of it? D'you think her ladyship's not good for the money, Mrs. O'Brien?"

"I think no such thing, Mrs. Doherty. 'Tis because I know she's good for it that I undertook the work." Kath's voice rose. "Any road, I'll thank you now for six guineas to cover the work done thus far, finished or not. Of course you must hold back the remaining ten shillings and sixpence until I finish the embroidery on the two napkins. That is only fair. But I want my money now, because I am in desperate need of it. And I'll have my three guineas for the bed linen as well. That is only fair, too."

"Well, Madam!" Mrs. Doherty bristled. "You've kept us waiting all this time, but you expect to be paid immediately! Now we'll see who waits. In any case, Mr. Lynch, his lordship's steward, is not here, and it is he who handles the money."

"I want to see Lady Roxbury then," Kath said, sticking her chin out and clenching her hands.

"So you want to see her ladyship, do you?" Mrs. Doherty replied, arms akimbo, her face turning a mottled purple. "The impudence! What makes you think her ladyship would see the likes of you? She has better things to do, woman. I'll have you know that I am the housekeeper here, and you'll deal with me! You'd best be off. Go on, be gone about your business!" Mrs. Doherty bustled to the kitchen door and wrenched it open.

"Is Lady Roxbury here, then?" Kath asked, standing her ground.

"It's no concern of yours where her ladyship is," Mrs. Doherty shouted. "Be off with you!"

Kath didn't move from the kitchen table. "Well, Mrs. Doherty, you owe me six guineas for this work here, and three guineas for the bed linen I delivered last December." Kath straightened her shoulders, drawing herself up to her full five feet two inches. "Please see that Mr. Lynch is informed of this bill and that I get my nine guineas as soon as possible."

The kitchen door slammed shut as Mrs. Doherty let go the latch. "Oh I see," Mrs. Doherty said silkily, advancing on Kath. "You want your nine guineas as soon as possible! And we all know why you're so desperate for it today. We know all about your two thieving sons. You want Lord Roxbury to pay you so you can help them, the very ones who stole his lordship's sheep! You used this table linen as an excuse to come here, hoping for the chance to snivel to her ladyship."

"What's wrong with you, Helen Doherty?" Kath asked, stepping nearer to her. "Have you no pity at all? Working for these English Protestants has made you just like them! You're Irish too, you know! And I suppose you've forgotten all about Cory Brody, now that you're so grand! Remember how you felt back then? Before your precious English hanged him?"

"Get out!" Mrs. Doherty screeched. She raised her right hand and slapped Kath hard across the face. "How dare you come here and demand money? I'll set the dogs on you! I've never seen such impudence!"

"Oh, so I'm beneath you now. You'll set the dogs on me, will you!" Kath's face flamed, her voice grew louder. "I'm Irish, with thieving sons, while you are the housekeeper for Lord and Lady Roxbury. Just remember I was married to John O'Brien! There was no finer man in all Ireland, save perhaps Cory Brody, and you know it! And I know that you were Cory Brody's sweetheart. If Cory had not been hanged with John, you'd be Mrs. Brody today."

Mrs. Doherty's eyes widened, her face blanched. But Kath wasn't through. She felt a thrill at hitting home, a deep satisfaction over the effect her words had on Mrs. Doherty, and now she couldn't stop herself. "So now butter wouldn't melt in your mouth." Kath wanted to lash out and hurt, make somebody pay for her own sorrows. "You didn't even have the courage to stand beside your man's coffin. Why, you couldn't have people know that you were mixed up with those filthy Irish Rebels!"

Mrs. Doherty seemed turned to stone. Mrs. Nugent and Sheila looked first at Kath and Mrs. Doherty, then at each other, like two hens with the gape.

Then Kath turned and fled through the door, banging it shut behind her. Pausing to see where the dogs were, she hurried towards the drive and the long walk back home. How stupid she had been, to think she could find help in an English lord's house. It was ridiculous to expect mercy, or even decency from the English!

Once under cover of the chestnuts, she stopped to take off her shoes. Both feet showed signs of blistering. Oh, she had done it now, she thought. Why had she blathered on about Corey Brody? Helen Doherty was the only person who might have helped her.

Suddenly anguish overwhelmed her. She leaned against a chestnut tree, buried her face in her arms, and sobbed.

3

Bleary-eyed and spent, Kath collected her belongings from the bush by the gate and began the long walk home. This time no hope accompanied her. Putting one wooden foot before the other took all the energy she could muster. If only she could be home right now, she thought, she'd rip off her clothes and fling herself into bed. She just wanted to hide somewhere dark and warm, where nobody would ever find her.

Kath felt chagrined, not only by Helen Doherty, but also by her own indiscretion. Mrs. Doherty would probably *never* pay her now; she might not be able to pay *anyone* soon, poor creature. She would likely lose her job if Mrs. Nugent or Sheila talked. Kath couldn't worry about her now, though. She needed to think about Duncan and Kevin. What was happening to them? Where were they? If only she knew. Kath imagined them being tortured, beaten bloody and bruised, like Evan was. Also, stealing a sheep was a capital offence. They could be hanged for this if it was true. She could hardly see the path for tears.

Just then Kath became aware of creaking cartwheels, and turned to see old Jock McFadden, the gardener from Ballyvale House.

"Hop on, Mrs. O'Brien," McFadden said, stopping his sturdy brown donkey and holding out his hand to help her up beside him. "I'm just going over Creagh way to bring back some turf. That'll take me right by your door."

"Thank you, Mr. McFadden," Kath replied, swallowing hard. She knew he had timed his errand to help her out, and she was grateful for his kindness.

"There, lassie," the old Scotsman said. "I know your trouble. The news has spread like moor-fire. There's nowt ye can do about it. The Sassenach laird and his lady are like flint, there'll be no pity for ye there." McFadden glanced shrewdly at Kath. "I take it that was your real errand this morning?"

"It was," Kath replied, her voice low and hopeless. "And I got rough handling for my pains. Mrs. Doherty wouldn't pay me and threatened to turn the dogs on me. And she herself an Irish woman!"

"Aye, she's a hard one, Mrs. Doherty," McFadden replied. "Toadies to the English something awful. Makes ye sick to see it. She'll never help ye. Do ye know she's joined the Church o' England? Goes in all her finest of a Sunday morning and stands simpering by the door at the English as they leave." McFadden was a staunch Presbyterian, and didn't think much of the Church of England himself.

Kath was shocked. "You mean she actually turned her back on the Pope and the Catholic Church – just to curry favor with the English? Why, she'll be excommunicated and go to Hell!"

"Could be just the place for her," McFadden said, his lips twitching. "She'd have the run of the place in no time. The Devil himself would have to mind his P's and Q's, or she'd roast him on her pitchfork. They're probably cousins, anyhow!" Kath gave him a wan smile, in spite of her woes.

"Ah, that's better, lassie," McFadden said, squeezing her hand for an instant. "Now you've to think what's best to do."

"If only I knew where they've taken them. Very likely I can't do anything, but at least I could go and try to see them, find out what's happening." She twisted to look into his face. "Have you heard anything, Mr. McFadden?"

"Aye, lassie, I have," he replied. "They're in Ballycrana lock-up. The Sheriff came over for Mr. Lynch about nine o'clock this morning and I overheard. They're to be taken on to Londonderry. The English judge is there just now, and the assizes are to begin next week, with Judge Thwaites presiding. The Sheriff needed Mr. Lynch to prefer charges."

19

"Judge Thwaites! Isn't he the one who hangs everybody?"

"Aye, lass, 'tis he," McFadden replied, his blue eyes looking worried under tangled white eyebrows. "It doesn't bode well for your lads."

Kath felt numb. Her mind was in such turmoil she couldn't think. She had another spell of feeling faint, and Jock McFadden watched her with concern.

"Are ye all right, lass?" he asked. "I think ye could do with something to eat. Have ye eaten aught today?"

Kath shook her head. "Not since daybreak. I've been too worried to think of eating."

"Well, ye must eat something to keep up your strength," McFadden said. "Ye canna face trouble on an empty stomach, lass. I've some oatcake and a wee bit of butter, and a few cold 'tatties.'" McFadden turned and rummaged under a cloth in the cart.

Kath took the proffered lunch bucket and tried to choke down a cold potato. She knew McFadden was right, but although her stomach growled and her head ached, she had no appetite. The food was like sawdust in her throat.

The donkey rattled on down the dusty lane, each of his passengers quiet with their own thoughts. The sun painted the distant hills with gold and the green fields rolled languidly down to the bog over Creagh way. Small white butterflies played tag across the meadows. Kath was too miserable to appreciate any of it. They were nearly at Kath's cottage when McFadden spoke again.

"If ye'd be quick at your cottage I could wait for ye. I'll need to stop at the turf stack over Creagh, but it'll no' take long to fill this cart. Then I could set ye down by the road to Ballycrana. 'Twould save your feet a few miles – that is, if you plan to go over there this afternoon."

"Thank you, Mr. McFadden. I won't forget your kindness to me this day, putting yourself out."

McFadden drew up his donkey at the small huddle of cottages that was Ballyclough. Maggie stood looking out her door as Kath got down from the cart.

"How's Evan?" Kath asked, hurrying to her own door. "Was Mrs. Ryan able to help?"

"He's sleeping now, God be thanked," Maggie replied. "Mrs. Ryan gave him medicine to drink for the pain, as we'd no brandy. We got Mr. MacManus over to help set his collarbone. Evan fainted, poor lamb. It'll be awhile before we know how bad he is, but he's young and strong. We'll just have to wait and pray. Oh Kath, 'tis awful to hear his groaning! What news of Duncan and Kevin?" Maggie asked.

"Let Mr. McFadden tell you everything, Maggie," Kath said, pulling open her door. "They've been taken to Ballycrana. I must hurry, so McFadden can drop me at the crossroads. Have you any potatoes cooked? I'll need to take them whatever I can."

Inside, Kath gathered clothing, woolen blankets and all the food on hand – half a loaf of bread, a small crock of butter and some oatcake.

"Have you got any medicine I can take with me, Maggie? That Mrs. Ryan left, I mean?" Kath called as she closed her door. "My boys will likely be in a bad way. I don't know if I can see them, but it would be good to have something along if I can."

Maggie handed Kath a few cold potatoes wrapped in a cloth. "Here's all I've to hand," she said. "I'm sorry, Mrs. Ryan is gathering fresh herbs now for Evan. We used up everything she had."

Kath put her bundle in the back of the cart and clambered up beside McFadden.

"God go with you," Maggie called from her door. "I'll light a candle and pray to the Blessed Virgin for you."

"Thank you, Maggie," Kath shouted back.

McFadden slapped the reins on the donkey's back and they trotted off.

*

A mile beyond the two houses they called Creagh, McFadden halted his cart. Kath got down and helped the old man load dried peat clods from his stack. *Could it be only three weeks since they had cut turf for the winter?* Kath wondered. It seemed like years after all that had happened.

One of the excitements of their year was always the few days in May when families went to the bogs to cut peat. Bread was baked and eggs boiled, oatcake, butter and jars of milk were prepared the night before. Then, at four o'clock in the morning, everyone was up and soon eating thick bowls of oatmeal. By five, the young children would be loaded onto donkey carts. An adult hurried alongside holding the donkey's reins. Older children skipped and ran to keep up, their excitement mounting. Everyone wanted to be at the bog by sunrise.

Each family set to work, even the small children. The men and older boys used a spade to cut out the sodden turf from the soft bog-bank. Others threw the clods to the chain of family members, who slung them along from hand to hand, catching and throwing from brother to sister to aunt. At the family's stack the clods were stored to dry until autumn.

Kath stopped for a moment, leaning against McFadden's cart. That day had been perfect! The moor had been so still and lonely when they arrived, with the early-morning mist swathing it like a cloak. Milky-white flowers had been everywhere, glistening with dew. Then the families had arrived and the place had exploded with noise. Men whistling, the scrape of spades; people singing and laughing, children shrieking and running, playing tag, picking flowers. Little family groups dotted about, getting the backbreaking work underway. It was hard work, but that was all part of the fun. Kath smiled as she thought of the scrawny little donkeys wandering free, nibbling the soft new shoots of heather. It had been a holiday for the animals, too.

Soon the sun had crawled higher in the blue sky, sharing it with the larks and the smoke from peat fires burning near the carts, where the women made the dinners. She had been so proud of Duncan! He had cut his bog-bank just as John used to, with those same quick, even strokes. Duncan had won the men's turf-cutting contest for the very first time, beating fourteen other men, older and more experienced than he.

Kath smiled sadly at her memories. It had been less than a month ago. Suddenly she shivered. A feeling of dark foreboding came over her. Would they live to burn this year's turf? Kath swallowed a lump in her throat. She would show Mr. McFadden their stack. He could use it for himself if they were under the daisy quilt by autumn.

4

Kath had limped into Ballycrana just before seven o'clock that night. Ballycrana was the nearest market town before Londonderry for their part of Derry. At least a thousand people lived there, and the shops provided for the surrounding country.

This was Kath's birthplace, though she had no relatives there now. Her father, Breffney O'Neill, had been the town's doctor, and they had lived comfortably in a spacious house on a tree-lined street, with plenty to eat and fine clothes. She had attended the nearby convent school along with her three elder brothers, and life had been good.

Kath was about seven when the Nine Years War had begun to impact them in Ireland, and could remember her father putting on an officer's uniform to go and fight against the English. Mary, her refined mother, was tearful but tried to be brave. Mary needed courage in barrel-loads for the rest of her life, especially when her husband returned from battle without a leg, blinded in one eye, and other unmentionable damage to his person.

Breffney could no longer practice as a doctor, being constantly in pain and plagued with nightmares which left him listless and generally uninterested in life during the day. A learned man himself, he did his best to school his children, and taught them to read, write and do arithmetic. He tried discussing philosophy and to make them think for themselves. Mary made do without a servant and continued to do her part preparing Kath to marry well. Kath had to learn manners, sewing, embroidery, tatting and other fancy work; to sing, and to play the Irish fiddle.

Over the years Breffney's health deteriorated, and he suffered from an oozing wound in his thigh which eventually killed him in 1697, when Kath was fourteen. By this time the family's savings were exhausted. They had sold off whatever bits of land they had, for nothing near its former value, since Irish Catholics were barred from buying land, and the English Protestants would only pay a pittance. The family moved into ever meaner housing and, after Breffney's death, were turned out of their one-room cottage when they could no longer pay the rent.

The three elder boys took themselves off to the hiring fair and found laboring jobs on the farms roundabout. For all their learning, it was all they could find as Catholics. They could discuss philosophy with the cows if they chose. Mary and Kath went to stay with a spinster cousin of Mary's who begrudged them every morsel.

Mary died the year after Breffney, worn out from worry and the strain of raising her children with no income. This left Kath in a quandary, which a dashing John O'Brien soon solved by insisting she marry him. They would live in the small cottage on his family property in Ballyclough. The pair had known each other ever since they were children together in school, and even then Kath had been in love with John. It didn't take her a moment to agree, and the banns were announced that very Sunday.

The O'Briens had also come down in the world. After the Battle of the Boyne in 1690, many Irish Catholic estates were taken by the English Protestant victors. The laws were changed to prohibit Irish Catholics purchasing land, or passing their land by inheritance to only one heir (usually the eldest son), as had always been the custom in England and Ireland, ensuring the cohesion of family estates. Now Irish Catholics must pass their titles to all the heirs of the deceased, which broke the estates into ever smaller parts. Thus, after John O'Brien's father died, his land had been parceled out between his fourteen children. John and Patrick had chosen the Ballyclough cottage property and so each had a cottage.

*

Thus it was that, immediately after her arrival in the town, Kath sought out Father Kelly, the priest who brought communion to the outlying villages around Ballycrana. Surprised to see Kath, bedraggled, weary and footsore, Father Kelly invited her in, gave her a bowl of bread and milk, and then sent her to a respectable widow to spend the night.

The following morning, rested and fortified with good oatmeal for breakfast, Kath made her way to the military barracks where her sons were in the lock-up.

"I'm here to see Duncan and Kevin O'Brien," Kath told the English soldier on guard. Kath's words sounded strident and demanding in her own ears, so she added more quietly "That is, I'm their mother and I'm hoping you'll be good enough to let me see them, Sir."

The soldier leered at Kath. He took a swig of ale from a pewter tankard, wiped his mouth on the sleeve of his greasy tunic and belched. His protuberant eyes glittered as he took another bite of hard soda bread and chewed with his mouth open, all the while insolently undressing Kath with his gaze. "Oh aye?" the soldier said at last. "And who might Duncan and Kevin O'Brien be?"

"The two lads brought in yesterday for stealing a sheep from Lord Roxbury," Kath replied stoutly, her courage waning.

"Oh, aye. Those 'uns," the jailer said, taking another gulp of beer. "And what have you got to offer for the privilege?"

"Nothing, Sir..." Kath looked away, then back at the man. "I only have a few cold potatoes and half a loaf of bread. I was hoping to give them a bite to eat. But you can have my cloak, if you like, it's all I've got to hand."

The soldiers looked at Kath's patched cloak and his lip curled. "Keep your tatty cloak, Missus," he said. "It might do for my dog to lie on, if I had a dog, but I don't. And on second thoughts, it would probably give it fleas. So it'd do my dog no good neither, if I had a dog." The man scratched his armpit, laughing at his own wit. "But stay – take it off anyway."

Kath obediently took off her cloak and stood before the man in her Sunday best dress, which she still wore since her visit to Ballyvale House. The soldier guffawed. "'Struth, woman, you're nothing but a bag of bones! Small ones at that! Now, if I had a dog, happen it'd like a good gnaw of you. Meat for men, bones for dogs. But I don't bark! So you're no good to me! No, Missus, I'm a man likes a bit of meat on my bones!" He laughed again, showing stubby black teeth. Kath waited, playing with her fingernails.

"All right," he said, bored by now. "I'll take you to 'em. It's likely the last time you'll clap eyes on 'em..."

Taking a ring of keys from a peg on the wall behind his desk, he stood and stretched himself, scratching his armpit again. The soldier jerked his head, indicating that she should follow him down a smoky dark passage with rush lights burning in niches along the wall. At the end of the passage was a heavy oak door, with a large iron lock. The soldier inserted a key and swung the door open, bowing as low as his bulk would allow, motioning Kath to enter. She had to brush hard by him in passing.

As soon as Kath walked through the door, the soldier banged it shut. She heard the lock snap to, a jangle of keys, then the soldier's guffaw and receding footsteps. Panic gripped her. She could see nothing in the dark room. She could hardly catch her breath; the air was fetid with smoke, unwashed bodies, vomit and slops. She gagged, then whimpered as a hand grabbed her arm.

"Mam! It's me, Kevin!"

It took a moment for Kath to calm herself. Kevin hugged her tightly, burying his face in her hair. "Oh Mam," he said, "I'm so glad you've come. I've never been so scared in all my life!"

Kath stroked his back. "Me neither."

As they stood clasped together, Kath became aware of low moaning and scratching sounds in the room. There was a small, barred window high up on one wall, admitting air and a little daylight. Gradually her eyes grew accustomed to the dark and she could make out several people sitting propped up against the walls. There was dirty straw strewn over the floor. Several large rats scrabbled on a couple of tin plates left lying about.

Kath's skin crawled. She scratched her legs – fleas jumped onto her hand. The place was full of fleas, and who knew what else! She fought for control as a wave of disgust overwhelmed her. "Where's your brother?" Her voice sounded thin and shaky.

"Over in the corner. He's in a bad way, Mam. He *would* sass the Sheriff. You know Duncan – always the brave hero."

Kath disentangled herself from Kevin's grasp. Holding on to his arm, she went across to the figure slumped in the corner. Dried blood matted Duncan's hair and swollen black bruises distorted his face. It made her sick to look at him. She covered him with her cloak, speaking softly to him as she tried to make him comfortable. Duncan stirred, but did not wake up. Kath smoothed hair from his face, peering at his cuts in the dim light.

"Any water in here?" she asked, turning away. "He's roasting with fever."

"No, Mam," Kevin replied. "They'll likely bring us some by and by. I hope they'll bring some food too. I haven't eaten since breakfast yesterday."

"I brought a few cold tatties and some bread," Kath said. "It's all I could find when I left."

Kevin attacked the potatoes with gusto. "Now, Kevin – why would you steal a sheep?"

"I didn't steal it, Mam. Duncan did."

"All right," she said patiently. "Why did *Duncan* steal a sheep? I want the whole story, mind!"

"Oh Mam, it was horrible!" Kevin began, his face in his hands. "The Sheriff came to Sumner's Farm for us. At first they wouldn't tell us what it was about. Someone had seen 'one of the O'Brien lads' over Ballyvale way, where they'd found the lamb's fleece. The shepherd was out looking and his dog dug it up."

Kevin gulped his mouthful of potato. "They took us to the Sheriff's office and started hitting us, asking about the sheep. Then they tied Evan up – he was the smallest – and started in on him. They made us watch. Duncan couldn't stand it, so he confessed, thinking to put an end to it.

" 'How do we know you're telling the truth?' they asked. We were all crying and pissing ourselves in fear. I even threw up, Mam. They just laughed at us. 'You Irish scum aren't the brave lads you thought yourselves, hey? 'Tis one thing to kill a lamb – 'tis another to be a man!'

"It was just awful, Mam," Kevin said, covering his face with both hands. "They untied Evan. He fell to the floor and couldn't get up. Those English bastards just threw him onto some sacks. He was moaning something awful, but we couldn't go to him. They had our hands tied, anyway.

"Then the Sheriff questioned me. I said I didn't know aught about it, but somehow they knew Duncan and I'd been gone Monday night. We just came clean, after that. No sense in getting any more punishment. So they're holding Duncan for theft and me for aiding and abetting," Kevin said finally.

"And how can they do that, if you had nothing to do with it?" asked Kath.

"Well, I helped Duncan slaughter the sheep," Kevin admitted, taking a bite of bread and chewing it slowly.

"But why, Kevin? Why?"

He looked around, then leaned close and spoke softly. "You know the Gradys over Kinlough way?" Kath nodded. She had known Connie Grady since they were girls; she'd kept up with Connie's news, when she'd married, had her babies.

"Well, Duncan's been courting Molly for the past two months. You know how poor they are, especially since Will Grady died. Mrs. Grady has five little ones, Molly's the eldest, and she's only fifteen. Well, they're under notice to quit their cottage. The rent hasn't been paid for three years. And they've no food, Mam, hardly a tattie. The family's been living on dandelions, watercress, mushrooms, eels – whatever little William can find in the stream. Mam, they're so thin and draggled looking..."

"I can imagine," Kath replied, nodding. "It grieves my heart to think of Connie in that state. We were great friends as girls."

"Well, Duncan has been taking them whatever he can lay his hands on," Kevin continued. "We boys at the farm would lay by a bit of our oatcake and cheese to send, and Duncan takes any cabbage ends and such that the cook throws out. You know he's taken some of our eggs, and vegetables from our own patch – but he's always careful not to cut you short, Mam!

"Well, last Sunday, Duncan went over to see Molly. He'd snared a rabbit and they stewed it for Sunday dinner. Mrs. Grady said she didn't like rabbit, but Duncan knew it was only so the young ones could each have a bone. A rabbit doesn't share very far."

Kath nodded in sympathy. A rabbit was nothing, even when only the three of them had one.

"Well, Duncan said he wasn't hungry either," Kevin went on. "He went outside with Mrs. Grady while the others ate and they sat on the wall and talked. Mrs. Grady told him about her life, how she missed her husband, and had nothing to look forward to any more. How she'd dreamed of a better life, when she was Molly's age.

"While they talked, she mentioned how much she would love a bit of roast lamb. Duncan says her poor pinched face took on such a longing he could hardly bear to see it."

Kevin paused.

Kath waited.

"So Duncan decided to get her a nice fat lamb, that's all," Kevin said in a rush.

"I see," Kath said. It was simple. Get a bit of roast lamb for a starving family, pay for it with your life. She sighed, dropping her head in her hands. How could they have been so naïve, so stupid? She shook her head as Kevin continued.

"After dinner, Duncan left and went towards Ballyvale – you know the old Ballyvale Common, which Lord Roxbury enclosed as his own? Well, Duncan saw a ewe with two lambs, just right for eating. He didn't want to take an only lamb, since the mother would bleat a lot. So he snatches this twin lamb, takes it to that old tumbledown cottage, and ties it behind some gorse by the wall. There was plenty of grass to keep the lamb fed until we could get back there the next evening and no one nearby to hear if it bleated.

"Duncan told me about it Sunday night," Kevin recounted. "He came back to the farm late, and I knew straight away that something was wrong. Anyway, I wrung it out of him. After he told me, I was worried and tried to persuade him to take the lamb back, but he wouldn't listen. He said he'd already stolen the lamb and if he was found taking it back he'd swing just as sure as he'd swing for eating it, so was I coming to help him butcher it or not?

"Well, I went with him, Mam," Kevin admitted. "I couldn't let him run the risk alone. It was easier with two, and we'd need to work fast even so, to be back at the farm before daybreak Tuesday for work.

"So we did it, and left the meat wrapped in a gunny-sack by Mrs. Grady's door. But you're the only one who knows about the Gradys, Mam," Kevin said urgently, dropping his voice to a whisper. "Duncan 'n' I won't say anything about them. They've enough trouble as it is, and they didn't ask for the lamb. But the English would make them all hang for it, or transport them to America. They'd send a troop of soldiers to pick them all up in a wagon.

"No, we'll take our punishment like men, Duncan and me!" Kevin said, sticking out his chin and holding his head high.

*

Like men, thought Kath, looking away and blotting her eyes with the back of her hand. Like men! Her father had been a man, and had taken his punishment like a man, with pain and

31

suffering for years. Only her mother, her brothers – she – had paid the price as well. Her husband John had been a man, and he took his punishment like a man. Strung up on a gallows, dying in agony and shame, but shouting impotent defiance until the end. Her uncle; Corey Brody; and dozens more men she knew had died the same way, all taking their punishment like men. All their families paying for it.

Tears ran freely down Kath's cheeks now. Blessed Mother of God, would there be no end to this 'taking it like a man' that took all of a woman too? Here were her sons, fourteen and sixteen, with all their lives ahead of them, playing at being like the men they knew and admired. When would these men learn that there was no honor in dying at the end of a rope, jerking, staining their pants, their eyes and tongues leaping from black faces?

"For Ireland," some of them said.

There was no glory in it. To die like that was to die like a dog. A show for strangers, that's all it was in the end. Strangers, making a holiday picnic, so they could watch the hanging. And how could that help Ireland?

What was wrong with dying of old age, in bed? Kath wondered. Was that to die like a woman? She had this surge of longing for peace, for the struggle, the hardship, the misery, to cease. Mother of God, was there nowhere that people dwelt secure, happy, with their loved ones around them, with enough? Kath yearned for the expectation of sunny days and tomorrows, until, old and satisfied, she could die in her bed with comfortable things about her and the noise of grandchildren playing outside. She knew what her life's ambition was.

Men seemed to despise what was her greatest hope.

5

"Come in, Mrs. O'Brien, come in!" Father Kelly held his door open for Kath, as she stood scratching, smelly and forlorn at his door.

"Thank you kindly, Father," she replied, remaining on the threshold. "That lock-up stinks to high heaven and I know I'm covered with fleas. I don't want to bring the wee beasties in with me."

"Don't you worry," the priest reassured her. "Just come in and have a wash by the fire. You'll be needing a bite to eat and a rest. Then you can tell me everything."

Kath accepted his offer gratefully. The priest's boy, Clancy, filled a large basin with warm water and the two men left her to her ablutions. Kath was soon presentable, and told Father Kelly her morning's experiences while she ate a piece of bread and cheese.

"I came back to you in the hope that you'd know someone who could go and see my Duncan. He's been badly beaten. I have nothing to pay a surgeon, but I'd happily work for him, if he'll only go."

"Yes, Mrs. O'Brien, I know a man who'll go," Father Kelly replied. "One of the priests at St Margaret's is a skilled man. He'll go, and for no charge.

"Boy, run over to Father Malone and ask if he can go to the lock-up to see Duncan O'Brien. Then come straight back here. I want you to take Mrs. O'Brien home in the cart.

"So you've no money," the priest said turning back to Kath. "But your boys were working on a farm, you said?"

"Yes, Father. They worked for an English Squire, Mr. Sumner, on his farm."

Kath told Father Kelly all about the money the Roxbury's owed her, and how she had tried to get payment – leaving out her heated exchange with Mrs. Doherty, of course.

"Well, I know the Squire, at any rate," Father Kelly said. "He's a fine man. He was born in Ireland and his father before him. I'd say he was *Anglo-Irish*, rather than *English*. I'll write him a letter, ask him to pay your lads for the quarter – less the days they haven't worked, of course. Quarter day is only ten days away. Perchance he'll do it."

Father Kelly jumped up and went to rummage in his curtained alcove, emerging with paper, quill pen and ink. "If the Squire will pay up, I can collect the money after Mass on Sunday and get it to your lads on Monday morning. That'll be a comfort. I doubt the soldiers will move prisoners out to the Assizes until Tuesday or Wednesday." Father Kelly set to work at the table, his quill scratching industriously.

Soon the priest's boy returned. "Father Malone said he'd go straight away," he reported. "I'll put the donkey to the cart, Missus, if you're ready."

"Yes, do that boy," said the priest. "And I've a letter for you to deliver to Squire Sumner after you've taken Mrs. O'Brien. You're to wait for his reply."

*

Kath finally arrived home that Friday night, numb with fatigue. Maggie rushed out to meet her, with her brood tumbling after her. The little convoy swept Kath into their cottage, with everyone asking questions at once. She slumped onto Maggie's kitchen table and laid her head on her arms, squeezing her eyes shut.

"Here, Kath. You need something hot and sweet to give you strength," Maggie said. "You children give your Aunty Kath some room! Can't you see she's tired out?" Maggie dished up a bowl of hot oatmeal and a mug of chamomile tea. She put a good dollop of honey into both and stirred them for Kath.

"How's Evan?" Kath asked, looking around but not seeing him.

"Not too good," Maggie replied, her blue eyes sad. "Mrs. Ryan says he'll mend in time. There's no space here for him to be quiet with all these children, so Mrs. Ryan's taken him. She wants him handy, anyway, so she can nurse him. God bless her!

"Now tell me everything Kath!" Maggie demanded. "What's happening with Duncan and Kevin?"

Kath told Maggie the story simply, without embellishment and without identifying the Gradys. It would eventually be common knowledge, but she didn't want to betray Kevin's trust. If by some slim chance the English found out later, perhaps the bloodlust would have subsided and they would let the matter rest.

When Kath finished, everyone clamored for more details, with Maggie trying to keep order. The noise in Maggie's house was more than Kath's nerves could stand. "Forgive me, Maggie," she said at last. "I'm just too exhausted to go on. I can tell you more in the morning. Right now, I only want my bed."

"Of course, my dear," Maggie said, understanding at once. "Cullen has run in regularly to keep your fire going, so your place should be nice and warm. You know what they say, 'when the fire goes out, the soul goes out of the people of the house.' We can't let that happen!"

"Thank you, Maggie," Kath said, giving Maggie a loving stroke on the arm as she moved to leave. But when Kath stepped through her own door, the cottage was cold and the fire out. She sighed and set to work with tinderbox and kindling. The souls of this house were already gone, she thought. The fire going out only confirmed it.

*

Early the next morning Kath gathered her sons' Sunday shirts and breeches, adding their tin mugs, bowls and spoons. Everything was so shabby! Her eyes filled as she handled their things. She folded their old blankets, remembering how lovingly she had knitted them years ago.

They would need them, until they needed nothing. Kath swallowed the lump in her throat, then collected her own things, adding her crucifix, the small picture of the Virgin and her sewing kit. She would try to get to Derry Assizes. Perhaps she could pay her way with her needle, especially if she had to stay at an inn.

The packing didn't take long, since they had so little. Kath rolled everything up in the blankets. When she was through, she tidied the cottage.

She made herself some oatmeal, but had to force down the food. Would she ever lose the heavy, sick feeling in the pit of her stomach? She stroked the wood of her table, remembering how proud she and John were when they got it. Kath couldn't shake the leaden feeling of despair and foreboding which covered her like a mist. She moved about the small room, touching each stool and bench, saying goodbye to everything, remembering the years of her marriage, small happenings with her sons.

Now Kath leaned against the doorpost and looked into her small home. These walls held most of her life. They had welcomed her when she came into their protection as a bride, had seen her love and sorrows, peace and pain. The dirt floor, the rough rubble walls, the byre at the end where their cow, now dead, once sheltered. The hearth, with its stack of peat blocks and firewood beside it, the cauldron hanging above the fireplace. Her only stewing pan on a hook by the wall, and the few shelves, bare of everything they'd held. Such small, poor things which the Lady Roxbury's of the world would not deign to touch, let alone love. But they were all she had, and she loved them.

Kath turned around, looking at the view that was as familiar to her as her own hand. Her eyes filled, dissolving the soft green grass and dry-stone wall with its clambering pink roses. Would she ever see it again? Her chest ached. She felt as though she'd swallowed a whole boiled egg, and it was stuck midway.

Then she hustled back into the cottage. How could she have forgotten? She took the old wooden box from the mantle shelf which held her precious pieces of paper. Her marriage lines, a copy of her father's Will, a love letter from John. A note from John, written from Londonderry the day before his hanging. Kath unfolded the letter and read it yet again.

"My Dear Wife, believe me my Hart is broken to think I must leve you. I don't mind the thot of Swinging so much as the thot of leving you and our Young sons alone in the World to live how you might. It cuts me even to the Hart that you have nothing put by you and no-one to lean upon. I am writin my Brother Patrick, to Pray him and Wife Maggie to be Kind and look out for you and the boys. If onley I could see your lovely Face before deth closes my Eyes. My Dear Wife, you know how I ave Loved you true, no other Woman have Ever Run into my Mine since ever I saw your Face, and that were when I were a lad of Seven year. Tis onley you Forever my Dear Kath. If only we could live a Peeceful Life together with our boys, and sit by the fire as old uns, we shoud be so Happy. So Goodbye for aye, My Loving Wife, and Goodbye from me to Duncan and Kevin. Tell em their Father wishes they be good boys and Mind their Mother.

I have asked Colin O'Kane to see you get this after I Die. And may God be Mersyful to me. God Bless You, Kath. I kiss you with all my Soul."

Kath put the pages on the smoldering peat, one by one, watching as the edges turned brown, curled, then burst into flame. She fed the love letter to the fire, then her marriage lines, then her father's Will.

So much for it all – it was gone, past, finished now. The few shillings her father had left were long gone, and now the sons John had left were going too. She had nothing any man had given her with love. Even the cottage was not hers. The English Popery Laws had made sure of that, the property was split between Duncan and Kevin.

Kath took out a fresh piece of paper, and trimmed the old quill lying in the box. She made a paste with some soot and water, then wrote:

"This is the Last Will of me, Katherine Elizabeth O'Brien. I leave all my belongings to Mistress Margaret O'Brien, my dearly beloved sister-in-law with my Hart Felt Thanks for all her Loving Kindness to me and my boys."

It needs to be witnessed, she thought. Two people had witnessed her father's Will. She stood and looked out her door, wondering whom she could ask. Down the lane she saw three men riding. It looked like the Sheriff again! He would make a good witness...

Panic surged through her, as the men turned in at the O'Brien gate.

"Oh no! Blessed Virgin, *please...*" she pleaded, wringing her hands. The men reined in, dismounted and walked over to her, looking grim.

"Mistress Kathleen O'Brien?" Sheriff Twynam asked.

"Yes..." Her voice sounded reedy and unsteady.

"I have a warrant for your arrest."

6

"For *my* arrest? *Why?* What have I done?" Kath asked the Sheriff, her face white. Maggie came running over from next door and put an arm around her.

The Sheriff looked at his warrant. "You are accused of stealing a silver cup, the property of The Honorable Master Charles Roxbury, from the kitchens of Ballyvale House, on Thursday, the Fourth day of June in the year of Our Lord One Thousand Seven Hundred and Sixteen." He looked up at Kath. "That's the day before yesterday."

Kath stared at the men before her door, her mind racing. She struggled to bring her thoughts together. Maggie looked at her, her large blue eyes questioning, waiting for her denial. "But I was only at the kitchen door for a few minutes. I never went more than ten paces into the room. I went to deliver some fancywork for Lady Roxbury. Mrs. Doherty can vouch for me."

"Aye, that's as may be," said the Sheriff. "But 'tis not Mrs. Doherty who will vouch for you. 'Tis Mrs. Doherty who is accusing you."

"But this is ridiculous!" Kath sputtered. "When could I have stolen anything? I was never alone, there were others present the whole time I was there."

"Save it for the judge, Missus," the Sheriff said. "I have this warrant, and you must come with me. We'll search these cottages for stolen goods before we go."

"All right, I'll come quietly. And you're very welcome to search mine; you'll find nothing," Kath said, her eyes blazing. She flung her door wide with a crash.

"Please may I speak to my sister-in-law here for a moment?" Kath asked the Sheriff, as the men got busy searching her cottage.

"Yes, but stay in plain sight."

"I have nothing whatever to hide, Sir," She put down her packed bundle outside the door, by her stand of tall pink hollyhocks, put her arm through Maggie's and they walked over to lean against the garden wall.

"What could Mrs. Doherty be thinking?" Maggie asked. "Surely you didn't take any silver mug!"

Kath looked over at her garden. She could not look Maggie in the face. "When I asked to see Lady Roxbury, Mrs. Doherty and I had words. I ended up mentioning her relationship with Corey Brody – and right in front of Mrs. Nugent and Sheila Monaghan. You can imagine how stuck-up, English Mrs. Doherty liked *that!* I was a stupid fool, Maggie. I must have been out of my wits!"

"You never did!" Maggie said, shocked.

"Och, if the others tell, she might lose her fine English job..." Kath replied. "Well, it's too late for me to do anything about it now. I've told her dirty secret in front of her underlings, so she's done this to spite me. And she's done a good job of it! Mrs. Doherty knows I would have no chance before an English Judge. Accused of stealing from an English Lord, a warrant taken out by his Steward, another Englishman. And my two sons before the Courts at the same time for stealing from that same English Lord!

"No doubt Mrs. Doherty's got the others primed to agree with her story, and I have no witnesses." Realizing the full extent of her danger, Kath's eyes grew large and she buried her face in Maggie's neck, holding her tight. "Oh Maggie, I'll probably be transported to the Colonies!"

Maggie gently disengaged herself and pointed to the Sheriff, who was beckoning Kath to come. "We must go back, now," Maggie said gently.

"Ever since yesterday, I've had this feeling that something awful would happen," Kath said. "I packed some things for the boys and myself. The furniture and everything else in the house are yours if we don't come back, Maggie.

"If you and Patrick don't need my cottage right away, please let Connie Grady use it for a while. Kevin says they're being turned out of their place. You know Connie was my best friend when we were girls, and her husband died a few years ago leaving her with five little ones. I'd like to think we could help her.

"Oh – and I showed our stack of turf to old Mr. McFadden yesterday, when we passed through Creagh. I told him to use it if anything happened to us. He was so kind to me."

*

"Will you witness my signature on this paper please?" Kath asked the Sheriff. "It is my Will. I don't know what may happen to me."

Kath signed her name, then the Sheriff took the paper and quill from her and scratched his name on the bottom. He was surprised that Kath could write. He wondered why a woman whose work was in demand by Lady Roxbury would stoop to steal a child's silver cup. What would she want with it, anyway? It made no sense. He had been surprised when his men had found the cup stuffed into Kath's bundle.

"I'll need another signature," Kath said, turning to one of the men. "Would you sign, Mr. Grant?" Kath asked. Grant looked embarrassed, and shook his head. Both men finally admitted that they could not write, so Kath wrote down one of their names and the man marked his X instead.

"Thank you," Kath said, handing the paper to Maggie. "Now may I also take some clothing and personal things with me? I suppose I'll be away for some time."

"Yes," the Sheriff said. "Just don't take too long."

"Indeed not, Sir. I'm nearly ready to go. My things are in that bundle by the door."

"You'll find that's lighter now, Missus," the Sheriff said, waving a small silver cup in her face. "We've removed this cup belonging to the Hon. Master Charles Roxbury."

Kath turned beet red. The shock and disbelief on Maggie's face pierced her heart. "If you found it, you must have known just where to look, since I've just cleaned the house from top to bottom and never saw it!"

She turned to one of the Sheriff's men. "You brought it with you, didn't you, Hugh Grant?"

"Don't be daft, woman. Why should we ride all the way over here to put a child's cup in your house?"

"Where are you taking me?" Kath asked, her body prickling with shame.

"To Ballycrana Lock-up and then to the Assizes at Londonderry," the Sheriff said.

"Och, Sheriff, that's just where I was headed," she said, refusing to look at Maggie. "I'd as soon ride with you as go on shank's mare!"

7

They arrived at Ballycrana barracks about noon, where Kath was handed over to the Charge Officer. She was grateful that it wasn't the soldier who 'didn't have a dog'. She couldn't bear to go through that again.

After the minimal paperwork was finished, the Charge Officer put Kath in leg irons. The soldier grabbed her arm, shoving her along the same dark passage as she'd gone down before. The grating key opened the same black dungeon where Duncan and Kevin were held. Filled with despair, Kath shuffled through the door. The soldier threw her bundle in behind her, hitting her forcefully in the back. As she fell headlong onto the filthy straw, she heard the lock snap home once again. This time she was on the wrong side of the door, here to stay.

"Mam!" What are you doing here?" Kevin's voice demanded. He rushed to help her stand.

"Oh son! They arrested me for stealing a silver cup from Ballyvale House!"

"Stealing? Ballyvale House?" Kevin asked, confused.

"Never mind about that now. How are you? How's Duncan?"

"He's mending," Kevin answered. "He's asleep. How could you steal anything from Ballyvale House?"

"I'll explain later. Tell me about your brother."

Kevin picked up the bundle. Kath's eyes were adjusting to the dark now; she and Kevin crossed the room and sat beside Duncan.

"Father Malone has come to him twice," Kevin said, "... and the fever's broken. He ate some gruel this morning. He's sleeping a lot. Awful stiff, he says but his pain's better. Father says he'll be alright."

"We'll not be here long, Mam," Kevin said. "We hear they're taking us to Londonderry first thing Monday morning."

"Oh no!" Kath was aghast. "How can we get a message to Father Kelly? If he gets your money from Mr. Sumner tomorrow, he must bring it straight in to us!"

"Oh Mam, don't go dreaming," Kevin responded. "D'you think for a minute that Mr. Sumner cares about the likes of us? You've got a hope. He cares more about his sow Jolene!" Then Kevin's bruised face lit up with excitement. "Jolene's just farrowed twenty-two piglets, Mam! She's a prodigious sow!"

There was a chink of irons as Duncan woke and sat up, a frown on his brow. "Mam? You here?" he asked.

"Yes son, they've arrested me for stealing too..."

"It's all my fault that we're here!" Duncan said. "If only I hadn't been so cocky and stupid. I don't mind what the English do to me, but you and Kevin..."

"No, Duncan, it's not all your fault," Kath said gently, smoothing matted hair out of his eyes. "I know you were the leader, and should have been a better example to Kevin, but he went along with you of his own choosing. And I have made my own problem." Kath quietly explained her situation.

"I must do my best at the trial to prove how impossible it was for me to have taken the cup, that's all." She put an arm around each of her boys and pulled them closer. "Och, it gives me comfort to be here with you! Since we're in peril, then at least we're in peril together."

She smiled sadly. "I was planning to follow you to Londonderry Assizes anyway, which is why I had all our things in a bundle. This way, I've been spared the trouble of transport and lodging!"

"That's cold comfort," Duncan replied. "If not for my stupidity, we'd all be snug at home this afternoon, rooting about in the garden, feeding the hens and checking on the bees!"

"Any road, there's naught we can do about it now," Kath said softly. "Let's not be miserable, we don't know what will happen. We may not be together again after Monday, they may separate us."

"What do you think they'll do to us?" Kevin asked, in his high child's voice.

"I don't know," Kath replied. "I asked Father Kelly what he thought. You know that stealing a sheep is a hanging offence. Being Irish, they may hang us all. The English don't care a fig for age or sex." Silence reigned for a few moments. "Och, if we're to die next week, let's not be moaning about it," Kath said. "It can't be helped now. Let's try to remember the good times we've had and be as merry as we can be."

"What good times?" Duncan asked. "I only remember how hard it's been to live, how hungry and cold we've been on a few moldy potatoes. I won't mind dying! It'll save doing it slowly, anyhow."

Kath was determined to keep their thoughts out of the hangman's noose. "What good times? Think of the summer days when Da was alive, and he'd come home after work. There'd be eggs for supper, and buttermilk, and fluffy potatoes and butter. We'd have strawberries and cream, apricots and a knob of cheese. Wasn't that good?

"And the times we went to cut peat! Remember how Da always won the turf cutting? I was so proud when you won last month, Duncan, just like your Da! And the hay making. How about all those hot apple dumplings and bramble tarts?

"And Duncan," Kath continued – "a little bird's whispered to me there's a bonny lass named Molly who can cheer your thoughts!"

"No, Mam," Duncan said. "Don't tease! I've no cheerful thoughts of her now. If she's not already choked on the meat, she's choking for fear they'll be taken for receiving stolen property. Then she'll choke again from a hemp knot. Likely she's cursing the day she ever laid eyes on me."

"Yes, son, that may be! It's too late to worry about that

now. You should have thought about it first. But I doubt not that her throat is choked from crying for you, and her heart is choked with pain at the thought of your dying. She'll be blaming herself all her life for your love-gift. And likely she'll never love another as she loves you."

"Oh Mam, what a mess I've made for everyone!" Duncan buried his face in his mother's lap. "I wish I'd never been born!" His tears wet through the thin stuff of her dress. She stroked his hair and back, then held him to her and rocked him gently, as though he was still a little boy.

"Molly's not the first lass to suffer, nor will she be the last. She'll get over it in time and make a life for herself somehow. I only wonder how she'll ever be content with another man, after knowing she had the likes of you." Kath smiled down at her son, sprawled before her, large, raw-boned and solid, his dear face swollen and discolored.

"Och, Mam, Tom Monaghan's probably sprucing himself up now to call on her tonight," Duncan said, his lips twisting. "He's always been keen, lurking about her whenever he could. But I beat him out, or so I thought. Guess I was wrong, and he'll win her after all. He'll not be as stupid about a sheep."

"No, that he won't," Kath said, and laughed. "He'd never dare. He's nowt but a sheep himself!"

Gradually their mood changed. If this was to be their last time together, then they'd make it a holiday. The specter of death hung quietly at the back of each mind, but was not allowed on their tongues. They told tales of their childhoods, traded secrets, and talked of their cousins and friends.

As the afternoon grayed into evening beyond the barred window, a nightingale sang from a field nearby, its thin, reedy song reaching them in melancholy stillness. Eventually the chill night closed upon them. They spread one of their blankets on the damp straw and spooned themselves together under the other two blankets. Comforted by memories and the warmth of each other's bodies, somehow they slept, despite the running of rats and biting of fleas.

8

Just before daybreak on Monday morning the weather changed. Kath woke with a start, not knowing where she was. She lay nested between Kevin and Duncan, listening to the rising wind in the trees. The smell of damp earth wafted in through the barred window and she heard the faint spatter of rain. She rose and shuffled over to relieve herself in the slop bucket. It hurt to move about with the foot shackles, which were chafing her ankles raw. Lightning flashed, followed by the roll of distant thunder. Soon the rain came in torrents, spattering in on them through the window. The air grew colder. The three huddled closer together, shivering under their blankets.

An hour later the door flew open and two red-coated privates came in with a steaming cauldron. "Get up! You're leaving soon," one of them said. "Shift yourselves if you want to eat!"

Father Kelly had managed to get the boys' wages from Squire Sumner, and Father Malone, who had come to check on Duncan, had returned to bring it on Sunday night. They had divided the money between them right away.

"We mustn't keep all our eggs in one basket," Kath had reasoned. "We might be separated, or one of us might be robbed. This way will be safest. And in the morning we'll each take our own belongings, just in case."

Now they scurried to make three bundles and joined the other prisoners, who were shuffling into line holding out their bowls. From outside came muffled shouts and the rattling of horses and wagons.

"You boys eat mine," Kath said. "I've no appetite."

"Force it down, Mam!" Duncan replied. "We don't know how long we'll be on the road, or when we'll see food again."

Kath swallowed the thin, glutinous gruel, nearly gagging. The soldiers began moving the prisoners out to the wagons. A pretty, round-faced girl of about twenty was the only other female in the dungeon. She was unkempt and wore her bodice very low, but she had a ready smile. She gave Duncan an appraising look.

"What're you in for, then?" she asked, flicking a wing of greasy hair out of her brown eyes.

"Stealing a bit of English lamb," he replied with a crooked grin.

"My name's Cara..." The two bantered while they waited to get on a wagon. Kath was pleased to hear Duncan being more his usual self again.

Three wagons waited, with high, barred railings, standing like crouching cages in the misty drizzle. Each wagon had four carthorses, their heads hanging miserably. Kevin was just ahead of Kath and was the last prisoner in the second wagon. Kath, Duncan and Cara went along to the third.

Kath struggled to get into the wagon, hobbled with her irons. One of the soldiers grabbed her and swung her up. Cara was already in the wagon and caught Kath as she staggered. "You'd best sit down, Missus," Cara said. "It takes some getting used to, those irons."

"This is my Mam, Kath O'Brien," Duncan told Cara, as he stowed their bundles beneath the bench. He looked up at Cara. "Where are your things? Don't you have anything with you?"

"Just my bowl and spoon. I wasn't home when the soldiers grabbed me, and my thieving landlady kept my belongings for rent." She swore volubly, venting her spleen on soldiers and landladies.

Kath was amazed. She'd never heard another woman swear like that. Then she thought of how miserable she would be without her things, or the few shillings nestled in her bodice. Only by Providence was she different from Cara.

"I don't have much, but we can share it," Kath said. "Would you like to use my comb?"

"Thanks Missus, but it makes no difference now. Between the drizzle and the wind, there's no helping it."

The carts lumbered ahead, grinding over cobblestones and muddy puddles. It was a long way to Londonderry, still twenty bone-shaking miles. It would take all day to get there.

*

It was a relief when the portals of Londonderry prison opened to receive them. The weary horses clopped into the large inner courtyard and the prisoners slowly got down. They were wet through, stiff and cramped almost unable to stand. Kath shivered uncontrollably; she felt as though all her vital organs had the ague.

Reception formalities were blessedly brief. Soon the guards herded their prisoners down yet another smoky damp passage and put them into cells for the night. Kath and Cara went into a cell that already held two women, while Duncan and Kevin went further along the corridor.

The cell door clanged shut and, once again, a key rasped the lock home. Kath jumped when Cara spoke behind her. "What elegant chambers these English provide for ladies!"

Cara went over to one of the unoccupied straw mattresses lying on the ground. Kath sat on the other. She scratched her forearm; her fingers found a round, rancid-smelling bedbug. The only light came feebly through the wrought-iron grill high on one wall, and the stench of the place was overpowering, especially after a day in the open air.

The four inmates introduced themselves; the two women already occupying the cell were Rose and Martha.

"Do you know when the Assizes will begin?" Cara asked. "We've just come in from Ballycrana."

"They started this morning," Rose said. "Our cases were heard this afternoon. We're both to be transported." She spoke prosaically, but her voice shook on the word 'transported' and Martha sobbed aloud.

"Don't cry, lass," Rose said. "Happen it'll no' be as bad as we fear. Any road, there are thousands who've gone before us and there'll be thousands after. It might be a better land than here."

"How better?" Martha asked. "I've heard about those black people, and wild Indians. We'll be eaten by heathen savages!"

Rose snorted. "Don't be such a simpleton! Nobody's going to eat ye. For my part, I'd as soon be eaten as not have enough to eat meself. And victuals have been scarce these past years. It's my little 'uns I'm fretting about." Her voice quavered again. "They'll go to the poor house, poor wee creatures."

The women talked for a while, the room growing completely dark with the setting sun. Cara was up on a prostitution charge. Martha, a lady's maid, had stolen a brooch, while Rose was guilty of stealing food from a market stall; she'd been desperate to feed her children. They were soon silent, each overcome by fatigue, apprehension and hopelessness.

*

The Assizes were held in a large rectangular room, with sharply arched leaded windows. Spectators packed the room, sitting on long oak benches.

Judge Coleman Thwaites sat on a platform at one end, a large table before him. He was resplendent in red robes and black shoes with large silver buckles, and he wore a full-bottomed white wig. He had a high, square forehead and a long nose, which sported a pair of wire spectacles. His mouth puckered above his receding chin, which disappeared into the snowy ruffles of his jabot.

The Clerk of the Court was a scrawny man of middle age. He was swathed in a voluminous robe of black stuff, with white linen bands at his neck. On his head was a wispy gray wig, frizzled on each side, and with a limp pigtail behind. He sat just below the judge's table looking like a brooding black bird of prey, a look that his beaked nose, bad posture and claw-like white hands only enhanced.

Duncan's case was the first to be heard that morning, as he had already confessed to the Sheriff. He waited in the prisoner's dock, leaning jauntily against the rail. He was trying his best to be brave, but his callow youthfulness stuck out of every awkward limb.

Judge Thwaites peered over his spectacles, looking down at Duncan. "What is your name?"

"Duncan John O'Brien." The Judge scribbled on a sheet of paper, then looked irascibly down at the prisoner once more.

"Duncan John O'Brien, you are charged with stealing a lamb from a flock belonging to Lord Roxbury on or about the First day of June, 1716. How plead you, are you guilty or not guilty?"

"Guilty!" Duncan thrust out his chin and glared up at the judge.

"Have you anything to say for yourself?" asked the judge.

"No, nothing," Duncan replied, a muscle rippling in his jaw.

"No, nothing *My Lord!*" the Clerk corrected.

The judge put a black cloth over his wig and rapped his gavel.

"Duncan John O'Brien, I hereby sentence you to be taken hence to the place from which you have come, and held there until you may be taken thence and hanged by the neck until you are dead."

Duncan's bravado faltered. His face blanched and he groped behind him for the railings surrounding the dock. The Sergeant at Arms opened the door and motioned him to descend; he stumbled down the two stairs, his fetters chinking.

Kevin was sitting on an oak bench awaiting his turn, and he stared aghast at his brother when the judge pronounced Duncan's sentence.

Then the Sergeant at Arms rapped the floor with his rod. "Kevin O'Brien to the prisoner's dock."

The soldier in charge of the prisoners grabbed his elbow and lifted him to his feet, hustling him over to the dock. The procedure began again.

"Kevin Patrick O'Brien, you are charged with stealing a lamb from a flock belonging to Lord Roxbury on or about the First day of June, 1716, in association with your brother Duncan John O'Brien. How plead you, are you guilty or not guilty?"

"Not guilty," Kevin said in his piping young voice. "I didn't steal the lamb. I only helped my brother slaughter it."

"Did you know the lamb had been stolen when you helped your brother?" asked the judge.

"Yes, Sir, I mean, yes Sir My Lord."

"How old are you, boy?"

"Fourteen Sir, I mean My Lord, come August."

"Old enough to know better! I find you guilty of conspiring with your brother Duncan John O'Brien to handle stolen property." Judge Thwaites scratched with his quill again, then looked down at Kevin.

"I think there is nothing for it. You will have to be transported to the Colonies..." The gavel descended and the sentence was formally read.

*

The afternoon came, and with it the women were brought before the judge. Kath and Cara sat beside each other on the bench, listening as the proceedings droned on, feeling listless, hungry and numb.

Soon the Sergeant at Arms rapped the floor with his rod. "Katherine Elizabeth O'Brien, to the prisoner's dock."

Kath stumbled up, almost tripping with her leg irons, and made her way to the dock. The judge went through the same procedure as he did with everyone, and when he asked if she was guilty or not guilty, Kath said stoutly, "Not guilty, My Lord."

Witnesses for the Prosecution were called; Sheriff Twynam; Hugh Grant; and Lord Roxbury's Steward. All Kath could say was what she had already told the Sheriff: she had not taken the cup, she had had no opportunity to do so, being always in the company of others. Her own defense sounded thin even in her own ears; her accusers had found the cup in her belongings. What chance did she have, a small dirty Irish woman, bedraggled and scratching, against these smartly dressed English. It was no surprise to anyone when the judge pronounced his decision.

"It is therefore ordered and adjudged by this Court, that you be transported upon the seas, beyond the seas, to such place as His Majesty, by the advice of His Privy Council, shall think fit to direct and appoint, for the term of seven years."

The gavel descended with a staccato rap, underlining the sentence. Judge Thwaites sat impassively at his table on the rostrum at the front of the court and pronounced Kath's sentence with stentorian relish, his small black eyes gleaming down upon her in the dock.

Kath goggled back at the judge, his red robes and white lace jabot swimming before her eyes. Someone grabbed her arm and pulled her down from the dock, the leg-irons tearing into her flesh.

What happened? Kath wondered. *What does he mean, "... transported upon the seas, beyond the seas..." are they going to throw me into the ocean?* Her mind refused to understand anything.

She sat again on the oak bench with the other felons, waiting until the court adjourned so they could be taken back to jail. The voices of the Clerk of the Court, the Judge, sometimes another prisoner in the dock, droned on around her. That queer rushing noise in her ears was back. She couldn't understand what they were saying. Then, in silence, she heard that strange sentence again.

This time she grasped it. She was being transported. Banished from Ireland, from all she'd ever known, ever loved. Seven years might just as well be forever, Kath thought. She thought about her boys. They were younger, stronger, and they could adapt to change. Perhaps it might even be a good thing for them, to go to a new country and make a fresh start, even as indentured servants. They might manage. It was the best she could hope for – God willing they would not be hanged. Well, she would soon learn their fate.

Eventually the proceedings were over for the day and the prisoners were taken back to the lock-up. Now they all went into one large room. Men, women, children, no matter what their crimes, be they forgers, embezzlers, rapists, murderers, petty thieves, innocents or highwaymen. There was no distinction between sexes, ages or offenses – they were all felons, all damned by society as the Criminal Class.

Brutality was commonplace. Sewage creamed over the floors, rats were everywhere, not even waiting until dark to nose about the fetid rubbish. The only small ray of comfort, one tiny blessing was this: Duncan, Kevin and Kath were together in the same room.

9

"I could see it if I'd killed a *man*! But to die for killing a *lamb*, an animal born and bred to be killed and eaten!" Duncan's tears gushed down, forming white runnels on his face. He buried his head in his mother's chest, and the rest of his words were muffled. "I'll come back and haunt that Judge if I can! He'll never know another night's rest after Thursday!"

Kath's heart plunged. She leaned away from him, pulling his head from her. *"Thursday?"*

"That's when I'm to hang!" Duncan clutched her, holding fast, making her stagger back. "I'm so scared," he whispered.

"Holy Mother of God! Why so soon?"

"So they won't have to feed us. They need the space for the next lot of poor devils!"

*

The next day was desperate and tearful for the O'Brien family. They counted down the hours as they huddled together, watching the light change through the window. Kath encouraged Duncan to spend his share of money on something from the food vendors, who came to sell outside the window. There were fresh fruits, bread, pancakes, pasties and fruit tarts, all sorts of good things to tempt prisoners with money, but Duncan refused to spend anything on himself. He was already grave filling, he said, and he was going where nothing like that mattered anymore. His Mam and Kevin would need every penny to keep themselves alive, and so he shared his money between the two of them.

Wednesday evening a priest came to hear Duncan's

confession and administer the sacrament for the last time. He intoned the rite of extreme unction, then moved on to the next prisoner on the roster for hanging.

They slept little, but eventually sheer exhaustion made them drop off. They woke in alarm Thursday morning to find the damp gray dawn creeping through the window, and hearing soldiers at the door.

Prisoners were shuffling stiffly to line up when their names were called. Speechless, Duncan hugged Kevin, then clung to his Mam for the last time before making his way to the line when they called his name. A few minutes later, the prisoners clanked through the door, which closed with an echoing crash.

Then Kath and Kevin went to the window overlooking the inner courtyard, the other inmates moving away out of pity, giving them space to look out at Duncan for the last time. They watched as the condemned prisoners climbed into the cage-like wagons. The red-coats swung open the great gates of the courtyard, and the wagon drivers slapped the reins over their horses' backs, geeing them into a slow walk.

Kath thought her heart would break. There went her pride and joy, her firstborn son, now a tall, handsome, stalwart young man. She had poured years of herself into him, to make him into a man who could hold up his head, a good Catholic, husband, father and friend. A person of worth, looking forward to a life with meaning.

"God be with you, Duncan," Kath shouted out, her voice cracked and ragged. Duncan turned, and their eyes locked until the wagon passed through the gate. Their last sight of Duncan was of his blurred face and a hand raised in farewell, as their tears began to fall.

*

The next two weeks passed somehow. Days were monotonous, dank and hopeless. Malnourished, sick, desperate people fought among themselves, stole from each other and took basic pleasures whenever they could. Squabbles were continuous, the poorer wheedling from those with a few pence in their pockets. Women sold themselves for morsels of food or scraps of clothing.

Kath tried to pray, to say the Rosary, but her mind was blank. She knew that Jesus Christ had also suffered like this, but it had no relevance to her own situation. Christ had been innocent and was put to death. The Blessed Virgin knew all about mourning an executed Son, but somehow it was just something Kath had heard about. It had no meaning to her now that she was in the same situation. Christ had died for sinners, so the priest said; Christ's death had a purpose. Duncan's death was pointless, had no meaning whatsoever.

She removed herself by sinking into a secret place inside her. She didn't initiate anything. If someone spoke to her, she looked at the speaker, sometimes answered. She smiled at Kevin and Cara, tried to swallow what they offered her. She couldn't tell what she chewed, was not aware of any flavor or texture, whether it was hot or cold. She obediently swallowed because it seemed to please them. Mostly she curled herself into a ball under the ragged blankets and slept.

One day the soldiers put them into the wagons again. Kath sat quietly between Kevin and Cara during the whole long ride, passing mountains on one side, sea on the other. Beyond cliffs, meadows, hills, through villages and towns, to Belfast. In the towns, people stopped to jeer and shout comments as they passed. Small boys threw refuse and rotten fruit at them, running along sticking out their tongues and trying to whack the wagons with sticks.

They were blessed with fine weather, and they enjoyed feeling the sun on their faces. Kath saw the flowers, the fields of rustling corn, smelled the sea; but it was at a strange remove, from somewhere outside of herself. She was no trouble. She did whatever they told her to do.

*

At Belfast, the prisoners transferred to a large sailing ship, the *"Lady Jane"*, and early the next morning they sailed south out of Belfast harbor. Once underway the soldiers removed their irons, and they were permitted to exercise above decks for part of the day. The rest of their time they were crammed into the smelly hold amidships.

They were put in irons again when Cork was sighted. The *"Lady Jane"* hove to, and the prisoners were rowed across in longboats to huge ships anchored in rows in Cork harbor, their oak sides rising up like sheer cliffs from the heaving gray sea.

Then the unthinkable happened: Kath was put on a ship bound for Jamaica and the West Indies, while Kevin and Cara were sent to a ship bound for Virginia.

10

Kath held onto the rail around the *Lydia's* deck, looking hopelessly towards the longboat that still held Kevin. It pulled away from the side of *Lydia* and rowed over to the *Edward*, anchored two hundred yards further along the line. The hard knot in her stomach seemed to smash open at last. Tears flooded from her eyes. She threw herself onto the deck, coughing and moaning, racked by the storm of her buried emotions.

"Get up, woman," a weathered English sailor said, prodding her with his toe. "You can't stay here! Prisoners belong in the hold amidships!"

Kath lifted her swollen red face to her tormentor. Her nose was running and there were sprigs of straw in her straggling hair. She was filthy and smelly, her legs raw and oozing, the picture of abject misery. A surge of pity washed over the old sailor, as a memory of his own daughter weeping after the death of her first baby flashed across his mind. This woman looked like the scum of the earth, but she was still one of God's creatures.

"Come," he said more gently, offering his hand to help her up. "You'd best go along and secure your place. There're plenty more will be coming aboard. There'll be hardly room to breathe." He waited while Kath stumbled to her feet. "They'll take those irons off once we're underway. It will be easier. Come now...I'll take you to the hold you'll be in."

Kath wiped her face with her sleeve. "Thank you, Sir," she replied, hiccupping. "I could use a rest."

"I don't think you'll rest. That hold will soon be crammed

full of prisoners. You won't be able to breathe down there."

"Where's the best place to be, if I can?"

"You're small. I think you could tuck in right down in the bottom deck, the hold, we call it. There are a lot of stores down there, barrels, casks and such, but there's likely room for a small person to sleep.

"Y'see, if we are becalmed in the tropics, when the heat comes down hard, you'll be below the waterline, which will be cooler. It's bad however you slice it, but not as bad as at the top, when all the hot air and smell rises.

"And sleeping with barrels has to be better for a woman than sleeping with a hundred other bodies! You go right on down to the bottom. You'll likely find a shelf to sleep on."

"Thank you, Sir," she replied, giving him a tremulous smile. "I know nothing of ships."

The sailor led Kath over to the hatch where a Redcoat Captain was checking his manifest of prisoners.

"Name?" he asked, without looking up.

"Katherine O'Brien, Sir." He flipped through his list until he found her name, ticked it and nodded his head towards the open hold. "Go below."

"Excuse me Sir... Do you know what's to become of me now?"

"Am I God woman?" the Captain snarled. "How the devil am I to know what's to become of you?"

"I – I meant, whether you know what will happen to me once we arrive in Jamaica..."

"You'll be damned, for all I know! You're an indentured servant, you'll work for whoever takes your indenture in that Colony for seven years, and then you'll be free to come home again, if you live."

*

Clutching her precious bundle, Kath clambered down the ladder to the first deck, her chains rattling against the ladder. It was dark and damp below decks. A noxious odor of tar and urine and rotten meat assailed her nostrils as her head came below the hatch. Gradually her eyes became accustomed to the twilight below decks, and she could see rows of bunks, upper and lower, about six feet square. The ceiling was about five feet high, she could not stand without bending her head, and she wondered how full-grown men would fare.

She threw her bundle down the shaft to the next deck and followed it down the ladder, through two levels, until at last she was on the bottom among the casks. As she descended, Kath heard other prisoners coming below, with great clanking, curses, groans and coughs.

The bottom deck was pitch black. The sea gurgled against the hull, ropes and planks creaked and groaned. This ceiling seemed lower than the decks above, and Kath moved carefully among the casks and boxes, searching with her hands along the damp hull. At last she found an empty shelf, about three by five feet, with a four inch lip along the outer edge, mid-way up the hull. There was only the one shelf. Relief flooded her mind when she realized she might be able to sleep alone, unless the sailors needed it for storage. Her hands explored the length of the shelf. Angry squeaks and scampering erupted as she disturbed a rat's nest. She snatched her hand back, quivering, biting back the scream in her throat. Hands over her heart, she calmed herself. The ship was likely full of rats, just as the jail had been. She could manage this. She would rather four-legged rats than the two-legged kind.

She brushed off the bunk as best she could with her hands, then lay down and cowered under her own blanket. She would stay there, tucked away, unless someone came to make her move.

*

Kath woke to sounds of shouted orders, creaking ropes straining through pulleys, thumps and running feet. Then came the sound of the capstan and the sailors heaving the ship's great anchor up from the seabed. She had no way of knowing the time in the blackness of her deck, but she knew she was hungry and thirsty. How would she be fed if she stayed in her shelf down on the bottom deck, with nobody knowing she was there?

She was glad she had not been found out, made to move; happy at the thought she might have this space all to herself for the whole trip. She would have to listen carefully, though, and make her way up to the deck above – or wherever – when the victuals were being dished out. Now she felt her way back to the ladder, and crawled up to see what was happening above. Thank the Blessed Mother, she was in time for breakfast.

That night the fine weather broke and seasickness began. As the ship rolled with the ocean swell, heaving and pitching, the prisoners groaned as one. The prisoners down in their bunks were still in irons.

The hatch above their hold was tightly shut, and a stout oak beam held each hatch-cover closed between the decks. Everyone was penned in, with no fresh air. They were unable to crawl to the slop buckets or help themselves in any way, which added to their anguish. Some called on God and the Blessed Virgin; others screamed, swore, and blasphemed.

It seemed interminable. Alone in the hold, Kath's misery was worsened by dehydration. The old ship let in seawater, which came seeping through the planks in heavy weather. By the time it reached the hold where Kath huddled on her shelf, it ran down the hull in rivulets. She felt too ill to be afraid. *It will not be for long,* she told herself. *I'll die very soon now.*

She didn't die – and, on the third morning, awoke to find the ship was sailing calmly and that she was thirsty, famished and wet through with sea water. Kath crawled up to the top hatch, now open, and emerged into a new world. Rapid blinking soon accustomed her eyes to the brilliant sunlight, and the air was fresh and sweet. There was dark blue sea as far as she could see in any direction.

"Strike the prisoners' irons off, Mr. Walsh," Captain Hilary ordered his First Mate. "We're in deep water now, there's no chance of escape."

"Aye, aye, Sir!"

"Sluice them under the deck-wash pump," Captain Hilary ordered. "Fresh salt water will clean 'em up. And have Mr. Mason, the new surgeon, look at anyone who needs his attention. I want no sickness on this ship!"

"Aye, aye, Sir."

"Starting this afternoon, prisoners are to exercise, in shifts, on the main deck for two hours each day when weather permits," the Captain continued. "And they are to sun their bedding in rotation every two weeks."

Kath joined others on the sunny deck to have her shackles removed, and then under the deck-wash pump. The cold seawater left her gasping and shivering, but at least she was clean!

*

As the weary weeks crept by, the prisoners repeated horror stories they had heard about other prison ships. They were all thankful for Captain Hilary, a better man than they had expected. Thanks to his humanitarian care, there had been no raging fevers or infections aboard the *Lydia* so far.

Mr. Mason did his best. As soon as anyone was sick, the kindly surgeon came with his assistant and his bag, to bleed, purge or make suggestions. He treated the prisoners just as he did the sailors. "Pestilence is no respecter of persons," he often said. "He is just as pleased to visit a captain or sailor as visit a prisoner. And I, for one, do not wish to shake his hand! We'll keep this ship clear of Mr. Pestilence, if we can." It was his little joke.

The drinking water was always tepid and stale, flavored by the wooden kegs from whence it came. There was never enough of it, and whenever a squall threatened, the sailors rushed to put out tubs and stretch tarpaulins in the hope of catching some rainwater. Thus far, their ration was two quarts each per day – enough to keep thirst at bay, even in the sub-tropical heat of August.

The ship's staple diet of salt beef and hardtack biscuit was not so bad. Everyone soon developed the sailors' habit of rapping the biscuits sharply, to make the weevils crawl out before eating them. Twice a week they ate rice and salt beef, twice a week, salt pork; if the sailors were lucky with fishing, they ate fresh fish. There was always bread of a kind, chalky, gritty stuff. Rations for the prisoners were slim and they were always hungry.

Sundays were always special though, a day of rest and relaxation for the sailors. They did not have to work on the decks on Sundays and, when the weather was fine, their other regular duties were minimal. Sunday afternoons the sailors would play games, sing to their guitars or recorders, and repair their clothing. There was usually a special treat for everyone at Sunday dinners, too. Several times they had pickled beets, and once, even a small slice of steamed pudding!

There was no fraternization between prisoners, soldiers and sailors. Each group stayed to themselves, though sometimes the soldiers and sailors would talk together on a Sunday. As for the prisoners, there was always a sentinel stationed at the hatchways. Thick bulkheads filled with nails ran from side to side in between decks, behind the main mast, to ensure separation. There were holes to permit the soldiers to fire at the prisoners between decks in case of rioting.

Long months of incarceration and deprivation had made brutes of many of the prisoners. But in fact few of the prisoners had energy to do much, except argue and fight in the close quarters. The soldiers kept a close eye on the prisoners, were alert to any bickering or breach of order, and were quick to punish the offenders. For a small offence, it was the cramping box; for a more heinous offence, it was flogging.

*

Sometimes Kath didn't know whether to be glad she was alone in the hold or not. The disadvantage of not having a porthole was no light and no possibility of fresh air, but it seemed to her that the advantages of living alone below outweighed even those necessities.

On the one hand, she was thankful for her space, and

freedom from the constant bickering, stealing, and sexual attentions which plagued the other women in the upper decks, where prisoners were crammed together and four people slept in each six by seven foot bunk.

She was always pleasant to the others, but kept her distance. She didn't want her fellow sufferers to think her snobbish, but she wanted even less to be drawn into the constant squabbling that went on among them.

On the other hand, she was desperately lonely.

Kath made one friend – a wiry ten-year-old boy named Jem. She found his monkey-face endearing. His jug-handle ears stuck out beneath a thatch of wiry brown hair, and freckles dotted his little pug nose. Jem's blue eyes seemed to dance with mischief, and they always managed to have a laugh.

One breathless afternoon they were sitting on deck, in the shadow of the mainsail. "Tell me, Jem," Kath asked. "What did you do to land in jail at your young age?"

"Well, Missus," Jem replied, "I was working along with my Da, ever since I was seven years old. We had a few sheep. We took them up in the hills for the summer and brought them back near home for the winter. But last winter we all got sick. We had to sell the sheep, one by one, to buy us food. By March, we had nothing left. My Da was coughing up blood. He got so weak he couldn't walk and he had to take to his bed.

"I tried the farmers around, to see if I could make a shilling, but nobody wanted me. They said I was too meager and weak to help them. I had a bad cough myself and I must have looked sick." He sighed, and the earnest expression on his face made him look more simian than ever.

"Anyway, I started selling peat from our stack, but we'd used it all winter, and there wasn't much left to sell. Most people had their own peat, anyway, they didn't need to buy any from us. So we starved.

"See, Mam had four more behind me. Well, she had seven altogether, one before me, and they buried two after me. I was the eldest and the three after me was girls. They stayed home with Mam. They planted vegetables and sewed a bit, did the cooking. We all did what we could to get by.

"One Market Day I was in the square. Sometimes I could get a few old tatties, a bad cabbage or carrots – whatever was thrown away – to take home to Mam. It was awful cold. I saw a man take off his jacket and sling it aside while he lifted some crates for a woman." Jem wiped his nose with the back of his hand. "I wanted that jacket more than anything! I didn't think about it, I just grabbed it and ran! O' course somebody saw me.

" 'Stop thief!' this woman started screaming, and a man caught me and brought me back. They threw me in the lock-up, then sent me down to the 'Sizes at Dublin. Now I'm to go to Barbados for seven years."

Jem broke off his narrative, biting his lip and twisting his hands in his lap.

"I don't know what's happening at home. I don't know if they found out about me, or if they think I just left them and ran off! Likely they all died of cold and hunger, anyway."

"We can write them a letter, Jem," Kath said gently. "And I can send it with one of the ships going back from Jamaica, telling your family what's become of you. Then when you're settled in Barbados, remember to get someone to write to them again, saying you're well as can be expected, so your Mam won't worry. Give them an address where they can write you back."

"Thanks, Missus," Jem replied. "It won't do no good, 'cause none of us can read or write."

"Well, Jem, there'll be the priest who can read it for them," Kath replied. "And he can write back to you. That way, you can stay in touch. You can find someone to read what he says, and write to your Mam again. I'll try to get some paper and a quill, and we'll do it next time we're on deck," Kath promised.

But the letter was never written.

11

Over this time, the *Lydia* had been dropping well down the map. During the third week of September they crossed the Tropic of Cancer, and the weather became increasingly hot and humid. It had been impossible to sit in the sun between ten and four o'clock for some time, since the decks threw off terrific glare and heat. Nights were wretched down in the hold. No air circulated, and everyone ran with sweat.

They had watched as rainsqualls dumped precious water into the ocean, but not one squall had rained on the *Lydia* for nearly two weeks. The prisoners were rationed to three pints of drinking water a day. It was warm and ill tasting, but everyone was desperate for it.

That night the wind died completely, and the *Lydia* floated idly on the current, the indigo sea heaving its tired bosom in an oily-looking swell. The sickening smell, heat and humidity seemed unbearable.

Sequestered down in the hold, Kath could hear squabbling and violence in the decks above. One man was beating a woman.

Dear God, she thought, *I'm in Hell even before I die!* Kath could bear her wet clothing no longer and stripped it all off, lying in her shelf naked but no cooler. Her salt-caked hair hung in wet rat-tails down her back. She screwed it up on top of her head, skewering it with a long pin fashioned from a salt-beef bone. One or two of the prisoners were clever with their hands and made scrimshaw from the bones left after meals, and one Sunday Kath offered to mend a man's shirt in trade for the hairpin.

Just before dawn the soldiers opened the hatch to the main deck. No wind came down below but the night seemed cooler. Moisture dripped from the railings; the decks and sails were wet. Sound traveled clearly on the still air.

"Mr. Walsh!" called Captain Hilary to his First Mate, "the glass has been dropping all night. We're in for some weather. Reduce sails to topsails only, and reef them."

"Aye, aye, Sir!"

Then came the sound of the order being relayed to the bo'sun, the hubbub of sailors moving about the decks and the sails creaking down and being stowed.

"Mr. Walsh!" Captain Hilary called again. "Get everyone fed as soon as possible, then extinguish the galley fire."

"Aye, aye, Sir!"

Then the order was repeated to a midshipman, and there was the sound of his feet hurrying towards the galley. Then the faint clatter of cooking from the galley, followed by the tramp of sailors going for their food.

"Captain Taylor!" Captain Hilary called the captain of the guard. "You'd best get your soldiers fed! Then the prisoners!"

"Yes, Sir! Right away!"

Everyone heard the order. There was immediate commotion from the prisoners above her. Kath struggled into her wet dress again. "Get up here, you scum!" a soldier bellowed down the main hatch leading to the prisoners' hold. "You're to have early breakfast! Up here on the double!"

It was a relief to get out of the hold and breathe fresh morning air, still and hot as it was. The sky was overcast, with a strange, brassy-yellow light. Ominous dark clouds filled the southwest; sheet lightning flashed, and there was the rumble of distant thunder. The prisoners filed up to the galley door, where two soldiers ladled gruel into wooden bowls.

Kath finished and went onto the main prisoners' deck. There was a slight eddy of air, bringing the scent of rain. Overhead the brassy light was brighter, but the angry dark clouds still scudded below a solid gray canopy. There was no sun, and no wind at sea level. The *Lydia* wallowed and groaned as the violet ocean heaved in weary fatigue, the red and white pennant, identifying the *Lydia* as a convict ship, drooped from the masthead.

Prisoners milled about on their part of the deck. One woman raked her hand along the dew-wet railing and dabbed at her face. Kath caught her eye and smiled. *What I wouldn't give for a swim in Ballyclough pond,* she thought, wiping her own sweating face with the back of her hand. She licked her lips, tasting salt. Sweat ran down her legs and her long sleeves stuck to her arms. A jagged bolt of lightning shot down into the sea, followed by a deafening crack of thunder. A hot wind started blowing, spitting rain.

"Land Ho!" the lookout shouted from the crow's nest.

Captain Hilary was on the quarterdeck. "Mr. Walsh, he bellowed, "Get the decks cleared and ready!"

"Aye, aye, Sir!" Mr. Walsh turned and began shouting orders.

"Send everyone but the watch below," the Captain continued. "Tell the men to sleep if they can, we'll be needing all hands soon. We could be in for a hurricane."

"Aye Sir!"

Everyone hurried to the hatches, their fear palpable. A solid line marked the edge of rain falling on the ocean from the squall moving rapidly upon them from the southwest. Lightning flashed constantly now, rippling from cloud to cloud in frantic bursts, followed sometimes by rattling booms of thunder. The wind picked up, howling, snapping the masthead pennant to stiff attention, slamming the blocks and rigging against the masts like gunfire.

Prisoners were hustling down the hatch. Kath moved to the end of the line. The fierce beauty of the on-coming storm excited her, and she hoped she'd get caught in the rain. Suddenly the squall was upon them, torrents of rain driven horizontal before the shrieking wind.

Blinded and gasping, rain stinging her like a million bees, Kath held onto a rail, hardly able to keep her footing in the deluge sweeping over the deck, deafened by the tumult. Then the *Lydia* bucked and plunged, mighty waves slammed into the prow, their foam hissing over the decks. She barely heard Captain Hilary's screamed orders, but saw sailors running to the bilge pumps. There were four men at the wheel now, battling to control the ship. Mr. Walsh sent a midshipman hurrying below, screaming to men to relieve the tackles.

A soldier grabbed Kath's arm and raked her across the deck to the hatch, throwing her in. She tried to grasp the ladder, but a soldier at the bottom grabbed her legs and pulled. They both sprawled in a heap as the *Lydia* plunged, and the hatch banged shut. Somehow Kath managed to crawl down through the two decks to the hold. She held onto barrels feeling for her shelf, then went sprawling into it as the ship lurched again. Her knee caught on her skirt. Already rotten from constant wear, her dress ripped at the armpits, and the skirt came away from the bodice.

The ship continued its sickening plunging. Seawater streamed in through the seams in the ship's planks. Kath fancied she could hear the low murmur of the bilge pumps working, though it was hard to tell above the groaning and creaking of the ship, the water smashing against the hull. Then some barrels broke loose, adding to the noise and confusion. Kath cowered at one end of her shelf, hanging onto the edge, trying to pray. The wild swooping of the ship went on for hours, and she lost all sense of time in the blackness, motion and noise.

Then the noise stopped. The ship's plunging moderated, and all was calm.

*

Holy Mother of God! The storm is over, Kath thought. She heard the tramp of sailors moving around on the decks above, shouted orders, and the sound of axes chopping away masts and rigging. *We survived it!* The hard lump of fear in her stomach began to uncoil and she was abruptly sick. She lay back, exhausted. It was fiercely hot, so she stripped off what remained of her dress and lay naked, drifting into a doze, spread-eagled on her shelf.

She startled awake. The noise and plunging were beginning again!

There was a loud retort from the stern, like a cannon exploding. The ship seemed to be spinning, heeling over further than ever. She was thrown against the hull of the ship. There was a shuddering wrench, and more kegs and barrels broke loose; terror gripped her as they bounced and rolled around in the dark.

The *Lydia* careened completely over onto her port side. Then came a terrible grinding, and the rush of seawater pouring in. The vessel heaved back over on her starboard side with a mighty shudder. Kath fell beneath the shelf. Barrels bounced above her, hitting the ledge of the shelf and rolling away. One small cask landed right beside her and she grabbed it, hugging it for protection.

It was only then that Kath realized that she was able to see. Dim light filtered through a large gash in the side of the hull – and she could see daylight.

The ship was jerking now, with awful ripping noises. The water level was rising rapidly in the hold; she tried to stand, but couldn't find her footing. There was the horrible din of trapped people, doomed people, pounding the sides of the ship and screaming.

Then she was floating in the water, clutching the small empty cask, surrounded by other barrels that were floating too.

*

I have to get out, Kath thought. *Somehow I've got to get through that hole at the top. If I can get underneath it, when the water fills this hold, it'll float me up and I can get out.* She began kicking her way through the bobbing barrels, shoving them aside with her keg.

The hold deck was filling rapidly, and within moments Kath was under the hole. Now water began streaming through the hole, its force ripping it larger, taking more planks, but the incoming water was pushing Kath away from the hole. She grabbed the edge of the hole and held on tightly with both hands. Soon there was only enough air space for her head.

My mouth must be the last to go under, she thought. *I'll take a big gulp of air, then force myself through. The ship hasn't sunk completely yet. I should pop out like a cork from a bottle. I must not panic! I've got to concentrate!*

Her moment came quickly. There was still a current of water pushing in through the hole, but it was weaker now, as the water in the hold equalized with the water outside, but she could feel the current from the waves surging around her. *Lydia* was sinking! Kath filled her lungs, let go and started kicking, up and through the hole.

Gasping and spluttering, Kath took another great gulp of air. A mighty wave slammed into her, bashing her against the side of the ship. She managed another deep breath. Her hand closed briefly over a rope. Then another wave hit her. The rope was gone. Up, up, up she rode on the crest of the swell, away from the boat, beyond the rigging.

Kath had a fleeting impression of the *Lydia* wallowing under the waves, her three masts and rigging swirling in a tangle beside her, her yardarms pointing up to the sky. Kath could hear nothing but the screaming fury of the storm, could see nothing through the white torrents of rain.

She tried to swim. Her arm hit a piece of wood. Pain shot into her shoulder but she grabbed at the wood, holding onto it with both arms, kicking both legs. The waves were towering green mountains flecked with foam. Kath was swooped into their valleys, then hurled up to their fifty-foot crests. Totally helpless, terrified, clinging to her plank, Kath remembered the nun's telling them the story of Jesus calming the storm.

"Jesus save me!" she cried aloud. "Save me!"

Immediately came a sense of peace, as though God was holding her in His hand. She knew He had heard her cry. Somehow she knew that she would live.

For a long time Kath clung to the wood, arms and legs scraped raw from holding on, as it rode the billows, sweeping up their crests, and plunging into the deep valleys. The rain seemed to come in bands, heavy downpour, then light drizzle.

From the top of a wave, Kath saw the olive green of land looming through the rain, and heard the boom of sea crashing against rocks, could see its spume flying high into the air. Then she would be swept down, down into a deep valley of angry water, where nothing but surging ocean existed. But the terror had left her now; she was no longer afraid. God hadn't brought her this far only to destroy her on rocks. He would save her, she was sure.

Closer and closer Kath came to the rocks. Soon she realized that the waves were carrying her beyond the rocks, around a point, along the coast. She was floating in a current that knew exactly where it was going, and taking her with it. Then she saw a break in the rocks. The waves were pushing into a bay, flinging themselves against grass-covered sand dunes.

Waves took her nearer and nearer to the dunes, until eventually she could see that the next breaker would dump her ashore. She let go of her plank and abandoned herself to the surge, kicking to stay afloat, swimming on the crest. Suddenly she crashed hard onto the sand, in a maelstrom, tumbling, rolling over and over, her lungs bursting. Then she felt her face smash hard against solid sand. She fought for breath – somehow, she caught a breath. The surf thundered around her, the receding wave was sucking her back out into the sea.

Kath scrabbled at the sand, trying to dig her fingers in, to get a hold. It was no good. She was tumbling again, in a soup of seaweed, sand and pebbles, swallowing water, inexorably caught in the undertow. Her lungs were burning. She couldn't see, but she sensed the swell of another breaker. Instinct made her paddle, turn around and paddle with the wave. She was up on the crest, then there was a free-falling moment and the wave hurled her ashore once more.

This time her grasping hands found a tussock of wiry roots. She grabbed them as the wave receded, clawing herself further up on the dune. I must rest, she thought. But the next breaker washed over her legs, nearly sucking her back into the maw of the sea. *Can't stop here,* she thought. *Must go higher, must get further away...*

With her last ounce of strength, Kath crawled another fifteen yards through the leathery, scrubby grass. Then she knew no more.

12

Kath woke shivering, her body wracked with pain. She sat up and looked around, not remembering what had happened, or where she was. She came to with a jolt. *Shipwrecked... Washed ashore somewhere...* She looked around. It was hard to tell how long she had been asleep, or what the time was. The sky was leaden, but the rain had stopped, and the terrible wind had ceased. The sea still raged, but she noticed that the tide was much lower. The breakers now spent themselves on a sloping white beach, hissing in retreat from the sand.

Kath cleared her throat and spat. Her mouth and throat were full of sand. She put her face in her hands. Her skin burned. Gently she felt her cheek. It was swollen, terribly sore. Her fingers explored a cut on her forehead. She looked down at her naked body. I'm bruised and cut all over, she thought. *All sandy and salty and bloody...* Slowly she brushed herself off. Everywhere hurt. She had raw scrapes all over her body from riding the plank in the water. She touched an angry red gash across her stomach. *So thirsty...head hurts! Must have water...*

It was agony to stand. Her legs buckled, refusing to support her. She staggered a few steps, then managed to straighten up. Hobbling through the dune grasses was agony too. There were prickles – straw colored, vicious things that dug into her feet. Long vines caught at her ankles, tripping her. She stubbed her toe on a jutting rock, and pain shot white-hot through her. She collapsed on a patch of clear sand and sobbed.

Blessed Virgin, Holy Mother of God! What have I done to deserve all this? Have I ever wronged anybody? Was I unfaithful to my husband, did I break my vows? What? Why must I suffer like this? Have you spared my life from the sea so I can die more painfully? I've tried to live a good life. I've gone to church... said my confession, taken the sacraments. What do you want from me, God?

Look at me! I'm all scratched and bruised... My hair is tangled, full of sand. I'm so thirsty... and hungry. Help me!

She got up again, stiff in every joint, and picked her way to the top of the dune to have a look around.

Kath saw a thick wood, tortured by the storm, growing on the other side of the dunes. Trees were uprooted, fallen in drunken snarls against their neighbors. Mangled, black, stripped limbs reached up in supplication to the sullen sky. All was desolate. No bird called, no cricket chirped. All she heard was the melancholy boom of the surf.

Those trees will give me some protection, Kath thought. *At least I can sleep there.* She stumbled on through the scrub and rock, heading for the trees. Once there, she found the ground marshy, and that rain had settled a couple of feet deep under the trees. Kath crouched and drank from cupped hands until she was full, then lay in the fresh water. She washed slowly, discovering new bruises wherever she touched herself. She got most of the sand off and untangled her hair in the soft rainwater, combing through it with her fingers.

So tired... somewhere to sleep, Kath thought. She spotted a large rock sticking out of a dune. There was a small indentation beneath it – hardly a cave, but it seemed inviting. She trudged over to it and mechanically scooped out sand with her hands, making herself a hollow in which to sleep. *I'll think about it all tomorrow... I can't bear another minute of this day!*

*

When she woke the next morning, the sun was high, beating on the blinding white sand, sucking water from the soil. The air was already hot, but the sky was clear, deep blue, with puffy white clouds strewn across it. There was no sign that Mother Nature had had a terrible tantrum the day before and done her utmost to ruin everything in her path. Then she looked at the land, the broken, uprooted trees, the snarled grasses, and the flotsam on the beach along the high water mark. She had not dreamed the hurricane, it had definitely happened!

Kath hurried over to the pool beneath the trees. She slapped at her leg. Something was biting, a sharp pinprick, itchy. More bites, all over her body now, but she could see nothing. Carefully inspecting a new stinging spot on her arm, Kath saw a tiny black dot. It was the smallest possible fly, and it was making its dinner from her tender skin!

Quickly she drank her fill, then, thinking that perhaps the flies would not be on the beach, she tackled the dunes again, with their clumps of coarse grass, prickles and scrub. Tangled sea oats were everywhere, their heads snapped, jagged and bedraggled.

There was a gentle breeze down on the beach. Although the waves still beat themselves to froth on the rocks, the tide was out again. Kath's stomach rumbled. *A few pieces of oat-cake with butter and milk would be handsome right now,* she thought. *What am I going to eat?* She looked around, abjectly miserable again as the full realization of her situation dawned upon her.

The sea blazed with splintered sunlight. The water was a wonderful color, one she had never seen before, a bright, translucent turquoise. Its sheer beauty made her catch her breath. Then she saw it. A barrel, bobbing in the surf. At the high water line on the beach there was more flotsam. Things littered along the edges of the dunes...

Her pulse raced at the thought that perhaps she wasn't the only one to escape. Maybe there were others from the ship. And since she had got out of the hold, maybe other barrels had broken out too. The food stores were in there. That very same barrel might be full of ship's biscuit, or salt beef! Her mouth watered. She would have to wait until the tide brought it in.

Dear God, please grant it is so! Let there be food, let there be other people! Then she remembered. *Holy Mother, I'm stark naked. I can't let anyone see me like this!* Eyes narrowed against the sun, Kath carefully scanned the beach and the rolling surf. There was no sign of anyone else.

Holy Mother, please send me some clothes, Kath took up her silent prayer again. *Let somebody's trunk wash up for me... Maybe a dead body will wash up and I can have its clothes,* she thought. *That's not a kind thought, Kath,* her conscience admonished. *Well, if I do find a body, it'll have no need of clothes and I certainly need them,* she told herself firmly. *This is no time to be squeamish about pillaging the dead.* The idea made her shudder. *I'll just have to be practical. My skin's turning red, I'm roasting in this hot sun. And I'm getting dizzy,* she thought. *Have to find shade...shade behind the dunes, but those stinging flies... Maybe I can build some cover on the beach.*

Kath plodded wearily along the sand, looking for something to use, and something to eat. At the end of the crescent strand, where the jagged rocks began, she found a broken spar with torn canvas and cut ropes. Of course – the sailors had cut away the rigging after the masts toppled over.

She tugged at it. *Waterlogged, too heavy to drag onto the beach. Wait until high tide, then float it to that gap in the dunes. Hold onto the rope, stop it going back out to sea. Then drag it higher, make a kind of tent.*

What do I do in the meantime? She looked around wiping sweat from her eyes with the back of her hand. She noticed that the dunes were casting a shadow on the blazing sands beneath. *I'll go up there,* Kath thought, *above high-water mark. I can dig a hole in the shade, cover myself with sand. That will be cool and will keep the sun off my skin.*

As Kath dug into the sand about a foot deep, water welled into the hole. Ever thirsty, she tasted it... it was fresh. Rainwater was seeping from the land into the sea. She grabbed a piece of wood from the debris on the beach and finished her trench, then covered herself with a mound of sand, protecting her eyes with her arm. The cool, wet sand was like a balm to her feverish body.

*

Slowly she woke. *It must be four o'clock,* Kath thought squinting at the sun. *I've slept for hours!*

Breakers were rolling in, crashing onto the sand to die in cascades of green and white lace, the remnant of each swirling back, in time to join the suicide leap of the next. Although the ocean swells were mighty, the terrible rage had moderated. The breakers were no longer gouging at the dunes, though their wash still reached the top of the beach. Kath crawled out of her hole and crouched at the edge of the waves, washing the sand from her body. Her stomach sent grabbing, painful signals that she needed food.

Please God, give me food and shelter. Rescue me! Surely You haven't saved my life to take it by starvation! Kath plodded along the top of the beach, her pleading prayer becoming a litany in her mind. There were several barrels toiling in the surf, rolling in and out with the motion of the waves. Kath watched for a while, thinking how best to get one to stay up on the beach.

Working up her courage at last, Kath plunged in after one of the barrels. She grabbed hold of it as the breaker crashed around her, rolling it up the beach with the incoming water. The barrel jammed itself into the sand, and the wave receded without it. She tried to right it onto one end, but it was too heavy for her. Well, she would work out how to open it later.

Two barrels and one small keg later, Kath sat to rest. *I must not give in to despair,* she thought. *I have to keep doing things, thinking how to solve my problems rather than worrying about my fate.* She noticed that the tide had turned, was ebbing now. The waves no longer reached up to the barrels.

I must have another drink, she thought, digging a new hole in the sand beside the last rescued barrel. The sand kept collapsing into the hole from under the barrel. She made the hole wider, then turned the barrel until one end was near the edge of the hole. She dug the sand from under the end until the barrel canted down into the hole. Lying on her back, Kath pushed the barrel with her feet until it slid into the hole, then pulled it upright.

Now what? Kath wondered. *I still have to open it.* She put a short piece of wood planking against the bung in the top of the barrel and pounded the end of the wood with a rock, gradually working around the circumference of the bung, pushing it in. She looked inside. Small wheels of cheddar, wrapped in waxy cheesecloth! Quickly she unwrapped the top wheel and dug into it with her bit of plank, stuffing down the crumbs as fast as she could chew.

After her feast and more water, Kath felt stronger, more optimistic. She remembered the spar and canvas then, and went looking for it, but she could not find it on the beach. *Maybe it's caught in the rocks,* she thought, and picked her way up onto the rocks, but found they were razor-sharp, and she soon gave up the struggle. She went back to her sleep-hole on the beach.

Loneliness enveloped her like a shroud. Kath nibbled some more cheese, thinking with longing of her life in Ireland – and her beautiful, fine sons, whom she would never see again. As hard as life had been after John's death, still there had been a kind of peace, a kind of security in having her own tumbledown heap of stones, with her own hearth, her garden. She smiled to herself, remembering spinning flax for the itinerant weaver to make into linen; the deep pleasure she took in sewing, and designing her embroidery. A little gossip with Maggie next door, minding the children, tending her bees, feeding the chickens, going to Mass when the priest came to see them every quarter.

The English Protestants had taken it all from her! Kath had spent hours on board the *Lydia*, lying on her stinking dark shelf, immersing herself in hatred. Before all this with Duncan and Kevin, she had hated the English more as a cultural stance, at one with her Irish Catholic people. She blamed them for her father's injuries, her husband's hanging, but that had been through their own decision to go to war, and to be a part of the Rebellion. Her hatred of the English was to some extent at a remove from her center. Maggie had felt it more forcefully than she had.

Now her hatred was personal, and she found herself grinding her teeth and balling her fists when she thought of their injustice, their cavalier manner with stealing Irish land, not paying for their purchases.

Their selfishness, their snobbish attitudes, as though God had made them a different species, far above the rest of humanity. She had come to understand fully what her people had known all along. The English Protestants were the scourge of Ireland and the Irish. Now she truly hated them, and wanted vengeance. Vengeance for Duncan, for Kevin, for dear little Jem, herself... *for this!*

*

Kath watched as the sun sank behind the horizon in fiery red, casting a blazing path across the ocean. The sky was shot with brilliant pink, peach, gold and turquoise. Puffy white clouds, like grazing lambs, floated lazily about. Gently the colors faded into a translucent deep blue, then violet, then velvety purple, then at last into black. Stars crept out, one by one, until the sky was riddled with winking diamonds.

I'm totally alone, she thought. *I'm naked, homeless and hungry. I have nothing. Everybody I've ever loved, everything I've ever had, is gone. My whole life is gone forever, as though it had never been. John, Duncan, Kevin, all the people who gave my life purpose, everything that defined my very self, no longer exists.*

"Who am I, God?" Kath shouted to the sky. Her voice came out cracked and ragged, like the cawing of a rook. *"What do You want from me? And what will You do with me now?"*

She waited, but of course there was no reply. As usual, He was hiding from her. There was only the monotonous boom of the surf, the sough of the wind in the broken bent grasses on the dunes.

The moon peeped above the heaving ocean, then rose quickly in golden magnificence. Then the splendor of the scene, the awesome miracle that she had survived at all, filled Kath's desolate heart. Surely the God who had made all that – who had created and ordered the earth, the sea, the stars, the moon – had made and ordered her, too. She would not despair. She felt certain, she knew, that God would take care of her. Whether He spoke to her or not.

13

Kath woke early on the third day since the hurricane and made her daily inspection of the horizon and the beach. There was the merest white spot, way out to sea. As she watched intently, it slowly grew larger.

It's a sail, Kath told herself. *It's definitely a sail! Oh, if only I had a fire! How can I get their attention? How can I make them stop for me?* Kath's mind twitched feverishly over the questions, like the tail of an angry cat. A fire would be the best thing, but she had tried several times to make one without luck.

She had longed for fire. One of the barrels held salt pork. Two days of damp, wormy ship's biscuits and cheese had left Kath yearning for variety. Her mouth watered at the thought of the salt pork. She tried a gob of it straight from the barrel; it was pickled meat, it should have been fine – but it made her retch. With fire she could cook it, could have cheer at night, smoke to discourage the swarms of biting flies and mosquitoes. And she could build a bonfire to attract a ship, should one pass by.

The next best thing would be a flag – but she had no cloth, since the sail and rigging she'd found earlier had gone back out on the tide. Then she thought of the cheeses. They were wrapped in cheese cloth! She unwrapped the cheeses and tied the stiff, waxy cloths onto the ends of the longest planks she could find. Then she stuck them into the highest sand dunes. Maybe the lookout on the ship would see them with his glass.

Kath walked up and down the long beach, leaving footprints above high water mark. She stuck her 'flags' well above the line of the surf, ending at her sleeping place under the edge of the dune. She planted her last flag here.

What more can I do to get their attention? Kath wondered. Then she had an idea. She ran into the bush and broke armloads of branches from the leafy boughs of the trees which had been felled by the hurricane. She took the largest branch she could drag and stuck it into the sand, just above the edge of the waves. Then, walking directly up to her sandy burrow, she planted a line of smaller twigs. *That ought to lead them straight to me,* she thought.

Next, she gathered driftwood and seaweed and spelled the word 'HELP' in large letters on the white sand.

Then, exhausted, she sat down to watch as the sail drew nearer. Finally the ship was just outside the bay. *Holy Mary, Mother of God, please let them see me! Please make them stop here...*

The ship was tacking... was coming about... was sailing into the bay! Wild with joy, she jumped up and down, waving a branch.

Kath watched the ship drop its sails and anchor. It all seemed to take forever. Then she realized they would see her naked, so she crawled into her sandy nest and covered herself with branches. *If they miss all my signals, I'll just have to run out to them naked.* She grew warm at the idea that the person with the glass had already seen her!

There was a lot of activity on the deck, a man examining the shore with a glass at his eye. Then they lowered a boat, two sailors got in and began rowing towards the beach. Slowly they came in, beaching by her planted branch.

"Hoy!" Kath shouted, waving another branch. "Hoy! Halloo! Up here! I'm up here! Come over here!"

The men waved, then pulled their boat up onto the sand and secured it with a small anchor. They were both large, and about six feet tall. One was black and held a cutlass in his hand. The other was mahogany brown and carried a musket. They wore dirty white breeches and no shirts. Their powerful muscles gleamed in the sun, and their hair and beards were wild and woolly.

Kath's heart thumped in her chest. *Holy Mother, what will they do to me? These must be black men,* she thought. *I've never seen anybody so dark – and huge!* Kath fought an intense desire to jump up and run. She would just have to brave it out.

Suddenly the thought came to her that they were afraid as well. Their weapons were for defense, not to harm her. They didn't know who they would find. Maybe they thought she was a decoy... that they would be ambushed.

"I'm alone!" Kath called. "I've been shipwrecked and I have no clothes!"

The sailors stopped about fifteen feet from her and conferred a moment. Then the black one came over, his teeth flashing and his eyes crinkled in a smile as he looked down at her.

"Vell, Missus," he said, "Ya sure can't come aboard like dat!" His voice was soft, a deep, rumbling bass. "We'll need t'bring ya somethin' t'cover yaseff wid. An' we gatty tell Cap'n Grev 'bout ya. Don' fret! Ain't nobody goin' hurt ya! You's safe wid us. We ga be right back."

Kath watched with some apprehension as the dinghy went back to the ship. She didn't understand what the man had said, but she felt reassured by his gentle voice and obvious respect. Anyway, she thought, I have no choice.

*

Four men, including the two from the first trip, returned to the beach. One was dressed in a straw hat, white cotton shirt, which he wore open in front, and black breeches. He came towards Kath carrying a folded cloth over his arm. The others fanned out above him, their muskets ready and their eyes searching the dunes.

This will be their captain, she thought. Kath's heart beat faster as he came nearer. She had never seen anyone so commanding and exotic.

Like his men, he was tall, muscular and darkly tanned. His face was triangular, with a pointed chin, high cheekbones and a broad, high forehead. His shoulder length dark hair was streaked with white, tied back with a black ribbon. Deep fissures ran from his aquiline nose to the corners of his mouth, which was wide, with full lips that smiled to reveal very white teeth. He wore his beard short, shaved around his cheeks and jaws, and his mustache was neatly clipped. Heavy dark eyebrows guarded hazel eyes, surprising in a face so brown. He wore a small, thick gold hoop in his left ear.

The Captain stopped a few feet from Kath, swept off his hat and bowed, presenting a well-muscled leg.

"Your servant, Ma'am," he said in a vibrant baritone voice. "I am Captain Greville Knowles, of the *Swan*. My men tell me you've been shipwrecked and have lost everything."

"That's so, Sir. I am Kathleen O'Brien, from Ireland, and much obliged to you, Sir. I was aboard the *Lydia*, out of Cork, bound for Jamaica when we were caught in a hurricane several days gone."

"Are you truly the only survivor?" he asked, looking around.

"I have searched this part of the island as best I could, Sir. I have found no others, dead or alive. There may be others washed ashore around that point. I was unable to walk upon those sharp rocks to explore further."

"We will take a look," Captain Knowles said. "Are you in need of anything immediately, Ma'am? Have you had water, and food?"

"Yes, Captain, I thank you! There is rainwater settled behind the dunes and food washed ashore in those barrels yonder."

"I'll spread this sheet over you, Ma'am, and leave you to cover yourself. Then please wait in the boat until we come back."

Captain Knowles spread the sheet over Kath up to her chin, then bowed from the waist. He turned and walked towards the far end of the beach with his men, who were still keeping a sharp lookout. As soon as he had moved well away, Kath scrambled from her sandy berth and wrapped the sheet around her. She walked down to the boat and waited, while the men examined the flotsam along the beach.

She was painfully aware of how she looked. Naked, sandy, her skin red and blistered from the sun and insect bites, her hair in snarled strings. She was desperate for a bath. The men had moved along to the other end of the beach, they couldn't see her if she took a quick dip in the sea to get rid of the sand. She went around the side of the boat away from the men, dropped her sheet, then plunged into the water, rubbing the sand off and scraping it out of her hair. Then she let her hair float behind her head, ducked her head back into the water and stood up. Her hair now fell tidily down her back. She walked out of the sea and wrapped the sheet around herself like a toga, tying it over one shoulder.

She leaned against the boat, drying herself in the sun. Squinting in the glare, she watched as the Captain easily climbed the highest dune, put his glass to his eye and carefully swept the interior of the island, then examined the rocks on either side of the bay.

While Captain Knowles made his inspection, his men were bringing the barrels down to the edge of the sea. They made heaps of the wooden planks and other things they found, then the men separated – two went along the rocks, while one returned to the boat with the Captain.

"We'll take you aboard now, Ma'am," Captain Knowles said. "My men are searching for wreckage. We'll take this keg and a barrel with us now, too, Horace," he told the sailor with him.

The boat was loaded to the gunwales as they set out across the calm bay towards the *Swan*. Kath soon understood why the men wore no shirts; the sailor's body poured with sweat as he rowed. The *Swan* was a white schooner, with beautiful lines.

"What a fine ship, Captain Knowles!" Kath said warmly.

"Thank you, Ma'am!" he replied. "We're very fond of her too!" His face glowed with pride as he looked up at his ship. Still smiling, he looked straight at Kath with his tawny hazel eyes. Again she felt her pulse race. There was a swift moment of recognition, a sense of having known this man all her life. She dropped her eyes and held onto her sheet.

There was another sailor aboard the *Swan*, leaning over the side, waiting to catch the rope from the boat. After the little boat was secured, the men stood ready to help Kath aboard.

"Excuse me, Ma'am," the Captain said. "I think it best, in the circumstances, if I hand you up to the man..." at which point he put both hands to Kath's waist and lifted her easily up towards the deck of the *Swan*.

"Careful, Harry, Mistress O'Brien mustn't lose her winding sheet!" the Captain called.

Kath's body burned from the feel of his hands, as he held her like a straw doll in the air. She clutched her sheet to her, hugging herself as Harry swung her onto the deck. She waited, flustered, as the Captain leaped nimbly up beside her.

"That was neat work, Ma'am," Captain Knowles said, smiling down at Kath. "Welcome aboard the *Swan*. Please wait aft, until we get these barrels aboard. Then I'll lend you some clothes and see to your comfort."

14

"Well, Mistress O'Brien!" Captain Knowles said, coming up behind Kath, who was leaning over the rail lost in her own thoughts. She turned to find him right behind her, with a big smile on his face. Her pulse raced.

"Oh, Captain Knowles! You startled me!"

"Let's go to my cabin, if you please, and see to your needs," he said, oblivious to her discomfort. "No doubt you long for a wash and a hot meal. I've set Harry to work in the galley. He's quite a good cook. We still have a few luxuries we've been hoarding since Jamaica. Like butter – and eggs! I know old Harry will be falling over himself to produce something tasty for you. We don't often have the pleasure of a lady's company on board."

"Please, Captain Knowles, do not concern yourselves on my account. I don't need to have your special delicacies! I can never repay you for saving my life, as it is."

"Well, we'll soon be home – and the men's wives and sweethearts can make delicacies for them then. I think you need something light at first, to break your fast. Perhaps a jam omelet? That's my favorite!"

As he spoke, the Captain took Kath's elbow and steered her towards a hatch. "This is my cabin, Ma'am, which I propose you shall use until we make landfall. It is Spartan, I'm afraid, and small, but I trust you will be comfortable here."

"Oh Captain, please do not!" Kath turned to him, his kindness causing her throat to close up. "I will happily sleep in any cranny you can find – anywhere that I shall not be in the way."

"I will not hear of it, Ma'am, and there's an end to it. You have just come through the most dreadful tribulations. You need food and rest. Whatever small comfort this ship can provide shall be yours.

"Now, there is my wash basin," he said, pointing to his chart table. "Ah – and here is Ned, with some fresh water and a clean towel for you. And a mug of good Jamaica coffee... that should put you right. Did you put a tipple of rum in it, Ned?"

"Yeth, Thir, Cap'n Grev, Harry put it in."

Ned placed a towel and tankard on the table, and put a bucket down beside it. He'd lost most of his teeth and his mouth had caved in. His prominent chin spouted several days' grizzled growth, and greasy hair flopped on his forehead. He was no beauty, but his crooked grin beamed eager goodwill.

It was all too much. Kath collapsed on the chair by the Captain's table and put her face in her hands, her body shaking.

"Hey Mithus, there'th nothin' to cry fer," Ned lisped, putting his warm, gnarled hand on her shoulder. "Ye're thafe with uth! No harm'll come to ye now! We'll look after ye! If there'th anything ye need, ye've only to thay..."

A muffled howl answered him.

Captain Knowles strode to the door. He was always flummoxed by a woman with the vapors. "Well, I'll leave you now," he said.

"Oh – I was forgetting..." he reentered the cabin and rummaged in a small locker. "Here are some clothes, Ma'am." He threw a pair of draws, some white cotton hose, a pair of black knee breeches and a frilled white shirt on his berth. "I know they'll be too big, but happen you can fix them to fit somehow.

"Now rest! Rest as long as you care to. Harry will be along by'n'by with something to eat. Come, Ned! Your servant, Ma'am." Captain Knowles bowed to the bawling Kath, moved quickly up the ladder and closed the hatch.

Kath soon recovered. The coffee smelled inviting. She

didn't know what it was. She looked at it, and took a sip. Hot. It was bittersweet, potent – unlike anything she had ever tasted before. It felt good going down. The liquor in it made her tingle. Her stomach growled.

I'd better get washed, she thought. Harry will be appearing any moment, and I must apologize to the Captain and Ned for my outburst. Poor men, they don't know what to do with me. She smiled, thinking of their hasty retreat.

Kath found soap in the basin. She washed her hair first, then did the best she could with the rest of herself between sips of the delicious coffee. It was wonderful to feel clean again, to be looked after, and to feel safe at last.

She turned to the clothing the Captain had left out for her. His white stockings were so baggy she had to pinch the tops, screw them into a ball and tuck them in. His drawers and breeches ballooned about her petite body. They were big enough for two of her, and his knee breeches fell to her ankles. The frilled cuffs of the shirt flapped below her fingertips, and the neck threatened to reveal all of one shoulder.

There was a knock on the hatch cover.

"Yes? Come in," Kath called, hugging the clothing to her body. "It's me, Harry, Ma'am," came the reply. The opened hatch revealed a short, wiry young man holding a loaded tray. He burst out laughing, hardly able to hold the tray.

"S'cuse me, Ma'am, but you do look comical in that rig! S'truth, it swamps you. You look like a brig under full sail, you do."

Kath looked ruefully down at herself and laughed too. Harry set the tray on the table and looked at Kath again, twinkling eyes lighting his angular brown face. "We must see if we can't find you something better to wear. You'll never be able to go about a ship in those clothes."

"I know, Harry, but I've none of my own. Tell me, do you have a needle and thread? And perhaps a pair of shears? I can make myself something out of this sheet, if it can be spared."

"Yes, the Mate has some sewing things. But I most believe my spare pair of breeches will fit you better'n Cap'n Grev's. They're almost clean. And maybe Ned has an extra shirt – I'll ask. The rest of the crew are all big men, like Cap'n Grev. But between Ned and me, we should be able to get you decent until we get home tomorrow evenin', God spare life. We'll be checking the shore on the way home, too. Happen we'll find something from the wreck that might fit you. But don't worry 'bout that now. Come and eat your nice dinner. I cooked it especially for you."

Harry brought the chair up to the table and held it for Kath. He had brought a trencher holding a yellow porridge of some sort, with a slice of ham and two soft-boiled eggs. A knob of butter melted on the porridge. The fragrant meal made Kath's mouth water.

She bowed her head and made the sign of the cross. Harry leaned against the cabin door, waiting for her to eat. She dipped the spoon into the food, starting with the porridge. "What's this yellow porridge Harry? It's very good."

"Why, that's grits, Missus. You ain't never tasted grits before? It's ground up Indian corn, cooked soft, with butter to give it flavor. We eats it all the time. It tastes good with anything, specially boiled fish. That's what we'll be having for dinner. We caught a nice barracuda trolling this morning. I'll save you some for your supper."

Kath could hardly understand what Harry said. He used words she didn't know and spoke with a lilting accented English that sounded quite foreign. She smiled and began to eat with gusto, and that seemed enough for Harry.

"You must be most awful famished and tired. It's been three days since that hurricane. You'd best eat slow to start, though Ma'am – your stomach's not used to food no more." He sighed and straightened up. "Well, Miss, I best be going about my duties. Just leave everything on the tray when you get through. I'll come to get it later. I still got the fish to clean and cook, and Cap'n Grev wants to get underway soon as the others get back from the island."

"Thank you, Harry. You're a good cook. I'll be looking forward to my supper."

"S'nothing, Missus. It's good to have you aboard. Breaks the monotony, like." Harry departed.

They're all so kind and friendly, as though nothing was too good for me, Kath thought. *They're like my neighbors back home. Not at all like those stinking English, with their airs and graces. But I wonder how they'll treat me when they find out I'm a prisoner, on my way to be sold as an indentured servant? I won't tell them right away, until they know me better and realize that I'm not a thief.* She finished the last bite of grits and yawned. The Captain's bed looked very inviting. She took off the Captain's clothes and crawled naked between the sheets.

*

Kath woke slowly, relishing the feel of the sheets on her body.

They had a sweet, musky smell that made her think of Captain Knowles. She looked through the porthole and saw the sky streaked with vermilion and peach. It was hot and humid in the cabin. Her body was drenched with sweat, her skin felt stretched and sore. The ship creaked and she could hear the gentle gurgle of water. *We're underway already,* she thought. Faintly she remembered the sound of scampering feet and sails hoisting.

Her stomach rumbled. She thought the men were probably eating supper by now, so she wrapped the sheet tightly about her body, opened the hatch and peered out. Outside on the threshold was a smaller pair of knee breeches and another shirt. She tried them on – these were much better. At least she could walk in them.

She stood on the ladder and looked out of the hatch. The crew were drinking coffee on deck. She was disappointed that the Captain was not among them.

"Good evening to you, Missus O'Brien," Harry said. "Are you ready to try a little boiled fish and grits? It was so good dinnertime, I had a job saving some for you."

"Harry's bragging again," said the large black man who had come ashore and found her. All the men stood as she came up on deck, snatching off their hats. "Come and sit with us, Missus O'Brien... Come and meet the crew. My name is Horace," the same man said, stabbing his chest with his right forefinger, and continued pointing: "That's Ned, Harry, who's also our Cook, and Obediah, our Mate. We call him Obie." Each man gave a little bow as his name was called. "That's it, the crew of the *Swan* at your service!"

Kath smiled. "Sit, if you please! Do not disturb yourselves on my account. See, I'm wearing breeches, too. I expect to be working as one of the crew."

"I doubt Cap'n Grev would have that, Ma'am," Obie said, his face lighting up. "We're honored to have you aboard as our guest. We don't often have the pleasure of a lady's company, let alone a heroine such as yourself."

"Thank you kindly," Kath replied with a catch in her voice.

"How did you manage to stay alive, all alone? We found two corpses thrown up on the beach around the point, badly battered by the rocks. We're eager to hear your story."

Harry gave her a steaming bowl of boiled fish and grits. "Let her eat first," he commanded. Kath tasted it and coughed, her eyes watering. The fish was seasoned with red pepper, all-spice, onions and lime juice.

"Quick, some water," Ned said. "She's not used to all this pepper, Harry!"

"I forgot," Harry replied. "I just seasoned it as usual."

"I'll get used to it Harry," Kath replied after a drink. "It's very tasty, even it if bites!" She smiled at him and took another taste. There was a general silence. Kath looked warily at the bowl. She was hungry enough to eat a horse, but this spicy dish...

Obie laughed. "Missus O'Brien reminds me of Jimmy's cat, Tab!"

Kath looked at him, puzzled.

"Jimmy was our ship's carpenter several years ago," Obie explained. "He loved cats, and one day he found this scrawny little tabby hanging around the dock in New Providence. He brought her on the ship, to help keep down the rats – and to be company, you know." Obie looked around the company, warming to his subject. "Well, that cat was a thief!"

Kath's face turned bright red, but Obie held every eye. "We couldn't put anything down without that cat getting into it. If we caught fish, Tab would take her share while it was seasoning before cooking. If salt beef or pork was in soak, she'd scoop out a chunk. She would even jump on a table to steal the food from a man's plate, the minute he looked away." Obie looked around to make sure they swallowed this assertion. Horace sniggered. "That's true as I sit here! Tab would snatch a man's meat from his plate and scoot away." He brushed his hands together with a smack, to illustrate how quick Tab was.

"We all got sick and tired of this. Tab was a nice little thing, and she did catch rats and all, but this t'iefin' habit was hard to take.

"One day the cook came up with an idea to teach Tab a lesson. He rubbed a piece of fish with some of those hot ladyfinger peppers and left it on a table near the cook stove. We moved away and waited a minute." Obie took a gulp of coffee.

"'T'wasn't long, all you could hear was cat cussin'! We looked to see old Tab on the table, her fur frizzled out, back arched, tail big and fluffy. She was spittin' and a-yowlin', a-growlin' and a-hissin', but still chewin' on that fish!"

Everyone laughed. Obie took out his tobacco pouch and filled his clay pipe. "Yes, we laughed that day! It was a good joke, but it didn't cure Tab a'tall. She went right on t'iefin' till she died."

Kath looked down at her fish again. Obie turned quickly to her. "Oh Ma'am, I beg your pardon. I didn't mean you looked like Tab eating that fish, or anything. It was just how you were looking at that peppered fish, made me think of old Tab..."

Kath laughed. "It's all right, Obie. I understand. If I could have hissed and spit and put my hair on end, I probably would have, after tasting that fish!"

"Here's some johnny-cake and guava jam, Missus," Harry said, putting a chunk of biscuit-bread before her. "That won't 'bite' you like the fish! And some good hot coffee."

The Captain came up on deck then, and Kath's heart gave a lurch.

"What's the joke?" he asked. "Oh, I see, you're entertaining our fair guest, Obie!

"Good evening, Mistress O'Brien. You must watch out for Obie. He's our storyteller. Don't let him get you cornered, and don't believe everything he says as gospel." He clapped Obie on the shoulder.

"Harry says you will make landfall by tomorrow night," Kath said, looking at the Captain. "Where are we bound?"

"We are going home to Fortune Island, Ma'am," he replied. "All our families are there. We used to live on Eleuthera, and New Providence Island, but the pirates have made it their nest now. Decent people can hardly live there because of them. They live a lewd, licentious sort of life, carousing and carrying on.

"Any more of that coffee, Harry?" Harry handed him a steaming mug.

"A group of us decided to move down this way in '03, after we were raided by the Spanish and then the French," the Captain continued. "The men in our group – those not on a regular boat – sail down this way to chop hardwood and rake salt, in the salt season anyway. It's nearer for them to find their work, and it is directly on our sea route. We call in to bring supplies and pick up cargo whenever we go back and forth to Jamaica."

"You have a regular route, then?" Kath asked.

"Yes. We carry cargoes. We start in Charleston, or sometimes we go up to Virginia, or Bermuda, depending on what cargo we can get. We bring cargoes down to New Providence, then pick up hardwood, like lignum vitae, salt, dyewoods – like brasiletto or logwood – and sometimes a little rendered seal oil, or anything else we can take down to Jamaica, mostly for onward shipping. There we load up with sugar and rum, then head back to New Providence. It's quite the place for trade these days, what with the pirate plunder and all. Sometimes they consign their takings to Charleston, for sale."

The Captain sipped his coffee. "My compliments on your new clothes, Ma'am," he said, looking at her, smiling. "Harry told me what a sight you looked in mine!"

"She wants to sign Ship's Articles, Cap'n Grev," Obie said.

"Indeed! What think you, Horace? I hazard she'd make a tolerable cabin boy for the *Swan*."

"A cabin boy?" Kath raised her eyebrows. "I don't aspire to being one myself, Sir, rest assured. I was relieved when Obie turned me down as crew. Though thankful enough for these breeches, I look forward to donning a gown again."

"We'll see that you are properly outfitted as soon as we get home," Captain Knowles said. "If you will tell me what you need, I can buy materials in New Providence or Charleston, and send them to you by the next ship sailing this way."

Kath dropped her eyes. "You are very kind, Captain. As you see, I have no money." She paused, then looked up again. "Nor have I any hope of earning any, seeing you have dashed my bid to join your crew and thereby pay my way!"

Everyone laughed. *They are all so warm and obliging,* Kath thought.

"Seriously, though," she continued, "what am I to do? Is there anyone at Fortune Island who might employ me? I should not feel comfortable going to a Pirates' Nest to beg employment in my present state. I would prove a wretched pirate's apprentice, in any event. But I am an accomplished needle woman. I can spin, sew, embroider and do fancy work. Indeed, I have made my way in the world thus far by my needle. And I can read, write and keep books, should there be a man of business who could use a clerk."

"Well, Ma'am, as it happens, I do know of work you could do at Fortune Island," Captain Knowles replied, tapping his nose with his right forefinger. "You could work for me." He gave Kath a searching look.

"My old grandmother lives alone in the settlement. She is very spry, and still able to keep her garden and what not. But I am away so much, and I worry about her. I fear she has not the energy to cook for herself and manage things as she used to. If she became ill, or had an accident, there would be no one to care for her. I wonder, would you consider living with her? It's isolated on the island, and she loves a bit of company. I would feel easier in my mind, knowing you were her companion. It might be a boon to the three of us."

Kath sniffed, as her throat closed up. "Nothing could please me more, Captain Knowles," she said gruffly. "I am used to a quiet country life and my family about me. To be alone in the world – as I am now – is a most unhappy state." She blotted her eyes with her arm.

"Your grandmother shall be to me as my own! You have saved my life, and now you have given me a purpose to live..." A tear slid down Kath's nose and she choked up. The men looked at their hands, or off out to sea. Horace bounced his knees, and Harry spat over the rail.

"Well, that's that, then," Captain Knowles declared, giving the table a smart rap with his knuckles. "Now let's have some music, hey? Horace – Obie? How about tickling your guitars for our guest? We can't have Missus O'Brien thinking we hold wakes after supper..."

15

Early the next afternoon the *Swan* dropped anchor in the clear turquoise waters of Fortune Island's harbor. The crew quickly stowed the sails and put all to rights aboard. They drew straws to see who would take first shore leave. The lucky winners put the *Swan's* boat into the water and hopped into it with their duffel bags the moment the *Swan's* anchor was set. Nut-brown little boys swam out to meet them, turning around to accompany the boat to the shore. Others swam all the way out to the *Swan,* to swing on the anchor rope and call up to the two men on duty. Men, women, children, dogs and a pig were all down on the shore, joking and laughing, barking and squealing, calling out to the men.

Kath sat apprehensively in the middle of the boat. All that day the crew had been telling her of their wives and children, the settlement, their huts and animals. She had looked forward to arriving. She had tried to make herself presentable, tidying her waist-length hair with the Captain's comb and tying it back with a piece of string. Now, however, she felt self-conscious of her men's clothing and peeling, sunburnt skin. She looked up to find the Captain's hazel eyes shining on her. A slight smile played about his lips.

"You'll be grateful enough to land, I'll wager, Ma'am," he said.

Kath put a hand on her heart, for some strange reason, his rich baritone voice always startled her. "We'll soon have you comfortable. I can see my Gammie now, waiting on the beach with the others. See her there, at the top of the beach?"

he asked, pointing. "She'll be delighted with what I'm bringing her today!" Kath looked in the direction he pointed. "I hope you'll be happy here with us."

She saw a woman standing apart from the others on the beach, petite and dainty and black. Now her joyous smile lit her face as she threw up her arms, hands fluttering like butterflies. "Grev, Grev, over here!"

Greville was over the side the moment the boat scrunched onto the white sand, splashing through the water's edge. He raced to his grandmother and bent almost double to scoop her into his arms. "Oh Gammie, my dearest Little Mouse, I've missed you! And I've brought you such good presents!"

Horace and Obie were out of the boat in a flash, lifting it high onto the beach before Kath could get out. "You stay in the boat, Miz O'Brien," Horace said, grinning. "No need for you to get wet. You so small, you don't weigh nothin' a'tall."

Wives were clamoring around the men now, their children were jumping up and down, dogs were barking and jumping too, with their gay tails wagging. There was general pandemonium. Obie helped Kath out of the boat, as several little children peeped at her from behind their mother's skirts. The news of her rescue streaked through the crowd like lightning.

"This is Mistress Katherine O'Brien, Gammie," Captain Knowles said, materializing at Kath's side with a wiry old woman. She wore an old brown dress, fashionable ten years before, tied about with a gunnysack apron. Her silver hair was parted in the middle and plaited like a laurel wreath around her small head, held erect on a long neck.

She had wrinkles, but not many; she was old, but seemed so young and alive it was impossible to say her age. Her intelligent dark eyes were shining with happiness, and Kath knew instantly that she would love her.

"This is my grandmother, Mistress Evangeline Burrows, he said with obvious pride. "Everyone calls her Miz Eva."

"Pleased to meet you, chile," Miz Eva said, grasping Kath's hand.

Kath winced. Miz Eva's callused hand delivered a power-ful grip. "The Good Lord's sent you! I been asking Him for a friend – only I expected it would be Greville's wife," she said, twinkling up at Captain Knowles and nudging him with her elbow. "When you going to get married, boy? Time now for some great-grand."

"One day, Gammie," Captain Knowles replied, putting one arm around his grandmother and slinging his bag over the other shoulder. "When the right one comes along, I'll come ashore. And what about you? Have you seen any swain to fancy while I've been gone?" They headed towards the path leading to the settlement.

"No, I haven't," she said, shaking her head. "Hasn't been a new soul on this rock!

"We're especially glad to see you this time, though. We were worried about you-all, with that hurricane blowing through. I told people you had sense enough to duck into a hole somewhere. I prayed long and hard, anyway. We all did. Happen it's my prayers that's saved Miz O'Brien."

"Happen Miz O'Brien said some prayers of her own, Gammie," he teased.

"I certainly did pray, Miz Eva," Kath replied. "And I know that's the only thing that saved me."

"We searched for two days, Gammie," Greville said. "But we didn't find anybody else alive. We did find some wreck, though. Miz O'Brien had *a whole barrel of cheese* to herself. What do you think of that, Little Mouse? Wouldn't *you* like to be marooned with a barrel of cheese! Well, you shall have a large chunk for your supper."

While the two were teasing and catching up, Kath walked silently behind them on the sandy path. It was very natural, she did not feel slighted. She was glad to have a chance to take her bearings and look about her. The other two seemed to understand this, only seeking her opinion occasionally in their playful banter.

They were soon among the small huts in the settlement. These were made of rubble walls, conch shells and stones with wattles, held together with what the islanders called "tabby," a kind of cement the men made by burning coral and adding sand and water. The roofs were thatched with palmetto leaves. Each hut was rectangular, with two doorways, one on the windward side, the other on the leeward, and windows on all four sides. Doors and window shutters were made of scrap lumber.

Dry stone walls, just like in Ireland, surrounded one or two fields, and these walls also made enclosures for several scraggly sheep or a few goats, with prickly dry brush placed on top of the walls to prevent the animals escaping. Cocks strutted about with their hens and chicks, their iridescent green tails in rich contrast to the russet of their necks and bright red combs.

There was a grove of coconut palms, but the rest of the vegetation seemed similar to what she'd seen on the other islands they'd sailed by. It was thick, thorny, and olive green. The soil was sandy – what there was of it – in pockets between outcroppings of rock. There were no rivers or streams that she could see, though she noticed several wells, and barrels filled with rainwater. The warm southeast wind smelled of the sea, and of flowers.

They walked through the settlement, the path climbing through more bush, eventually emerging into a clearing on the top of a hill.

"This is Miz Eva's home," Captain Knowles said. "Isn't it pretty?"

"Oh *yes!*" Kath agreed. The hut had whitewashed walls, with pink and white periwinkles tumbling from the rocks around it. A bright red bougainvillea cascaded down from its thatched roof. There was a small outside privy behind, to leeward, and a separate kitchen built at some distance from the hut, as a precaution against fire.

Looking around Kath saw the *Swan* at anchor in the harbor. The hill commanded views over the whole island and beyond the foaming reef to the sapphire ocean. A humming bird whirred by, flashing iridescent red and green, as it explored the possibilities of the bougainvillea. Kath took a deep breath and sighed.

"It's not too remote?" Captain Knowles asked, concern creasing his handsome face. "Could you be happy here?"

Kath turned to him, her eyes suspiciously bright. "Yes, oh *yes!* I've never seen such a perfect place. Why, it's even more beautiful than... than Ballyvale House!"

A little brown puppy waddled out from behind the hut. "Here's my surprise for you, Greville," Miz Eva said. "Reena Sturrup's dog whelped just after you left. I thought a pup would give me some company. I've named her Treacle!"

Kath and Greville both crouched and called "Treacle!" at the same moment. They looked at each other and laughed. The pup toddled over, investigating one hand, then the other with her wet nose. The Captain stroked her silky body, his face glowing.

"What a little beauty you are Treacle! What do you feed her, Gammie?" he asked, standing up again.

"A little bread and milk. She's just eaten enough to pop – look at that fat stomach!" Miz Eva picked up the pup, which immediately squirmed around and licked her face. "Ugh! Play with puppy, puppy lick your mouth!"

Captain Knowles laughed. "That's a saying we have here, Miz O'Brien. It means that, if you become friendly with people beneath your station in society, you shouldn't be surprised when they take liberties and treat you as an equal."

Kath smiled and looked away. She was now beholden to the Captain and Miz Eva; she was their servant. Besides, she was a convicted criminal, and he was a ship's captain. She was definitely beneath his social station. Her heart sank. *That's why he's always so formal and correct with me,* she thought. *Well, I'll watch my step. I'll not presume to 'lick his mouth.'*

Inside, the hut was one large room containing a small table and two benches, a narrow bed along one wall, with a grass-filled sack mattress, and two chests, one with a candle and a family Bible on top. On the table stood two oil lamps, a tin basin, and a pitcher of water. Some pottery bowls and plates were stacked on two shelves nearby. Plaited straw mats covered the hard-packed dirt floor. Everything was tidy and clean.

"Go get a stick of fire for me, chile," Miz Eva asked Greville, and he headed out towards the kitchen. "It'll soon be time to light the lamps," she continued. "Let me see now... Grev's hammock is in that chest on the left. Get it for me, please Miz O'Brien. He'll likely sleep 'board the boat, but we need him to hook it up for you to use."

"Please call me Kath, Miz Eva," Kath said as she opened the chest and took out the hammock. "You're all the family I have, now."

"Poor lamb! And here's Grev and me prattling on, forgetting how strange you must feel." The old lady peered into Kath's face, stroking her hair. "Such beautiful hair! Just like my Eliza's used to be. She's gone to glory now, praise God. God knows I need another daughter to love after all this time."

Kath's face crumpled. She put her arms around Miz Eva and buried her face in the old woman's neck.

"Hush, chile, don't you weep no more," Miz Eva said, rocking Kath in her arms. "You're safe here with us. This'll be your home. We'll have each other for company. We'll be family, and everything'll be alright. My Lovely Lord Jesus has not abandoned you."

"What are you two up to?" Captain Knowles demanded. He came in holding a stick of wood, a glowing coal at its end. "Here's your stick o' fire, Gammie. I'll light the lamps for you."

"Kath and I are just getting to know each other, Grev," Miz Eva said. "We're going to be fine friends."

"So I can see! What's for supper? Got any johnny cake? That would go down well with our cheese... I'll go and boil the coffee."

"These men don't want to see a woman cry," Miz Eva said, winking at Kath, who managed a wan smile. "They'd rather cook, even!"

Supper was prepared and the three sat down. Miz Eva and the Captain bowed their heads, while Miz Eva thanked the Lord for the *Swan's* safe arrival and His bounty in bringing the cheese. Kath made the sign of the cross.

After they had eaten, they sat sipping coffee. Captain Knowles brought the big Bible over to the table. "Where are you at, Gammie?"

"In Isaiah, around chapter 49 or 50. But any chapter will do, son. Every chapter has something good to hear."

"Then let's read in Acts. That's one of my favorite books. There's a chapter describing a hurricane and Paul's shipwreck on an island... here it is, chapter 27." Captain Knowles read the chapter in his fine voice, then said a short prayer of thanks for the *Swan's* safety and Kath's survival through the hurricane.

Kath's thoughts were in such turmoil she could hardly listen. *I'm in trouble again,* she thought. *These people are Protestants, Puritans, likely. And I'm a Catholic. They don't pray with the Rosary. They talk about "the Lord Jesus" and "Heavenly Father", as though they were friends. They never even mention the Blessed Virgin, the Holy Mother of God.*

Oh Mother of God, what am I to do? Likely there'll be no priest here among them, nor another Catholic soul. How will they treat me when they find out I'm a Papist, as they call us? Maybe I'm cursed, having to live with heretics about me. First the English in Ireland, now more of them here!

I'll make myself a Rosary as soon as I can. A bit of thread and some dried peas should do. That'll help me to remember my true religion.

*

Captain Knowles left right after supper. The wind was picking up and he wanted to be sure the *Swan's* anchors held against the surge of the changing tide. He might have to move the *Swan* to the other side of the island, too, if the wind changed, since there was no room for her to swing at anchor in the little harbor.

The two women sat down together on the front step, in a comfortable silence. Miz Eva held Treacle on her lap, fondling her silky ears, looking out to sea. Kath's thoughts ran riot.

There was so much to digest.

I'd better tell Miz Eva all about what happened in Ireland, Kath thought. *If she hears it later somehow, she'll never trust me again. I'd hate anything to come between us. I love her already. And I'd better tell her I'm a Catholic, too, right now. If she wants nothing more to do with me, I can go to New Providence with the Swan.*

Kath swallowed hard. The very thought of leaving brought on a wave of panic. She clenched her hands in her lap and took a deep breath. "I want to tell you about my life at home in Ireland, Miz Eva…"

Just then a familiar voice hailed from the bush by the path. "Good evenin', Miz Eva! Dis Obie. I come t'bring Miz O'Brien some clothes."

"Hello, Obie! Come in." Miz Eva called back. "You had a good trip?"

"Yes, thank ya Ma'am. De wedder wuz li'l rough in spots, but de Lord brought us through."

"The women in the settlement put these things together to start Miz O'Brien off," he said, coming over to the hut. "Maria woulda come with me, but she's puttin' the chirren to bed…"

"That's just where I was thinking of going, myself," Miz Eva replied, yawning. "I've had too much excitement for one day. Besides, I was awake before sunup. I'm getting too old for all this." Miz Eva clutched the small of her back as she rose, staggering a step or two into the hut. "You children sit out and talk a li'l while. Make yourselves at home. You won't disturb me none."

"Good night, Miz Eva, and thank you for everything," Kath said.

"Good night, all," Miz Eva said, and, once inside the hut, she closed the doors and the window shutters.

"And thank you, too, Obie," Kath said, turning to look into the bundle he'd brought. "These clothes look to be just the right size! Please tell Harry and Ned that I'll wash their clothes and return them tomorrow."

"Do you want to go to bed now too, Miss O'Brien?"

"No! I'm still too excited to sleep. Besides, the sun hasn't set yet. Let's go sit over by the kitchen, so we don't disturb Miz Eva."

The few days Kath had spent on the *Swan* had removed all her fear of black people. They had treated her with unfailing courtesy and kindness, as an equal, without any bias about her color, nor had they mentioned religion. They'd talked and joked with her enough for her to understand their accent, and she was now completely comfortable among them. She was glad that Obie could stay and be company.

The two sat making small talk, then fell silent as the sun descended into the horizon, turning the sky bright rose, shot with orange, yellow and luminescent blue. Below, the *Swan* rode quietly on her anchor in the darkening blue-green sea. A cloud of white-crowned pigeons flew across the harbor towards an outlying cay and home to their nests. Sounds from the settlement below floated up, people chatting, a goat bleating, and the clack of coconut fronds in the wind. A faint fragrance from the bush wafted on the breeze, from some tree encouraging evening insects to visit, and a tinge of wood smoke, from the settlement at the bottom of the hill. Underlying all was the gentle suck and sigh of sea against rocks, and the swish of waves as they washed onto the beach.

Eventually they began to speak again, and inevitably the subject came around to the *Swan*, her crew members, and to Captain Knowles.

"Miz Eva keeps teasing him about getting wed," Kath began. "Has he never been married?"

"No, he hasn't, and he's getting on, he's thirty-three now. His father was a sailor. Cap'n Grev says he watched his mother pine for his father, when he was out to sea for weeks on end. Says being a sailor's wife is hard on a woman. Says he's vowed he would never marry as long as he was wed to the sea."

"But surely he has a lass somewhere? At one of your ports of call?"

"Well, maybe." Obie gave Kath a sidelong look.

"You know, but you're not telling, Obie?" Kath asked with a smile, raising her eyebrows.

"Well, he stays with Miz Nancy Lou Lilly every time he's in Nassau. He's pretty faithful to her." Obie sniggered. "Don't tell anyone I told you..."

"Certainly not! What's she like?"

"Well, she's good looking, painted smart, plenty flowers in the garden. She can get noisy sometimes, but mostly she's quiet. And comfortable. She knows how to provide good victuals and ale for a man – and doubtless a nice, comfy bed. Nice, if y'can afford such. But Cap'n Grev don't have no chirren, no wife to feed and clothe."

Kath was silent for a few minutes. They watched the first stars begin to twinkle in the deep violet dome of the heavens. Sadness squeezed her heart. "Well, Obie, I'm tired now, too." She sighed and stretched. "It's been a full day. Perhaps I should join Miz Eva."

"Beg pardon, Miz Kath," Obie said, leaping to his feet and holding his hand out to help her up. "Didn't mean to keep you up!"

"Good night, Obie. You didn't keep me up, I enjoyed the company. I'll see you tomorrow."

"Good night, then," Obie said. He flashed Kath his toothy grin and melted into the dark bush.

16

Kath woke with a start, at first not knowing where she was. She could hear Miz Eva moving stealthily about the hut.

"Good morning, Miz Eva."

"Morning, chile. Don't get up, it ain't daylight good yet. You go back to sleep. Little Treacle and I are going to throw a bucket of water on my garden. Then I'm going to sit a spell with my Lovely Lord Jesus. We talk this time every morning. Come, Treacle!"

Kath shifted in her hammock. There she goes again, she thought. *Talking about her Lovely Lord Jesus as though He was a personal friend, who comes to sit and talk to her. Maybe she's a little crazy. No wonder the Pope excommunicates them! They're blasphemous! But maybe this is because they have no priest, and they've never been taught the true religion, they just don't know any better.*

Then her thoughts shifted. *Obie said the* Swan *would sail on tonight's tide, to make up for the time they lost over the hurricane. That's just as well. I don't want to have any more to do with Captain Knowles. My heart can't bear any more pain.*

I wonder whether Kevin is all right. I wonder where he is now. I wonder if Cara looked after him. Oh, Mary Mother of God! Both my boys! Kath's throat closed, and tears trickled down into her ears. *Perhaps I should ask Captain Knowles if I can sail with him to Virginia next time he goes,* she thought. *I could look for Kevin... But not without money. I have no money! I must think how to earn some.*

Kath could see daylight sparkling through a crack around the door. *Time to get up and face life again,* she thought, rolling out of the hammock. She stumbled stiffly over to the table, washed, combed her hair, and then tried on her new clothes. The women had made up a complete ensemble – pale yellow pantaloons and petticoat, with a mint green skirt. The stomacher and bodice were cream colored, and the neckerchief was fawn with a touch of embroidery. There was even a little white cap, with a snippet of lace. Everything fit passing well.

Just then there was a knock on the door. "Good morning! Are you ladies decent?" Called Captain Knowles's voice.

Kath's face lit up. "Indeed we are, Captain," she responded, dashing to throw open the door.

Captain Knowles stood transfixed. He blinked, then took a deep breath; he opened his mouth and closed it again. His eyes met Kath's in an incredulous stare. Her cheeks colored.

"Good morning, Captain Knowles," she said, flashing a dazzling smile. "We have been up betimes! Miz Eva is already in her garden..."

"I, ah... I, um... I c-came to bring some provisions," he stammered, putting down a large gunnysack. "These are some things I bought for Gammie in Jamaica." His words tumbled out in a hasty stream. "Now there are two of you, though, so I have asked Ned and Harry to bring some of our ship's stores along as well. I don't know exactly when we'll be back. And I don't want you to run short in the meantime."

"Thank you, Captain. I am much obliged to you, yet again. Please, come in! I was just about to go to the kitchen and start a pot of coffee..."

"Oh, allow me... I know where everything is," the Captain turned and headed briskly towards the kitchen. Escaping, again.

"Then perhaps you'll be good enough to show me?" Kath called, running to catch up. "This will be my happy duty from now on!"

The Captain overcame his confusion and they cooked breakfast together. Kath had her first lesson in the preparation of corn grits, which was the staple in these islands, just as oatmeal was in Ireland.

"We'll be sailing on the evening tide," Captain Knowles said. "We're behind schedule, due to the hurricane. Have you thought what dry goods you would like me to buy? There will likely be another vessel passing this way in a few weeks."

"Thank you, Captain Knowles, I have thought. I'll give you a list. Would you be willing to send some materials for me to make Miz Eva something too? She might enjoy a new gown."

"By all means! That would be capital. I was wondering what nice thing I could do for Gammie, for Christmas. 'Twill be here before we know it."

"Indeed it will!" Kath looked up from the pot she was stirring. "And... and Sir, if you could see your way to doing so, could you send me some needles, a length of fine linen and some embroidery silks? That is, if it's not too much to ask. I have been thinking of how I may earn my bread." She paused a moment, then went on in a rush. "If you could advance me the money – that is the materials – I could sew dainty articles: table cloths, or women's caps, or stomachers. Then, when you pass through here, you could collect the finished work to sell in Charleston, or Jamaica. The money would repay your loan to me, your hospitality, and buy more materials. That way I could make a few shillings for myself and not be a charge on you."

"What a splendid idea, Miz O'Brien! Every time I come through, I can bring you fresh materials – and perhaps orders, from the shops in Jamaica, or New Providence – or even Charleston. Then I can deliver the completed goods. It would give you some occupation, as well. Life can be tedious and dull on these islands...

"But you're not to think of yourself as "a charge" on me. It's a great relief to me, knowing that Gammie will not have to struggle here, all alone. And don't think of paying for your keep! I owe you a salary, and we should discuss this."

"Certainly not!" Kath retorted. "Let's say we are even, then. I'll do my best to care for your grandmother, and you will give me food and shelter."

I should tell him now, about Ireland, Kath's conscience screamed, and her heart thumped. *He might not want to leave me here with Miz Eva...*

"What are you two hatching up?" Miz Eva asked from the kitchen door. "I hope it's breakfast! My stomach thinks my throat's been cut..."

*

It seemed no time at all before the whole settlement was down on the shore again, waving goodbye to the *Swan*. Kath never had another chance to talk privately with Captain Knowles.

On the one hand, she was relieved not to face telling him the truth about herself, facts that would only prey on his mind during his long weeks of absence. She shrank from the pain of bringing herself down in his eyes, and from causing him concern about leaving Miz Eva in her care. On the other hand, Kath felt burdened by having lied, by omission, to one who had treated her with the utmost respect, kindness, and generosity. He had saved her life, supplied her with food, the means to earn money, and hope for the future. He had left her with his grandmother, his most precious possession. She felt keenly that she owed Captain Knowles an all-encompassing obligation, which she was betraying.

Her guilt, and her caution to avoid any presumption, caused Kath to behave with reserved coolness towards the Captain upon his departure. She was also protecting her battered heart, which *would* insist on skipping beats whenever Captain Knowles was near. This same heart twinged now, as she remembered the Captain's puzzled look at their formal farewell.

As the white sails filled and the *Swan* heeled off the wind, people began gradually to head up the sandy path to the settlement.

"Come, Kath," Miz Eva said. "This would be a good time for you to meet your new neighbors. Shall we make the rounds? I know you'll want to meet the women who donated your clothing. And I know they're longing to meet you!"

Kath was glad of the distraction. She linked her arm through Miz Eva's and tried to forget a pair of hurt hazel eyes.

They went to Obie's house first, to meet his wife, Maria, and their three children. Then they moved on until they had called briefly at all fourteen huts in the settlement. Everyone welcomed Kath warmly, obviously curious about her. Miz Eva lessened her stress by giving witty sketches of each occupant before going into the huts, turning Kath's anxiety into an amusing pastime.

I am going to have to tell them the truth, Kath realized, her heart sinking again. There could be no secrets in a place this small. Everyone was so open and sincere, she could not be otherwise. She decided to let all that come in due time. She would have enough to do, remembering their names and faces and who belonged to whom.

Miz Eva left her favorite friend, Reena Stirrup, to be their last call. "That way we can stay and have tea before we head up the hill," she said. Reena seemed to be expecting them. She had supper all laid – fever-grass tea, bread, guava jam, and some of the salvaged cheese waiting ready on a wooden tray.

17

"I was interested to see all the different colors in the people here," Kath said to Miz Eva at breakfast the next morning. "Some people are quite dark – black, I would say – while others are different shades of brown, or have a yellow cast to their skin. And Mistress Lowe and her family are blonde, with blue eyes and a white skin. Yet everyone seems to get on tolerably well with his neighbor."

"Well, we're all poor, you know, chile," Miz Eva replied, putting down her coffee mug. "And poverty is a great leveler. Anyway, most of us in this settlement have a lick of the tar brush, or some Indian.

"I'm what they call a mulatto, half white, half black. My mother was an African slave, and my father was a white indentured servant. My husband was white, with maybe some Spanish, and his mother was English, but since he never knew his father, he never knew exactly what he was. And it didn't matter. Our daughter, Eliza, Greville's mother, married a man from Virginia whose mother was a half-breed American Indian, and whose father was English. So we're all mixed up."

Kath was silent for a few minutes, thinking. "How do you all come to be here together, Miz Eva? Usually people stick with their own kind. In Ireland, we Irish stay with our own and don't mix with the English, who stay with their own."

"Well, that's true here too, chile. Although we get on, the whites usually try to marry their own color, and the browns marry each other. Many brown people try to "lighten their color" by marrying someone whiter than they are. The whites look down on dark people. In general it doesn't mean much, until people get into fights. Then they start calling each other names about their color.

"We're all at the bottom here, we got no pretenses. Nobody wants people like us, Kath. My Isaiah and I were both born free, in Bermuda. We met in the parochial school. Many of the people in the Bahamas, mostly white, came down from Bermuda. The first ones came for religion, but later, people came because they wanted room to breathe. If you don't want to slave for other people, and be looked down on, you have to go. Being colored and free, we decided to settle in New Providence. There were hardly any people, mostly poor fishermen, like my Isaiah.

"Isaiah used to go fishing. Turtling, raking salt, looking for ambergris, salvaging wrecked ships, whatever he could find. We chose New Providence because it was near to his work. We have plentiful turtles, fish, and conchs here, and I grew a few things to stretch our food, like I do now. We got by.

"That same Mistress Lowe came to the Bahamas from Bermuda about eight years ago. They deported her because she was too obliging to the men – and she had an illegitimate child. Probably the father was someone high up, scared she'd embarrass him by telling his friends he was the father of her child. I'm sure she obliged men who sat in judgment of her, too. You know her husband – she married Ned, on the *Swan*."

Miz Eva took another sip of coffee and looked out the door at the sea. "Here, we're free of all that. We have our own huts, such as they are, and as much land as we need to farm. Nobody lords it over us. But in Bermuda – or Jamaica – we'd be poor colored folks, with nothing of our own, taking abuse, likely having to beg for bread."

Kath looked down at her hands and played with her fingernails. "Miz Eva, I understand about that." She looked up, her face troubled. "Now it's time I told you everything about myself, and my life before I came here. I should have told you – and Captain Knowles – before he sailed. In case you won't want me living here anymore."

Miz Eva drew back a little from the table and looked straight into Kath's eyes. "Nonsense, chile. I *already* love you. I would never stop wanting you to live with me."

Again Kath stared down at her hands, fidgeting with her thumb. "Here you don't have to worry about your past," Miz Eva said gently. "It's over. Finished. You have a new beginning now. You came naked into this New World, just as you came naked into your Old World, as a baby. Now it's up to you to clothe yourself in righteousness and truth. The folks here will take you as they find you."

Kath did not look up. Miz Eva reached over and took her hands, wrapping them in her own. "I been watching you, chile, ever since you got here day before yesterday. There's something eating away at your insides. You'll never be free until you spit it up. Then we'll move on."

"Tell me," she coaxed.

Kath snatched her hands from Miz Eva and covered her face. "I'm a Catholic!" She dropped her hands and glared at Miz Eva, who stared quietly back at her. "I know you're all Protestants and you hate Catholics!" There was a moment of silence.

"That's it?" Miz Eva asked. "We're Protestant, you're Catholic, and so we hate you... that's it?"

"Not all of it," Kath said, looking out at the sea. It was already getting late, the sun was climbing higher, promising another hot, humid day. A flock of laughing gulls breakfasted noisily in the big wild fig tree at the edge of the yard, and the cicadas had started their intermittent ear-splitting buzz in the bush.

Kath sighed, and turned to face Miz Eva again. Her mouth twitched, and then words tumbled out. "I was charged with stealing a child's silver cup, in Ireland. I was found guilty and was being transported to Jamaica when that hurricane hit and sank the ship. I was on a convict ship."

Miz Eva looked down at her coffee, then took another swallow. There was another thoughtful pause. "You say you were 'charged with stealing' and 'found guilty,' Kath. You did

116

not say you stole, or that you were guilty." Miz Eva looked her straight in the eye. "Chile, did you steal? Were you guilty?"

"No!" Kath burst out. She glanced at Miz Eva defiantly, tears spilling from her eyes. Then her eyes slid away. "No, I did not steal any cup. I was not *guilty!*"

Miz Eva continued to search Kath's face; she would not meet her gaze.

"All right then," Miz Eva said softly. "I believe you. Now tell me the whole story, sweeting."

At this tender endearment, Kath's face crumpled, her body heaved with sobs. At last she could speak. "Oh, Miz Eva, I did steal that cup," she blurted, her nose running. "I was guilty! But the English Protestants made me do it! They owed me a lot of money, for nine months of work, and they wouldn't pay! We had nothing, and no way to get anything. We had all this trouble and no money! I took the cup because they owed it to me!"

Miz Eva reached for Kath's hand. "Oh, chile! Don't take on so. Life is so hard, especially for women alone with children. And anyway, none of us can live without doing things we're ashamed of. The Bible says "for all have sinned and come short of the glory of God." You're heartily sorry you took it, I'll bet."

"Oh yes, Miz Eva, there's not a day passes but I don't ask God a thousand times to forgive me..."

"Then He has. His Word promises that if we confess our sins, He is faithful and just and will forgive us our sins, and cleanse us from all unrighteousness. He has forgiven you, chile. You don't need to think on it no more. Now you need to forgive yourself... and that's the hardest part. We always have to live with the regret, and the result of our actions."

*

Kath began haltingly to tell her story, then her words tumbled out. Telling the truth at last brought her overwhelming relief, and Miz Eva never once interrupted. When Kath finished, the old woman got stiffly to her feet. She stood behind Kath, stroking her hair, then put her arms around her and held her, rocking her gently back and forth. At length she spoke.

"You sure had a heap of sorrows, Kath. I know you'll ache till you die for your sons. Whatever happens in your life, you'll never finish mourning them. When I lost my Isaiah, and then Eliza – Greville's Ma – I like t'died myself. But it heals somewhat, with time. Life has a way of rolling on over the bitterest things.

"As for your being a Catholic, chile, it won't matter here. Let the white people over yonder fight about it. It don't affect our life a'tall which King reigns in England. Be he Catholic or Protestant, our hardships are the same.

"This Catholic and Protestant hating each other is all about power. Most of those people fighting for Catholic or Protestant don't know what they're fighting for. Nor do they care. They're put in the army or the navy, they're made to serve, to kill and be killed, and they don't know why. They only know their lives are horrible, they're going to die, and it's all for some rich white people half the world away.

"Times past, everyone was Catholic. There were still good and bad people. People who knew the Lord and tried their best to please Him with their lives. And there were others, who didn't give a fig for Him, who used religion as a means to an end. Nothing has changed since then, nor ever will. Human nature will always be the same – sinful – be they calling themselves Catholic or Protestant."

Miz Eva walked to the hob and poured some fresh coffee. "No, as long as you respect our beliefs, we'll respect yours, and let you go your way. We have no priest or church here. Old Mr. Cartwright tries his best to preach under the coconut trees Sunday mornings down in the settlement, but otherwise, it's up to people what they want to believe."

Miz Eva moved over to the door and looked out. "You have no objection to reading a chapter every night after supper, I hope?" she asked, looking back at Kath. "You read it so nice last night."

"No, Miz Eva, I love to read aloud. I used to read to my

old Granda, when he was going blind. I've never read the Bible before; it's always read by the priest in our church, in Latin. I want to read it for myself, to know what it says."

"I'll be glad of that. My eyes aren't too good anymore, for close reading.

"Now, chile, I'm going back out to the field. When you finish tidying here, come find me there. I want to show you what's what. Put on that hat," Miz Eva said, pointing to a straw hat hanging on a nail over her bed. "The sun's hot."

*

"I been thinking how best to tell people about you," Miz Eva said, looking up from her weeding. "It would kill you to go through that story twenty times. Bad enough you had to live through it."

Worry sprang into Kath's eyes. "I was thinking maybe they don't need to know anything? You said I could start my life all over again." Kath put her hands to her temples. Suddenly she had a throbbing headache.

"Yes, and you can. But you have to tell 'em something." Miz Eva pulled a few more weeds. "Nobody can keep secrets here. You're a nine days' wonder, chile, the most exciting thing that's happened to us for a long time. You can't think to fall into our midst, like a God-angel from heaven, and be accepted just like that. Everyone wants to hear all about you."

"Couldn't you do it for me, Miz Eva?" Kath asked irritably. Her eyes ached, and her back, her legs, her joints. She couldn't bear to think. "You'd know what's best to say. I don't want to be a side-show at the fair."

"Yes, I know what you mean. I think I'll tell Reena, and ask her to tell a couple of the women. They get together on Sunday afternoons to sew. We can trust Reena to tell it straight."

"Thank you, Miz Eva," Kath said, her stomach in knots. "I've been worried sick about it."

"Well, don't worry 'bout it no more. I'll take care of it."

Kath rocked back on her haunches, her head spinning.

Miz Eva's face seemed blurred. Nausea washed over her. "If you don't mind, Miz Eva, I'm going to lie down a little. I don't feel well."

Miz Eva looked up sharply. Kath's face was flaming. "What's the matter, chile? You sick?"

"I hope not," Kath answered, staggering to her feet. "Maybe just too much bending over in the sun. But I feel so tired, and painful."

Miz Eva felt her brow. Kath was raging with fever. She was too ill to argue when Miz Eva helped her back to the hut, out of her clothing and into Miz Eva's own bed. Kath sank instantly to sleep, sweat beading her face. All afternoon Miz Eva sat beside her, putting wet cloths on her body to bring down the fever. Kath was fretful, plucking at her blanket, tossing and turning. She became delirious in the night.

"'Tis the yellow fever, I believe," Miz Eva told her the next day, when Kath roused enough to drink some water. "We call it Yellow Jack."

"Miz Eva, leave me," Kath pleaded. "Suppose you catch it too? Then what will we do? I feel like I'm dying."

"'Tis a scourge in these islands, for sure," Miz Eva said, placing a fresh wet cloth on Kath's brow. "But once you've had it, you never get it again. I had it myself years ago. Don't worry 'bout me chile, I won't catch it from you." Miz Eva's face puckered. "But I'll not lie to you either, my sweeting. Many people die from this fever, it wants careful tending."

Miz Eva warned the settlement folk to stay away. Every day their neighbors sent them cooked food, brought by someone who already had had the fever, or left at the top of the path into their yard. They gathered bush medicine for boiling into tea to bring down the fever. Miz Eva bullied Kath into drinking pints of the disgusting tasting stuff. Four days later her fever broke and she began to feel better, though very weak.

"Don't do anything yet, chile," Miz Eva instructed. "You rest yourself, and keep on drinking the tea. That fever can come back. It can go away for a few days, then come back worse. Like a hurricane.

"Sometimes you only get one good blow. Then another time, the eye will pass over you, nice and quiet, and you think everything's all right. Next thing you know the hurricane's down on you again. Yellow Jack's just like that. You rest up 'till we see what happens."

Kath was glad to comply. She felt washed out, good for nothing. She dozed on a grass-filled sack, put out in the dappled shade of the old fig tree, or stared up into the branches, thinking over her life. From time to time her face crumpled and scalding tears came again. As the days slipped by, though, blue and gold and warm, Kath's heart began to heal along with her convalescing body.

Almost imperceptibly her mood shifted and her thoughts came into the present. She watched a pair of mockingbirds, listening to them singing to each other across the bush. One of them, singing from the very top of a tall tree nearby, would leap into the air four or five feet and land back on his branch, singing all the while as though he could not contain his joy. She had never seen birds do that before.

Sometimes she gazed out to sea, or at the harbor, remembering the *Swan* at anchor, thinking about the crew, her new friends, and wondering where they were now and what they were doing. Thinking, too, about Greville, and what would come of her feelings for him.

Often Miz Eva brought her stool to sit beside Kath under the tree. She had dried silver-top palmetto leaves which she stripped evenly and plaited while she told Kath funny stories. She was an excellent mimic, and her wrinkled brown face aped the characters she talked about. The laughter, as much as sleep, sun, good plain food and Miz Eva's loving touch all had their desirable effect.

After a week of lazing and lying down, Miz Eva allowed Kath to begin doing simple chores. Then one morning, while Kath was fixing breakfast, Miz Eva received her reward. She heard Kath's pure, sweet soprano singing an Irish ballad for the very first time.

18

Several weeks slipped by. Everyone treated Kath as an exotic pet, a romantic addition to their humdrum existence. They loved her simple manner, and ready acceptance of them. She was without the airs they had come to expect in people from the Old Country. They loved her too, because of her devotion to their own Miz Eva.

In the weeks since her fever, Kath had gently integrated herself into the life of the settlement. She started by helping Obie's wife, Maria, with her mending. Maria hated sewing and, with three active little boys, her sewing basket was always full. Kath had been looking for ways to thank Maria for the clothing she'd donated. Now she was glad to help with the darning, and finished it in an afternoon. Maria had baked bread that day and insisted that Kath take one of the warm loaves.

"I could earn bread in other ways too, Miz Eva," Kath said, as they munched the delicious bread for supper that evening. "If we didn't have to bake bread and work so long in the field, I'd have time to do all sorts of things." She looked out to sea, her eyes glazing slightly. It was her habit now, when she needed to think. "I could start teaching school and the parents could pay me with grits, fish, or anything they had on hand. Maybe the older children could draw our water from the well, and help with the chores about the place. I could trade my sewing for gardening in your field." Kath looked back into the room. "What do you think, Miz Eva?"

"I think it's a fine idea." Miz Eva gave her usual sunny

smile. "We could live like ladies and have our hard work done for us. To tell you the truth, I'm feeling like a dead old woman these days. This morning I couldn't straighten up for the longest time, I was so painful and stiff."

Soon Kath had eight pupils of varying ages trudging up the hill every morning. Classes were held from nine until one o'clock, under the old fig tree. Kath taught reading, writing and arithmetic, and Miz Eva told Bible stories. Kath sewed in the afternoons and evenings, and Miz Eva often took naps now.

News of Kath's excellent handiwork spread like hot jam in the settlement. Within the week, Kath had as much sewing as she could handle. Several people had cloth on hand, waiting until they could find time to make clothing. Even more people had mending that needed doing. They were delighted to trade food, or a couple of hours of easy labor, in exchange for something they found to be a chore.

Early one morning during Miz Eva's meeting with the Lord, she noticed a white sail on the horizon. When she finished her prayers she went looking for Kath.

"See if you can read the name, chile," she asked, handing Kath a battered brass spyglass.

"It's the *Stella Maris*, Miz Eva."

"Oh, that'll be Mr. Cartwright's son, Jonah. Happen he'll have the things Greville bought for you in New Providence."

The usual hubbub followed later, down at the shore. Jonah Cartwright turned out to be about thirty years old, tall and tan, with crisply curling dark hair. Miz Eva and Kath waited until he greeted his family, then went to ask after Captain Knowles.

He has the nicest face, Kath thought, as they were introduced. She watched his eyes crinkle up and disappear when he smiled – and he had an infectious laugh.

As for Jonah, he held Kath's hand in his own callused paw for just a moment too long. He looked deep into her green eyes and felt his pulse quicken. So this was the woman that the men on the *Swan* had rescued! His smile broadened. Maybe his luck had changed. He was expecting nothing but boredom on Fortune Island, looking after the old man, but things were looking up! Mistress Kath O'Brien was a delicious tidbit, and he had two whole months to make his move.

*

Miz Eva and Kath had just finished breakfast the following morning when Jonah's large shadow loomed at their door.

"Hello, this house!" Jonah called, sticking his head and shoulders into the hut. "I brought the package from Cap'n Grev."

"Come in Jonah," Miz Eva replied. "We're just having a cup of coffee. Come sit a spell and tell us the news."

"Well, there's nothing new in New Providence," Jonah replied, his teeth flashing against his tanned face. "The pirates are still swarming there, with the usual whoring, brawling, cussing and fighting. And the dogs are still there too, scrounging for something to eat all day, howling all night. The noise was so bad the last few nights we were there, Cap'n McPhee anchored down the eastern end of the harbor so we could sleep. Now you know, Miz Eva, for tired sailors to do that, there had to be a racket!"

"The same as always," Miz Eva said, her eyes sparkling. She was delighted to have male company. "How long will the *Stella Maris* lay over here?"

"She's leaving before noon today, Ma'am, if there's any wind." Jonah replied. "But I'm not going to Jamaica with her this trip; she'll stop for me on the way back, after Christmas. I heard my Pa wasn't doing too well. I want to see for myself how he's getting on."

"Reena's been boiling bush medicine for him, but she says he's not getting any better. I'm glad you've come, Jonah. We old people need to know somebody cares about us."

"Well, I'll likely be here six or eight weeks. I'll have to see what can be arranged if Pa's no better by then. In the meantime, I can tend his field and see to the creatures, maybe cut some hardwood. Spend a little time with the old man."

"Happen you might find a mermaid to look after your Pa like Greville found for me," Miz Eva said, glancing fondly at Kath.

"I'll be looking on every beach from now on, Ma'am," he said, his dark eyes dancing with mischief. "Especially if I can find one as pretty as yours..." But he doubted he could. He hadn't so far. Maybe he'd just have to steal Kath away from her. His Pa and he could use some looking after. Suddenly Jonah had the strongest hankering for a wife. He almost drooled he wanted one so much. His shining eyes washed over Kath in a lazy caress.

Kath's cheeks pinked. "Let's see what's in the package, Miz Eva," she said, changing the subject. She found the bold stares of the Bahamian men unnerving. Jonah made her stomach plunge when he looked at her that way.

Jonah laughed. "Now, there's something to see, Miz Eva. The women in New Providence can't blush like that!" He pushed the parcel over to Kath. "Greville said he bought some dry goods for you to sew, Miz Kath. Said you're a seamstress. I hope you'll have time to make me a shirt or two? I'm sorely in need. My Pa, too. I brought some cambric home, just in case."

"Why, yes, Mr. Cartwright, I'd be happy to sew for you," Kath said, opening the package.

Captain Knowles had sent three dress lengths of sprigged muslin, with solids in matching colors for petticoats. There was fine handkerchief linen and ten yards or so of a coarser weave, some calico and some cambric. There were needles, pins, a pair of scissors and some embroidery silks.

"Well, your grandson is an excellent shopper, Miz Eva," Kath said, pleased with the purchases. "He's sent everything I asked for. I can get started this afternoon."

"I know you're busy now, so I'll be going," Jonah Cartwright said to Kath. "But may I call on you later this evening, Ma'am? This island can be powerful dull. I hope we can become friends."

Kath's cheeks bloomed again and she looked at Miz Eva with pleading eyes. *So you're coming after my little chicken,* Miz

Eva thought. *Just like a fowl snake!* This was going to be fun. *Well, just you try to get her, Jonah Cartwright. My Greville's a better man than you, any day.* Miz Eva quickly gazed out the door, trying to control her wicked grin. Kath was on her own.

"Y-yes, Mr. Cartwright, you may call if you wish," Kath managed to stammer. "I can measure you for your shirts," she said briskly. "And any friend of Miz Eva and Captain Knowles is always welcome here. You don't have to ask me."

"Then I'll say goodbye, for now, and see you after supper," Jonah said, getting to his feet. "I'm so glad to find somebody new on this island."

"Zounds, what a woman!" he said to himself, as he went whistling down the path into the settlement.

*

The whole settlement had watched Jonah as he walked up the path to Miz Eva's hut the morning after his arrival. Everybody immediately started joking about Jonah and Kath 'keeping company' and the gossips had a high time speculating about the possibility of a wedding.

Everybody, that is, except Miz Reena's sixteen-year-old granddaughter, Shirley.

Shirley was a precocious girl and she was lonely. The two boys who had been in her age group had gone to sea with their fathers several years before. Becky Harding was the nearest person to Shirley's age, and she was only twelve, no companion for Shirley. Anyway, Becky preferred playing with ten-year old Amy. So Shirley spent hours by herself, lying on the beach, collecting shells, looking out to sea. She escaped her mother's chore list and her own doldrums by floating in romantic daydreams.

When the *Stella Maris* had arrived the day before and Jonah Cartwright stepped ashore, Shirley's heart gave a leap. She'd known Jonah all her life, but up until now had considered him an old man. Suddenly she saw him afresh. He was no longer 'old' but 'older,' a man of the world. At her exalted age of sixteen, she might now aspire to his interest. Shirley felt a stab of envy when she saw Miz Eva go over to Jonah and introduce Kath.

As people drifted away from the shore after meeting the ship, Shirley decided to go visit her Granny Reena. While she walked over, she dreamed of what life would be like with Jonah. She imaged several delightful sessions alone with him on the beach, when she would dazzle him with her wit and surprising sophistication. He would be fascinated, would not rest until her Pa agreed to their marriage.

Shirley stopped to sit under a coconut tree and design her wedding dress. It would be in shell pink and have a very low bodice, laced up tight to show her tiny waist. There would be festoons of lace and pink satin roses on the skirt. The whole settlement would talk of nothing else for the next year!

Shirley smiled, as she imagined how jealous Kath would be. She would mope on the shelf as she sat stitching the most elegant bridal gown of her career – for someone else. Kath would defer to Shirley, ask her for style ideas to use later, when making clothes for the other women. Shirley would be kind, but firm. The soon-to-be Mrs. Jonah Cartwright would be too busy with her wedding plans to help an old maiden seamstress.

Pulling herself from her reverie, Shirley jumped up and walked with jaunty steps over to Granny Reena's. After chatting of this and that, she casually brought up the subject of old Mr. Cartwright.

"I guess Jonah's come to check on his Pa," she said. "How is he doing?"

"Not too good, chile. Poor man's got everything wrong with him. I have some gale'o'wind grass boiled up now, to help his appetite."

"I'll take it over for you, Granny Reena."

"Thank you, chile. That'll save my old legs. Mind you bring back the jar when he drinks it. I got most of my jars over there now. Maybe you can ask Jonah for them, and bring them back."

Shirley took herself off, skipping along the road to the Cartwrights' hut. She took off the white neckerchief that she wore over her low-cut bodice. Her breasts were high and round, her skin a beautiful, smooth caramel. She looked down at them with satisfaction before she knocked on the Cartwrights' door.

"Evenin' Jonah," she said, giving him a simper that she thought was her most devastating smile. "I brought this gale'o'wind grass tea for your Pa."

Jonah looked at her, tilting his head to one side. "Well, it's little Shirley Stirrup, Miz Louise's girl, ain't it? My, how you've grown up!" Jonah gave his lazy, audacious grin as he took the jar from her hand. "Come in." Shirley felt a hot flash sear through her body as his hand touched hers.

"Have you got anything for supper?" she asked. "I know you just got here. I could fix you something to eat, while you rest from your trip."

"Thank you, Shirley," Jonah said. "I brought victuals home with me. We'll be fine. But thank you kindly," he said again, firmly. "I'll just pour this tea into a mug for the old man and let you have your jar back..."

Shirley lingered, tried to draw Jonah into conversation, but he only answered in an absent kind of way. He was tired and exasperated with the little brat. He believed she was actually trying to flirt with him, and he was twice her age! He wondered if Miz Louise knew she was visiting two men with her bodice laced low like that.

"Goodnight, Shirley," he said at last, holding the door open. "I'm going to be here for a couple of months, you know. We'll have plenty of time to catch up."

There was nothing for her to do then, but go. She did a little jig on the way home, skipping from one foot to the other, hugging Jonah's news to herself. *He's going to stay a couple of months*, she thought, wildly happy.

That first night of Jonah's return, Shirley couldn't sleep for the longest time. Her imagined future with Jonah Cartwright grew more fantastic as the night wore on.

The next morning Miz Louise kept Shirley busy with the household chores that she had managed to avoid earlier in the week. Shirley was working about the house when Granny Reena came in with the juicy gossip that Jonah was already up on the hill, visiting Miz Eva and Kath. Shirley broke a precious earthenware plate and made such a clatter with her bucket that her mother and Granny couldn't hear each other speak.

Right after supper, about six o'clock, Shirley tidied herself, pinched her cheeks, bit her lips and set out on the road through the settlement to call on Jonah. She turned a bend in the road and there was Jonah himself, striding towards her, all spruced up. He was so beautiful Shirley could hardly believe her eyes.

"Hello, Jonah," she called gaily, and Jonah waved back. *Zounds*, he thought, *there's that pesky brat again.* If she caught him, she'd be yammering all night, batting her lashes and pushing out her chest.

Shirley leaned against an almond tree, took a deep breath, and expelled it slowly with her eyes closed. He was coming to see her, she thought. She must think of what to say. But the moment was too delicious, and no clever words came to mind. Shirley opened her eyes and – consternation – Jonah was gone. He'd turned off onto the hill path leading up to Miz Eva's hut. She caught a glimpse of his white shirt disappearing fast through the brush in the darkening twilight.

Shirley clenched her teeth and balled her fists. Stamping her foot, she said a word her mother did not know she knew. Slowly she turned and went down to the beach, sat on a rock and glared out to sea. But not for long. The mosquitoes and sandflies were out in force. Shirley slouched home. Granny Reena's dog bounced out to meet her, and received a sharp kick for her greeting.

*

Jonah Cartwright was at Kath's door several evenings that first week. Kath and Miz Eva both looked forward to his visits. Jonah had a devilish sense of humor, and it was fun to hear of his travels and the gossip down in the settlement, all told with his droll twist.

Shirley burned with jealousy and aggravation every time she saw Jonah going up the hill path to visit Kath. And of course, with her special interest, she managed to know exactly when he went up and when he came down.

Why should Miz Kath have everything? Shirley fumed to herself. Kath was everyone's precious darling – and why? Shirley herself was younger and prettier. Kath was so old. She was forty if she was a day. Well, Shirley wanted to leave Fortune Island, and Jonah Cartwright was the man to help her do it. She had had enough of this boring place, where nothing happened day in, day out.

*

Shirley's mood did not improve over the following week. She made several stabs at trying to see Jonah, without much success. He was busy and worried about his Pa, he said – *but not too busy or worried to visit Miz Kath,* Shirley thought angrily. Well, if Jonah wouldn't come to her, she'd just have to go to him.

One afternoon Shirley ripped a piece of lace on her Sunday-best petticoat and took it along to see Miz Kath right after supper.

"I was wondering if you'd please teach me to sew?" Shirley asked after their greetings. "I have this torn lace, and I'm so clumsy with a needle. It's my best petticoat, the only bit of lace I have. It used to be Granny Reena's when she was a bride, and then my mother's. Would you show me how to mend it please?"

"Of course, Shirley," Kath replied, putting her own embroidery aside and reaching for Shirley's work. "My, it's lovely lace. You're a lucky girl to have it…"

Miz Eva took herself outside to sit on the step with her clay pipe, leaving the two younger women at work around the table. A little later, Jonah's voice greeting Miz Eva made them both start.

"Still teaching classes, Miz Kath?" Jonah asked in his customary drawl.

"No, I'm just helping Shirley with a bit of lace." Kath smiled up at Jonah. "We're just finishing."

"Good evening, Jonah," Shirley sang out.

Kath handed the petticoat back to Shirley. "I'm sure you can manage on your own now. I've been sewing all afternoon, and I want to enjoy my company."

"Thank you, Miz Kath," Shirley replied. "I'll just keep at it here where you can oversee me. I don't want to ruin this lace."

"Just as you like," Kath replied. "Shall we sit outside Jonah? We can watch the moon rise."

They were not outside long before Shirley came looking for them.

"I've made a mess," she said. "My thread is all tangled up and my stitches don't look neat like yours, Miz Kath."

Shirley sat down on a rock the other side of Jonah. "It's such a beautiful evening," she said breathlessly. "What a wonderful view over the harbor!"

For the rest of the evening, there was a threesome in the moonlight. When Jonah rose to leave, Shirley went with him down the path, her petticoat 'forgotten' in Miz Eva's hut.

Shirley became a regular visitor after that. The next time, she came to collect her petticoat. The time after, to bring Miz Eva a piece of coconut tart from Granny Reena. Then she decided to teach Kath how to plait straw from the silver-top palmetto leaves that grew on the island. This would be a welcome change from her sewing, was Shirley's kind thought.

Miz Eva enjoyed the show. She was in two minds about Kath's suitor anyhow. Jonah was a good man, she'd known him from a boy, and if Kath's fancy lay that way, well, so be it. She still cherished hopes for a match between Kath and Greville, however, and the *Swan* would be home for Christmas in a few weeks. The old lady puffed on her clay pipe, speculating. Life sure had picked up since Kath's arrival.

After Kath's initial amazement and annoyance with Shirley, she began to get used to her being around. Kath missed her boys and it was nice to have a teenager about the house again. Besides, Kath was curious to see how many excuses Shirley could find to weasel her way into their evenings.

"I was married to John by the time I was Shirley's age," Kath told Miz Eva one morning when they were talking about Shirley. "I can remember how sweet it was to hold my own man. And my son Duncan was sixteen, and he was already courting Molly Grady, which is what got him into trouble."

Kath sighed. "There's no one on this island for Shirley, Miz Eva, not even another girl of her age to talk to. Can you imagine how dreary life here must seem for a lively young girl like her?"

"It was dreary for a girl like me, too, before you came," Miz Eva said, smiling at Kath. "And I'm seventy years old. There's nothing to do on these islands. The monotony can drive you crazy. I must say, it's very generous of you to let her come visit with you and Jonah. The Lord will bless you for it."

"It's hard to see where it will all lead," Kath said. "As for me, though I enjoy Jonah's company, I'm not ready for courting. I need to feel more settled in myself before I become involved with a man. Too much has happened to me this past year. Besides, he hasn't said anything to me. The island is boring for him, too. If we lived anywhere else, Jonah might not spare me the time of day."

Kath reached for her sewing basket and began to work.

"It's a blessing you know how to sew so well," Miz Eva said. "I guess it's stood you in good stead over the years."

"Yes, it has," Kath agreed. "I'm glad my Granda prodded me to keep at it when I was a girl. He used to tease me about marrying John. He could get me to do anything that way. I doted on John from the time I was a wee thing, you see.

"'You'll need to learn to read and figure, if you're to marry John O'Brien when you grow up,' he'd say, and I'd rush to my copybook. Then he'd say, 'You have to learn to sew like your mother, Kathy. You know John O'Brien descends from the great kings of Ireland, and his wife must sew like a lady.' No matter how disgusted I was with my sampler, I'd pick it out and do the stitches again. Just so I'd be worthy for John to marry me." Kath looked up from her stitching and gave Miz Eva a broad grin. "Those lessons weren't the reason he married me, though…"

"I'll bet they weren't!" Miz Eva laughed. "Well, we'll watch and see what happens with little Miss Shirley Stirrup."

19

Little Miss Shirley Stirrup was not making the conquest she had imagined. It was discouraging, but she was a determined girl. It was the middle of December, and Jonah was due to leave Fortune Island early in the New Year. At sixteen already, with no prospects, Shirley felt time was running out for her. She was in danger of becoming an old maid.

Desperate situations demand desperate actions, and she was not one to quibble about doing whatever was necessary.

Each night when she and Jonah had left Miz Eva's and were alone on the bush path back to the settlement, Shirley had done her best to show Jonah what a superior female she was. She tried to engage him in elegant conversation, only to have him look baffled and ask her if she was all right. She had stumbled on the path and fallen against him, crashing them both into the dark bushes. He solicitously helped her up and brushed her down, with nary an improper touch. She had asked for his arm and cuddled it close by her breasts. Jonah had looked at the stars, begun to name them for her, and started explaining celestial navigation.

The company at Miz Eva's was boring Shirley, if she would but admit it. However, her own sense of impending spinster-hood, and the challenge of playing with the grown-ups, of besting Kath O'Brien, drove all doubts from her mind. Jonah Cartwright was the man – the *only* man – for her, and she would have him. She would just have to turn up the burner.

Jonah himself was beginning to find Shirley as tedious as a biting horsefly. Everywhere he turned, there she was, simpering up at him, plucking at his arms, his clothes or his mind. It was flattering initially to be so doggedly sought after. He was amused at the interest the settlement took in his visits to Miz Kath, of being the center of a stir among his own people. He was just an ordinary seaman, experienced enough to get by, but showing no talents of leadership or specific ability. Becoming a big fish is always pleasant, no matter what size the pond, and Jonah enjoyed his new status.

Over the previous weeks, however, Jonah had enjoyed more than fame. He had come to look forward to seeing Kath at the end of the day, to making her face wreathe in smiles at the sight of him. Her blushes entranced him, used as he was to swarthy women, or the hard-bitten females who frequented the waterfront. He liked to watch Kath bent over her embroidery, her hands delicate and sure, producing exquisite results. He took pride in the fact that she found him acceptable, she of education and ability, he of none. There was a comfort at Miz Eva's that he had never known before and he attributed it all to Kath.

Jonah began to feel that marriage to Kath would be a highly desirable thing, and to have a few fantasies of his own. Why should Kath be looking after Miz Eva, when his own Pa needed someone caring to ease his old bones into the grave? And Jonah could sell Kath's finished garments just as well as Captain Knowles. He would probably do it even better, since Kath would be his wife. Life at sea was hard and brutal. Fancy having Kath to dream about all during the long, lonely voyages; to know that there was a place of warmth and love waiting for him ashore!

Jonah decided to pop the question, and began to look for his best opportunity. God willing, Shirley would give him space.

The settlement was watching for the *Swan* any day, bringing the crew home for Christmas with their families, along with toys for the children and special treats of food and drink. There was an undercurrent of excitement in the air.

Kath was excited too, though she found it strange to be

contemplating Christmas with a blazing hot sun and palm trees. She had finished new dresses for Miz Eva and herself, and a dress shirt in white handkerchief linen for Captain Knowles. She had made a calico shirt for Jonah and a lovely embroidered mob cap for Shirley. She and Miz Eva had chosen a hen to fatten up for Christmas dinner and were planning whatever delicacies they could contrive from their field to go with her. The oranges and limes were ripe, and there was a bunch of bananas ripening on the hook over the table in the kitchen.

Just after noon four days before Christmas, Jonah came to the door of Miz Eva's hut. "Afternoon, Miz Eva, Miz Kath," he said, holding his straw hat in his hands.

"Afternoon, Jonah," the two women chorused.

"This is an unusual time for you to call," Kath said. "What is it? Has someone sighted the *Swan*?"

"No, not yet," Jonah replied. "I was wondering if you would come for a sail with me this afternoon. I've borrowed James Harding's dinghy and the wind is just right."

Kath looked at Miz Eva. "Go on, chile," she encouraged. "A li'l sail would do you good. It's so nice on the water, and you've been slaving over that sewing for weeks without a break."

Kath snatched up her hat and ran down the steps. It was not until she and Jonah were almost down to the shore that her delight gave way to a sliver of unease. Jonah was looking very spruce for sailing in a dinghy, and he was behaving peculiarly. She could not say exactly how, just that he was not his usual breezy self. He seemed quiet, and, well, a little nervous.

As Jonah handed Kath into the boat and pushed off from the sand, Kath's heart sank, and her delight gave way to dismay. She sat quietly on the stern while Jonah hoisted the sail, then came aft to the tiller.

"She's a sweet little mover," Jonah said, as the sail filled and the dinghy heeled over. "I been wanting to bring you out for days, but the weather's not been right. No fun in getting wet." A lacy bow wave trailed hissing aft and a pair of gulls

136

swooped by. Jonah grinned at Kath. "It's kind of nice to get away from the old and the young, to be on the water all by ourselves."

"Yes," Kath agreed, wondering how to get the conversation back into safe territory. "I guess you've been very busy with your old father. He's bedridden now, isn't he?"

Jonah nodded. "I think he must have had some kind of stroke in the night. He wasn't talking good today." He paused, looked at Kath and then up at the masthead. "But that's not what I meant. I mean, it's nice not to have Miz Eva and Shirley sittin' with us. You must know by now that I don't come up the hill to sit with them."

Kath smiled and trailed her hand in the water. "Yes, I know. But it is Miz Eva's home, and poor little Shirley has no company of her own."

"I been watching you Kath, these past weeks. You're always thinking about somebody, or doing something for someone. You're just plain nice..." Jonah reached over and smoothed a tendril of hair out of her face. Kath flushed at his touch; Jonah flashed his sparkling smile. "And you blush! Anybody says something nice to you, you blush. Anybody touch you, you blush. That's the first thing I noticed about you, how you blush. And I love it!"

"Thank you Jonah. I can't help it, you know."

"That's what I mean. You can't help being nice and modest and sweet." He looked back at the island, now left behind in their wake, then turned to Kath and took her hand.

"I love you Kath. I want to marry you. Will you marry me?"

"Oh Jonah, I don't know what to say..."

"Say yes! Just say 'yes'..."

"No. That is, I need to think about it..."

"What's there to think about? I been sitting up with you for the past six weeks. If you don't know me now, you never will. I know you like me..."

"I do, Jonah, very much..."

"Then what's wrong? The *Stella Maris* will be back for me

in a week or so. If we're going to have any time together, we have to decide now."

"I know, Jonah. But this is all so sudden..."

"How could it be sudden, when the whole settlement is placing bets on the date? Don't tell me you didn't know, that you haven't thought about it. Why would I have been visiting you all these weeks?"

"Yes. No. That is...maybe. I mean...Jonah, I'm a Catholic. I don't wish to marry someone who is not of the same faith. Even if you converted, there's no priest on Fortune Island and I don't know about New Providence. How would we be married without a priest? That wouldn't be right for me."

"Kath, there're no priests in any of these islands. People get married by telling everyone they are, then having a party to celebrate it. This ain't like the Old Country, where everything has to be done with a piece of paper. Our word's good enough." Jonah looked pleadingly into Kath's troubled eyes.

"We could get Captain Knowles to marry us on the *Swan*, maybe," he suggested hopefully. "Captains can do all sorts of things on their ships."

Kath's cheeks pinked, then paled. She looked doubtfully at Jonah, her brow wrinkled.

Jonah spilled the sail and put the boat in irons. She wallowed on the ocean swell, her rigging tapping softly against the mast. He reached for Kath's hand again.

"Don't you care for me, then?" Jonah's voice had a catch of heartbreak, as though stating the question brought him pain.

"Oh Jonah, I *do* care for you! I just don't want to get married right now. I'm still recovering from my shipwreck, the yellow fever, and mourning for my boys. You don't know anything about my past life, who I am."

"I do so. Miz Reena told me all about how they convicted you for stealing in Ireland and they transported you. But you were shipwrecked and you were the only one to survive. That proves to us all that you're innocent. God wouldn't do that for you if you were guilty. Besides, now everyone knows you. We *know* you wouldn't steal from anybody. And even if you did, I love you." He took a deep breath and looked up at the horizon.

"Look – a sail!" Jonah pointed to the west. "Looks like the *Swan's* here at last."

Kath's head whipped around to look. Her heart gave a huge lurch and hammered in her chest. Her blood roared in her ears.

"The settlement will be wild with joy," Kath said, waiting for the rush to subside. Then she turned back to Jonah, and looked into his earnest face again.

"I need some time to think about all this. Must I say yes or no right now? If we marry, it will be for the rest of our lives. It's too important to rush, just because the *Stella Maris* is due back. If it's right, it'll keep and grow stronger between us. By the next time you pass through we'll both know if we should marry or not."

"You mean, *you* might know. I know *now*. I'd hoped you would, too." Jonah turned the bow off the wind again, filling the sail. "I've never asked another woman to marry me, Kath, and I won't browbeat any woman to marry me now. But I don't want to go away with this thing unsettled between us. Please try to answer in a day or two."

"All right, Jonah, that's fair enough. I promise to give your offer serious thought and let you know by Christmas Eve. If we decide to marry, we can announce it to the settlement on Christmas Day and celebrate it then. Let's keep this between ourselves for now though, please."

"Agreed. By Christmas Eve *morning?*"

Kath smiled. "All right, by Christmas Eve *morning*, mid-morning! And I thank you Jonah. You've done me a great honor by asking. You're a fine man and any woman would be proud to be your wife."

Jonah's mouth twitched. "But not you, eh?"

"Oh Jonah! You know that's not what I mean! I can't say anything right today."

Jonah smiled. "And the right thing would be so easy! Say 'yes'..."

Kath laughed. "I told you I couldn't say the right thing today. But at least I haven't said 'no'."

"That's true, you haven't, so I can still hope." Jonah squinted up at the sun. "Let's enjoy this lively lass a bit before we go home again. I know a lovely cove about a mile away. We have plenty of time to get back before dark."

*

By the time Jonah brought the little sailboat back to the settlement, the *Swan* had anchored and everyone was down on the shore.

Captain Greville Knowles had been as eager as a schoolboy for his Christmas holiday this year. He had given the *Swan* as much sail as possible on the way down to Fortune Island, and still she seemed to creep. His restless eyes had scanned the beach as his men rowed him ashore. He quickly spotted Miz Eva, but his eyes roved on among the crowd, seeking yet another.

Captain Knowles had just stepped ashore and was kissing his grandmother when he sensed a commotion among the crowd. He looked up to see Jonah Cartwright helping Kath out of James Harding's sailing dinghy. He felt as though someone had whacked him in the chest with a two by four. *So that's how it is,* he thought, his merry heart crashing. *Looks like I've come home too late...*

Shirley was down on the shore, too. She had been moving from group to group looking for Jonah. She, too, noticed the nudges and knowing looks between people as they watched Jonah helping Kath out of James Harding's boat. *So that's how it is,* she thought, her body prickling hot with envy. *We'll soon see about that!*

Jonah's chest stuck out like a pouter pigeon's, and he held his head high as he offered Kath his arm to walk up the beach. He'd timed it just right, arriving back when the whole settlement was down on the shore to see they had been sailing alone together. It would be a perfect time to announce the wedding. If only Kath had said yes...

A surge of disappointment washed over Kath. Of all the times to be compromised, why did it have to be in front of Captain Greville Knowles?

20

Kath struggled for composure, then headed over to where Miz Eva and Captain Knowles waited, almost dragging Jonah in her wake. Shirley was also plowing through people and sand, towards collision with Jonah and Kath.

"You naughty man," she called gaily to Jonah, wagging her finger. "Why didn't you tell me you were going sailing? I would have loved to go. What a wonderful afternoon it was for a boat!" She came up and took his free arm, so that Jonah was escorting both ladies by the time he reached Miz Eva and Captain Knowles. For once Kath was glad for Shirley's silly audacity, which diluted the impact of her own arrival alone with Jonah.

"Welcome home, Captain Knowles," Kath said warmly, disentangling her arm from Jonah so she could shake hands.

"Thank you, Mistress O'Brien," Captain Knowles replied, bowing over her hand. "How d'ye do, Jonah. And this charming young lady is Shirley Stirrup, I believe? I hardly recognized you Shirley, you've grown so much."

Shirley smiled and inclined her head. "Indeed, Captain Knowles." She did not offer her hand, for to do so she must give up Jonah's arm. She clung on with limpet tenacity, using both her own.

Kath now threaded her arm with Miz Eva's, drawing the old lady close to her side. "I thank you, Jonah, for the afternoon's sail," she said. "It's the first time I've been in a boat since Captain Knowles rescued me last September." *At least he'll realize that I have not made a practice of sailing alone with Jonah while he's been gone*, she thought.

Captain Knowles turned towards the path up the hill.

"Will I call on you this evening, Miz Kath?" Jonah asked quickly, his face glowing with adoration.

"I think not," Kath replied. "Perhaps Captain Knowles and Miz Eva would like to be quiet at home for the next day or so. But I shall see you on Christmas Eve, as agreed."

Jonah's face fell. "But that's two days from now! Surely you can spare a few moments for me before then."

Kath had not intended to cause such despair. "Well, there will be all the Christmas preparations to make, cooking and so on, and I will need some time to myself before Christmas Eve morning," Kath said firmly. "Remember, too, that I'm a guest in Captain Knowles's home."

"Nonsense, Kath," Miz Eva interjected. "Come whenever you like, Jonah." Kath pinched Miz Eva, who hastily added, "...so long as you realize that we *will* be very busy with our housework...

"Well, children, shall we head up the hill? All this excitement has worn me out."

"Of course, Gammie," Captain Knowles said, tucking her free arm through his own. "I bid you goodnight Jonah, Shirley..." With that, Kath, Miz Eva and Greville headed up the path to their home on the hill.

*

"Well!" Shirley said, as she and Jonah watched Kath disappear up the bush path with Miz Eva and Captain Knowles. "We can see when we're not wanted! Now that the dashing Captain is back, she has no time for her everyday friends."

"Shut up, Shirley," Jonah snarled. He was concerned enough about how dashing Greville looked without Shirley's mosquito-whine in his ear to remind him. "Captain Knowles is just back from a three-month voyage. I know how tired I'd be. A man has the right to a quiet evening in his own home when he gets ashore. Kath's right, as usual. She always thinks of others rather than of herself – unlike some I could mention."

Soundly squelched, Shirley began a new tack. "Well, that

leaves us at loose-ends for the evening," Shirley said, smiling sweetly. "Would you like to come and have supper with us? Maybe we could eat at Granny Reena's – she was baking coconut tarts this afternoon."

"No thanks, Shirley. My Pa had a bad turn last night. He was talking funny this morning. I've got to get home now to see how he's doing."

"I could bring you something to eat, then stay and help with your Pa."

"No, thank you kindly. I have things to think about."

"I see Miz Kath isn't the only one who's forgetting who their regular friends are!"

"Go play with your own little friends, Shirley. I got things to do." Jonah turned on his heel and walked off towards home, his head bowed. He kicked a twig from the path, then bent and picked up a stone, which he shied into the bush at a mockingbird singing in a treetop.

Even Shirley's optimism took a spill at this turn of events. She, too, headed for home. Jonah wasn't the only one who had things to think about. How was she going to hook a fish that wouldn't bite her bait? *When a fish won't eat conch, sometimes it'll bite crawfish,* she thought. She had to decide how to change the bait.

*

The three hill dwellers spent a talkative evening together, catching up on the latest news from the outside world as well as the doings on Fortune Island.

Captain Knowles had brought Kath some beautiful materials from Charleston. He seemed delighted that she had started her little school and had already been sewing for the local folk. Kath was as animated as Miz Eva at Greville's return. After the Bible chapter and evening prayers, Miz Eva shooed the 'children' out of the house, claiming she needed her bed early.

"How has it been for you truly, Miz O'Brien?" Captain Knowles asked when he and Kath were sitting outside in the starlight. "You and Gammie seem very close, but I know it's hard work caring for the elderly. The old girl looks ten years younger. I'm in your debt for that."

"In *my* debt?" Kath cried, amazed. "The debt is mine! I owe my life to both of you. After you left I caught yellow fever. She cared for me constantly, all by herself, for more than a week. I would have died, but she pulled me through. She showed me so much love that she made me want to live. It's amazing how she's shared her home and all she has with me." There was a catch in Kath's voice. She paused, then continued.

"Please don't ever think that caring for Miz Eva might be a burden to me. I love her like my own mother. I would go to the ends of the earth for either of you. You are my family now.

"And, would you *please* call me Kath?"

She could see his face soften in a smile. "Only if you will honor me by calling me Greville. I would very much like to be your family, Kath. Having saved your life, I am now responsible for it." He turned to look at her, and his steady gaze made her tremble. As he shifted his position on the stone bench, he accidentally brushed her fingers lightly with his own. Kath felt a rush of heat and caught her breath.

"Thank you, Greville. I will try never to be a burden." The tremor she heard in her voice dismayed her. Her eyes prickled and she swallowed hard. She knew her tears made Greville uncomfortable and she hated how emotional she became around him. She was grateful when he suddenly changed the subject.

"Shirley Stirrup seems much attached to Jonah."

"Yes! She follows him around like a puppy. Jonah can hardly breathe without smelling her perfume..."

"Did you enjoy your sail this afternoon? Do you like boats?"

"Yes, I do like boats. At home in Ireland, we thought a boat trip the greatest treat. I like to fish, too."

"Indeed! We need some fresh fish, it's our tradition to have a good boiled grouper Christmas Eve morning. Will you come out with me tomorrow?"

Kath's pulse quickened. She was glad the starlight hid her excitement. "Yes, thank you. I'd like that more than anything!"

"What other victuals do we have for Christmas?"

"We've planned a sweet potato bread, some banana bread, and there are yams and cassava ready, some black eye peas and green pigeon peas, some onions, fresh thyme, a bunch of plantains, and grits, of course. We've been saving things right along. We have a pot of guava jam from Miz Reena, so we can have jam roly-poly, or a duff. Oh – and Jonah tells me that James Harding will slaughter a sheep, and that we can have a leg. Also we have a nice fat hen..."

"I've brought several treats as well," Greville said, taking up Kath's enthusiasm. "There are candied fruits from Cuba, which I bought in Nassau, and a smoked ham from Charleston. We have some good Jamaica coffee on board, which is so much better than what we manage to grow here. And, as a special treat for Gammie, I have a few ounces of China tea and three bottles of sherry! We'll feast royally, Kath. It'll be the best Christmas ever!"

Kath had a sudden pang, remembering other Christmases in Ireland. Greville seemed to notice the change in her mood.

"Well, perhaps we'd better turn in," he said with a sigh. "I'm glad I thought to bring that other hammock. I'm too tired to row back to the *Swan* tonight."

Kath's stomach fluttered at the thought of sleeping in the same room with Greville, although Miz Eva would be there too. *He's so casual about it all,* she thought. *He's already treating me like his sister.*

*

Kath heard Greville's even breathing and Miz Eva's quiet snores, but still she lay rigid in her hammock, her mind in turmoil. She tingled with excitement when she thought of going fishing with Greville. She recalled the gentle rocking of the boat, the sun and breeze on her body, the crack of the sail, from her afternoon's trip with Jonah. Her mind swooned with delight as she imagined Greville beside her instead of Jonah. Greville proposing, saying she was his heart's one desire, urging her to throw religion and caution to the wind. She imagined Greville's full mouth tenderly exploring her own, Greville's large square hands caressing her back, then riveting her body to his as the passion of their kiss exploded. Her heart soared, her stomach tightened, and her pulse raced.

Then her heart failed her as she wrestled with how to tell him that she was a Catholic and a convicted criminal. Miz Eva had made light of those things, but Miz Eva was a loving old woman. She'd lived beyond the age where many things in life bothered her. Greville was a man in his prime, well-traveled and versed in the political opinions of the outside world. He took his religion seriously, and Catholicism would likely be anathema to him. Just as his Protestant beliefs were anathema to her. It was easy for Jonah not to mind her religion, since he seemed to have none of his own. Greville was a very different man.

Then her mind would switch back to Jonah. She ticked off his attributes: he was a good man, the salt of the earth, honest, strong, good looking, hardworking, affectionate, amusing, reliable, and popular. He would make a loving husband. He adored her and she was fond of him. He wouldn't hold her religion against her, he knew about her past and thought nothing of it. Also, he had already asked her to marry him and was anxious for her decision. The whole settlement had been watching them 'keeping company' for the past six weeks and expected them to marry.

Suppose she did marry Jonah. Where would she live? Would Jonah expect her to move in with old Mr. Cartwright, to nurse him while Jonah worked? What of Miz Eva? Would she have to live alone again, or would she move in with Mr. Cartwright too? Or could they manage to bring Mr. Cartwright up the hill to Miz Eva's? But the house wasn't Miz Eva's, it belonged to Greville. What would Greville think about having an old people's home in his cottage? She owed her life to Greville and Miz Eva, she owed them her loyalty and love.

Indeed, she did love Miz Eva. And she had to admit, she also loved Greville, or very easily could, if he showed any inclination in that direction himself.

Then her heart would leap again, at the thought of their fishing trip on the morrow. What did Greville have in mind? Would he confess his love? Several times that evening she'd noticed him looking at her. She knew his eyes followed her about the room, seemed to brighten when she returned to the hut after a trip to the kitchen. What did they say, those intense hazel eyes? They were the windows of his soul, but she was afraid to read them and be wrong about what they said. But just suppose he loved her?

It seemed no time at all before Kath heard the cocks crowing and Miz Eva's stealthy scuffling, heading out for her morning meeting with the Lord.

21

Right after breakfast Greville and Kath went down to the shore, where the *Swan's* battered wooden boat awaited the Captain's pleasure. Ready to go fishing, Greville had put on a pair of faded pants, cut off to mid-thigh, and an old shirt he wore open and tied at the waist. He carried a bucket with hooks and fishing lines, a couple of sharp knives, a small hatchet and a chopping board. Kath wore one of Miz Eva's old shifts and a straw hat.

Greville helped Kath aboard, shoved the boat out, and then clambered in himself. He picked up the oar and sculled the dinghy from an oarlock in the stern, moving along the shore until he found a sandy area that was dark with turtle grass. He shipped the oar, then peered overboard through a glass-bottomed bucket, which he called a 'water-glass'.

"We're looking for our bait, Kath," he explained. "I'm hoping to find a few conchs."

He soon spotted one, stripped off his shirt and dove overboard. He bobbed up with a gasp about twenty feet from the boat, holding a large pink conch shell in his hand. A few sure strokes brought him back. He dropped the shell into the stern, then hauled himself into the boat. He picked up the oar again, stopping every few yards to scan the grass.

Kath sat in the bow of the boat watching. Greville's well-muscled, bronzed body awed her. *He's like one of the men from those old stories, when the Great Kings ruled Ireland,* she thought, as he dove again with hardly a splash. When his hands gripped the gunwale, she held her breath in anticipation of his body shooting up out of the water, his chest rippling with the effort of hauling himself back into the boat. His pants clung to his hips, and water dripped from him as he towered above her.

"Found two that time," he said, pleased. "That's enough for bait, but maybe we should get some for us to eat. Gammie loves conch." He began sculling again, with his left arm pumping at the end of the oar, rocking his body and right arm with the rhythm. Greville gave Kath a questioning look and smiled. The thick gold ring in his left ear glinted in the sun. Searing desire rose in her. She caught her breath and wrenched her gaze from him, turning to look out to sea to hide her flaming face. She trailed a hand in the gin-clear turquoise water. She had been staring at him! What would he think of her?

Greville soon had eight conchs. "These will be enough for us," he said and sat on the thwart with his legs spread around the heap of conchs in the bottom of the boat. He pulled out the hatchet, a knife and the board from the bucket and set to work. He chopped a hole at the back of a shell, then inserted the knife blade to release the mollusk, which slipped out from the front. He threw the empty shell overboard, and Kath watched in fascination as he scraped the soft, slimy parts of the creature into the bucket, then cut its meat into strips on the board.

"We'll use this conch slop to chum up the fish if we need to," he said. "We'll use the meat on our hooks, and tempt them to have some breakfast. We'll go over to a reef where I usually find a grouper or two. If we don't catch any, we can always eat the conch."

Kath's face puckered in disgust. Greville laughed. "Haven't you eaten conch yet? I'm surprised. We eat it a lot in these islands, especially when the weather's bad and we can't go fishing. Miz Eva's conch is delicious! You'll see when you try it."

"Don't go to the trouble for me," Kath said quickly. "I have had Miz Eva's conch before, but I've never seen it like this, right out of the shell. Usually Mr. Harding brings it to us cleaned and ready for the pot. Besides, we have a lot to eat over the next week."

*

They were soon over the reef. Greville bent overboard with the water-glass, to see if any fish were at home. "Good, there are lots of fish, just asking to be caught," he reported as he sat back in the boat. "I saw several large snappers, a Margate fish, some yellow tails and other small fish that are good for frying. Here have a look yourself. Then let's get those lines over."

He handed Kath the water-glass, and she looked below the surface for the first time. "Oh!" she exclaimed.

The reef was beautiful beyond her imagining. There were corals of all different shapes, sizes and colors, chrome yellow, lavender, beige and gray. Sea fans of deep purple and yellow, pink twig-like weeds, sea-feathers in purples and lavenders, and weeds with little berries, which she had already seen thrown up on the shore. Among everything swam many different colorful fish, dark blue and yellow, red and pink, green and black, gray and silver, striped and mottled ... and everything was gently swaying in the swell of the aqua water. When at last she had seen enough, Greville sculled a short way beyond the reef. He secured the anchor rope to the bow and threw it in and let the boat drift back towards the reef. When he was satisfied with the position, he sat in the stern. He cut a piece of conch, speared it with a fishhook and handed the cotton fishing line to Kath.

"Cast over that way," he said, pointing. "You want to be close to the reef without being on top of it. You don't want your hook to snag and get lost in the coral."

"May I watch you do it first?"

"Of course. Nothing to it though," Greville said, taking the line from her and casting it in a wide arc towards the reef. The lead weight landed in the water with a small plop.

"Ah... the small fry are picking at it," he said after a moment. "They'll tell the bigger fish there's something good to eat. Sometimes they eat it all, though." He held the ball of

151

twine in his left hand, letting the line flow through his right hand and lie gently over his index finger. Suddenly he jerked his right hand into a fist.

"Got one!" he exclaimed, pulling the line in, hand over hand, the ball now secured in his pocket. Soon a foot-long silver fish with a bright yellow tail wriggled and flapped in the bottom of the boat.

"A nice yellow tail," he said, taking the fish from the hook and throwing it into a bucket of water. "Want to try now?"

Kath shook her head. "I'll wait awhile." She watched the fish swim round in the bucket as Greville baited the hook again. "I have a lot I want to tell you."

"Oh?" Greville glanced sharply at her, curiosity clouding his eyes.

"Yes. I feel I've not been fair to you, accepting your hospitality without telling you about myself."

Greville looked back at his hands, busy with the line. "There's no need to tell me anything you don't want to, Kath."

"You've been so good, never pressing or inquisitive about my past. But I want to tell you. It's the only way we can have an honest friendship."

"Tell me, then. Just know that I don't sit in judgment of you. I believe you've had enough of that already."

"What do you mean?"

"Well, when we found you on the beach, you told me you were on the *Lydia*, out of Cork, bound for Jamaica. The *Lydia* is a convict ship, so I assumed you were a prisoner on the way to indentured service in Jamaica."

"So you knew, straight away, that I was a convict!"

"Yes, I knew. Also, when I lifted you from the dinghy up to the *Swan*, I saw the red scars left by the leg irons, which confirmed my assumption."

Kath sat in stunned silence, looking over at Fortune Island but seeing nothing.

"And all the others knew, too?"

"Yes."

"Yet you gave me your cabin. Everyone treated me like

royalty. You brought me to your home and left your Gammie in my care. All this, without knowing what I was capable of, whether I was a thief, or a murderess or, or..."

"Come, Kath," Greville cut in. "If you had murdered someone, they would have hanged you. It doesn't take much for the English to hang people. Your crime had to be petty, or you wouldn't have survived the legal system. I've known people caught up for the smallest things, their lives and families destroyed, all for nothing. I've met several who swore they were innocent, and I had no reason not to believe them. I once knew a ten year old girl who was transported for taking a hair ribbon from her friend." Greville smiled at her, his eyes compassionate.

"And after all, what would you steal from my cabin? How would you hide it, what would you do with it on Fortune Island?" He threw his line overboard again. "What could you take from my sweet Little Mouse that she wouldn't readily give you herself? Anyway, you couldn't put a foot wrong with that old bird. She's as sharp as a sword." He twitched his fishing line with his finger.

"Besides, I told her what I knew of the *Lydia* before I left you there with her. She'd have said if she'd felt nervous, and I'd have taken you on to Nassau, or Charleston."

Greville paused as he hauled another fish into the boat. "Actually, she said she'd been expecting you. She had been praying for a companion, and the Lord had promised her He'd send someone who'd be the joy of her old age. After she saw you, you wouldn't have been able to leave her! You were *hers*, sent by the Lord!"

Kath frowned down at her hands. Miz Eva had never once let on she knew anything. She had left her to confess in her own time.

"How did you come to know about the *Lydia?*" she asked.

"We had the berth next to her at Port Royal, Jamaica last year. She flew the prison ship's pennant, and she stank to high heaven. We finished our business and left in a hurry that trip!

"Also, her Captain – Hilary, I believe his name was

– invited me to supper ashore one night, to apologize for the stench of his ship. He wasn't a bad sort, as the English go. He hated captaining a convict ship, but England was at peace, and the Royal Navy had let most of their seamen go. With a family of ten to support, the poor man had to take what he could get.

"I was hoping to find some trace of him, which is why we spent those days looking around the cays after we found you. It wasn't just for the 'wreck-goods', as we call them. I reported the *Lydia* lost to the Vice Admiralty Office in Charleston."

Kath was quiet for a while, then decided she would plow on with her confession. "You know that I am Irish, and that I am a Catholic?"

"Holy Mother, and what will you be telling me next, Kath?" Greville asked, mimicking her lilting brogue. "And ye're never Irish!"

"What are ye telling me, boy-o, ye're never Irish yerself?" she asked in reply, laying her accent on thick. "Well, I'm surprised at that an' all!"

They both laughed. "Oops!" Greville exclaimed, yanking his line. "Got another one – a big one this time..." A large, ugly grouper made Greville a proud and happy man.

After the excitement of landing the fish, Kath told her story. Greville concentrated on his fishing, saying nothing as she unfolded her previous life. She told him all about John, Duncan and Kevin. About Duncan's theft of the sheep, her own visit to Ballyvale House and her subsequent trial, about living conditions on the Lydia, and how she got out of the ship from the hold during the hurricane.

Kath talked of her feelings, how she thought God had abandoned her, until she had cried out to Him in the midst of the storm and He had saved her. Then, when Greville had rescued her and treated her so well, she knew that God had not forgotten her after all.

When Kath finished, they sat quietly for a time, enjoying the peace, the feel of the sun on their skin, the gentle rock of the boat. They watched as seagulls and terns began plunging into the sea further out in the bay, feeding on small fry pushed to the surface by a school of larger fish feeding on them from below. Greville had nine or ten fish in the boat by now.

"I'm amazed that you all treated me so kindly," Kath said, breaking the silence. "Especially now that I know you knew my situation right away. You even gave me your own Captain's cabin!" Kath said, her throat closing up.

Greville glanced sharply at her. "Stop up the fountain, wench," he said, a note of warning in his voice. "You're safe now, there's no call for tears."

"You hate them, don't you?"

"Never know what to do, when a female starts with the vapors."

Kath sniffed. "I'm alright. It's just that my life was so hard. Alone on that island I didn't know whether to pray for life or death. Then you came along in the *Swan*, and everything changed like the sun coming out after the rain. I'll forever be grateful for you, Captain Greville Knowles. I shall never say another prayer without asking God's blessing on you and yours."

"Stop it, wench! If you get me blubbering like a babe, I'll never speak to you again!"

He wound up his fishing line. "Let's head back in. I have all these fish to clean and the sun's getting hot. I remember what it does to your pale skin."

Greville put his lines and tools back in the bucket. He hauled up the anchor and stowed it in the bow, then sat and let the boat drift on the tide back towards the settlement.

"You asked me why I gave you my cabin after we found you," he said. "You're right, it was an unusual thing for a Captain to do. But you see, I had an idea how you must have suffered in prison and on the *Lydia*. Then you'd survived a hurricane, and days of being naked, hungry and afraid on that barren shore, waiting for death to claim you. What kind of monster would I be, not to offer comfort to a fellow creature who had gone through such trials?

"I am a Christian, Kath. I try to live by the Book. We're told to welcome strangers, since we never know when they might be angels. As it turned out, the Lord had sent you in answer to Gammie's prayer. Besides, when I saw your poor burnt face buried in the sand, with your hair streaming out like seaweed, my heart went out to you. Being a Good Samaritan was easy."

"You knew straight away that I was Irish, too, didn't you?"

"Yes."

"And that I was most likely a Catholic?"

"Yes."

"And yet you were so kind! Protestants and Catholics hate each other!"

"It didn't matter! That's *religion* you're talking about, Kath, not true Christianity. Do you think the Lord Jesus was a Catholic? Was He a Protestant? Do you think He cares whether we're one or the other? Neither religion existed when He walked the earth. But in His day there were the Pharisees and the Sadducees, or the Jews and the Samaritans, or the Romans. There are always religions, and people to hate.

"What He did tell us was to love one another, and that we must follow His commandment. That's what I try to do." His eyes crinkled into a smile. "It's what my Gammie taught me."

Greville stood up, making the boat rock. He grasped Kath's shoulder to steady himself and a thrill ran through her. Her heart thumped a few rapid beats, but for the first time she felt no anxiety. As Greville took up his oar and began to scull them back to shore, she felt truly at peace for the first time since her whole miserable adventure had begun. Greville did not hate her. He did not despise her for her religion or her past, or who she was.

And by the God he worshiped, he was bound to love her.

22

It was about noon by the time Greville and Kath finished cleaning the fish and arrived back up on the hill. Miz Eva had already showed Kath how to season fish in the Bahamian way; how they cut diagonal slashes in the sides of each fish, then rubbed in a little fresh hot pepper mashed into sea salt, squeezed lime juice liberally over them, and left them to sit for a while before cooking.

"We have enough fish to invite Jonah and Shirley to supper if you'd like," Greville suggested. "I'll cook. We can have fried fish with peas and grits." He nodded and winked. "Good eating, wench!"

Kath's cheeks pinked at his mention of Jonah. She'd completely forgotten about him, and the answer she must give the following morning. Right after they had eaten some bread and cheese, Kath excused herself. "I'll go find Jonah and Shirley, to see if they'll come to supper," she said, though really she wanted some time to herself. So much had happened over the past two days, she hardly knew how she felt anymore. Kath headed down the path towards the beach. She liked to sit in a small grove of coconut trees and look out to sea. It was one of her places to think and dream.

She knew that she didn't love Jonah, although she found him attractive and good company. On occasion there had also been some sexual tension between them, especially at first. With Shirley's constant presence, however, the sexual attraction had dissipated and Jonah was now simply a friend of the opposite sex. While she felt friendship was good grounds for marriage, she wanted much more at this time of her life. She remembered the intimacy and lovemaking she and John had enjoyed. Her heart yearned to know that again; the deep devotion, the unity and satisfaction of two people who had become one.

Of course that might come in time, with Jonah, but Kath felt sure that such union would be possible with Greville. Now he had swept away her fears of his rejection of her, she had a surge of hope in that direction. There was no feeling of social superiority, either, which she'd feared before. Greville had never shown any condescension because he was a Captain and she was his servant, and a convict, at that. Both he and Miz Eva had treated her as an equal, like their own family.

However Greville felt about religion, though, she was still a Catholic, an adherent of the One True Church. Could she bring herself to marry a Protestant, someone who was a heretic, excommunicated by the Pope and damned to eternal Hell if he did not convert? The Church would not sanction her marriage to a Protestant and would consider she was living in sin, especially as there was no Catholic priest to perform the ceremony – even if a Catholic priest *would*.

It was the same with Jonah, too. Maybe she could influence the men to convert, if only for her sake. But how would she go about doing that? She didn't know enough about her own faith – or theirs – to know how they were different. She could remember most of the catechism, and she could teach them that, how to say the rosary. But there would be no priest available to confirm them, to give Holy Communion, nor did she know if there was a Catholic priest living anywhere within reasonable sailing distance. If one lived in Jamaica, for instance, was she willing to sail to Jamaica and risk imprisonment or indentured servitude? Kath's lips turned down and she shook her head.

She definitely wanted to marry again. She hadn't in Ireland, but that was because there was no man who struck her fancy. Also, she had her two boys and both her family and John's around her for support, though she never saw her brothers, year in, year out.

She had not needed a man then. Not like she needed one now. Now she needed someone to love, to wake up for, to share things with. She wanted protection, her own home and children again. And time was going by. She'd be thirty-three in March, she couldn't wait forever.

Holy Mother of God, with no priest, she could never marry, could never have children – at least in an acceptable way – could never again confess her sins, take Holy Communion, or worship God. She would die in sin, without extreme unction. Never mind these heretic Protestants going to Hell. *She herself was doomed too.* She dropped her head into her hands and stared at the sand. She was in a pagan land, beyond the reach of God, among heretics.

Gradually her eyes focused on the sand. She absently watched a column of black ants scurry back and forth, carrying white egg sacks to a hole in the roots of a coconut tree. Two small gray lizards lurked nearby, darting in to feed on ants and eggs. Suddenly a text from one of Miz Eva's chapters came to mind. "Whither shall I go from thy Spirit? Or whither shall I flee from thy presence?"

What was she thinking? God was never beyond reach. Wherever she was, she was still in His world. He was everywhere – even His ants seemed to be everywhere. God had saved her from the hurricane and He was definitely here. What's more, from what Greville had told her this morning, God had sent her here in answer to Miz Eva's prayers. If that was true, then God had sent her here for a reason. God wouldn't send her somewhere, save her from jail and servitude, a hurricane, shipwreck, and yellow fever, and then damn her to Hell, would He?

Kath rubbed her temples with her fingertips. If God had sent her to be with Miz Eva, then she had no right to marry Jonah. She was not free to leave Miz Eva. Anyway, she didn't want to become a geriatric nurse, the willing slave of old Mr. Cartwright while Jonah was off working. How often would she see Jonah? The *Stella Maris* had no reason to visit Fortune

Island as the *Swan* did. The *Stella Maris* had dropped Jonah off, taken on water, and left again within hours. Was that to be her future with Jonah? How would she conceive children like that? Even if she did manage to conceive, she'd be on her own, to raise children by herself again. Besides, it wasn't just the conception she wanted. It was the process, too! Her answer to Jonah must be a definite no. Her heart lightened instantly.

Kath looked out to sea again. Now, to think about Greville.

Greville gave her lingering, enigmatic looks sometimes which she didn't understand. Like when she was aware of his eyes following her around the room, and how his face lit up with a smile when she came into sight. Once or twice she'd noticed a sadness about his gaze, a vulnerability, a longing.

She loved the way he'd started calling her *wench*. "That's my wench," he'd said in the boat. "Good eating, wench," he'd said about his fried fish. There was a familiarity and affection in the way he said it that made her feel warm and very special. She'd never heard him use the word otherwise, in any general way. No, it was definitely an endearment, the same as when he called Gammie "Little Mouse". And when her Granda had called her "Kathy". Still, Greville had given no indication of deeper interest in her. He was always polite and kind, but he treated everyone that way.

No. *She* lusted after *him*, not the other way around. Kath breathed a heavy sigh. Then there was also Miss Nancy Lou Lilly down in Nassau to consider. Obie had said he was always faithful to her, always stayed with her in Nassau. Even if Greville accepted the One True Church, even if a Catholic priest stood ready to marry them, she still had no realistic hope of a wedding with Greville. He was already taken.

A bleak pall fell over Kath at this somber thought. As she was giving up Jonah, it would have been a comfort to look towards another man. With a sharp pang, she understood Shirley's rabid pursuit of Jonah all too well. Who else was there to come courting on Fortune Island? Only God knew the future, but she would give a lot right now to have a peek.

Kath stood and shook out her long skirt. Her calf cramped. She'd had no exercise for several days and she decided to take the long way home. As soon as the pain subsided, she set off along the beach. She'd return by way of the settlement and ask Jonah and Shirley to supper.

There was an outcropping of rock on the beach and the tide was high, so she cut across the rocks through the bushes to avoid getting wet. Sounds of conversation reached her on the still air, amplified by the water. That was Shirley's giggle, she was sure, with Jonah's voice answering. Kath smiled as she thought how she'd surprise them when she came out from the bushes.

*

"Don't you go flouncing off this morning, girl," Miz Louise warned Shirley right after breakfast. "Your Poppa's brought home a sack of dirty clothes and I've got all the Christmas baking still to do. Don't you run out on me!"

Shirley's heart sank as she took the laundry out to the washtub behind the house. It would keep her busy all morning. Then there'd be the dinner to get. She wouldn't be able to get away until early afternoon, if then.

Right after the dinner dishes Shirley saw her chance and took it. She made a beeline to the Cartwright hut.

"Afternoon, Jonah," she said, looking in at the door. "I came to see how your Pa's feeling today. Is he any better?"

"Yes, thank the Lord, he seems a little brighter," Jonah said, looking a little brighter himself at seeing some company at his door. "He ate a good dinner. Long as he eats, he'll keep his strength up."

"You been in all day?"

"Yes. Miz Lizzy brought us some fresh bread and sat awhile yesterday. Other than that, I been cooped up alone here with Pa since yesterday afternoon. Not a soul to talk to."

"I been helping Momma with the chores. But it's too nice to stay in. Can you come for a walk?"

"Yes, I could do with a stretch. I'm not used to being

indoors like this. Pa's sleeping now, anyway." Jonah grabbed his battered straw hat and closed the door behind him. "Sure has been nice, staying ashore this li'l spell with Pa, but I can hardly wait for the *Stella Maris* to come get me. I'm used to more action, more company like, not to sitting around in a lonely place like this. Time's soon up now, though. The *Stella Maris* should be here any day."

Shirley and Jonah headed down the path along the shore. "Do you have to go back to sea?" she asked.

"How else am I going to make a living? A man can't be idle if he ain't rich. Besides, I'm a sailor. I *like* going to sea."

"Couldn't you settle ashore, say in Nassau, or in Charleston, maybe, and do some other kind of work?"

"Like what? There's only farming and keeping creatures, or ship building maybe. Hardwood cutting and salt raking gives pretty lean pickings, especially since the war is over. No, it's the sea for me."

"Don't you want a home of your own, a wife and children?"

"Yes, I sure do! And I'm fixing to get that real soon."

"I could give you all that, Jonah..."

"*You?*" Jonah laughed. "Shirley, you're just a child to me."

"I am not a child, Jonah Cartwright!" Shirley turned to face him. "*Look at me!* You can't see me for looking at that old woman. Kath will soon be all dried up and finished." Shirley started tugging at the strings lacing her bodice.

"Look at me, Jonah! I'm a woman, with a woman's body, a woman's heart, and a woman's needs. And I love you!" Shirley seized his hand, kissed it fervently and held it to her breast.

Jonah stared at Shirley in dismay. Then, with a groan he clutched her to him, burying his face in her neck. They staggered a few steps, to lean against the trunk of a coconut palm.

"You been plaguing me since I set foot on this island," Jonah growled into her ear. "Like a she-cat on heat! If you're such a woman, I'm going to give you what you want!"

Passion surged in Shirley, a hot, sweet abandon she'd never felt before. She held Jonah to her with a cry of joyful elation as he kissed her face, her neck, and her shoulders.

Kath emerged from the bush at this very moment.

"Stop it, Jonah!" Kath shouted. "What are you doing?"

Jonah looked up wildly, his face flushed with desire. "Kath!"

Shirley groped at her bodice, her eyes stinging with angry tears, her heart pounding. She turned into the trunk of the coconut tree, feeling the scratch of its bark against her face. She felt sick at her stomach.

"Would you ruin her, Jonah?" Kath demanded. "She's hardly more than a child!"

"That's not what *she* thinks," Jonah mumbled, raking his fingers through his hair. "She thinks she's quite a woman." He looked defiantly at Kath, then dropped his gaze.

"That may be, but you're twice her age. 'Tis *you* must control yourself!"

Shirley wheeled around. "What business is it of yours?" she hissed. "What are you doing here, following us?"

Kath smiled. "Humph! Not following you. But looking for you, anyway." She sighed. "I was coming to present Captain Knowles's compliments and to invite you both for supper tonight."

"I want none of your suppers!" Shirley spat out, her arms akimbo. "I want to be left alone. Why must you come here and ruin everything?" Her lower lip trembled and her eyes dissolved in tears. "Nothing's gone right since you put your foot on this island!" she wailed, covering her face with her arm.

Kath put her arms around Shirley, who struggled to push her away at first, then collapsed sobbing against her. Kath rocked her, stroking her back.

"I know, Shirley," Kath said softly. "I know. It hurts something awful."

"Nobody loves m-me," Shirley hiccuped. "There's nobody for me! I'll die an old maid on this wretched island!"

"Shush, Shirley. It's not that bad. There'll be someone for you, you'll see."

Jonah sat on a log that had drifted in after the hurricane, his head in his hands. He was deeply ashamed. He felt ruined, devastated – and mortified. Kath was lost to him forever. She would never have him now. Still his mind raced for an excuse, some explanation that would remedy his situation.

"She tormented me day and night," Jonah said through his fingers. "Until I couldn't bear it no more! She was like the devil, never leaving me alone." He looked up, his eyes full of misery. "A man can take just so much before he boils over."

"I think the least said the better," Kath replied.

"I'm really sorry," he said, shaking his head. "I don't know what came over me. I promise it'll never happen again."

"Come, Shirley." Kath gently loosened the sobbing girl's arms. "Let's walk back together.

"Will we see you for supper tonight, Jonah?" Kath asked, looking back.

"No, I'll have to stay with Pa. But don't forget we have an appointment tomorrow morning."

"There's no need to keep that Jonah," Kath said, her eyes troubled. "I can answer you now."

"No, Kath!" Jonah pleaded. "Don't decide now. Sleep on it and tell me in the morning, as we agreed. We can talk more then."

"I see no point in waiting, Jonah."

"You promised, Christmas Eve, mid-morning. I'm holding you to it!"

"Jonah, I've made my decision and it has nothing to do with this," Kath said firmly. "I will not marry you for my own reasons, and there's an end to it."

Jonah's mouth set in a harsh line across his face. His chin puckered and he looked away, his chest heaving.

Shirley sniffed. A hopeful look flitted across her face. Kath noticed and gave her a conspiratorial smile.

"Come walk back with me Shirley, and I will tell you why *not*."

23

Christmas Day was sunny and warm. Greville was up first and slipped quietly out to the kitchen to make his special Jamaican coffee.

"Merry Christmas!" he shouted, waking the women on his return, bearing mugs full of the fragrant brew. Muffled Merry Christmases echoed in reply.

"Grev! You Devil," Miz Eva exclaimed after her first sip. "You've put a splash of sherry in it!"

"Yes, Little Mouse – and I've a deal more sherry to be drunk on its own later today. I bought a few bottles in Nassau for your Christmas treat."

"Kath and I have a few treats planned for you, too, son." Miz Eva swung her legs over the side of the bed and coiled her hair into a topknot. She bent over and pulled out a large kadeque, the large straw basket traditionally used in the islands for taking things in and out of the fields. "I had Lizzy make this for your Christmas present," she said, handing Greville the handsome basket, designed with rope handles for slinging over his shoulder. "I noticed the last time you came home that yours was looking raggedy."

"Thank you, Gammie!" Greville swept her up into his arms and gave her a resounding kiss on the cheek. "It's just the thing I needed most! Mine was blown overboard last month." He stopped to examine the basket. "It's beautiful, Gammie. Miz Lizzie is the best basket maker on the island, I bet."

"Yes, she's pretty good," Miz Eva answered. "And here's one for you too, chile," she said, holding a much smaller one out to Kath. It was plaited out of silver top and coconut frond, making a pattern of beige and dark brown, and clearly created for a woman to carry her personal things rather than to bring vegetables back from the field.

"Thank you, Miz Eva," Kath said, giving her a hug and kiss.

"Greville and I have a gift for you, too," Kath said, giving her a mysterious smile. She went to one of the sea chests against the wall, pulled out a rustling skirt in deep garnet over a gray petticoat and shook it vigorously. She held it out to Miz Eva, whose eyes grew as round as her open mouth. There was a black bodice and pearl gray embroidered stomacher, with a gray neckerchief embroidered to match.

"That's never for me," Miz Eva said quietly.

"It is indeed, my lady."

Miz Eva had watched Kath making the ensemble, noting its progress with interest, stroking the fabrics as Kath worked. But she had always thought the gown would be sent with Greville for sale – and for good money, too.

"Oh Kath, sweeting," Miz Eva's eyes were misty. "'Tis the most beautiful thing I've ever owned in all my seventy years. It's too fine for me!"

"Nonsense, Little Mouse," Greville said, his eyes shining with pleasure. "Put it on! I chose the material especially for you. Kath and I planned this since last September. Let's see you in it!"

Kath draped the outfit over Miz Eva's arm and she shuffled off to the screen in the corner of the room. She soon reappeared, smiling shyly, her head bent slightly to one side. She rubbed the muslin of the skirt between her fingers. The gown fit her perfectly.

"Your Majesty!" Greville said, bowing deeply and kissing her hand, while Kath held her nightdress out and curtsied low. "You're beautiful, Gammie. The other women will have no chance at all with the fellows when you're wearing that gown!"

The loving look Miz Eva gave them was priceless. Kath wondered who was happiest with the dress – Miz Eva, because she owned it, and had admired it so much during its sewing; Greville, because he'd made it possible; or she herself, because the other two were so impressed and delighted by her handiwork.

"I've made something for you, too, Greville," Kath said, handing him a folded white shirt. Greville held it up to look. It was made of white handkerchief linen with small tucks down the front. Its sleeves were flowing, gathered into cuffs with a short frill at the wrists, edged with tatting. Small seashell buttons marched down the front. Greville's mouth opened as he examined it.

"Kath! Thank you, my wench," he managed to say when he'd caught himself. He held the shirt up to his chest. "I've never owned such a wonderful garment. Are you certain you would not prefer that I sell this in Charleston? It would bring an excellent price from some shopkeeper there."

"I'm glad you like it," Kath replied. "Please try it on. I really meant it for you, though you may sell it in Charleston if you choose. I know that I owe you money, and the things I have for sale might not make up the amount. But I wish you would keep it for yourself."

"Of course I'll keep it! I wouldn't part with it for the world! It's just so – so fine!" Greville reached for Kath and hugged her. She turned scarlet, and Greville let her go as though she had scalded him.

"I – I've made myself a new gown, too," Kath stammered. "We can all wear our new clothes this Christmas. I'll just go and put mine on, shall I?" Kath buried her face in the sea chest and took out another dress, then disappeared behind the screen. She came out in a gown of salmon pink over a cream petticoat, with a brown and cream striped bustier and stomacher. A sheer muslin neckerchief draped her shoulders, and she wore a matching white muslin cap.

"Oh Kath, sweeting, how beautiful you look!" Miz Eva exclaimed, while Greville simply stared. "How you've managed to do all this sewing in two months, I'll never know."

"One thing's sure," Greville said, looking grave. "Your

talent is wasted here in this island. I think you must consider going to live in Charleston, where you can dress elegant people. They would pay a lot for your services."

"And leave Miz Eva and you, and Fortune Island, and all the people I know and love, and who have taken me into their hearts? No thank you! Those 'elegant people' bespeak work, then treat you like dirt when you ask them to pay their bills. I'll stay here, if you please."

While Kath had been changing into her new dress, Greville had gone out to the kitchen and returned with a lovely little spinning wheel. "This is your Christmas present from Gammie and me," he said, pulling it out from under the table. "I thought you might like to spin some of the cotton that grows wild here. I believe long staple Sea Island cotton is supposed to be quite good quality."

Kath clasped her hands when she saw the spinning wheel. "Oh, thank you Greville! It's perfect!" She stroked the smooth cherry wood of the wheel. "I've been longing to spin some of that cotton. In fact I picked a basket full of it only last week! Thank you, *thank you!*" Kath was almost dancing in excitement. She wanted to fling her arms around him and kiss him, but couldn't find the courage.

A timely visit saved her from her dilemma. "Merry Christmas!" Shirley's voice sang out from the door. She came in with a basket of goodies from her grandma Reena for Miz Eva, and a snappy straw hat, which she had made for Kath. Shirley had put a string of golden shells around the crown for a hatband. Kath gave Shirley an exquisite embroidered muslin cap in exchange. Shirley was thrilled, and tried it on at once, turning her head this way and that to get their reactions.

"Why don't you let me teach you how to sew after Christmas?" Kath asked her. "It's a good thing for a woman to be proficient at, Shirley. You never know when it will be useful in life."

"Even after you saw the mess I made with my petticoat, Miz Kath?" Shirley asked, laughing. "You have a strong heart."

Kath was glad to see Shirley in good spirits again. After

Kath had explained to her the disadvantages of marrying Jonah, Shirley had grudgingly agreed. She had been somewhat strained at Captain Knowles's fried fish dinner later that evening and had not come up the hill since. *Licking her wounds*, Kath thought. Now things seemed to be back to normal.

"Captain Knowles was just saying that a good seamstress can go anywhere to work, Shirley – even Charleston. It's something you should think about perhaps."

Shirley's face brightened. "Do you really think I could learn to sew well enough to move away from here?"

"I don't see why not! Let's start you tomorrow. You can help me later, when you have some experience. Then we can both make money by sending things with Captain Knowles for sale.

"Well, I must take off my finery now and begin Christmas dinner," Kath said with a sigh, heading once more for the screen in the corner.

"And I must go and help Momma," Shirley replied. "We have a lot to do too."

"Come up again Shirley," Greville said, "after dinner, mid-afternoon. Jonah will be having dinner with us and no doubt we'll find something to amuse ourselves with later."

"Thank you kindly, Cap'n Grev," Shirley called as she disappeared down the hill. Kath smiled to herself as she headed for the kitchen. Everything was turning out just fine.

She had felt sure that Jonah's pride was hurt far more than his heart, so the day before she had taken him a sweet potato pudding and an invitation for Christmas dinner. She had found him abject and miserable, unable to meet her eyes. He had spent the whole of the previous night tossing and turning, eating the bitter, cold leftovers of regret. He could never be easy in her presence again he had told her. He was full of shame and self-recrimination.

Kath had sat and listened for a while, then put a gentle hand on his knee. "And is it *your* fault that God made you such a beautiful man that young women lose their senses around you?" she teased. "I'll bet yesterday was not the first time you've been ambushed in the wilderness by a passionate female! It's not hard to see why the fair sex find you irresistible, Jonah. You're only lucky I did not set upon you as well!"

Jonah managed a crooked smile at the thought. " 'Twould not have been two of you for long!"

"Och, man, these things happen in life. You've naught to worry about. Come to Christmas dinner with us," she coaxed. "We're to have roast chicken and a leg of lamb, with peas and rice and sweet potato bread. And we've got some good Jamaican coffee, and even a drop of sherry!"

Jonah sat shaking his head, looking down at his hands and waggling his knees. "Will you never come to see us again, Jonah?" Kath asked. "Is that to be the way of it? Och, man, you're not an eedjit. How can you pass up a feast like our good Christmas dinner? And what will you do for Christmas, stay indoors with your poor old father the whole day? He sleeps much of the time now, doesn't he?" Eventually she had succeeded in cajoling Jonah, who had promised to come.

Jonah appeared around noon Christmas day, bearing a lovely little scrimshaw box for Kath and some bone hairpins for Miz Eva. He was delighted with his new cambric shirt.

Thus Christmas came and went on Fortune Island, leaving everyone as pleased as it was possible to be in the circumstances.

*

On New Year's Eve afternoon Greville spotted the sails of the *Stella Maris* in the distance and went to give Jonah the news.

"What will you do about your father, Jonah?" he asked.

"Well, I've asked Miz Reena and Miz Lizzy if they can look in on him for me," he replied. "I can't bear to be kicking around here any longer, doing nothing much. I need to be earning some brass again. Besides, I'm not a nurse. I'll gladly hand over my pay to the women if they'll care for my Pa. I was hoping to take care of the situation in another way, but that was not to be..." Jonah trailed off, leaving Greville to deduce what he liked. Greville struggled to hide his smile.

"Well, you'll be leaving in the morning, no doubt," Greville said, "and the *Swan* will be following hard on your heels the day after. We're heading down to Jamaica."

Jonah breathed a sigh. "So it goes! It doesn't seem so long since you were arriving and we were all so merry." Jonah looked away at the horizon, his eyes filling as he remembered his afternoon sail with Kath.

Greville clapped him on the shoulder. "Take heart, old son. All of us who go to sea have this hardship. Every time we go, we leave our loved-ones on the shore, wondering if God will grant our safe return – and if He will keep them safe in the meantime. It's the hardest part of a sailor's life."

"Yes – and in some ways, the best," Jonah said reflectively. "Our shore times become especially precious because they're never for long. But you know, Cap'n Grev, I love the sea. There's no other life for me."

"I understand that. For myself, though, I would come ashore if there were a reason – and if there were anything else for a man to do.

"Well, I'll let you get on with your preparations," Greville said, extending his hand. "I'll just say goodbye to your Pa, then leave you to it. We'll cross paths again somewhere, no doubt."

*

Miz Eva had watched the lingering looks between Kath and Greville, but she had decided to keep her tongue behind her teeth. After all, things were bound to work out to her satisfaction eventually. She had managed to say nothing all through the holidays. Now Greville was about to leave without things coming to a head, as far as she could see, and she was positively bursting to find out exactly how the cat jumped. Kath was out in the field picking vegetables when Greville returned from his visit to the Cartwrights, and the old lady couldn't resist such a heaven-sent opportunity. She took the plunge.

"You'll be leaving in a day or so, I guess."

"Yes, Gammie. On January second, 1717, bright and early

if the weather's fair."

"Have you spoken to Kath?"

"What do you mean, 'have I spoken to Kath'? Is that any business of yours, Little Miz Nosy Mouse?"

"Well, it is and it isn't," she said tartly. " 'Tis I must watch your mooning cow-looks. How you both look at one another! I wonder your eyes don't ache in your heads at night, flicking back and forth all day. You're both so careful not to let each other catch you staring. But I can see you."

Greville gave her a sheepish grin and walked over to lean on the doorpost, looking out to sea.

"You had a lucky escape with Jonah Cartwright, if you ask me," Miz Eva continued relentlessly. "Suppose she'd agreed to have him?"

"You mean he actually asked her?" Greville looked back into the room.

"She hasn't said, but something was up that afternoon you arrived. Jonah was so desperate, with his hair all smarmed down, and Kath so cool. Any fool could see the way it stood."

"Jonah would never do for Kath, Gammie."

"Why not? He's as fine a man as these islands generally have to offer. Hard working, decent, affectionate..."

"Spare me the song of praise, Gammie," Greville said, lifting his hands palms out. "He's admirable as men go, I grant you. But still – I say Kath is too fine for the likes of him."

"She's still a young woman, Greville. If not Jonah, who is she to have then? *You?*"

"I wish it could be so. You know how fond I am of the wench." Greville looked wistful, then grinned. "And it would secure a life-long companion for you too, Little Mouse. I think that was one of Jonah's aims, all right."

"You mean to mind his Pa?"

"Yes."

"But not the only aim, Grev. Kath's a good woman – sensible, funny, pretty and hard working. It's a rare combination, especially in this benighted place. Old King Solomon knew her value. 'Who can find a virtuous woman? For her price is

172

far above rubies,' he said in the Proverbs. Kath fits that to the letter, if you ask me," Miz Eva said.

"Well, nobody's asking you," Greville answered, smiling down at her. "I agree, she's a rare woman. But I worry about a couple of things, Gammie.

"First she's devoted to her own religion and probably won't marry anyone who isn't Catholic. I don't want a household at odds every time the Europeans start their 'Protestants against the Catholics' wars.

"Second, I'm anxious about color. I know that now it means nothing to her that I'm a colored man. Now she sees herself as a despised Irish Catholic convict. But in other places – if we lived in Bermuda, or Charleston, or Jamaica – she might come to feel it keenly. I don't want a wife who's looked down on because she married me, and I don't want any wife of mine to think she's better than I am because she's white."

"I know, son," Miz Eva said with a sigh. "Can't you just decide to live here on Fortune Island? It doesn't matter here."

"There's nothing to do here. I would come home from the sea if I married. That means I need an occupation, like a plantation, or running a plantation for someone else. That means going outside."

"I know." Miz Eva sighed. "Well, son, you have your own life to live. Mine is nearly over. You do love her, don't you?"

"Yes, I do love her, Gammie," Greville admitted, nodding his head. "I've loved her from the first moment I saw her, lying in the sand. This past holiday has made me care even more deeply." Greville turned tormented eyes to Miz Eva. "I've waited so long, been so patient. I've been so lonely, all these years. It seems God doesn't hear my prayers, and that he doesn't care that I'm alone. But I cannot, I *will* not ask a woman to marry me until I'm sure she loves me, and doesn't care about anything else. Life is hard enough even when two people agree on everything."

"I do understand, Grev," Miz Eva said softly. "I'll let the matter rest with you. What should I tell her if she asks me why you haven't spoken to her? She isn't stupid. She must have an inkling of your feelings."

"I doubt she'll ask, but you can be straight with her. She doesn't want to marry anyone who's not a Catholic and she'll understand my not wanting to marry anyone who doesn't believe as we do. As for the color problem..." he shrugged. "There's nothing I can do about that. Maybe my biggest problem is that I've been looking everywhere for a woman just like you, my own Little Mouse," he said smiling at her, and reaching down for a hug.

"You rascal!" she said, moving into his arms.

Greville canted his head to listen. Light footsteps were pattering towards the door, accompanied by an Irish ballad sung in a lilting soprano. For all his determination not to make a fool of himself over a woman, his heart beat faster with the knowledge that it was already too late.

24

Life on Fortune Island continued in its usual peaceful way. The day after the *Swan* left, the children straggled up the hill to their lessons once more. Shirley joined them, sitting under the fig tree working her sampler. Soon she decided she wanted to learn how to read and write, too, and began doing the exercises the younger children did. Shirley was a quick study and soon became a sort of monitor, helping Kath with the children, and working on her sewing during Miz Eva's story time and in the afternoons along with Kath.

Everyone looked forward to Miz Eva's story time. Her stories were not always from the Bible – sometimes she told them about Brer Bookie and Brer Rabbie, two characters who got up to all sorts of mischief, or other fables which she had learnt from her African mother.

Kath started spinning the local cotton during story time, with excellent results. It was tricky at first, as the cotton had finer, shorter fibers than the flax and wool she was used to spinning, but she soon got the knack of it. She decided to ask Greville to take her yarn to a weaver in Charleston. In the meantime, she spun all the cotton she could find and cleared additional bush to plant her own cotton field with the seeds she gleaned from the bolls.

Now that Shirley saw sewing as a means of escape from Fortune Island, she applied herself with a will. Her stitches were neat, her fingers nimble, and she was soon able to help Kath with the basics. Kath was delighted to find that Shirley had a natural flair for design. In a few months Shirley was able to modify cloth patterns for size and unusual cut, and she created artistic embroidery patterns in unusual color combinations that were very striking.

Shirley blossomed under Kath's attention. Excited by the discovery of her own creative ability, she threw herself into her new endeavor with focused energy. Sewing gave her self-respect and she was pleasantly surprised when others showed respect for her abilities. She did the household sewing now, while her two younger brothers did the dishes and the hated, laborious laundry. Her mother no longer nagged her, and was proud when the neighbors began bringing her work. The funny thing was that she still mooned and daydreamed, only she sewed the while.

One day when her father, Horace, was home from sea, Shirley was gratified to hear her mother bragging to him about her new skills. He called her to him and asked to see the piece of embroidery she was working. He looked at her with shining eyes, his face full of admiration. "That's beautiful, Shirley," Horace said, stroking the silk plumage of a bright bird with his callused index finger. "I've never seen anything so lovely! To think that my own little Shirley can do something like this!"

His praise meant more than anything to Shirley. At last she counted for something with her own people. She had a future, was finally being accepted as an adult – and she was no longer bored.

*

Now it became Kath's turn to feel restless and lonely. Miz Eva and Shirley were good companions, as far as they went, but Kath longed for a man, and her own fulfilled life as a woman. Often she would dream of Greville, and she would wake in a sweat, filled with desire.

As for Greville, he continued his usual sailing route with the *Swan*, arriving back from Jamaica in February, then heading out again to Nassau and Charleston, arriving back at Fortune Island early in May, thence to Jamaica again. Kath would build up her hopes between his visits. When the *Swan's* sails came in sight, her stomach would knot and her heart beat faster, and she was filled with expectation almost to the point of anguish.

Greville's eyes would search hungrily for her as he neared the shore and he would make a beeline for her the moment his feet touched the sand. Kath knew now that it was for her his eyes searched, not Miz Eva. When he returned from Jamaica in February, she had contrived to be talking in a group of people, away from Miz Eva but facing the water. He rushed over to her, not to his grandmother. Her heart pounded in jubilation as he made his courtly bow before her and kissed her hand.

She took his arm and they walked together over to Miz Eva. Walked? Kath had floated!

It was all for nothing. Although Greville's eyes spoke volumes every time he came, his lips never did. He was unfailingly kind. He brought her thoughtful presents and beautiful materials to work. He praised her handiwork and proudly repeated all the compliments it brought from the shopkeepers in Jamaica and Charleston. He called her "my wench" and "wench" as affectionately as ever. However, never once did Greville speak of his feelings for her, or allude to the possibility of a future together.

He always invited her to go fishing, and she always accepted with high hopes, working herself into a lather the night before these trips, hardly sleeping. The nights after the trips were agonizing, too, as her feverish mind relived the trip over and again, treasuring every touch, every glance, every word spoken, and searching for hidden nuances. The memory of his glorious bronzed body, wet and straining with effort as he dove, hauled himself back into the boat, or sculled, tormented her. It was as well that Greville had taken to sleeping aboard the *Swan* during these visits to Fortune Island, or she thought she might lose all responsibility for her conduct.

Kath could only think that Greville was not free to speak to her, that he was already committed to this Nancy Lou Lilly in Nassau. Kath knew that his integrity, his deep sense of personal honor, would never allow him to betray anyone. Although she thought he was in love with her, he was obligated in some way to another, and unless he could be released from his obligation, he would not speak. If this were so, then why didn't he tell her? If she knew the truth of the situation, she would be better equipped to deal with her own feelings. Oh, it was cruel!

Then her mind ran to the contrary. He *wasn't* obligated to anyone else, but he couldn't make up his mind to leave the sea. He'd taken a solemn vow never to marry whilst a sailor. He must be certain before he took such a step as giving up his captaincy of the *Swan*. When he was sure of her, and of what he could do ashore to make a living, he'd speak.

If only he'd speak, say *something*. She could reassure him, say that she could live with his remaining a tar, if he would but love only her. He could come ashore later, when times were better and there was something else for him to do. She wanted him beside her every day and every night, not only when his ship came into port. She would say nothing to discourage his giving up the sea, but she would take him just as he was.

Kath prayed every day for Greville's safety. She suffered whenever there were thunderstorms or rough seas, remembering the hurricane of the year before, thinking that Greville was at risk once more. She prayed for herself, for Kevin, wherever he was.

She prayed for her friends and relations in Ireland, but Ireland was receding into the past like a dream imperfectly remembered. It was no longer entirely real to her. She couldn't remember John's face, or recall his smile, or the sound of his voice any more. The sharp pain that lanced her whenever she remembered Duncan began to wane to a dull ache. He was a part of her that was gone. It was simply a fact, she had borne a son named Duncan, long ago and far away, and he was now dead. It was no longer an immediate, all-consuming sorrow. She asked God's forgiveness, that she should love a man more than she loved her own children, her own people and country,

even more than the Catholic Church. She was horrified to realize one day that she only had a dim recollection of Duncan
and Kevin's faces. Greville's face, smiling down at her, looking
grave, mischievous, teasing Miz Eva, seemed always to slide
into her mind's eye.

She was no less horrified to realize, too, that she no longer
prayed with her pea rosary. She wasn't even quite sure where
she had left it. She prayed directly to Heavenly Father now,
like Miz Eva did every night, and not to the Blessed Mother.
She was losing her religion, and she would be damned to hell.

*

On his side, Greville suffered much as Kath did. He longed
to return to Fortune Island while away, longed with all his
soul to see Kath's dear face again. His arms ached to hold her.
His dreams, too, contained countless sunlit visions of Kath,
the smell of her, the imagined taste of her kisses. He heard
her voice in the whisper of spray from the bow, her song in
the wind, her laughter in the chatter of the lines against the
mast. He found himself willing his ship to sail faster, to fly, if
it could, so he could be with his wench again.

One trip to Charleston he was sauntering along the main
street when a ring in a jeweler's window caught his eye. It was
a half hoop of pigeon's blood rubies and diamonds, sitting in
a shaft of sunlight breaking through the thick glass window-
pane. He walked into the shop before thinking. The jeweler
placed the ring in the palm of his right hand. It was elegant,
and exquisite; the band was of yellow gold, and he thought
it would fit a small hand he knew. Greville held it up, and the
sunlight splintered into myriad rainbow lights reflected from
the diamonds. He had to have it for Kath.

It had cost him nearly four months' pay.

*

Thus the year slipped by.

The *Swan* put in to Fortune Island on her way from
Jamaica, headed towards Charleston in October. They would

only stop in for a day and two nights, the wind had dropped and they were behind schedule. If they wanted to be back home in time for the Christmas holidays, they must press on.

Everything went as usual. Greville nearly spoke to Kath on their fishing trip, but decided to put it off until Christmas. He had decided that Kath was the only woman for him, and come what may, it was not fair to leave her dangling. By now he was irritated with his own prevarication, which was not at all like him. Normally decisive and firm, he was being dilatory and insecure, even stupid, he told himself. If she refused him, well, he would know for sure. He could rule his longings out and get on with his life.

Later that evening, after their fried fish supper, Miz Eva asked Greville to stroll with her out to look at their field. He looked at her inquiringly, noticing how she had seemed to age suddenly. Her carriage was still as upright as ever, but there seemed a hesitation in her step, an indefinable slowness in her ripostes to his teasing. Miz Eva sat on her favorite stone and patted the place beside her. Her faithful dog Treacle flopped panting at their feet in her customary position, with her head down between her front paws, and her back paws stretched out in line with her tail, like a great brown frog.

"Sit down, chile, I got something to tell you."

Dread cast its shadow over Greville's heart. "What is it, Little Mouse?"

"My Lovely Lord Jesus has told me I'm going home soon."

"No!" Greville's head snapped around. "Surely not, Gammie, you look as well as ever!"

"Hush, son," she said, patting his arm. Her hand felt as insubstantial as a moth fluttering against his flesh. "The Lord is kind. He told me it isn't going to hurt. It will be sudden, and it will be soon. I will not see Christmas, nor will I see you again after tonight, my darling boy. He told me to tell you goodbye."

"Oh Gammie dearest, my own Little Mouse!" Greville said, gathering her into his arms. She felt small, frail, as though he could break her in two with one swift squeeze. Tears prickled his eyes as she nestled into his chest. Her breath was warm against his throat. He kissed her cheek, her plaited hair; he rested his head on hers and rocked her. "Please say it isn't true!" he pleaded, his voice breaking.

"Yes, Grev, it is true. I know my Master's voice."

"How long have you known this?"

"I guess a week or so. I've been putting things in order, setting my mind to rights, and going to see everyone in the settlement. I haven't told Kath. I wanted to speak to you first." Miz Eva sighed and snuggled deeper into Greville's embrace. She rubbed her face into his chest, breathing in his scent. She had helped Eliza birth him, and had been breathing in his scent ever since he was born. Eliza had died when Greville was eight, so Miz Eva was the only mother he had cherished through the years. She loved his scent, she loved her darling grandson, and she was proud of the fine man he had become. Her one regret, now that she knew she was leaving, was that he was not happily settled with someone to love, and who would love him and appreciate all his qualities as much as she did.

"It's mainly Kath I want to talk about," she said, her voice muffled against his chest. "Greville, if you don't see your way to marrying her, you must take her to Charleston after Christmas. She's such a loving little soul. She does a power of good here in this island, and everyone loves her, but she's slowly dying inside. The place is too small. She needs a husband and a family of her own to care for. She loves you dearly, and I can see it eating away at her."

"I love her too, Gammie," he said, his voice husky. "I'm planning to ask her at Christmas."

"Why don't you ask her now? I may be gone by Christmas, and I would love to see you promised to each other at last."

Greville winced. His arms jerked tighter around her. "You talk about your death just like I talk about going fishing, Gammie. Are you sure the Lord wants you home now?" His voice was ragged and he sniffed, as tears trickled down his cheeks.

"Yes. Yes, I'm sure," she said sadly. "It's my time, Grev. I have nothing more to do here and I long to see my Savior's face. Don't try to keep me. I'm sad to be going now, in that I would have liked to know that you and Kath are settled and as happy as can be expected in this world. And I would have loved to see a great grand. But my living has nothing to do with that. You're in God's hands, right where I put you from the beginning. God will take care of you."

Greville fished in his pocket for his handkerchief and blew his nose.

"Don't you go mourning me, Greville Knowles! I've had a good long life, and a good old time of it – more than most. And I'm ready to leave. Would you have me get ill, maybe paralyzed like poor old Mr. Cartwright? He's helpless on his bed, day in, day out, his mind going and coming, sometimes he can't even tell you what he wants. He's younger than I am." Miz Eva looked out at the ocean. "No, I welcome the Lord taking me suddenly, without pain. It's a wonderful way to go."

The sun was starting its drop into the western ocean, lighting the sky with gorgeous shades of pink, orange and turquoise. The blue, brilliant day was softening to its close. Mosquitoes whined in their ears, bumbling around their faces. Miz Eva slapped one.

"Remember how, when you were a little boy, you used to love hunks of fresh bread and guava jam? Especially in the afternoons, after you'd been out swimming..."

Greville smiled. "Yes. And you always baked extra so I could have my hunk! And you made those crusty small loaves, especially for me, because I loved the crunchy crust!"

The two sat on together as night sifted down around them, remembering old times, people long dead and incidents not recalled for years. At last Greville helped his Gammie up off the stone. Her stiff knees creaked as she stood.

"See – my joints are longing for rest. Won't be long now, old things..."

"Let me carry you back, Gammie!"

"What, and risk you pitching me down on this hard

ground? No thanks. Shanks mare will still take me!"

They walked slowly back, companionable and close, relishing the tender feelings between them.

Back at the hut, they found Kath sitting on the doorstop before a merry little fire, the smoke keeping the bugs at bay.

Greville held Miz Eva close for a long time, his heart too full to speak. He wished she had told him sooner, that he could somehow stretch out the minutes and hours of this day, and that he could somehow savor her presence more.

It was time to leave.

"Good night, my own Little Mouse," he said softly. "And may angels speed you to your rest."

"Good night, son," she replied, smiling tremulously at him. "I'll see you in the morning." She turned and went slowly into the hut.

"What time are you leaving, Greville?" Kath asked. "I thought you planned to sail at dawn."

"Yes, Kath, we'll sail at dawn if the wind is right." Greville took both her hands and kissed them, one after the other, looking into her eyes. It crossed his mind to ask her, now, but his heart was too heavy. He wanted it to be perfect when he asked her to be his wife, only about the two of them, with time to kiss and to dream, and plan their future together.

"Good night, my wench," he said gravely. "I will see you at Christmas, God willing." His voice broke and he turned quickly away, dashing his eyes with his shirtsleeve as he headed down the path to the settlement.

25

The following morning Kath noticed that Miz Eva was not her usual exuberant self. She had not gone out to sit with her Lovely Lord Jesus, and now at mid-day dinner, her main meal, she was only picking at her food. Truth be told, her spirits had seemed a little low for the past week or so, but when Kath had asked how she was feeling, she said nothing was wrong. Kath was truly concerned; Miz Eva had never been off her food before.

"What's wrong, Miz Eva?"

"Nothing, chile, not really. I don't feel so good today, that's all."

"You minded Greville leaving this morning, didn't you? He only stayed a day this trip." Kath had minded him leaving, especially the strange, quick way he had gone last night. She wondered what Miz Eva had told him. They'd sat out in that field for a long time.

"Yes, but it's not that. I feel like I might be coming down with a cold."

Kath reached over and pressed her palm to Miz Eva's forehead.

"You don't feel feverish," she said. "But perhaps you should go back to bed. Let me make you a toddy, and some bush tea."

"No, thanks, nothing like that. But I will go back to bed." Miz Eva slept the whole afternoon. Kath cooked some grits and a soft-boiled egg, and took it in to her at suppertime. "How are you feeling now, Miz Eva?" she asked. "It's time you ate a little supper. I've made a nice cup of fever grass tea for you, too."

Miz Eva struggled to sit up in bed on one elbow. "I don't fancy anything to eat, sweeting, but I'd like the tea. My throat is parched." Kath sat on the side of the bed and cradled Miz Eva up against her chest, holding the cup for her to drink. "My throat's so sore, I can hardly swallow."

"The tea will do you good. Are you sure you can't eat a little grits and egg? You've had nothing all day."

"You eat it, chile. I have no appetite. I'll just drink this, then go back to sleep."

*

"Kath... Kath, wake up."

"What is it, Miz Eva?"

"I've got things to tell you. Come and sit in bed with me."

Kath rolled out of her hammock, landing on the packed earth floor with a thump. "Can I bring you some water?" she asked.

"Yes, please..."

Kath plodded over to the bucket and brought back the water. "What do you want to talk about, Miz Eva?" she asked, yawning.

"I want to tell you that I'm leaving soon."

"What do you mean? Where are you going?"

"I'm going home to be with my Lovely Lord Jesus."

"You're not going to die, Miz Eva," Kath said, yawning again. She took the water from Miz Eva and put it on the bedside table. "You've just caught a cold. You'll be all right in a few days, dearest." She crawled under Miz Eva's cover and cuddled her.

"No. The Lord's told me. I'm going home soon."

Kath sat bolt upright. "Did you tell Greville that last night?"

"Yes. We said our good-byes."

No wonder he was strange, Kath thought. *He must have been worried out of his wits.* "Did you tell him you were feeling sick?"

"No, because I wasn't. I only started feeling odd around dinnertime. This sickness won't carry me off. It may have something to do with it, but the Lord said it would be sudden and painless. This isn't painless. My throat aches."

"When did the Lord tell you this, Miz Eva?"

"About ten days ago."

"Why didn't you tell me before? Is that why you've been going to see everybody in the settlement? I wondered why you were doing all the visiting."

"Yes. I've been telling everyone goodbye, though they didn't know it. But I want to talk to you now, about all sorts of things. I knew I had until after Greville's visit, because the Lord told me to tell him goodbye. But I don't know how much time I have left."

Kath was wide awake now. Being Irish, she accepted these things. The Leprechauns often told the old ones when they were about to die – her Granda had known, and her mother, too – and she was only forty-one. People sometimes knew when they would die.

"Lean against me, Miz Eva," Kath said, getting under the cover again and sitting up against the wall, shifting the old woman's body against her. "Are you comfortable? I'm here. I'm listening."

"I want to tell you how much I love you and I want to give you my blessing. I've asked my Lord Jesus to grant you a healthy, happy and good life. I've asked Him to provide you with a fine husband, a new family, and enough money that you will never suffer want again." Miz Eva paused to clear her throat. She took another sip of water.

"You've been the joy of my old age, sweeting, just as the Lord promised. I was so lonely before you came. You made my life interesting and happy. You did all the heavy chores, you read and sang to me. I enjoyed your friends visiting, the children at your school, the sewing and fancywork. You included me in everything." Miz Eva paused for a moment.

"I appreciate your loving, respectful ways," she said with

a catch in her voice. "Younger people often get huffy with the old. They 'take over'. You've never been impatient or cross, and I know I'm cantankerous sometimes. I've asked the Lord to bless you especially for that."

Kath's throat closed and her eyes burned. "That was my pleasure, my lady," she said thickly, tightening her arms about her. "It was easy to love you. I loved you from the moment I saw you, there on the beach. You took me into your home, a naked, hopeless convict, and you treated me like your own daughter. You shared your friends, your food, your wisdom and your grandson with me, without holding anything back. I'd go to Hell for you, Miz Eva."

Miz Eva patted Kath's arm. "Luckily that won't be necessary," she said with a glimmer of her usual humor. "I'm going to be with my Lovely Lord Jesus, to walk on streets of gold."

Kath swallowed the lump in her throat. "It pains me to think you may be dying soon, without a priest to hear your last confession."

"I don't need any priest. I confess my sins every day to my Lovely Lord Jesus. He's our Great High Priest, the Bible tells us."

"All right, Miz Eva," Kath said warily. She didn't want to agitate her into any long Biblical explanations. "Let's agree to disagree, as we always have."

"I want you to have my old Bible. And I want you to promise that you'll keep on reading it every day if you can, like you have while you've been here with me."

"Thank you, Miz Eva. I'll treasure your Bible, and I promise to read it." Kath rolled her eyes in the dark.

"Another thing," Miz Eva said after a moment's silence. "I want to talk to you about that hard, unforgiving streak in your spirit, the grudge you hold against the English Protestants. It flows into your own life, and in time it will blight your happiness and your freedom. You don't talk about it much, but I know it's there, I've seen it from time to time."

"Now, just a minute, Miz Eva," Kath interrupted. "The English Protestants have always given me good reason to hate them! They have made themselves hateful all my life, and to all my people, my whole country! Living here with you, I've come to understand not all Protestants are like them, but..."

Miz Eva cut in. "Now listen to me, Kath, chile, this is important!

"Yes, powerful people can make you a slave. They can hurt you, do all sorts of harmful things, and take all that you have. No matter what they do to you, that's just your body, they take things that are outside your true self.

"But they can't make your soul a slave. Only *you* can make a slave of your true self, and this happens when you hate. Hating the English, the Protestants, the Catholics, black people, the pirates – anybody – shackles your mind, your true self, just like slave irons shackle your body.

"My Lord Jesus says "Love one another," and He came to set the captives free. We are freed by love, Kath! And as hard as it is, you must learn to love everyone, even the people who hate you. Especially the people who hate you."

Kath lay rigid throughout this homily, with her teeth clenched, and it took several minutes for the air to settle between them again. Miz Eva reached for her water and took another swallow, then began again.

"Now I know you're in love with Greville," Miz Eva said. "He loves you too, but he doesn't want to marry a woman who doesn't believe as he does, just as you don't want to marry a man who isn't a Catholic."

Kath exhaled and relaxed a little. She would certainly prefer to talk about Greville, than all that 'love everybody, forgive others their trespasses.'

"I do love Greville, Miz Eva. And I know my being a Catholic may be a problem, but I think there's another woman in his life. Obie told me about a Mistress Nancy Lou Lilly down in Nassau. I think he's already promised to her."

"Nonsense. He's never mentioned any Nancy Lou Lilly to me, and Greville tells me most everything. He would certainly have told me if he was engaged to a woman."

"Well, if there's nobody else, why hasn't he spoken to me?"

"I think he's afraid you'll reject him because of his color. As you said once yourself, in the outside world white people don't associate with black people on an equal footing. He worries about how other people would treat you if you married him – and that you'd come to despise him later on, hold his color against him. How do you feel about it?"

Kath shifted her position in the bed, stretching her neck. She had not thought about this before, but she had noticed the two white families on the island seemed to have an edge of superiority in their dealings with everyone else. Suddenly she did not know how she truly felt. It had never crossed her mind.

"You must think carefully about this, Kath." Miz Eva continued. "In the outside world they treat black and colored people like slaves, whether they are or not. You must decide whether you love Greville enough to stand up to this. I believe he may speak to you about marriage when he comes at Christmas, and you must be sure of your feelings. You will not always live on Fortune Island. You will have to go into the outside world, where Greville can earn his living. Be honest with yourself, chile, and with him."

"I'm used to ill-treatment from the English," Kath said. "It wouldn't make any difference to me."

There was silence as their thoughts ran on.

"What will you do when I'm gone, chile? That is, if you don't marry Greville?" Miz Eva's soft voice interrupted Kath's train of thought. "Will you stay here on Fortune Island? I'm sure Greville would want you to live in this hut. Have you thought about moving to Charleston and sewing for rich folks, like he suggested?"

"No, I haven't. I don't want to live in Charleston or Jamaica. I'd live in fear of someone finding out about me and making me serve my sentence. I don't fancy Nassau either, with all those pirates and scoundrels and rogues. What I've heard about that place makes my blood run cold. I'd best stay right here."

"It'll get awful lonely here, sweeting. You need a husband

and a family to care for. There's nobody suitable for you here."

"Jonah Cartwright's still available, I believe?"

"And when was he here? Last August, for one day! That's no use. Besides, he's not a Catholic either. No, you must give this careful thought, about what is truly important to you, about where you should live and with whom. Maybe you should try to find Kevin after the seven years is up. Nobody will know you haven't served your time if you turn up then. A former indentured servant is common in the Colonies."

Miz Eva shifted her weight from Kath's shoulder. "What will happen to Treacle?" she asked "Can you take care of her? I know you love her, but if you move from Fortune Island, it might be best to give her back to Reena. She said she'd have her if you didn't want her. Dogs can be a pest aboard ship."

The two women talked on into the night, from this thing to that, until roosters began to crow. Treacle sat up, listening intently to something, then settled down again. About dawn, Miz Eva dozed off and Kath followed swiftly behind her.

*

"Wake up, Miz Kath!" Shirley's voice was shouting. She was banging on the door, rattling the doorknob. "Wake up, wake up!"

Kath woke in an instant, surprised to find herself in Miz Eva's bed. Her arm tingled from the weight of Miz Eva's body. Treacle was barking madly.

"Just a minute, Shirley," she called, gathering her wits and lurching groggily towards the door. "What's the matter? What's happening?"

"There's a Spanish ship coming into the harbor! Everyone in the settlement is already in the bush. We saw it just after dawn. Then I noticed you and Miz Eva weren't with us, in the bush, I mean, so I ran back to get you. Hurry!"

"Hurry? Why?" Kath asked. She felt stupid, as though she didn't understand something important.

"Because the Spaniards will kill us if they find us! And they'll burn our houses! Get dressed – put on as many things as you can. Get your things and run into the bush! Bring whatever food you can, too! They'll burn our fields! They'll soon be here!" Shirley's eyes were wild, her hair uncombed. She was wearing all three of her dresses, one over the other.

"Miz Eva, wake up!" Kath rushed back to the bed to shake her. "The Spanish are here! We're being raided by the Spanish!"

Miz Eva roused, but seemed confused. "Here, Shirley, you try to get Miz Eva awake while I dress. Put on her Christmas dress for me..." Kath was already diving into her petticoat, her mind working frantically. "There's a sack of dried peas and a sack of corn in the kitchen. Let's throw them into the bush – we can't carry them. And Greville left me a fishing line – throw that with them.

"Oh and Shirley, hide this cloth Greville just brought. I'm finished dressing now, I'll take care of Miz Eva."

Shirley grabbed the bundle of sewing things and the sewing basket and rushed outside. "The boats are on their way to shore!" Shirley wailed. "They'll soon be here! I'm going! Make haste!" Shirley ran down the path leading to Miz Eva's field and disappeared into the bush.

Miz Eva sat on the edge of the bed looking befuddled. "Come, Miz Eva! There's no time to waste!" Kath seized her up by the elbow and thrust her out the door. Miz Eva sat on the doorstep and started coughing.

"Kath, you go. I can't run," she wheezed, tears streaming down her face. "I'm too weak."

"You catch yourself, Miz Eva," Kath said gently stroking her shoulder. "Start down the path to the field. I'll go to the kitchen. Please, please try!"

Kath dragged sacks of foodstuffs to the edge of the clearing and heaved them into the bush. She threw their few pots into the bush as well, along with anything else her hands came upon. She grabbed their pail of water and doused the fire, then slung the bucket into the bush too.

Miz Eva sat on the front doorstep, elbows on her knees, her head resting on her arms. "Why won't you try to save yourself, Miz Eva?" Kath panted out, grabbing her by the arm. She tried to lift her.

"It's no use, I can't run! I'll hide behind the fig tree. You run! I'm an old woman, they won't want me. You run, chile, and the Lord go with you."

Treacle was wild with enthusiasm for this new game. She ran back and forth, barking up a storm. She bounced around Kath as she threw things into the bush, then danced back to Miz Eva, her tongue waving like a pink pennant from her grinning brown face.

Kath could see the men swarming ashore from the boats. Gun shots rang out below, and shouted commands in a foreign tongue.

"Miz Eva, *come!*" Kath almost dragged her over to the fig tree. "Sit here, then. Tuck your skirt in, so they can't see it from the other side of the tree."

Miz Eva sank to the ground amidst her cranberry red skirt, looking old, drawn and gray. She hunched over, hugging her knees. Kath's heart broke with pity, and with foreboding.

"Goodbye, sweeting! Run, run!" Miz Eva said.

Treacle was heading down the path to the settlement, barking as she went. Kath panicked. She turned and ran along the path towards the field at the back of the hut and the safety of the bush. Treacle appeared running at her side, barking. *This dog is going to give me away,* Kath thought. She stopped running. "Go home, Treacle," Kath commanded, pointing. "Go home!"

Treacle looked woebegone, but turned obediently and trotted back towards the hut. Then Kath realized that Miz Eva was still there, hidden behind the tree – Treacle would go to *her*, would give *her* away...

"Treacle, here Treacle..." Kath called. But Treacle was barking furiously now, not her happy, game playing bark, but a serious, menacing bark that Kath had never heard before. Kath realized that the Spanish were likely in the home clearing. Frenzied, she plunged into the bushes, heedless of scratching thorns and whipping branches. A shot rang out nearby.

Then Treacle's barking was coming closer, along with the sound of running footsteps. Kath saw the trunk of a large gum elemi tree and made a quick decision. Adrenaline coursing through her veins, she leapt into the lower branches and crouched trembling in the leaves.

Treacle crashed through the bush after Kath, barking and barking... now Treacle was jumping up at the bottom of Kath's tree, tail wagging, her pink tongue flailing, and so pleased to have found her!

There was some more cautious crashing in the bushes. Then Kath saw a head of dark hair with gold streaks, a tarred pigtail behind. A swarthy man with a pointed beard and tobacco-stained teeth looked up at her. He laughed and jabbered in his foreign tongue. He was waving a blunderbuss, motioning her to come down.

26

Kath's body prickled with gooseflesh, and her blood pounded in her ears. Slowly she picked her way down from the tree. She was wearing both her dresses, and her skirts got in the way, tangling in the branches. The sailor grabbed both her legs and yanked her crashing down on top of him, knocking the breath out of them both. Kath was up in an instant, scrabbling away from him. The Spaniard rocked to his haunches and tackled her, bringing them both to the ground again. Treacle bounced around them, barking.

The man laughed. "*No, no, bella dama, ven aquí!*" he said, shooting to his feet in one lithe bound, dragging Kath up with him. He pulled her close and started kissing her. His body stank and his breath smelled of garlic and spirits. Kath screamed and fought, but she was no match for him. He clamped his hand over her nose and mouth and jerked the butt of his gun up into her diaphragm.

She could not catch her breath. Everything was covered by a gray mist, which quickly turned to black. She sagged against him. The man moved his hand and she doubled over, heaving, her lungs sucking in gasps of air.

Waving his gun, the sailor shoved her towards the path back to the hut. She felt the muzzle of the blunderbuss in the small of her back as she pushed through the underbrush, holding the branches so they would not whip back into his face. She didn't want to anger him further. Once on the path, the Spaniard grabbed her elbow and pushed her along in front of him. He was of medium height, with a powerful chest and strong, muscular arms. Now his fingers dug into the tender flesh of her upper arm.

Miz Eva was waiting behind the rainwater barrel. As they rounded the corner of the kitchen, she yelled and jumped out, whacking the Spaniard on the back of his head with a piece of firewood. He howled and spun, squeezing the trigger. There was a loud crack and Miz Eva staggered back, the stick flying from her hands. She crumpled to the ground, then toppled over onto her back to lie with a surprised look on her face. It was over in a moment.

"Miz Eva!" Kath shrieked, dropping to the ground beside her.

Blood welled out of a gaping hole in her left breast, spreading over her bodice, her scarf, and down into the sandy soil. Kath pressed both hands over Miz Eva's chest, wrenching at her scarf, frantically trying to stuff it into the wound, wailing in anguish. The sailor pulled Kath to her feet, shoving her towards the path down to the settlement, just as more men boiled into the clearing their guns ready and cutlasses flashing in the morning sun.

"*Hola, Alfonso!*" they greeted her captor. There was a staccato exchange in Spanish, then one of the sailors went over to Miz Eva and nudged her body with his foot. "*Está muerta,*" he said, spitting on Miz Eva's corpse and kicking dirt in her face.

Kath screeched, kicking and scratching at Alfonso, smearing him with Miz Eva's blood. He shook her, then slapped her hard across the face. She staggered, then went for him again. The others laughed and jumped back. Now they formed a ring around Kath, baiting her, touching her back to make her swing around, and then someone else would touch her from the other side.

Treacle bounced around, barking furiously. One of the sailors kicked her. She yelped and moved out of the way. He threw his cutlass at her, and it caught her in the neck. She lay twitching, arterial blood spouting into the air.

Kath stood still, staring at Treacle. Alfonso grabbed her hands and wrenched them behind her back, twisting them up towards her shoulder blades.

"*La llevo por El Capitán,*" he shouted to the others as he pushed her stumbling down the path to the settlement. The captain had asked him to bring back someone pretty from the island.

Down in the settlement Kath saw Spaniards everywhere, ransacking the huts and setting them ablaze. A couple of men were herding Mr. Harding's loudly bleating sheep down to the beach.

Alfonso pushed her along, shouting to his mates "*Para El Capitán!*" They all laughed, shouting comments in reply.

Kath felt as though she was in a nightmare. She staggered woodenly along, one foot in front of the other. Down on the shore, Alfonso tied her hands behind her back with a piece of rope. He made her sit in one of the boats that was already filled with plunder, then he shoved off, jumped in himself, and began sculling out to the galleon.

From the dinghy, Kath saw billows of smoke rising from the huts and fields. She seemed to be the only captive, but she didn't know whether others had been found and killed, or whether the Spaniards were content just to burn and pillage the settlement.

Sick at her stomach, Kath turned to look up at the ship. She was royal blue, and huge, with four soaring masts webbed with rigging and furled canvas. Flags and pennants fluttered gaily in the wind, and she bristled with gun ports. Intricate gilt carving covered the stern, with gilding all along the gunwales. More gilt carving festooned the ship's name, "*Jacinta de Chavez.*" A carved and painted female nude with flowing gold hair proudly adorned her prow.

As the boat came alongside, sailors on the top deck lowered a canvas sling by block and tackle down to Alfonso. "*Sentar!*" he commanded, pointing at the canvas sling. She sat and he untied her hands. Soon she was sailing high above the water, her heart in her mouth, clinging for dear life to the ropes. By the time they lowered her onto the deck, Alfonso had already climbed up the side of the ship. A knot of curious sailors clustered around her, grabbing at her clothing and gabbling in Spanish.

"Leave her alone!" Alfonso bellowed in Spanish. "She's a present for the Captain. He asked us to bring him someone pretty from the island and she's the best I could find. It's poor pickings over there."

They sent a cabin boy to tell the Captain of Kath's arrival. The Captain emerged from the great cabin, high on the poop deck, strolled to the railing and leaned over to look down into the waist of the ship.

"So Alfonso," he said in Spanish. "You found someone interesting to bring me after all! Bring her up! Let's have a look at her!"

Alfonso took Kath's hand and led her aft, pointing up at the Captain, who waited for them at the head of the stairs.

The Captain was in his mid-forties. He was short and sturdily built, and he wore a white wig of the latest fashion in Madrid. His clothes, too, bespoke wealth and fastidious attention to detail. He had an intelligent, sensitive face, with a high forehead and an aquiline nose. The interest in his dark eyes, coupled with his pleasant smile, dispelled Kath's fright somewhat.

"Welcome aboard the *Jacinta de Chavez, Señora,*" the Captain said in heavily accented English, as he doffed his hat and bowed, extending a well-muscled leg. "I am Don Francisco Adriano de Cornego y Orlando, *El Capitán.* You may call me Don Francisco de Cornego, if you wish.

Don Francisco de Cornego was about to extend his hand, but pulled back when he saw the state of Kath's hands. "I see you need to compose yourself, *Señora.* I will have you taken below to a cabin." He turned and gave orders to Alfonso in Spanish. Alfonso took Kath's hand again and nodded his head towards the stairs. Kath wrenched her hand from his grasp.

"I will follow you, Sir," she said haughtily. "There is no need to drag me." Don Francisco de Cornego laughed and translated for Alfonso.

Kath smoothed her billowing skirts towards her back as she carefully descended the ladder below decks. They came down into the dining area of the ship. The cook was preparing the mid-day meal in a vast boiling cauldron hung over the range fire. The heat and smell were overpowering. The ripe stench generated by too many people closely packed together for too long at sea rose up to meet her. She gagged and retched, holding tightly to the ladder until her nausea passed. Once below, she followed Alfonso in the dim twilight of between decks.

Alfonso stopped before a small door opening into a cabin that was no more than a closet. There was a narrow bunk and a shelf, on which a basin and ewer of water stood. Kath went in and Alfonso shut the door behind her. One small porthole allowed some light to filter into the gloom. Kath sank wearily onto the bunk and dropped her face in her hands. They reeked of blood! She blinked, then recoiled at the sight of Miz Eva's blood, smeared and dried all over her hands and clothes.

She poured water into the basin and washed with a piece of soap she found beside the basin. She looked down at her dress. Luckily she had put on her best dress first that morning, then her everyday one over it. Now she struggled out of her clothing and examined her good dress closely. It showed no bloodstains as far as she could see in the dim light. She poured more water in the basin and rubbed at her stained gown.

There was blood caked under her fingernails and in her cuticles, too. She sat on the side of the bunk and left her hands to soak in the basin, then attacked her fingertips again. The water in the basin had turned russet, and brown scum floated on top. When she felt that she was as clean as she could be in the circumstances, she lay down on the bunk, suddenly overcome with fatigue and anxiety.

*

Kath closed her eyes. Miz Eva's body, lying contorted, lifeless and bleeding on the ground swam before her, quickly followed by a flash of Treacle in her death throes. Kath gasped, breaking out in a cold sweat. *Dear God,* she thought, *must violence and death follow me for the rest of my life? Am I to lose everyone I love?*

No, not everyone... she answered her own question. *Greville's still alive.*

Greville. Would she ever see him again? And if she did, what then? He had never spoken of love, or a future. All she had to go on was his longing looks, his hazel eyes clouded by a nameless misery, his hand trembling when he touched her sometimes. All during their fishing trips, the long hours at the hut during his visits to the island over the past fourteen months, he had never spoken.

I might just as well face it, she thought sadly. He is not free to speak to me, or he would have by now. I must stop thinking of him. In any case I'll probably never see him again.

Tears seeped from her eyes and ran down into her hair, pooling in her ears. She heard her heart thumping. It felt like a granite boulder, bigger than her chest could possibly contain. How would she be able to walk again with the weight of it? It must forever bear her down, crushing her into dust at last. She gave a mewing cry, like the shriek of a seagull. Whimpering softly, she balled up and turned her face into the musty straw sack on the berth.

27

From far away came a knocking and a rattling. Kath opened her eyes. It was pitch black and she couldn't remember where she was for a moment. Turning her head, she saw a crack of light around a door.

"*Señora, Señora...*" a voice called, and the banging and rattling began again, coming from the door. Kath sprang up and fumbled for the latch, opening it to find Alfonso standing with a lantern. He smiled and gabbled quickly in Spanish. She could only make out one thing – *El Capitán* – and understood that she was being summoned.

Hurriedly she raked her fingers through her long dark hair and shook out her dress, wiping her eyes as she followed Alfonso. They went up the ladder to the top deck, then along to the stern and up another ladder to the quarterdeck. Alfonso rapped lightly on an ornately carved mahogany door, then opened it. Light spilled out onto the deck as Alfonso bowed and motioned her to enter.

Kath blinked rapidly and looked around, gaping. The room was large and airy, with rich furnishings. There was a bed bolted to one side, piled with cushions and covered in crimson brocade. Near it was a long sea chest with a large gold and ivory crucifix hanging on the wall above. A thick carpet hid most of the dark planked floor. On the far side were four windows and a door, which stood open to a balcony beyond.

Don Francisco de Cornego rose to his feet, stretching one leg forward as he made a courtly bow. He was splendidly dressed in a sky-blue coat of silk brocade, with its cuffs and lapels sporting bright silver buttons. His waistcoat was primrose yellow, worn over a fine shirt with frothy lace at the neck and wrists. His breeches were buff, with silver buckles at the knees. He wore thin white silk hose and high heeled shoes of black kid leather, also with silver buckles. His wig was freshly powdered and very white.

"Come in, *Señora,* I hope you are refreshed," Don Francisco de Cornego said in his charming accented English. "I understand from Alfonso that your capture was quite shocking."

"Yes Sir. Your men killed my old mother and our dog, in cold blood." Kath's chin went up defiantly and her green eyes narrowed.

"For that, I must beg your pardon, *Señora,*" he said earnestly. "It is against my honor to kill harmless women and animals. My men know this, but they forget sometimes in the lust of the moment. Alfonso told me that the old woman – your mother – jumped out from behind him and hit him with a wood. He shot before he knew his enemy. If this is true, it is not his fault that she is dead." He confused the English 'y' and 'j', turning 'you' into 'ju', and 'jumped' into 'yumped.' As upset as she was, Kath had to fight a desire to giggle. She was no longer afraid.

She dropped her gaze. "That's true, Sir."

"Well, I offer my apologies, and also for Alfonso, who cannot speak English. We are very sorry. You speak Spanish, *Señora?*"

"No, Sir."

"Please sit down," he said, his hand indicating an exquisitely carved mahogany chair. Padded in needlepoint, it showed a pastoral scene in lovely soft colors. Kath would have loved to inspect it closely. Carefully positioning his coattails, Don Francisco de Cornego took a similar chair next to the table, which was set with gleaming china, crystal and silver, ready for supper. Tapered candles shone from a silver candelabra. He crossed his legs at the ankles, glancing down at them with a satisfied smile, then looked up at Kath again.

"Alfonso is my boatswain, and a professional sailor. Some

of my men are vicious, but he is not among them. He would not choose to harm an old woman."

Kath swallowed the lump in her throat and turned an anguished gaze to Don Francisco.

"A little wine will help, I think," he said, pouring from a ship's decanter set in the middle of the table. He held one of the thin goblets out to Kath.

"Have a drink, *Señora*," he coaxed, "...and let us talk of more pleasant things. I know you are mourning, but I will try to cheer you. The past cannot be changed, however one might wish it."

"Thank you, Sir," Kath replied, accepting the glass. She took a sip and her heart twisted again. It was a cream sherry, Miz Eva's favorite.

She swallowed the wine in three quick gulps, then set the glass on the table with a slight rap. Then she looked Don Francisco straight in the face. "Tell me, Captain, why you should raid a poor place like Fortune Island? It must have been plain to see that we have nothing of worth."

He returned Kath's frank look. "Well, you do have something of worth. You have fresh water and vegetables and meat animals. Perhaps sacks of flour, and cheese without those detestable worms. These things are worth more than gold to us, now that we have none of our own." Don Francisco filled Kath's glass again and topped up his own.

"And may I say that the English habitually raid our Spanish settlements, however small and poor, as a matter of course? They rape, pillage and burn, killing anyone who tries to defend himself. They are not as kind as we are being to Fortune Island."

"Kind!" Kath snorted. "You are leaving a whole settlement to starve."

"Yes, *Señora*, kind!" he replied heatedly. "We have not killed them. We have not burnt their fields or poisoned their wells, all of which the English have done to our people in the past."

Don Francisco de Cornego gave Kath a conciliating smile

and dropped his voice. "We have just made a most difficult crossing from Cadiz, in *España*. The wind died, then blew only fitfully for weeks. Then there was a storm in the middle of the ocean and we did not see the sun for five days. We had no idea of where we were. At last we picked up the trade winds and sailed with them, hoping we would find somewhere we knew before our supplies ran out.

"We set out with two other ships, the *Jacinta de Chavez* being the mother ship. We lost sight of the others in the storm – I do not know whether they are lost, or whether they are already in Havana. It is a great worry." He sighed and looked at Kath with troubled eyes.

"I know we are in the *baja mar*, the shallow sea, and that the English now claim this territory." He took a sip of sherry. "As you know, there is no love lost between us. We had to go ashore expecting to fight, though none of us had the heart for it. We are starved and thirsty. But – what could we do? Our water is putrid, our biscuits full of insects. We ate our chickens and animals weeks ago, and our brined meats are rotten.

"Every man has attended Mass each day, *Señora*, to plead for safe haven – and food. The Priest will say a Mass of Thanksgiving in the morning."

He smiled slightly as he toyed with his glass, then with the lace cuffs of his shirt. His hands were brown and fine-boned, as smooth as driftwood. His nails were manicured, they looked like pink and white shells at the tips of his long tapered fingers. He wore an emerald ring on his right hand and a heavy gold signet on his left little finger, embossed with his family crest. "You say this place is called Fortune Island?"

"Yes, Sir."

"Fortune Island. A good name for it. It has certainly been fortunate for us."

"But not for the people who live there," Kath replied bitterly.

"Your mother and your dog were the only ones to perish, beside a few sheep," Don Francisco said. "I ordered my men not to hunt down the townspeople. All your friends and relations are safe, *Señora*."

Kath crossed herself. "God and the Blessed Virgin be thanked," she said softly.

"You are Catholic?" Don Francisco de Cornego asked, eyebrows raised.

"Yes, Sir." Kath drew herself up, jutting out her chin.

"Then you are not English? All the English are Protestant nowadays, no?"

"Yes, Sir, most of them are, I believe."

"And these people on Fortune Island, they are Catholic?"

"No, Sir. They are Protestant. Only I am Catholic."

"That is very... unusual, no?"

"Yes, Sir, it is..." Kath looked up and smiled at him for the first time.

"This is interesting. I love mystery." Don Francisco stroked his beard. "So Alfonso brought me the *only* Catholic on Fortune Island?"

"Yes, Sir."

"How do you come to be the only Catholic living among Protestant English on Fortune Island? A rare puzzle. Let me see if I can solve it for myself."

There were three staccato raps on the door. "*Pasa, Garcia!*"

A steward entered bearing a covered silver tray. He set it down on one corner of the table and began putting food out. There was a leg of lamb, potatoes, yams and pumpkin, and a dish of green pigeon peas. The smell made Kath's mouth water.

"Please, let us dine," Don Francisco de Cornego said, holding another chair for her at one of the place settings. "You must be hungry."

"I am indeed, Sir. I have not eaten today."

"I beg your pardon. I should have seen to it when you came aboard."

"Thank you, Sir, but I could not have eaten then. This is just at the right time."

Garcia ladled clear broth into soup plates, poured red

wine into their goblets, and then stood behind the Captain's chair.

Don Francisco crossed himself, bowed his head and gave thanks in Latin. Then he smiled and nodded at Kath, who watched to see which of the gleaming silver implements he would pick up. She followed suit, carefully mimicking him as he scooped his broth.

"I normally dine with the Padre and my officers, but tonight I asked their indulgence." He smiled slightly and looked directly at Kath. "I wanted the pleasure of getting to know you all alone. I hope you do not feel this is improper."

Kath had not stopped for a moment to think of impropriety. She was astonished at the careful, polite deference this aristocratic man paid her. Of course, he was Catholic, not one of those English Protestant dogs. That made all the difference in the world.

"Are you ready for the meat, *Señora?*"

"Yes, Sir, if you please."

Don Francisco motioned to Garcia. They watched as he removed their soup and began carving the joint, expertly placing slices onto their plates.

"Here we are, at supper together, and you are still an enigma. I do not even know your name."

"Oh, I beg your pardon, Sir! My name is Katherine O'Brien."

"O'Brien? Then you are not English at all. You are Irish. Aha! I have solved the mystery. You are an Irish Catholic!"

Kath blushed beet red.

"Have I embarrassed you, *Señora?*" he asked.

"N-no, I'm not embarrassed. It is as you say, I am an Irish Catholic."

"All the more reason for us to become friends. The Irish Catholics have helped the Spanish for centuries – and we both hate the English!"

Kath took another sip of her wine. She was beginning to like Don Francisco de Cornego more and more. He was handsome, a gentleman, a Catholic, and he hated the English

Protestants. She felt a great relief that he did not despise her for being Irish.

"Now you know about me, Sir. But you are still a mystery to me. May I ask...?"

"Please do." He gave her an arch look. "And if I do not wish to answer, I will be silent."

"How do you come to speak such excellent English?"

"Ah. It's not such a mystery. I had an Irish nursemaid, and she taught me the language when I was a boy. I have read English books as often as I could to exercise my knowledge. Whenever I can, I speak English, like with you tonight. It is for this reason that I asked Alfonso to bring me a pretty English captive. But he did better than I asked. He brought me a beautiful Irish captive!"

Garcia finished his food service, poured more wine and returned to his place behind Don Francisco's chair. Don Francisco tackled a piece of meat with his knife and double-tined fork. Kath had never seen anyone eat with a fork and knife together in that way, but her agile fingers copied him with assurance.

"I see you know the fashion in Europe," Don Francisco commented, noticing. "I think you have been gentle born."

Kath smiled but said nothing, chewing demurely. The meat had been braised in wine with garlic and dried rosemary, things she had no knowledge of, and she had never tasted anything like it before.

Everything was foreign and fascinating. Silence reigned as they ate. If Don Francisco de Cornego believed her to be well born, so much the better. There was no need to tell him she was a criminal, an outcast from her own land. And there would be no way he could find out. Her secret was safe at last.

In any case, Don Francisco was a proud man. He would not deign to consort with her if he knew the truth. He would throw her out again, probably give her to the crew for their pleasure. She decided she would spin a pleasant tale for her antecedents. She would keep it simple, say nothing except in response to direct questions. She knew she could suggest a lot without saying things specifically.

"Will you read to me after supper, *Señora?*"

"With pleasure, Sir."

"Won't you call me Don Francisco? I am craving for female friendship. On board this ship, I am always *El Capitán.*"

Kath inclined her head graciously. She vowed she would try to think of herself as an aristocrat from now on. That way she might be able to pull off a rise above her station, if only for the time she was on this ship. She would try to remember everything her mother had taught her.

"And then I will read to you," Don Francisco continued. "And you must correct my pronunciation. I need to hear English and also to speak it." He wiped his mouth with the snowy napkin in his lap. Kath imitated him again. "Oh we shall have – how d'you say? – such a jolly time!"

"May I ask another question, Don Francisco? Why are you so keen to speak English?"

"More food, *Señora* O'Brien?" he asked.

Kath shook her head. "No thank you, Sir."

He spoke to Garcia, who cleared the table and left, leaving the wine.

Don Francisco leaned back in his chair, took a gold cigar case from his coat pocket and removed a cheroot. He closed the case, then flipped it open again and offered it to Kath. She shook her head. "Forgive that I smoke in your presence," he said. Kath smiled and inclined her head again.

Don Francisco held a candle to his cheroot and inhaled deeply, exhaling a fragrant cloud into the room. "You should try this tobacco, *Señora* O'Brien. It is the best – from Cuba."

"No thank you, Sir. I do not use tobacco."

Conversation ceased for a time, as Don Francisco savored his cigar. There was the inevitable sound of men pumping bilge. Kath hoped she had not angered him with her question.

"You asked about my desire for English," he said eventually. "It is that sometimes I have hours with little to do. My officers take care of the ship when there is no wind, or it is constant. At such times, she sails herself. When this happens,

I keep my mind busy." He took another drag from the cheroot.

"England and Spain have been enemies for centuries. We are always at war!" He chopped the air with his hand. "The English prey on Spanish settlements in the New World, and we Spanish return the favor, just as we raided your settlement today. The English license privateers to take our treasure ships, and we retaliate on any vessel that we suspect is English.

"Although we are not at war now – to my knowledge – it can change in a moment. Our most recent war, the War of Spanish Succession, ended only four years ago, after thirteen years.

"So I have a burning curiosity about the English. I read their books, their scientific papers, whatever my agents can find. To me, knowing my enemy is as important to defeating him as winning a battle." He puffed his cheroot, then watched through narrowed eyes as smoke curled from its tip. "Alfonso's instructions for today, in addition to bringing you back, was also to bring back any books or printed materials they found.

"The answer to your question is, I suppose, that I want to know English so I may do my best to beat the English. As I say, we are at peace, presently, but it pays a fighting *Capitán* always to be ready." He shifted in his chair, then took a sip of wine.

"If there is peace between England and Spain now," Kath said thoughtfully, "...weren't you concerned about sacking Fortune Island? It is English territory. What you did may cause hostilities again?"

"I gave it some thought, for perhaps five minutes. There is no English government in the *baja mar*. It is a place full of pirates. In any case, it would be six months at least before a report could reach London. By then I shall be long gone. Any complaints by the English to the Spanish Court could be countered by complaints from our side against the English. Also, by then, who knows? We may be at war again!"

He lifted quizzical eyebrows. "*Señora*, don't you believe me, that we attacked only because of necessity? I am not a thief."

"Yes, I do believe you," Kath said slowly, flushing. She looked down at her lap as the memory of Miz Eva and Treacle flashed to mind, along with the sight of the burning settlement.

She thought for a moment. "You mentioned earlier that the English licensed privateers to prey on Spanish ships. Are these pirates in Nassau licensed by the Crown, then?"

Don Francisco's mouth twisted in a bitter smile. "No. Privateers and pirates are not the same. Though they behave in the same way as far as we Spanish are concerned – and we hate them both alike – the English draw a fine distinction between them." He got up and walked to the balcony door, threw his cheroot end over the railing and returned to the table.

"*Privateers* are gentlemen licensed by the King of England to fit out ships for the purpose of plundering and destroying enemy ships during war time. Privateers operate under a *Letter of Marque*, a document that gives them permission to attack enemy vessels with impunity. For profit on their investment, they are able to keep any treasure they take.

"In a way, privateers are a free addition to the English Navy, since the King pays nothing for ships and men who essentially help to fight his war. When peace is declared, the Letters of Marque expire and anyone plundering a ship of the former enemy is liable to be prosecuted and hanged." Don Francisco fumbled in his pocket and drew out his cheroot case, selected another one and lit it.

"Now, *pirates*, on the other hand, are groups of men who band together on ships – almost always stolen – with the express purpose of plundering any other ships they come across. It matters not to them whether there is war or peace, or to which country the ship belongs," he said waving his hand in the air. "The ship might be Spanish, French, Dutch, Portuguese – or even English. Any ship is fair prey. Pirates are sea robbers, a mixture of the scum of all nations. They are without honor, or religion, or loyalty to anything but to greed and themselves."

He leaned back and puffed on his cheroot. Kath opened her mouth to speak, but he held up his hand. He was not through yet. "Pirates are vermin. Stinking, vile and despicable. They are like packs of starving dogs scavenging in a refuse heap. They can be incredibly cruel, maiming and disfiguring their victims for no reason other than it pleases them to do so. They are swarming in these islands, headquartered in New Providence Island. If there is only one thing you pray for, *Señora*, then let it be this: *Pray that you will never fall into the hands of a pirate.*"

Don Francisco looked at Kath, her eyes grown large in her stricken, white face. "Do not concern yourself, *Señora* O'Brien," he said lightly, teasing her. "I will protect you from the pirates! There is no need for you to have night horses about them!"

Kath replied with a tremulous smile.

"But about my lessons again, *Señora*. I hope it does not disturb you to teach someone who may beat the English one day?"

Kath looked up and smiled broadly. She liked this man, and if she managed things right, he might be her means to freedom and comfort. "It would be my great pleasure to help you in any way I can to defeat the English! Where is the book you would like me to read? Shall we begin at once?"

Don Francisco smiled back, a slow smile of complicity. He took another drag on his cheroot and looked across at Kath through the haze of smoke. She was past her prime, but still pretty. Her complexion was a little brown for his taste – she had neglected it on the island, and her hands were red and rough. It did not matter. With a little grooming, staying out of the sun, some fine clothes, she could be all he would need in Havana.

And she was intelligent! He was delighted to find that she was exceedingly intelligent.

28

Kath woke in the middle of the night to bellowed orders and feet thudding overhead. Slapping, swishing and banging noises erupted as sailors stowed or dragged things across the decks of the *Jacinta de Chavez*. Men sang a sea chantey at the capstan, winding in the anchor. Sails creaked and flapped, as they were hoisted up the masts, the ship's timbers vibrating with each onslaught. They were getting underway.

She flounced onto her side, punching the straw mattress into new heaps and valleys. She was drenched with sweat, especially her neck, entwined with long wet tendrils of hair. She gathered it in her hands, spreading it out above her head to dry.

The noises took her back to her dark, dank hold berth on the *Lydia*. She remembered how that ship's sounds had terrified her at first, compounding her anxiety about what would happen to her at her journey's end. Her stomach knotted just thinking about it. Eventually she had come to find the sounds commonplace, almost comforting, the metronome of her squalid, humdrum existence on board.

The *Jacinta de Chavez* made similar noises. Her heart began to flutter like a captured bird. Here she was again, a prisoner incarcerated in another dark hole on yet another stinking ship, although it was a palace in comparison. But once again she had no idea of where she was going, or of what her future would be. What were Don Francisco's intentions for her? He had been a perfect gentleman the night before, but she was not naïve enough to believe he only wanted English lessons.

She recalled the sounds of the *Swan*. How different they had been from those on these larger ships. Perhaps it was because the *Swan's* sounds had meant that she was alive and not going to die on that deserted island. She smiled to herself, remembering her first sight of Greville coming towards her on the beach. And afterwards, how he had lifted her out of the ship's boat, the look of his tidy Captain's cabin, the feel and scent of his sheets, his enormous clothes, the jokes and laughter and kindness of the crew. It had been like heaven.

She sighed. Those sounds had filled her with anxiety too, but anxiety of a different kind. She had known nothing, then, about where they were taking her, or how their families would treat her on their island. Her attraction to Greville and her own insecurity, her poverty and feelings of inequality, had added to her discomfort.

Her trance of recollections turned again to Fortune Island, to Miz Eva and Treacle, to Shirley, to the children she had taught and the other kind souls living there. How happy, how contented she had been! Had she ever found the island too small, its people too inquisitive, too narrow-minded? She swallowed painfully as a tear slid down her nose.

Soon the gurgle of water against the hull of the *Jacinta de Chavez* changed to the hushed swish and chuckle that meant the ship was under sail. Kath scrambled to stand on her berth and peer out of the porthole, hoping for one last look. All she saw was a black smear of land against the star-studded sky.

The ship tacked to leave the mouth of the harbor. Kath glimpsed Miz Eva's house on the hill, a blur of white. Its thatched roof seemed intact. Maybe her quick dousing of the kitchen fire had saved it for Greville. It comforted her to think so, that she might have been instrumental in protecting his property, though he would never know it.

At least the old ones, Miz Reena, Mr. Cartwright, would be able to shelter there. The others would find the sacks of food and the cooking pots she had hidden in the bushes near the kitchen, too. At least she had done something to benefit the people who had so kindly sheltered her.

Her throat tightened, and she swallowed the lump that *would* keep coming there. Would Miz Reena and Shirley remember that Miz Eva wanted to be buried out by her prayer rock? Maybe they would put Treacle in with her, for company. Kath stood with her face stuck against the porthole until the land fell away, until all she could see was a vast expanse of black ocean.

*

The following morning Kath heard the ship's bell ring for the third watch of the day. Eight o'clock! She was hungry and thirsty, she needed to get up and find out where she might get some breakfast. Memories of the succulent lamb from the night before swam in her mind, pungent, moist and tender. Her mouth watered. She went along to the galley and mimed her need for breakfast to the cook, who gave her a tankard of water and a ship's biscuit.

Kath rapped the biscuit sharply against the tabletop, watching as a couple of fat brown weevils wriggled out, mashing them one by one with her index fingernail. She had forgotten how noxious shipboard food was. Forgotten that it was better to have a wormy biscuit than one with weevils, because the weevils left an unpleasant aftertaste. It took some getting used to, but she had better begin. She sighed and soaked the biscuit in her tankard of water to soften it, then took a small bite, which turned to bitter paste as she chewed. She cleared the floating weevils from her water and drank some.

She was just washing down the last of her biscuit when the Captain's steward, Garcia, came below and handed her a bulging cloth sack. Again, all she could make out from his voluble Spanish was "*El Capitán,*" so she took his burden, smiled her thanks and headed back to her cabin. She shook the sack out on her bunk and gasped with surprise.

Out fell a skirt of rose watered silk, with a rose and cream striped silk petticoat, an embroidered bodice, stomacher and gauzy neck scarf. There was a clever little cap to match the ensemble, and dainty cream silk underwear, trimmed with lace. Kath avidly examined each piece.

Everything was cut in a new, foreign way. The stitches were so fine she could hardly see them in the dim cabin.

Her excitement mounted as she realized that there was still more to come from the sack. She upended it, to find an exquisite turtle-shell and silver hand mirror, nail buffer, comb and brush set, with two carved ivory combs for her hair. There was a small brush – for her teeth, she thought – a bar of soap, a bottle of toilet water and a jar of moisturizing cream. She held each item to her nose, her eyes closed in rapture. They all had the same delicate fragrance, floral, spicy, yet musky. She had never smelled anything so wonderful.

She sat on her bunk and hugged herself, rocking from side to side, her heart soaring. She had never seen such finery, let alone possessed it. Gently she stroked the silk, tracing the beautiful embroidery with her finger. She picked up the mirror and looked at her reflection in wonder. Face flushed, eyes sparkling, brimming with excitement. She noticed her widow's peak and sucked in her cheeks to enhance the heart shape of her face. A tendril of dark hair had escaped from beneath her cap and curled down onto her neck. Absently she tucked it back behind her ear. Then she jumped up and took off her dress – her Christmas dress, which she had thought so fine before.

Kath shook out the new silk petticoat and a piece of folded paper fell out. She stood on the bunk, holding the paper up to the porthole to read the spidery black handwriting.

My dear Señora O'Brien,
Please accept these Gifts as a Gesture of Reparation for the Loss of your Mother and Pet Dog. I know that Nothing I do or say can ever Ease this Pain. I am almost as Bereft as you are at being the Unwitting Cause of your Sorrow. I Beg that you will signify your Forgiveness by wearing this Apparel at Supper this Evening, when it will be my Pleasure to Present you to the rest of the

Ship's Company.

> *I am, Señora,*
> *Your Humble and Obedient Servant,*
> *Don Francisco Adriano de Cornego y*
> *Orlando.*

Kath sat down on the bunk, the letter still in her hand. She must try to think. She was so overwhelmed that it was hard to bring her thoughts together.

Should she accept this gift, given in atonement for the death of Miz Eva? Hopefully Don Francisco had the best intentions toward her. After all, she was completely in his power. He could do whatever he wished with her. She was his prisoner, his spoil of war. He did not have to shower her with silks, placate her with perfume. Besides, if she was to pass as Quality, she had better begin to look the part.

There was Don Francisco's own position to consider too. He wanted her to be his companion, to read and converse with, to dine with his officers. She had to dress in a manner befitting that position, so as not to shame him. He was an aristocrat, the Captain of this mighty ship, a proud and fastidious man.

Also, it was true that Miz Eva had attacked Alfonso from behind. Her death had been an accident. Besides, Miz Eva had told her the night before the raid that she was expecting to die soon and was actually looking forward to it. Since God had ordained Miz Eva's death, why should anyone feel guilty about it?

Miz Eva was dead. Nothing could change that. Fortune Island was hours of sailing time away. Greville Knowles had been a girlish dream, the prayer and hope of her lonely woman's heart. She had given him every chance, every encouragement, but he had never spoken to her of love or a future together. She had best get over him and the sooner the better. Now another life beckoned.

The night before, after she and Don Francisco had read to each other, she had stood and stretched, then walked out onto the balcony. She had looked over at Fortune Island, silently brooding in the starlight. A faint whiff from its smoldering shacks floated acrid on the night air. She had leaned over the railing, wondering if she could climb up and jump. Would she survive the long plummet to the sea? If she did, if she could manage to swim with her heavy wet skirts, would the Spanish let her go, or would they fire their muskets into her flailing body? And, if she made it to the shore, what future lay there for her now?

She caressed her new finery, touching each of the toilet articles, tracing the silver inlay and the beautiful patterns in the gleaming turtle-shell. She smoothed some of the cream on her face, then rubbed a little into her hands, cupped them over her nose and inhaled deeply.

She sighed. She was in Don Francisco's power, like it or not. He could do whatever he chose with her. She could be outraged and difficult, or try to charm him and win him over.

You can catch more flies with honey than you can with vinegar, she thought. She would wear Don Francisco's finery, would ask him to teach her Spanish, take an interest in his books and ideas. She would grasp this chance for a privileged new life, and put the past behind her.

What's more, Don Francisco was a Catholic. *He even traveled with his own priest!* Miz Eva always said that God has a plan for everyone who listens to His voice. Well, perhaps this was God's plan for her life, to bring her back into a state of grace.

Anyway, it was the best plan that anybody had ever offered her. And it was all she could see to do in the circumstances.

29

Kath spent the rest of the day in her cabin, thinking and mourning. Sweet memories of Miz Eva crowded into her mind, abruptly interrupted by flashbacks of her body, lying crumpled and bleeding on the sandy soil.

She knew that this new adventure would help her to forget, in time. On the *Lydia*, Ireland had receded to unreality, still living in the court of her memory, but without urgency. Later, her shipwreck island had made the horrors of the *Lydia* recede, just as thoughts of Fortune Island had replaced the misery of her shipwreck.

Fortune Island would slip into that same hazy part of her heart, poignant with love and longing, but without today's searing agony. She had only to steel herself and wait it out. There was no escaping the pain in the present, however. Although it would come and go, with gradually diminishing intensity, it would not leave her soon. Diversion beckoned from these gifts and the elevated society of the Captain's cabin, but Don Francisco had been right. No words, no gifts, could spare her the anguish of Miz Eva's loss.

*

About five o'clock there was a tap at her door. She opened it to find Garcia proffering a bucket of seawater and a towel. Kath smiled her gratitude. She needed a wash before dressing for the party. Suddenly she felt a delicious nervousness, a tingling throughout her body, like a young girl the first time she was going to meet her lover. She dressed in a fever of apprehension.

An hour later, Garcia returned and escorted her to the quarterdeck. Once more came the signal tap on the ornate door, the luxurious great cabin opening before her, bathed in candlelight. Don Francisco made his courtly bow as the cabin door closed behind her, the click of the latch sounding strangely intimate... and somehow ominous.

"Good evening, *Señora* O'Brien" Don Francisco said, his accented tenor voice a honeyed purr.

Blushing, Kath dropped her eyes and swept the floor with a curtsy. "Good evening, Don Francisco," she said, her voice husky. She staggered slightly as she stood again, her knees unsteady. Her stomach fluttered as though she had swallowed one of the giant brown moths that flew during summer evenings at Fortune Island.

Don Francisco's hooded eyes glittered as his mouth curved in a slow, knowing smile. A smile of possession, Kath realized with a pang.

"I am gratified that you wear your new garments tonight. I am forgiven, no?"

"Yes Sir. There is nothing to forgive," she said, still flustered. She looked down at the dress, smoothing her skirts, then met his eyes. "I thank you for these lovely things. Indeed, I must thank you for everything."

"You are beautiful, *Señora* O'Brien. More beautiful than I had imagined. I admire your hair up like that. And the gown suits you well."

Heat flamed to her face and neck, then receded. "T-thank you, Sir. The clothes are a trifle large, but if you have a needle and thread, I can alter them."

"As you wish."

He moved to the table, where he unstopped the decanter of sherry and poured two glasses. "My officers are interested to meet you. I often bring something curious aboard ship, and they want to see my new pet."

He passed her a glass. "I have told them that this time my pet is a pretty, small animal, but she is mine alone. They are not to stroke her, nor give her sweetmeats, nor in any way to seek her affection."

"I shall snarl and snap should anyone try to do so, Sir."

He smiled and tipped his head. "See that you do... and report it to me. Only remember – show to *me* no fangs and claws..."

He held up his own glass for a toast. "Let us drink to our friendship and to happy hours together."

As they sipped, Garcia knocked. The door opened to admit the ship's surgeon, the priest and six others. Don Francisco introduced everyone, but between the unfamiliar Spanish names and titles, and his thick accent, Kath was none the wiser.

"None of my men speak English. It is unfortunate, but you have only myself with whom to speak."

"I should like to learn Spanish, Sir, if you can spare the time."

"Indeed, yes, it will become necessary for you. We are going to live in Havana, which is a territory of *España*. You will soon pick it up." He smiled again, that new, oily smile, between a leer and a smirk.

"We shall amuse ourselves in English, *Señora*. We will be always alone in that language, no matter who is present. We can be as rude as we like, without penalty."

Garcia poured sherry for everyone, then left. The men stood awkwardly in small groups, speaking in low tones, watching Kath surreptitiously.

Soon Garcia returned along with two other sailors and trays of food. Dinner was served, with Kath being seated on the Captain's right and the priest on his left. The officers ate with restraint, their conversation stilted. Kath thought they seemed embarrassed.

Kath had noticed during the introductions that one officer in particular had regarded her with hostile eyes, under bushy, caterpillar-like brows. Now she was aware that he glanced in her direction from time to time with unconcealed dislike. Although she was glad of a meal after her day's fast, the food stuck in her throat and she ate sparingly.

Padre Bonifacio said something to Kath in Spanish, which

Don Francisco translated with a wicked gleam in his eye.

"He wants to know why you did not attend Mass this morning, *Señora*."

"Please tell him that I didn't know what time it was held. Also, that I do not know my way about this ship."

He translated this, then turned to her again. "You had but to ask, *Señora*. You are not to consider yourself a prisoner here," he said mildly.

"I did think of it, Sir. I have not attended Mass in over a year and I need to make my confession. But when I thought that it was to be a Mass of Thanksgiving, I did not feel able to attend. I could not put my heart into thanking God for the slaughter of my mother, or the burning and looting of Fortune Island, after all."

Don Francisco inhaled sharply, his eyes registering hurt. It was as though she had slapped him. A chilly silence ensued for a time, then Don Francisco turned to Padre Bonifacio and the two began an animated conversation. In due course, he turned back to Kath.

"Did you notice that the wind dropped this morning?" he asked her courteously. "We were in one of those times I told you about last night. Did you wonder why I did not send for you?"

"No, Sir. But I noticed that we were hardly moving, and that it was very hot."

"Yes. Well, during that time, the lookout spotted a sail. We could not see what ship it was, or its flag. As I am still hoping to reunite with my flotilla, we took off sail and went very slowly, to wait on the other ship. The wind picked up this afternoon, so we anchored. It is not wise to sail at night in the *baja mar* in any case. Here one must cast the lead always, and look carefully at the color of the water. They will probably anchor too, and reach us in the morning."

"Suppose it is not one of your ships?"

"We are not at war with England or France at the moment. The Portuguese are our neighbors. The Dutch will not touch us. If they be pirates..." he shrugged. "We are a large frigate, manned by good trained men, with 40 cannon and adequate munitions. We would blow them into toothpicks. They would never dare take us on."

"You are not at war, but still you attacked Fortune Island. Suppose the English retaliate towards you now? And suppose they come in the night?"

"Do you question my decisions, *Señora?*" Don Francisco asked with narrowed eyes, his tanned face darkening. "I assure you that we are safe. That is enough for you. I do not tolerate contradiction." A muscle twitched in his jaw. *This is always the trouble with intelligent females*, he thought. *They think their own thoughts and that they know everything. I will have to curb this one sharply.*

Kath blanched, then turned crimson. She stared down at her plate through a blur of humiliated tears. "I-I beg your pardon, Sir," she managed to croak. "I did not mean to question your decision but only to converse."

"I, too, am sorry," he said, only slightly mollified. "It is early between us. You will come to understand my temperament. You will learn that I will not accept disloyalty."

Kath wanted the floor to open and swallow her. The others at table could not understand the conversation, but sensed the tone. They shifted uncomfortably in their places, glancing at each other. She picked up her fork and took a bite of meat, but it was like chewing string. The flint-eyed officer met her eyes, his mouth twisting in a derisive smile. Desperate, Kath changed the subject.

"Why does that man stare at me so?" she asked, inclining her head towards her antagonist. "Why does he dislike me?"

"Fernandez?" Don Francisco shrugged. "It is not personal, nor does it matter. Possibly he resents you because I have given you his cabin. He has had to sling his hammock in with the common sailors and he is not happy about it."

"I don't wish to take his cabin, Sir. I am happy to sleep in any corner."

Don Francisco raised one eyebrow and smiled, picking up his wine goblet. "You are sure? You wish to give Fernandez back his cabin?"

"Yes, Sir. I do not wish to be the cause of anyone's discomfort."

"So be it. I will make arrangements."

He said something in Spanish that caused a ripple of surprise at the table. Fernandez nodded and smiled slightly, looking smug. Garcia refilled the wine goblets, then left, closing the door softly behind him. He returned a few minutes later with a canvas duffel bag, which he put on top of a sea chest near the bed, beneath the gold crucifix.

Kath immediately had misgivings. What had she done? But Don Francisco seemed very pleased with himself and she was afraid of putting her foot wrong again. She decided to leave well enough alone until everyone left. Then she would ask Don Francisco where she was to sleep.

At last the ordeal of supper ended. Garcia poured brandy for everyone except Kath and passed around a box of Don Francisco's Cuban cigars. Kath excused herself and went onto the balcony to enjoy the night air.

The *Jacinta de Chavez* lay in a wide bay, near an island. A white sandy beach glowed softly in the starlight. It would be wonderful to walk on that beach and to feel the cool sand between her toes! Once more Kath debated jumping, but this time the thought of being stranded on another uninhabited island stopped her short. Any fate would be better than that.

She sagged against the railing, her head in one hand, looking up at the star spangled sky. She cringed inwardly as she thought about the dinner. She must take more care, weigh her words. Don Francisco had already indicated that he was embarrassed and ashamed about sacking Fortune Island. Why did she have to mention it again? And not just once, but twice! She shuddered. This new life was going to be fraught with difficulties. She knew nothing about being gentry, never mind the Spanish. Don Francisco was both, and a cultivated, complicated man as well.

She sighed. It was a relief to be alone with her thoughts again, if only for a few minutes. Then she thought she heard a splash, and she peered intently in the direction of the sound. Gradually her eyes focused on something dark moving in the water, some distance away. She shrugged. Probably off-watch crew going night fishing in a boat.

*

"*Señora* O'Brien!" Don Francisco called gaily out to her. "Come... we are going to have music now."

Kath gave a final, longing look at the ocean and went back into the smoky cabin. Everyone was standing. Don Francisco held a guitar, another man had a flute, while a third held two small, rounded pieces of wood in each hand, and was making a rattling, clacking noise with them.

"We often amuse ourselves after dinner in this way," the Captain explained, strumming his guitar, then playing a few bars of a plaintive melody. Looking around, Kath noticed that one of the common seamen had joined them.

"This is Carlos Sanchez," Don Francisco said. "He is a gypsy, from Seville. He is going to dance tonight in your honor, *Señora*. We will go out on the quarterdeck so that others can enjoy our music too. I have ordered a special issue of wine."

Each of the men took a chair from the table and headed out. Garcia took two chairs.

Don Francisco and Kath were alone in the cabin for a moment. She put a hand on his arm. "I beg your pardon for speaking as I did during supper," she said. "It was unforgivable. It is just that I am still mourning my mother."

"See that it does not happen again," he replied, tersely. "I warned you not to bite me. I will not put up with it, *Señora*."

Her face flamed. "No Sir."

"Let us forget it and enjoy the music now." He bowed and ushered her through the cabin door and onto the quarterdeck.

*

Enjoy it she did. There was singing and dancing such as Kath had never heard nor seen. Carlos Sanchez was a balding, portly man in his thirties, but he became something quite different when he danced. He stamped and snapped his fingers, throwing his head back in abandon with ululating cries. His audience clapped and yipped; his *Capitán* played with fire, slapping the box of his guitar to emphasize the beat. The castanets rattled away feverishly. Everyone seemed mesmerized by the music and the dancing.

When Sanchez cried off, bathed in sweat, the tempo slowed. Another man sang a haunting ballad, accompanied by the flute and Don Francisco's guitar. Then there were several guitar solos, then flute, back and forth, with various men singing.

"Do you sing, *Señora*?" Don Francisco asked Kath during a break.

"Yes, I do, a little. Would you like me to sing something from Ireland?"

"Oh yes, please!"

Everyone quieted when Kath stood up. She sang *'Danny Boy'*, her lovely voice soaring out into the night. She saw dreamy pleasure on Don Francisco's face as he listened, and the sight freed something in her bosom. She felt elated, powerful, and she knew that she had never sung better. When the last note died away, there was silence for a moment, then everyone applauded, with some of the crew banging the deck with their tankards.

"The men want you to sing some more," Don Francisco said.

Kath glowed. "If you wish. Do you know *'Greensleeves'* Sir?" and she hummed a few bars.

"Yes, of course, we sing it in *España*."

And so, far into the night, the people of the *Jacinta de Chavez* made merry.

30

Rosy with elation, Kath followed Don Francisco back into his cabin at the end of the concert.

"That was the most wonderful music!"

"I'm glad you enjoyed yourself, *Señora*. I am so happy that you sing, too. You have a beautiful voice! In Havana, we will have many soirees. When I am in port, I am the leader of culture there. No one can play the guitar as well as I, and of course I am invited everywhere. You must learn to sing Spanish songs, my little pet. I will take you with me, to sing."

"Oh yes! I would love that, Don Francisco."

"Would you, my little chicken?" He tipped her chin with one hand, bent his head and gave her a sensuous kiss.

Heat flashed through her body like lightning. She did not know whether it was desire or alarm, but her reaction was automatic. She slapped him.

"Sir! You forget yourself!" Kath said, stepping back and wiping her mouth with the back of her hand.

He reared his head. "Forget myself? *Forget myself?* No, *Señora*, it is you who forget. Do not play the virgin with me!"

He grasped her by the shoulders and crushed her roughly to him. She could smell his scent, a mixture of citrus cologne, tobacco, alcohol and stale sweat. She felt her heart pounding wildly against his. His mouth ground against hers, her head held fast by one of his hands entangled in her hair. When he had kissed her thoroughly, he let go. She staggered back against the edge of the table, panting.

Don Francisco laughed. He lurched towards her again, his face slack with lust.

"Stop! You led me to think you were a gentleman. Now you take advantage of me?"

"What is this?" he demanded, looking bewildered. "Take advantage? Certainly not! You have been asking for this all evening."

"Indeed not, Sir! What gave you that idea?"

Anger blazed in his eyes. "You wore the clothing I sent you. You accepted my presents. I was surprised, I thought it would be harder to win you. Then you come into my cabin blushing and flirting, smiling little secret smiles, dropping your eyes..."

Kath gasped. Her face turned as pale as wax, then flooded with blood.

"...And if that was not enough," Don Francisco continued, "...you dismissed the cabin I had provided for you, using the excuse that you wished not to inconvenience Fernandez. Ha! What was I to think? *Señora?*"

"It didn't mean that I was to be your strumpet, Sir!"

"What did it mean, then? Where do you think you can sleep, if not in my bed?"

"I-in *your* bed?" Kath asked incredulously. "I had no such thought..."

"Tell me where, then. You are on a ship with ninety-seven men. Where will you sleep? In a hammock below decks with the common seamen? On the deck? I assure you, I do not plan to give up my cabin!"

"N-no, of course not..." Kath stuttered. "I had not thought, Sir."

"Well, you had better think now, *Señora!*" Kath stood in consternation before him, wringing her hands.

"Bah! It is your problem!" he said, turning towards his bed. "It is time to sleep. I have a full day tomorrow. I will be meeting my other ships. It is late, and I am tired. I am not going to stand arguing with a stupid woman who behaves like a child."

"Where shall I sleep, then?" Kath asked in a small voice.

"With the devil, for all I care!" He walked over to the

226

trunk where Garcia had put the duffel bag he had brought in during supper. "Here are your things," he said, tossing the bag on the floor. Then he opened the chest, took out a blanket and pillow, and threw them on the floor as well. "...And here is a bed. Sleep where you want, and the devil take you."

Don Francisco strode over to his bed and began undressing, beginning with his wig. Kath was amazed to see that his head was completely bald. Next came his coat, waistcoat and shirt, which he flung on a hanger and slammed into a locker. He sat on the bed to take off his shoes, and Kath spun around to look in the opposite direction.

She did not know what to do. She was wearing the most beautiful clothes she had ever seen. She could not sleep in them, but she did not feel comfortable taking them off. She sidled over to the duffel bag and took out her bloodstained, everyday dress. She could sleep in that, but how would she undress and get into it?

Don Francisco's shoes hit the floor. She heard him stand up again, then fumble with his breeches. Scarlet with embarrassment, she grabbed the duffel bag and raced out onto the balcony.

"Do not think you will shut those doors, *Señora*," he said bitingly. "I sleep with them open in the tropics, and I sleep naked. But have no fear, you are safe with me. It is beneath me to struggle for my pleasures." He blew out the candles. "I bid you good night."

When her eyes grew accustomed to the dark, she took off the fine dress and put on her old one, then crept back into the cabin to find the pillow and blanket. The bare plank floor of the balcony was slick with dew. Kath curled onto her side, then tried to get comfortable on her back. She had a sour stomach from the rich food and wine. Her head ached. She looked up at the sky, extravagant with stars, and bit her lip.

Where are you, Miz Eva? She wondered. *Are you up there with God and the Blessed Virgin and Jesus and Joseph? Are you walking on streets of gold and drinking crystal clear water from the river of life? Can you see me? Do you know how much I miss you?*

Just then, a falling star shot through the sky. It seemed like a sign. Miz Eva was safe, with God and His angels. And Kath knew that she was happy, there with her Lovely Lord Jesus.

*

Kath woke with a start, her heart thumping. She sat up, listening carefully, waiting until the blood roar in her ears calmed. What was that loud bang? It sounded like an explosion. She looked around. Dawn was breaking; there was the merest hint of pearly gray on the eastern horizon. She crouched on her knees and peered around the balcony door into the dark cabin. Don Francisco had heard it too. He was sitting on the edge of his bed, reaching for his clothing.

There was a sharp knock on the door of the cabin before it was wrenched open and two men ran in, shouting in Spanish. Don Francisco asked a staccato question, hurriedly stuffed one leg into his breeches and started hopping towards the door, trying to get his other leg clothed. The three rushed out together. The ship was in an uproar, with loud, jabbered Spanish and shouted Anglo-Saxon profanity.

Kath ran to the cabin's front door and looked out. The main deck of the ship was crawling with men, waving cutlasses and muskets, and herding the Spanish sailors into groups. Their leader was a tall, wiry man dressed in a blue and white checked shirt, open at the neck, and wide, baggy red pants hanging to just above his bare feet. There was a red stocking cap on his head and a red sling holding four pistols across his chest. He had a dagger at his waist, shoved into a thick leather belt, from which hung a sword and three square case-bottles.

"You the Captain?" he demanded of Don Francisco in a hoarse voice. "You speak English?" Profanity punctuated everything he said.

"Yes, I am Captain Don Francisco Adriano de Cornego y Orlando, and I speak English," he replied with dignity. "Who are you?"

"John Martin, quartermaster under Captain Benjamin

Hornigold. Go pay your respects! Get your boat!"

"What the devil d'you mean, Sirrah? Who're you to order me about?"

"I mean, you dog, that we've taken your ship as a prize." He shoved the muzzle of a pistol into Don Francisco's chest, swearing vilely. "Now, get your scurvy backside in a boat, go over to that sloop and pay your respects to our Captain Hornigold," he said, pointing the cutlass in his other hand off the ship's starboard side.

Don Francisco's eyes followed, and he gaped in disbelief. There was a fine 65-foot sloop-of-war, with *Bonnet* proudly scrolled in gold on her dark blue bow. She was riding low in the water, her long, graceful lines and figurehead belying her sinister purpose, confirmed by the black flag at her masthead. Ten cannon bristled from open ports, and four swivel guns mounted on her rails pointed directly at the *Jacinta de Chavez*.

Don Francisco ordered his boat and waited, slumped against the ship's rail, one hand on his forehead.

"Hoy, you there, Craddock," John Martin shouted to one of his ruffians. "Did you find the woman?"

"Not yet. She's probably in the great cabin."

"I'll look. Everything's under control here now," he said, turning to mount the stairs to the quarterdeck.

*

Kath's blood turned to ice water. How did they know about her?

She looked around frantically to see where she could hide, but there was no time. She ran back onto the balcony and hid behind the door, looking into the cabin through the crack of the hinge.

In a moment, Martin was in the cabin. "Come out, Mistress," he called, looking under the bed, behind the drapes, rummaging in the chests. "We know you're here. We won't hurt you!" Suddenly noticing the tangled bedding on the balcony floor, he came out and jerked the door back, slamming it shut.

"Peek-a-boo! I found you!" he sang, wagging his head as though talking to a baby. He was a man in his early thirties, with greasy, crinkly dark hair escaping from his cap. His beaked nose and receding chin gave him the look of a ferret, and he stank of unwashed clothes, sweat, tobacco and rum. His grin showed rotten black teeth.

Kath stared at him, her green eyes huge.

"You come with me," he said, breaking her state of paralysis. "Captain Hornigold wants to see you. You're the one sang last night?"

Kath nodded dumbly.

"Any other women on board?"

She shook her head.

"Do as I say. Don't try any tricks. It's not worth what'll happen to ye. What's your name?"

"K-Kath O'Brien." Her voice came out high and squeaky.

"All right." He put his hand on her shoulder and led her ahead of him through the cabin and onto the quarterdeck. "Stay right here, in sight. Ye'll not be harmed."

"Thank you, Sir," Kath replied.

Martin cocked an eyebrow as he turned away. "Humph! *That's* a first..."

31

Captain Benjamin Hornigold looked up from the chart spread out on the large mahogany table and smiled a welcome at Captain Don Francisco de Cornego, who followed one of the pirates into the great cabin of the *Bonnet*. Hornigold rose from his chair, rolled up the chart and put it back on the table beside a pistol lying there. He straightened his blue brocade coat, stepped around the table towards his guest, and stretched out his hand. He wore a darker blue silk sling over one shoulder holding four pistols. A sword dangled from his left hip.

"Good morning, Sir. I am Captain Benjamin Hornigold. Welcome aboard!" he said affably, his teeth glistening between his gingery beard and mustache. He was a stocky man, barrel-chested, with receding sandy hair worn in a tarred pigtail at the back. He had shrewd blue eyes, nestled in a web of crow's feet. Broken veins on his weathered cheeks betrayed his liking for drink. Thick gold earrings shone from his ears. He gave an overall impression of geniality, capability, strength – and menace.

"I am Don Francisco Adriano de Cornego y Orlando," his visitor replied, hesitating before reaching to grasp his host's hand, "... *El Capitán* of the ship *Jacinta de Chavez*, out of Cadiz, España."

"Pleased to meet you, Sir, and very sorry for your troubles. Bad luck, I say."

Don Francisco gave him a savage look, then stared out a porthole, his eyes glittering. His hands gave a violent twitch,

231

and he clasped them together behind his back. "As you say, Captain Hornigold. Bad luck."

"Would you like some breakfast? Our cook is preparing salmagundi this morning, using a sea turtle we caught yesterday. It's my favorite, and he does a creditable job."

"No thank you, Sir."

"Still a trifle early for you, perhaps. Well, we have some Jamaica coffee aboard. Might do you good, with a little rum." Captain Hornigold rang, and someone came in with a fragrant pot of coffee. "Please sit, Sir. Make yourself comfortable," Hornigold said, pouring coffee and adding rum from a silver flask. He pushed a long-stemmed clay pipe towards his guest, along with a small leather pouch of tobacco, then took a sip of the coffee. He sighed in appreciation.

"Well, Captain Cornego, you are from Cadiz, Spain. And whither bound?"

"To Santiago de Cuba."

"With what cargo?"

Don Francisco's lip curled and he held his head a little higher. "No cargo. We are not merchants, Sir. We are a naval Frigate of His Majesty King Philip V of Spain."

"Indeed!" A look of annoyance flashed across Captain Hornigold's face and he swore fluently. Rotten luck, finding a ship on its way to pick up treasure, rather than on its return, heavily laden. Still, the King of Spain would not be sending an empty ship. There was bound to be something valuable in its holds, some domestic products that his loyal subjects in Cuba would pay dearly for. His countenance cleared as he reached for a pipe and began to stuff it with tobacco.

"Where is your gold?" he asked conversationally.

"We have no gold." Don Francisco sniffed and looked out the cabin door.

Captain Hornigold picked up his pistol from the table and idly cocked it. He looked calmly at Don Francisco and pointed the pistol at his chest. "Valuables, then, Captain. Jewels. Any interesting trinkets. Let's not quibble about this."

"There is a chest in my cabin. I'm sure your men have

found it. It's in plain view."

Hornigold nodded casually, then sprang forward in his chair, the pistol muzzle pressed hard against Don Francisco's jugular. "Anything else you want to tell me? It will go hard for you if we find more than you told us. Rest assured we'll look." Hornigold smiled nastily. "Believe me, my men are thorough lookers."

The suddenness of his movement and the cold steel of the pistol unnerved Don Francisco. He looked into Hornigold's narrowed eyes, as cold and steely as the gun. "T-there is some gold in the ceiling of my cabin. M-my carpenter will get it for you."

Hornigold continued to stare into Don Francisco's eyes, pressing the pistol harder into his neck. The Don's brow gleamed wetly, and a trickle of sweat coursed down his temple. "Anything more?"

"No! I swear. Any other riches are displayed in my cabin, for everyone to see."

Finally, satisfied, Captain Hornigold relaxed back in his chair and took another sip of coffee.

*

Kath watched from the quarterdeck as the pirates methodically frisked each man of the frigate's crew. Meanwhile, other pirates disabled the cannon on the *Jacinta de Chavez* by hammering nails into their touch-holes. Then all the ammunition, gunpowder and weapons were loaded into the *Bonnet*, which was now tied up alongside.

Martin separated the Spaniards. Don Francisco de Cornego, several of his officers and about a third of the crew had been taken aboard the *Bonnet*. The pirates put the rest to work helping them plunder the *Jacinta de Chavez*. Piles of clothing, valuables, extra sails and ropes, as well as spirits and foodstuffs grew on the main deck. There were also bolts of expensive cloth, lace and other luxury Spanish goods.

Don Francisco's cabin was the first area they stripped. Several of the pirates dressed up in the captain's elegant clothes. They put on his wigs and powdered their faces, like gentlemen of fashion. Plumed hats under their arms, they pranced about the deck in the Don's high-heeled shoes, bowing to one another, flourishing lacy shirt cuffs and brocaded coats while cursing in an affected falsetto. Their shipmates, well tanked with the *Jacinta's* spirits, gave them a raucous reception. Even the Spaniards had to laugh, despite their dire situation.

The men took a break mid-morning. Captain Hornigold came aboard the *Jacinta de Chavez* and inspected the ship and their plunder. Then he introduced himself to Kath. He had one of the pirates bring them some ale.

"So you're the lass who sang Irish songs last night?" he asked.

"Yes, Sir."

"We were anchored around that headland. I sent some of my men to reconnoiter in a boat and I was standing on deck, listening to the music. Water has a way of amplifying sound, you know. Suddenly you began to sing and tears sprang to my eyes. You made me think of my mother and sisters, of my home in England, lost to me now these many years. We used to sing a great deal at home, when I was a lad."

"We did, too, Sir."

"Where are you from? How come you to be on a Spanish naval frigate?"

"I'm from Ireland, Sir. And my story is a long one. But I'm on board because Don Francisco de Cornego's men captured me three days ago at Fortune Island. And I was on Fortune Island because of shipwreck, and being found and taken there by Captain Greville Knowles in the *Swan*."

"So *you're* the mermaid we heard about in Nassau! Perhaps you'll tell me your story one day." There was such a yearning in his eyes that Kath's heart softened towards him.

"Only if you will tell me your own story in return, Sir. Yours is bound to be more interesting than mine."

"Yes..." he agreed, looking away, then back at her. "I've had an interesting life, as you say. I've been many places, seen and done many things that I never dreamt of as a lad." His voice caught, and he gripped the railing convulsively, his tanned hands whitening with the pressure. "Unfortunately, Mistress O'Brien, many of the things I have done and seen I am too ashamed to recount." He looked out to sea, then back into her face. "But I'll tell you the good things. There have been one or two of those!"

"I'll look forward to hearing them, Sir."

"Now tell me. How long were you on board the *Jacinta de Chavez*? How did the Captain and his officers treat the common sailors? Did you notice anything in particular?" he asked.

Kath thought for a moment. "The men seem fond of the Captain. Also, he gave a dinner for his officers and made a party for the crew afterwards. He issued extra wine, so they would have a good time. I would say he commands respect, but treats them very well."

"And the officers?"

"I couldn't say, Sir. I've not noticed any cruelty, but then I do not speak the language. Nor have I been in amongst them."

Captain Hornigold nodded his thanks, then sent a pirate to summon Don Francisco back onto the quarterdeck of the *Jacinta de Chavez* to share a bowl of rum punch.

Kath was surprised at Hornigold's civil manner. From the stories told about the New Providence pirates, she knew that Hornigold was one of the main villains. Indeed, he was the 'Governor of the Pirate Republic,' as they styled their settlement at Nassau. Strangely enough, he didn't seem so terrible to her. He cursed and drank a lot, like the rest of his crew, but beneath his swagger he seemed like an ordinary working man. He treated Don Francisco politely in spite of the Spaniard's peevish indignation.

She stood in the sun watching the two men together. She wondered what would happen if the other Spanish ships arrived. What would happen to her? What would her life be like with either of these men?

She remembered Don Francisco's icy manner the night

before, as soon as he thought she was his possession. If she went with him to Cuba, she would be in a Catholic country, but she would be among strangers.

She would have to depend upon Don Francisco for everything. He had changed from a courteous host into an imperious master in a matter of moments. Would she enjoy being at his mercy for the rest of her life, no matter how comfortable her physical circumstances? Kath shuddered at the thought. Moreover, she felt that Don Francisco would quickly tire of his pets. She might soon have to earn her living in a place where she could not even speak the language.

As she watched the two men, Captain Hornigold looked up, his homely face crinkling into a smile. "Your good health," he said, tipping his tankard towards her.

Suddenly Kath knew what to do. "When you have a moment, I should like to speak to you, Captain Hornigold," she said.

32

Captain Hornigold sent Don Francisco back onto the *Bonnet* and crowded his own men onto the quarterdeck and in the great cabin of the *Jacinta de Chavez* for a general council meeting, since the company of pirates decided everything by majority rule.

"The woman tells me that there may be two other Spanish ships nearby," he said, looking around at his men. "The *Jacinta de Chavez* anchored last night because they thought our sails were their ships. We must think what's best to do."

The men looked at one another, excitement and greed dancing in their eyes. John Martin was the first to speak. "The *Bonnet* is heavily laden now," he said, "...and her bottom is foul. We were heading to Exuma to clean her when we spotted the *Jacinta de Chavez*. We can't take on two Spanish war ships in this condition. I say we go on our business, careen the sloop and divide the booty."

One burly pirate spoke out. "Why? We can do that later. Let's look for them. We might be foul, but they're worse, after crossing the Atlantic."

"We spiked 40 guns on the *Jacinta*," Martin replied. "How many do you think the other two have? They'd cut us to pieces."

The noisy debate went back and forth, between avarice and commonsense. Finally, the company decided to run with what they had. Then the meeting went on, deciding what to do with the *Jacinta de Chavez*, her Captain and officers. As they had treated their crew decently, they were not 'disciplined'.

The pirates voted to make the Spanish cook roast several of the sheep for their dinner, and to put the whole Spanish crew ashore for the night without a boat. Then the pirates could enjoy their dinner and make merry, while the Spanish listened and slapped at mosquitoes. It was only fair.

They also decided that they would take Kath with them.

*

The quartermaster detailed George Rounsivell, a large, raw-boned lad of about seventeen, to guard Kath below, in one of the officer's cabins.

Kath's anxiety mounted, as the men grew louder and drunker on deck. The musicians struck up and they danced and sang. About dusk, George brought her roast mutton and wine, staying to talk for a few minutes.

She felt better after the food and started to consider what her strategy should be. New Providence was two or three weeks' sail away, depending on the wind, with time added for careening the *Bonnet*. That was a long time to be alone with eighty drinking men. Would they continue to leave her alone? George had told her that, as long as she was on board the vessel, their Ship's Articles would protect her. Once they were ashore, though, anything could happen.

Her courage sank when she thought about the days to come. She must win the protection of one of the men who could defend her on the island somehow. Who would be better than Captain Benjamin Hornigold?

*

The pirates disabled the *Jacinta de Chavez* by chopping her mainmast and stealing her mainsails the following day. She would be unable to chase them and would have to head for Santiago de Cuba immediately, even if her flotilla found her.

The *Bonnet* weighed anchor and headed for the island of Great Exuma, where the men knew of a hidden cove ideally suited for careening. As the *Bonnet* slipped away from the *Jacinta de Chavez*, she passed the longboat bringing Captain

Don Francisco Cornego back from the island. The pirates gave him a clamorous goodbye, waving and whistling and shouting insults. Don Francisco shook his fist at them, which made the pirates roar with laughter.

Early that afternoon, the lookout spotted two sails coming towards them. This news threw the pirates into a tizzy. "Look what Providence has sent us," Captain Hornigold crowed, doing a little jig. "Two more unfortunate Spanish vessels as a sacrifice!" They took off sail, then each man made his weapons ready and prepared the *Bonnet* for action.

The on-coming ships were making good speed and Captain Hornigold was soon able to identify them with his glass. They were the *Success* and the *Greyhound*, out of Port Royal, Jamaica.

"No luck, lads, stand down," Captain Hornigold said. "These are Captain John West and Captain Holford, our good friends from Jamaica. We'll wait and see what news there is, and invite them to supper." The ships were in hailing distance within the hour. Captains West and Holford came aboard the *Bonnet*, welcomed with a large bowl of punch. The three captains exchanged the usual compliments, and soon settled with their drinks and pipes.

"Hornigold, we've been sent by Governor Heywood to find you," Captain West said, looking serious. He leaned forward to pass Hornigold a printed flyer. "Look at this."

" 'By the King – A Proclamation for Suppressing of Pirates' " Hornigold read aloud. "What's this, West?"

"It's an Act of Pardon from King George. It gives pirates up to a year to surrender to a Royal governor. If they do, they'll be pardoned. If they don't, they'll be hunted down with a large price on their heads. The Governor thought you should know about it as soon as possible, maybe call a general council in Nassau so you can discuss it."

"We're headed there now, after we careen," Hornigold replied. "What say you, Holford?"

"I've surrendered already. I think the best days for freebooters are over, anyway. Since the war ended in '14, every rogue seaman calls himself pirate. What's more, the King must find work for his idle Navy fleet. What better employment than hunting down pirates?"

Hornigold took a swig of punch and wiped his mouth with the back of his hand. He shifted in his chair and looked up, watching the water reflections dance and sway on the ceiling, enjoying the slight rock as his sweet *Bonnet* moved with the ocean swell. *Ye gads, she was a pretty lass*! She was a Jamaica sloop, made of red cedar. She had a steeply raked mast and raised gunwales, to protect her crew during a chase – and she was fast, seaworthy even in heavy weather.

His thoughts returned to the Proclamation in his hand. Maybe Holford was right. Holford had been his friend for years, and he was a man to respect. He was an ex-buccaneer, tough as old boot, a fine mariner, possessing great courage. The Navy had cleared the buccaneers out of the forests of Hispaniola, where they had made their living by hunting animals, smoking the meat and tanning the hides to sell to passing ships.

John West had sailed in consort with Hornigold on his first pirate voyage. They had done fairly well, and West had decided to take the money and 'go on the beach' in Jamaica.

Hornigold drank again and gave his beard its customary wipe. "Have you got more copies I can take to Nassau?" he asked. "They'd need to read it and think on it."

"Yes, we brought a good supply to hand around," West replied. The men sat in unusual silence, each enveloped in thought, listening to the creak and groan of the ship. Finally Holford spoke.

"I'm relieved to be finished with roving. It's been exciting, but I'll be fifty-two next month, and that's old for a rover. It's a wonder I've made it to this age. If they hadn't hounded us out of the bush those years ago, where we were harmlessly smoking meat, I'd never have gone 'on the account'." He puffed at his pipe, watching the smoke curl upwards.

"I think the same is true for you," Holford continued thoughtfully. "If they hadn't dumped you out of your ship in

Port Royal back in 1713, with no pay and no way to make your way, you'd probably never have sailed under the Banner of King Death. Well, you had to eat, to clothe yourself. They left a man no choice. It was either beggary or theft."

"I'm sick at heart, Holford, that's the truth," Hornigold said. "We were never gentlemen, but some of these people are more like fiends than men. I've no stomach for all this killing and cruelty going on. I have never suffered it on my ships, and I have tried never to prey on my own countrymen.

"Look at Charles Vane," Hornigold continued. "I tell you, that man's turned into a monster. He's a good sailor, has a shrewd intelligence, but he is given to every excess imaginable. And he attracts men with his own brutal tastes into his Company. God help the prey he finds!"

"Calico Jack Rackham, Edward English – all his people are vicious." Holford added. "And there's a dozen more companies like them. What man worth his salt wants to be counted among such vile rogues?"

Hornigold took another swig of punch and wiped his mouth, his eyes narrowing in thought. "I believe you're right," he said finally, nodding his head. "It can only get worse. Most of us went 'on the account' to get money and to be free. Not to kill, except in fight, and not in cold blood or for private revenge. But no matter how many lies we tell ourselves, or how we convince ourselves we are honorably changing the way of the sea, we're all just thieves awaiting a noose."

"I hear Bellamy's company call themselves 'Robin Hood's Men,' and I've heard countless scoundrels refer to themselves as 'gentlemen' and such," West added. "More and more are crowding into the business. The merchants are arming themselves and traveling with escorts. Soon there'll be nothing to take. And when the King puts his Navy to work on the problem, there'll be certain death for no chance of reward."

Hornigold nodded agreement. "No, I'm glad to have this news, my friends, very glad. And grateful for your trouble to deliver it. Jennings and I do not get on, but I know he'll be happy to hear this too."

Hornigold stood and walked to the door, staring out at the shimmering ocean, then turned into the cabin again. "I must write a letter," he said, "thanking Governor Heywood for sending you. I'd better do it now, before I get foxed. Will you excuse me a moment while I write it? Help yourselves to punch." He sat at his table, pulled paper from a drawer, sharpened a quill and set to work. Soon he looked up and read aloud:

" *'This is to acquaint Your Excellency that we have met with Captains Holford and West, who hath Brought us the Welcome Tidings of an Act of Grace from His Majesty King George, which we Embrace, and Return His Majesty our Hearty Thanks for the same. God Save The King.'*

"That should do it, eh Holford?" He shook sand over the page, then folded it and sealed it with blob of sealing wax, pressing it with his thumb. "I suppose we'll all have to come down to Kingston to surrender to Governor Heywood? Or go up to Charleston, or perhaps Bermuda..."

33

John Martin had ordered that Kath remain under guard in the bow of the *Bonnet*. He designed a cubbyhole for her behind stacks of plunder, with an old tarpaulin dropped across the opening for privacy. For two days now she had been sitting alone in the semi-dark, frustrated, seeing only her guard, George Rounsivel. How was she going to charm Captain Hornigold when she couldn't get to see him?

Below decks, the *Bonnet* had no inner walls or cabins. The sloop was wide open, with hammocks slung in every direction for the men and a galley in the stern. George told her this was because it was easier for fighting. Moreover, pirates were all equal, and none of them had their own cabins, not even the Captain. Although he used the great cabin, any crew member could come and go as they pleased, and might sleep there as well.

George was proving very useful for information. He told her that Ship's Articles, or rules, governed a pirate vessel. The company drew these up before each voyage, and every man signed them, or swore to them, binding himself to obedience. George said that the ship's company, or 'the council' as they called it when they sat to decide things, elected pirate officers, including the captain. The council also decided where they would sail, and whether to attack a ship.

"Pirate Captains don't have any special privileges, see, any more than an ordinary man," he said. "Nor the officers. They answer to the council, see, and the council can remove them anytime. The Captain is responsible for sailing the sloop and fighting, see. And the quartermaster is responsible for discipline and settling arguments, sharing out booty and such, and he leads the men in fighting and boarding the ships we take. Other than the Articles, we only have to obey orders when we're chasing, or fighting, or running away. We're all equal, see," he said proudly.

That might explain why Captain Hornigold showed her no special favors, nor came to see her, nor called for her. If *he* did, then any of the crew could, and probably would. The question continued to vex her. How was she going to see him? They would be at the careening cove in a couple more days.

In her long hours of detention she thought of things she could say that would show her interest, while remaining a lady. It was imperative that she not seem 'fast' or Captain Hornigold might not feel protective. Kath smiled when she thought of Shirley and all the tricks she had used on Jonah. Maybe she should try some on the Captain! She was willing to try, but she had to get his attention first.

She thought with a pang about Greville, and how differently he had treated her on the *Swan*. Well, that wasn't constructive use of her time, thinking of Greville. She was annoyed with herself for thinking of him at all, let alone almost constantly, as she did. It took her awhile to see that, like Shirley, she must ask for what she wanted.

"May I speak to Captain Hornigold, George?" she asked with her most charming smile.

"Yes, of course," George replied. "Anyone can speak to the Captain anytime, see. But Mr. Martin says you must stay here, see, so you can't disobey him and leave. The next time Jim relieves me, I'll ask if the Captain will come down to you."

*

"Captain Hornigold, how good of you to come," Kath said with a delighted smile, offering her hand. "Can you tell me how long I must stay bottled up in this stuffy place? Am I considered a part of your plunder?" she asked, giving him a Shirley-look. "I should love a breath of fresh air. Am I so dangerous that I need constant guarding?"

"Why no, Mistress, you're not a part of the plunder," he replied. "At least, I don't think so. We're not white slavers, y'know. I'm sorry we must treat you so. Even the animals go up on deck sometimes, after all. Martin and I thought it best that you remain below, for your own safety. You're not guarded against coming *out* – it is against others coming *in*. Some of our fellows are not as genteel as you might wish, and they haven't seen a female for two months. We'll soon be at Exuma and you can be free there."

"Thank you, Sir," she said, then dropped her voice to a murmur. "That concerns me, as well. How can I protect myself on the island? George has told me the men are not bound by Ship's Articles once ashore."

"That's true... I will give it some thought, discuss it with Martin. We've never had a female guest aboard. We'll come up with something, never fear."

"And my bag of clothing and toilet articles, Sir, are they considered part of the plunder too, or may I have them?"

"I will see they are returned to you, Mistress O'Brien." He turned to go. Kath stumbled with the roll of the ship, her breasts crushing hard against him. The Captain held her steady. "Thank you, Sir. I know you will do your best to protect me," she said breathlessly, giving him a melting look and taking her time about finding her balance.

"Your servant, Madam," Captain Hornigold mumbled distractedly, trying again to leave. Kath ran her hand lightly down the back of his upper arm as he turned away.

"On Exuma, Captain, I will sing for you alone," she purred. Hornigold fled.

*

Hornigold leaned over the taffrail of the *Bonnet*, watching her wake spread foamy white lace on the turquoise seas. He had much to think about and his thoughts were a jumble, going round and round. It was no wonder that most companies had an Article against bringing women aboard ship. The creatures could fuddle a man with a glance. They were worse than strong drink.

He stroked the smooth mahogany rail under his hand, then looked up at a screaming seagull. This was the life he loved! His ship had always been woman enough for him. Until now. Kath's delicate face swam into his memory, the tantalizing feel of her body against his, the sound of her voice, floating over the water from the *Jacinta de Chavez*. She filled him with longing and unease. Hornigold groaned.

He had definitely decided to surrender to the Governor. At least that was settled in his mind. He'd called a council meeting the morning after Captain Holford's visit. Most of his crew had decided to take the amnesty, though a few were going to wait and see what transpired at the general council in Nassau. All of them were younger than his own 37 years, only 'on the account' as the men called pirating, for a couple of years. He knew why they had no desire for a law-abiding life ashore, or in the Royal Navy or merchant service. There was neither freedom nor hope of advancement for common men, and conditions were brutal. He had gone to sea as a lad of eight years, had never since lived ashore, and he knew all about it.

He'd been a licensed privateer, sailing under a Letter of Marque in consort with different captains during the war, an honorable occupation. The same thing as being a pirate, but with Government approval.

Privateering had ended when the war ended, the Governments were at peace, and overnight privateering became pirating. However you looked at it, being at sea was an unstable and risky life. Uncomfortable, too, and he was getting older. For himself, Hornigold was relieved that it was ending. And here was a wonderful chance, Providence be praised! They could be pardoned, their misdeeds all forgotten, and melt back into normal society. He had been one of the successful ones and had made his fortune, most of which was stashed away at Harbour Island. In fact, he was a very wealthy man.

What would he do? Now that he could do anything, go

anywhere, what did he truly want? Go back to England, find some decent girl and set up house? No, too cold, and he didn't know anything about England really. No, he liked New Providence and sailing in warm waters. He could build himself a house on one of the hills overlooking the western end of the harbor, plant an orchard and vegetable garden, keep a horse and carriage. There was nobody who could look down their noses at him in Nassau. On the contrary, he could live like a Lord.

His heart quickened as he thought of this plan. He could let the Company have the *Bonnet*, go to Bermuda, take the King's Pardon and buy himself one of those neat little Bermuda sloops, one that would be a handy size to sail alone. He grinned at the thought of actually *buying* a boat. It would be his first time!

Still, what would he do, alone on his hill, alone on his new boat? Desolation flooded his spirit like cold seawater. It would mean nothing, without someone to share it. He thought again of Kath. Had Providence supplied him with a way of escape *and* a way to enjoy it fully?

*

At high tide, the *Bonnet* was run ashore as high as possible in the cove at Exuma. The men cleared her hold of their plunder and their personal things, which they piled on shore, well above high-water mark. They removed everything possible before careening, including her guns, which they mounted on shore as a precaution against unwanted surprise visitors. The sails and rigging were next. Finally, when she was as light as possible, the men attached a block and tackle between her mast and a huge gum elemi tree that grew near the water.

The sloop was turned on her side by using the block and tackle and floated further up, until one side bogged into the sand, leaving the other side high in the air. As the tide ebbed, the men scraped weed, barnacles and worms from the hull under the direction of Nathaniel Saunders, the ship's carpenter.

Kath found a flat rock next to a cannon where she could

see and hear, while remaining hidden herself. She wanted to be as unobtrusive as possible. The pirates rigged up tents with spars and canvas sails to protect themselves from the weather and to give shade for their off-duty drinking and gambling.

"Quartermaster, when will you share the loot?" one rowdy asked when the tide came in again, bringing work to a standstill. "We want to play dice."

"Now, if you like," Martin replied. "Call everyone in."

The pirates formed a circle around the pile of plunder. Martin began auctioning the clothing and small valuables, noting the bids on a bit of paper, or throwing any money paid into a chest which already held the gold and silver from the *Jacinta de Chavez*.

Captain Hornigold stood by until some women's clothing came on the block, then he began to bid. Kath was amazed to see several dresses, as well as petticoats and dainty underwear held up. Each piece brought lewd remarks, whistles and guffaws from the crew. The Captain ignored them and doggedly bid for each piece. When her own "good" dress came up, the Captain bid for that too and for the toilet kit Don Francisco had given her.

Kath bit her lip. She had never stopped to think that the Captain might be married, or have a sweetheart in port. So much for her pathetic scheme to attract him and gain his patronage. She looked down at herself, realizing what a sight she must look in her bloodstained, everyday dress. Perspiration stains spread darkly from under her armpits. She had not been able to comb her hair or wash properly for ten days, since before Don Francisco's dinner party. Her hands were dirty, her fingernails black with grime. She must smell like a stable.

What had she been thinking? Flirting with the Captain and looking like a slattern. Kath's face flamed with shame.

Soon the auction was finished. Martin announced that there would be another share-out after merchants in Nassau bought the bolts of cloth and various other dry goods. Then he turned to the money-chest and began counting.

"Just a moment, Martin," a raucous voice shouted.

"You're not finished yet. What about the woman? I want my share of her!"

34

"No, Jenks," Captain Hornigold said. "We'll not share the woman. Can't you see she's not the common sort we're used to?"

"What's that to us?" Jenks said. "Is she too good for the likes of us? We'll soon bring her down to our level." He laughed and looked around at the others for approval. Punch had been flowing freely all afternoon and now every pirate felt himself to be a king. The idea that Kath was a cut above them made them indignant. Jenks was right. Everyone was equal, and everyone should share in the woman.

"Quiet!" Hornigold bellowed. "I have no objection to sharing, and have always done so, according to our Articles. But not this woman!"

"What gives you the right to rule? We made you Captain and we can unmake you as easily! You're no better than us."

"A few days ago we talked about the King's Pardon," Hornigold shouted over the babble. "I told you I planned to go 'on the beach'. Well, I shall. And I shall have this woman as my wife."

There was quiet for a moment, while this stunning idea percolated through the alcoholic fumes in each head. Then the tumult broke out again.

"Who says you can have her?" Jenks demanded. "A lot of us are going 'on the beach'. Maybe we want wives too! I say we share and share alike. Or throw dice for her," he said, laughing at his new idea. "Eh, lads?"

"We could auction her," Hornigold said quietly.

"No," Jenks said. "We know you can out-bid us. That's not fair."

"It'll make the company all the richer," Hornigold said. "There'll be that much more in the chest to share out."

This thought gave pause to many of the company. They looked at one another with glittering eyes. But Jenks was intent on sport. He liked to fancy himself a leader of men and was always arguing, just to win.

"No, we have enough. We'll spend it in a fortnight, no matter how much we have. I say we want the woman!" He looked around at his shipmates and began to chant "We want the woman! We want the woman," rousing them with his right hand as though he was leading a choir.

"Tell you what, then," Hornigold said, shouting to make himself heard. "I'll fight for her. Any man you choose. If I win, I get the woman. If you win, she'll be yours to do with as you please. Fair enough?"

Here was another idea, one that provided sport as well as ample chance to gamble. Jenks rubbed his hairy chin and said "Done! We'll decide who'll fight, and the match can go on at high tide tomorrow."

"What will it be, mates?" John Martin asked. As quartermaster, he was responsible for officiating at duels and seeing fair play.

"Pistols and swords, as usual," the men agreed. "That's what's in the Articles to settle things between us."

"But wait," another man said. "It's Jenks who wants a fight. Let him fight the Captain. I don't see why anybody else should risk their skin. It's between the two of them. We're just as happy with the money!"

*

Kath crouched behind the cannon, hugging her knees to her chest. Her stomach knotted. What should she do? She thought of running into the bush, then reconsidered. Dying of thirst or starvation was not a viable option. She found a rock that was the right size for her hand. She could do some damage with that.

An hour passed and the wind picked up, blowing chilly

from the northwest. The full moon rose while the pirates bar-becued turtle meat on the beach and got roaring drunk. She was hungry, cold and stiff.

Looking around to see where she could find better shelter, she noticed a shadow slithering through the grass. Someone was coming. Why was he not walking plainly in the moon-light? Her blood seething, she felt for her rock.

A moment later, Hornigold's voice called low from a clump of sea oats. He was soon beside her with a blanket. "I thought you might be cold," he said, wrapping it around her. "I've brought you some supper, too." He handed her a piece of lukewarm turtle steak. "Gnaw on this – it's good!"

They sat in silence for a few minutes. "I suppose you heard what went on this afternoon?"

"Yes, Sir, and I'm distressed that you must risk your life for me."

"Oh, I doubt it'll come to that. Jenks has a loud mouth, but he's not particularly courageous. He may call it off by to-morrow. These men are like children. What interests them one moment bores them the next." He spoke lightly, as though the coming duel meant nothing. "In any case, I'm known for my luck in a fight... and my straight eye with a pistol, too. If anyone goes down, it'll more likely be Jenks than me."

He stretched his legs out before him and rocked back on his elbows, looking up at the moon. "Look at that! So beauti-ful! So pure! It's hard to understand why there's such evil in the world when the world itself is so wonderful."

He sighed heavily. "I have something else for you, Mistress O'Brien." He took her hand and put a pistol in it. "In case things go wrong tomorrow. Do you know how to shoot it?" He took the pistol back and showed her how to cock it and pull the trigger. "Don't hesitate.

"Those rogues will fall on you like dogs on a rabbit. Hold it like this," he said, putting the muzzle in his mouth. "Then pull the trigger. You won't feel anything. Can you hide it in your pocket?"

"Yes, Sir," Kath replied, her voice wavering. "But what

about you, Captain Hornigold?"

"Oh, I'm not afraid to die," he replied, looking out to sea. "In recent months, I've become weary of the stench of smoke and gunpowder and death. My ears are always ringing with the clash of steel, exploding cannon and the screams of injured men." He looked into her face. "Can you imagine what it's like?"

"No."

He was silent for a moment, then continued. "Your hand becomes numb, clamped so tightly to your gun, or your sword – or whatever weapon you have – that the steel becomes a part of your own flesh. You hit and hit, heedless of the shocks to your arm. All the while, you're screaming. The noise comes from the bottom of your soul, where Satan lives. But your voice is lost, like your soul.

"Soon all your senses shut down, too overloaded to take anything in. You don't smell the blood anymore, or anything at all. You only hear a far-off roar, like the sea raging. You can see, but the scene is meaningless, too dreadful for your brain to understand. Shards of flesh stick to the sails. Your feet slip in blood. Blood splashes your clothes, sweeps over the deck of the ship and floods into the sea."

He paused again, looked at the moon, then out to sea. "Sometimes in my sleep I fight. Every battle, every blow, every man I have ever harmed comes back in a screaming, sweating rush to haunt me. The only relief lies at the very bottom of a full bottle – and that for but an hour or two."

He groaned. "They say I am one of the lucky ones. I am rich. I made my fortune, and still live to spend it. But I can't help thinking that the dead are better off than I am. In death they may perchance have gone to heaven, whilst I must live in Hell and have no hope of anything to come, except more of the same – only worse, and forever!"

Kath took his hand and kissed it, moved by his pain. Hornigold folded her in his arms and clung to her like he was drowning. "Please save me, Mistress O'Brien!" he pleaded against her throat, his tears scalding her neck, his body wracked with sobs. "Teach me to live a normal, decent life. Tell me I am still a man and not a monster!"

*

All that night they held each other in the sea oats, taking comfort from the warmth of each other's bodies, seeking respite from their fear of the morrow. Sometime towards dawn, Kath woke and listened to the swish and hiss of gentle waves licking the sugar-white sand. She was still in Hornigold's powerful embrace, and she snuggled gratefully against his strong chest, reveling in the masculine hardness of his body, the slight scratch of his beard against her cheek.

Now that she had him, she would not let him go.

35

The men stopped work around noon the next afternoon, when the incoming tide washed too high on the hull of the sloop for them to continue. The ship's cook had prepared dinner over a fire on the beach and, as soon as everyone had eaten and drunk a liberal supply of ale, the company was ready for entertainment.

John Martin had a strip of ground cleared behind the dunes for the duel. Betting had started the night before and continued throughout the morning, the book running heavily in the Captain's favor. The pirates stood in two groups to watch. Jenks stood with a few friends, bragging and drinking. Captain Hornigold stayed with Kath, listening intently while she read a Psalm from a greasy prayer book.

Martin walked to the center of the clearing and the Captain and Jenks joined him immediately. An expectant hush fell on the company.

"You know how it's done," Martin said. "You stand back to back, then take fifteen paces and turn around. I'll count out the paces. When I give the word, you shoot. Then if you're both able, you fight with cutlasses. The first man to draw blood wins."

The two stood back to back. Jenks licked his lips and wiped his brow with his forearm. Hornigold bowed gravely to Kath. She bit her lip and fingered the pistol in her pocket.

Martin began counting. "One...two..." and the duelists walked their paces. As Martin said "...twelve...," Jenks turned and shot at Hornigold's back. Surprised, Hornigold turned and stumbled, falling onto his right arm and discharging his pistol. With a blood-curdling yell, Jenks threw his own pistol aside, grabbed his cutlass and ran towards Hornigold. Jenks's arm lifted. For an instant the sun flashed from his blade and then it plunged into the sand, just as Hornigold rolled aside. Jenks snatched it up, his face contorted with fury.

The company went wild, calling instructions, jumping up and down with excitement and blood lust. Kath's pistol was in her hand, cocked and ready. She was screaming, too, and running towards Hornigold. As Jenks's arm lifted the second time, Kath squeezed the trigger.

The cutlass flew high in the air. Jenks crumpled to his knees, clutching his stomach, his eyes and mouth wide. Blood spurted between his fingers. He stretched out his dripping hands, staring at them in disbelief. The pirates all laughed.

"Hey, wait," one of Jenks's friends shouted. "She can't butt in like that. Only those two can fight!"

"Jenks cheated," Martin said. "He didn't finish the count."

Hornigold was on his feet and beside Kath in a bound. He snatched her pistol and stuck it in his belt, then stood in front of her. "I'll fight anybody else who has the stomach for it," he said. "But as this woman is now my wife, I say it doesn't matter whether she or I shot Jenks. We're one flesh, the same person. Look in the prayer book if you don't believe me!"

"How could she be your wife? You didn't win her yet," one man shouted, but the pirates who wanted to collect their bets on Hornigold shouted him down. Jenks's faction angrily rounded on the Hornigold supporters, but there were far more for Hornigold, and they were laughing and shouting that Jenks had not played fair. They hoisted Hornigold and Kath on their shoulders and carried them back to the beach, leaving the ship's surgeon bending over Jenks.

"Let's have a wedding, then," Martin said, grinning. "Make more punch. I'll be the parson. Where's the prayer book?"

"Yes, Cap'n Hornigold," the company cried. "We'd see ye properly wed!"

"That's more fun than a public hanging!" Martin added. "And 'twill be good reason for us to celebrate!"

*

Within the hour, the pirates gathered under a large sea grape tree at the shoreline. The musicians were playing and punch flowed freely. Kath put on the finery that Don Franisco had given her and now Hornigold had bought back for her. George went into the bush and came back with a few sprays of the native yellow orchids for her bridal bouquet. Two wiry men wrapped themselves up in some of the elegant cloth from the *Jacinta de Chavez*, simpering and cavorting in front of Kath as her bridesmaids. The Gunner and his mate put on some of Don Francisco's finery and were best man and groomsman.

John Martin used the lower limb of the tree as his pulpit. He sat above the bridal pair, wrapped in a dirty tarpaulin for a cassock and with the prayer book opened at "Marriage". In his most sonorous voice, he began.

"All stand." The company stood, a little unsteadily.

"For this reason a man shall leave his father and mother and be joined to his wife, and the two shall become one flesh." Martin intoned. "Who gives the bride to be married?"

"We do!" the company shouted unanimously.

Whenever a response was required from the congregation in the service, Martin prompted and the pirates repeated it lustily. Martin skipped the Bible readings, but could not resist trying to give a sermon – on the harmful effects of too much punch. However, the company hooted him down and he had to give over moralizing.

Eventually the bride and groom exchanged their vows, and the whole matrimonial service was read through. Then a hymn was called for, and the company decided the only one they all knew was "A Mighty Fortress Is Our God", so the fiddle player tuned up. Some wag amongst them loudly hoped that the Captain wouldn't need a fortress, now he'd married a woman who'd shoot anyone who tried to harm him. More uproarious laughter.

Led by the happy couple, the company danced a con-ga-line back to the tents for more punch, endless toasts and ribald humor. The music and dancing continued until dark, by which time most of the men were too drunk to stand, including Hornigold.

*

Kath crept on hands and knees out of Hornigold's make-shift tent into the cool moonlight and lay on the sand. Her head was spinning, the beach going round and round. Her stomach churned like a basket of eels. She sat up and vomited, but felt little better. She thought about Jenks, and hoped he was all right. "Don't want to be a murderer," she muttered to herself, her throat constricting and hot tears stinging her eyelids. But her tears were for herself, not for Jenks. Strangely enough, she felt no guilt about shooting him.

She remembered Greville's face, his bronzed body, his elegant hands and gentle voice. Hopeless longing welled up in her. She had cherished so many dreams of marrying him, with Miz Eva and all of Fortune Island rejoicing. Somehow she felt she had been unfaithful to Greville, had committed adultery by marrying Hornigold. But what choice did she have? She was only a piece of wreckage, floating in the tide of her fate. Was pain never going to leave her? Must there always be this solid mass inside, constantly weighing her down? She wanted to kick and scream, to yank out her hair.

She dug her fingers into the cold sand and lifted handfuls up to press against her throbbing temples. One thing was sure, she thought bleakly. She was Mrs. Benjamin Hornigold now, the wife of one of the biggest pirates in New Providence, and she was probably a murderess, too. Greville was lost to her forever. She must forget him and concentrate on how to please her new husband.

*

Kath woke with a splitting headache and a foul taste in her mouth soon after daybreak. She was cold, wet through from dew and lying in the sand. She sat up stiffly, not remembering how she came to be there. Hornigold sat nearby, watching her with a little smile playing about his lips. "Come my Treasure," he said. "Have some breakfast. It'll make you feel better." He held out a tankard of coffee, a hardtack biscuit and a gob of salt beef with one hand, while offering the other to help her get up.

"Oh-h," Kath groaned. The thought of food made her shudder.

"You think you'll never want to eat again, I'll wager," he said, unbearably cheerful "This too shall pass!

"As soon as you feel better I'm going to take you on a honeymoon trip. We'll leave the lads to finish cleaning the sloop and take a longboat over to that small cay," he said, pointing across the bay. "You can sing to me alone, like you promised," he said, with a sidelong look. Kath blushed. Hornigold chuckled.

"There's a lovely little beach on the other side," he continued. "I'll make us a shelter and we'll take food for two or three days. We can get to know each other better, away from this horde of reprobates."

"That'll be nice," Kath grunted.

Hornigold laughed. "Have you ever been drunk before?"

"No," she said shortly, shooting him a look of sour resentment.

"I thought not," he said, giving her another sunny smile. "Well, you need not do it again. At least this will teach you to have pity on your fellow creatures when they've had too much punch."

A chilling thought made Kath catch her breath. "Jenks! What happened to Jenks? Is he dead?"

Hornigold clenched his fist. "Not yet. The surgeon's done his best."

"You mean he'll die?" Kath asked, stricken.

"Yes, he'll die, and soon." He sighed. "Not to worry. Fellows like him are always looking for death."

She felt as though someone had whacked her in the chest

with a plank. "I killed him! I'm a murderer!"

"He killed himself. He should have thought better of demanding a fight. Of course, he didn't expect to be fighting *himself*," Hornigold said, with a bitter smile. "I told you he was a coward. He didn't even fight fair. And you shot him in self-defense."

"I thought he'd killed you, Captain Hornigold. When he shot at your back and you fell, I – I..."

He regarded her evenly, a glimmer of admiration lighting his expression. "You killed for *me*, little one? Not for yourself? Knowing what they'd do to you, you avenged my death?"

"Well, I was so angry that he shot you in the back, and before he sh-should... I-I didn't th-think," she stuttered.

Hornigold reached for her and held her close. "Thank you," he said fervently. She felt his hot breath on her scalp and her pulse raced. She snuggled into his embrace.

"You saved my life, Mrs. Hornigold. For that, I owe you everything. And everything is what I plan to give you, for the rest of our lives."

36

Kath and Hornigold did not know each other, but the intensity of their short acquaintance gave them a familiarity beyond what might normally be expected. The initial strain of being alone on their little island wore off as they worked together, cutting thatch for shelter, gathering firewood and cooking.

Kath had been deeply moved when Hornigold had revealed the agony of his soul that first night on Exuma. He was an atrocious pirate, that may be – but he wanted to change, and he needed her to show him how to live the decent life he craved.

She knew this was possible, because she remembered reading in one of Miz Eva's chapters about how God would replace a heart of stone with a heart of flesh, if the person wanted it. She had seen plenty of cruelty and hardship in life and began to understand what Miz Eva had tried to teach her about love. She would learn to love Hornigold and teach him how to love her in return.

Hornigold was gentle with her, eager to please and anxious for her comfort. However, he had never married, having gone to sea as a boy, and his knowledge of females was limited to his mother and three older sisters – and perhaps a few prostitutes. Since his mother had been a bitter drudge, resentful of his alcoholic father, and his sisters had treated him like an oafish nuisance, he was wary of Kath at first. His early experience with the female sex had made him shy and abstemious. He had rarely engaged with the tavern women, feeling that he ran enough risks in his life without adding that of venereal disease.

They stripped and swam naked, Kath reveling in the freedom of feeling her body float, with her long hair streaming about her like mossy seaweed.

They walked the beach, collecting shells. They watched a flock of small wading birds scavenge nervously at the water's edge, running away to higher beach as the waves washed in, then racing back as they receded, to gobble whatever little bite they found left behind.

They watched as the dawn broke with an intense luminescent orange in the east. The sky otherwise was silver, gradually becoming more orange on the horizon, then turning the palest silver-blue. Blue-gray clouds hung low over the islands, later turning light gray and white, later still casting dark moving shadows on the water below. The sea was gun-metal gray at first, then turned silver in the east and blue green in the west. As the sun lifted above the horizon, the sea took on more color and changed to the medium blue-green of early morning, then finally to the translucent aquamarine of the Exuma waters.

They enjoyed the dawn chorus, birds twittering in the rustling bush against the gentle swish of waves kissing the shore. They enjoyed the gentle warm trade winds' caress. They became Adam and Eve, the first and only humans in creation. Beauty, peace and tranquility reigned all around them, and encouraged intimacy and trust.

Gradually they covered their personal histories, sympathizing with each other over the sad parts and laughing at the funny things. Hornigold occasionally noticed a woebegone expression on Kath's face as they strolled. He would put his arm around her, making her meet his eyes and give him a grave smile, but the pensive look would return. He did not press her to share her thoughts, however. He was content to learn things by degrees. He, too, had thoughts that made him sad and regretful, thoughts that he was unwilling to burden her with as yet.

She fretted about Jenks. Greville often surfaced in Kath's mind too, but she banished him to that locked place in her heart where her two sons stayed, where Miz Eva, Treacle and Fortune Island were put, and Ireland, with John, Maggie, and all her lost relatives lived. Occasionally the door unlocked and her heart gave a twinge of pain, but she soon regained her composure and slammed the door shut again. She was determined to live in the present, to live what *was*, not what used to be or might have been.

Captain Hornigold, or Ben, as he now preferred Kath to call him, had brought a bottle of rum and made a punch on the first night of their honeymoon. Sipping their drinks, they sat in their shelter looking out at the still, moonlit sea, feeling peaceful and cozy. The faint fragrance from flowers in the bush drifted on an eddy of air, tinged with wood smoke from the fire they built to keep the sandflies and mosquitoes away.

"Will you sing to me?" Ben asked. "You promised, on the sloop."

"What would you like me to sing?"

"The songs you sang that night on the *Jacinta de Chavez*."

She sang them, then sang two Irish love ballads. As the last note died away, Ben reached for her. "You sing like an angel," he said huskily, nuzzling her neck. "Your voice takes me to Paradise."

He licked salt from her throat, then gently licked and bit her ears and shoulders, as passion swelled within him. Kath moaned and shivered, heat flooding her body. She turned fully into his arms and kissed his hair, his eyelids; then their questing mouths found each other in a long, consuming kiss. They were both healthy and desperate for love. Ben was awkward and a little clumsy, but Kath used her experience to ease his anxiety. Her ready acceptance of him and the touching way she melted into his arms gave him encouragement and filled him with joy.

When they returned to the *Bonnet* at the end of three days, they were firmly a couple.

And Jenks had died, in horrible agony.

*

The pirates agreed to give Hornigold and Kath the great cabin of the sloop for their trip to New Providence, and promised not to barge in as they usually did. The men were in high spirits, looking forward to carousing in the taverns and bawdy houses on the waterfront. The trade winds blew steadily and the *Bonnet* zipped along on her clean bottom.

Early in the morning of the fifth day, the *Bonnet* entered the western end of Nassau harbor with her Jolly Roger floating out from the masthead and her pirates standing proudly on deck. There was a booming cannon salute from the shore, answered by the guns aboard the *Bonnet*.

Kath looked at Ben with startled eyes, her heart jumping. "The boys are welcoming us home," he said, grinning.

"Oh," she said weakly, her hands over her chest. "I wish you'd thought to tell me before. I thought the town was firing at us!"

"Not this town, my Treasure," he replied. "The people love us here, especially the merchants, the tavern keepers and whores!" He winked. "As soon as we tie up, I'll take you to the best inn in Nassau to freshen up. We can have bacon and eggs for breakfast! And a hot, fresh-water bath!"

People lined the wharf. There were women in bright, low-cut dresses, holding their skirts knee-high, ostensibly to keep them out of the mud. Horses and drays stood ready for hire, while small boys with dogs chased each other in amongst them. Market vendors sat with mounds of fresh vegetables and fruits, calling out to entice buyers. There were live turtles for sale, lying on their backs, their fins flapping feebly against the buzzing flies, and heaving great sighs. Chickens and ducks, with their legs tied, and sheep and goats. The sun already beat down upon it all, raising the peculiar wharf-smell of ozone, fish, tar, horse-droppings and rotten fruit.

Hornigold shepherded Kath off the *Bonnet* and over to a dray. "Take us to the Nancy Lou Lilly," he told the driver.

"What did you say?" Kath asked in astonishment. She had not heard that name since her first week on Fortune Island fifteen months ago, when Obie had said that Greville always

264

stayed with her in Nassau.

"I told him to take us to the inn," Ben replied.

"Nancy Lou Lilly?" she asked with a little smile. "That's the name of an inn?"

"Yes. Three maiden sisters, Nancy, Louise and Lilly own it. It's the best place to stay in Nassau. Those old biddies run a tight ship. No noisy drinking or harlots allowed in *their* place. I think you'll like it."

"Do you always stay there?"

"Well, no, not always," he said sheepishly. "Truth is, it's a little tame for me. Or, um, that is, was, before I um..."

Kath smiled sweetly. "I understand, Ben. Thank you for taking me there."

"Nothing's too good for you, Mrs. Hornigold," he said, his eyes soft with love.

That Obie! She thought. *He's got a lot to answer for! If I ever see him again...*

*

After breakfast and a bath, Captain Hornigold returned to the wharf. He and John Martin had to see about selling their plunder to the local merchants, and he wanted to make sure that the *Bonnet* was secure.

Kath stayed at the Nancy Lou Lilly, luxuriating in a large bathtub half filled with warm fresh water. She washed her hair, and dried it sitting in the sun slanting through her window on the second floor. She had a perfect view of the harbor. She manicured her nails with her little toilet kit, then put on her Christmas dress and went down to the lounge for dinner at two o'clock. After dinner, she had coffee on the porch, waiting for Ben's return. Suddenly her heart skipped a beat. Turning the corner a block away, and headed straight up the hill towards her, was Captain Greville Knowles.

Kath's first inclination was to bolt inside and up to her room.

Don't be ridiculous, she thought. *You'll have to face Greville sometime.* Besides, news traveled quickly on the waterfront.

He might already know. She swallowed hard and composed herself, looking down at her hands and playing with her fingers until his light tread on the porch floor told her that he had arrived. She looked up with a broad smile, her face a vivid rose.

"Kath!" Greville exclaimed in amazement. "What are you doing here?"

"Good afternoon, Captain Knowles," she said demurely. "I thought you'd be surprised to see me. A lot has happened since you left us last October."

"Tell me, then," he said, beaming down at her. "I'm so glad to see you, my wench. May I join you? I'm gasping of thirst... and I'm hungry, too," he went on. "I s'pose you've already had your dinner?"

Kath nodded. "Yes, I've just finished."

"Then I'll go see if Miz Nancy can find some for me. I'll wash and be with you in a moment," he said, disappearing through the parlor door.

Kath closed her eyes and took a deep breath. Her heart was racing. Oh why could it not be still? Why did it have to leap and thump like this every time Greville looked at her? I'm a married woman now, she told herself, but her heart had a will of its own. Your husband will be here any moment, she reminded herself severely, but she remained as breathless as before. *What will Greville say when I tell him I am married to Benjamin Hornigold?*

Greville ran straight back onto the porch, all thoughts of his dinner forgotten. "It's Gammie, isn't it Kath?" he demanded, his voice ragged. "She's gone?" His eyes were full of pain. "I suddenly thought, you would never leave her alone on Fortune Island. She's either here with you, or...she's..."

"Yes, Greville. I'm sorry..." she said softly. How could she be so stupid, so self-absorbed? He didn't even know Miz Eva had died.

Greville sank into the chair next to hers and dropped his face in his hands. "That night before I left, she said goodbye. I didn't know what to think, I didn't entirely believe her..."

Kath poured fresh coffee into her cup and pushed it in front of him. Her hand fluttered over his shoulder. She touched him lightly, then snatched her hand back again. She wanted to fling her arms around him, stroke his hair, comfort him, let him cry – but she was Mrs. Benjamin Hornigold now, not Kath O'Brien. She was no longer his 'wench'.

"Did you order dinner?" she asked quietly. Greville shook his head. "I'll go," she said, getting up.

Greville reached out and clutched her skirt, looking at her appealingly. "Don't leave me."

"I'll be right back. You need to eat. I'll tell you all about it." Kath bustled into the house and ordered dinner from the kitchen maid, then returned to the porch. She had needed that spurt of action to get a grip on her own emotions. She sat beside Greville again.

"Now I'll tell you how it happened..." she said, and began recounting the Spanish raid, Miz Eva's death, her own kidnap, and then rescue by the Nassau pirates. Greville sat in stunned silence, listening, sipping the coffee. When at last Kath finished, he looked up with a small smile.

"So Gammie actually jumped out and whacked that Spaniard!" he said with admiration. "My own dear Little Mouse! She was never one to back down from a fight, no matter what the odds." He finished off the coffee. "But *you*, my poor wench," he said. "You *have* had a time of it! And you arrived here only this morning?

"Have you given any thought to your future? What will you do? Of course you can't stay in Nassau alone, without male protection." Greville smiled his old smile, his eyes crinkling merrily, lips curved up to show his even, pearly teeth. "You can't keep gallivanting about the world on one ship after another, y'know, rattling around by yourself! I shall have to make a decent woman of you. You must come with me in the *Swan*. I know it's not the most romantic way to ask, but will you marry me? We can announce our engagement immediately and make our vows before the crew in the morning."

"I'm sorry, Greville," she said with a sob. "I am already

married to Captain Benjamin Hornigold! I – I had to, to avoid…"

Greville blinked, then nodded after a few seconds. "I see. Yes of course! Good of him to do it, and he's a lucky fellow, too." Again, he dropped his head in his hands. "Just give me a moment – all such a shock…"

Kath looked up, to see Ben trudging towards them two blocks away. "Here comes my husband now," she said.

Greville sprang to his feet, and bowed over Kath's hand. "Congratulations my dear Mrs. Hornigold. I will not stay to wish your husband happy, but be assured that I wish you both the very best, the happiest of lives together…" He choked up. Dashing his hand across his eyes, he said "I must go and see about that dinner. My poor stomach thinks my throat's been cut…" He strode to the parlor door, then paused and looked back at Kath, his face like a mask.

"I'd better say goodbye now, too," he said, in the same brittle tone he had used to congratulate her. "I must arrange extra provisions for the Fortune Island folk, and will leave very early in the morning. I doubt I shall see you again this trip."

He slipped through the door and closed it firmly behind him.

37

Captain Benjamin Hornigold came eagerly onto the porch, slightly puffed from his exertions with the hill. "Was that Captain Knowles with you Treasure?" he asked.

"Yes, but he's rushed off to swallow some dinner. I told him about the raid on Fortune Island and he's anxious to take extra supplies to them and leave as soon as possible. Have *you* eaten yet, Ben?"

"Yes, thank you. I ate with Captain Henry Jennings at the Mermaid's Tail." Ben went to the parlor door and stuck his head inside for a moment, then came and sat by his wife. "I don't see Captain Knowles," he said crossly. "I was looking forward to seeing him. Did you tell him we were married?"

Kath nodded. "He wished us very happy."

"He'll naturally be concerned for you. My reputation's not the best. I wanted to tell him about the King's Pardon, and that we're going to settle down here in Nassau."

"How long have you known each other?" Kath asked guardedly, intent on her fingers again.

"About twenty years, I should say. Ever since he was a midshipman on the *Fancy* under Sir Aynsley Luscombe."

"What sort of ship was the *Fancy*?"

"A brigantine! She was a beauty. Sir Anysley Luscombe was a lusty privateer, but he was also a gentleman and a scholar. He was a friend of Greville's father, y'know, and took Greville on after his parents died, since he only had his old granny left to him. It's Luscombe who taught him his manners and love of books."

"What happened to the *Fancy*?" Kath asked innocently, looking up from her hands.

"Luscombe sailed her back to England after the war. I remember he wanted Greville to go with him, but he stayed here to look after his grandmother. He had enough saved from the *Fancy's* prizes to buy himself a share in the *Swan*. I believe his two partners are in Charleston." He paused a moment. "But then you already know all this, I don't doubt."

"No," Kath said. "Captain Knowles rarely talks about himself."

"No. He's a modest type," Ben said, pulling out his gold pocket watch. "It's twenty minutes to four! I promised Jennings I would meet him and the others out by the Eastern Cemetery. Would you like to come, my Treasure? You could see a bit of the town... and," he added, his eyes brightening "...I could show you off to my friends!"

"The dead ones? Why are you meeting in the cemetery?"

"We're not. There's a small beach there, near the burial ground. Jennings, Auger, Vane, Burgess and several others have their sloops moored along there."

"How convenient! Not far to carry their victims," she said smiling. She jumped up. "But I'd like to come and meet these notorious friends of yours." She was glad of the chance to leave the inn – and avoid the possibility of running into Greville again.

"Well, they're not friends, really," Hornigold said with a grieved look. "We're in the same business, so to speak. So we know each other and have the same interests."

*

Kath need not have worried about running into Greville. The poor man was destined to eat nothing that day. He had scuttled up to his room, locked his door, thrown himself on his bed and buried his face in his pillow. He was too heartsick even to sob.

So this was what all his mental agonies had brought him! His sensitive restraint when he had first met her – he had not wanted to confuse her, she had just been transported from her home, lost her sons. Later, he wanted to be sure that she was not in love with Jonah Cartwright. Later still, he quibbled over her being a Roman Catholic, and not wanting to marry a Protestant. What it all meant was that he was too afraid to put his hat in the ring. As long as he did not ask, she could not reject him.

Bitterly, now, he faced the truth. All these excuses covered his one fear, that she would not accept him because of his color. And all these excuses were worth nothing now, since she had gone to a man who made no excuses or quibbles – a man who worried about nothing, who simply took whatever he wanted. *I hope she'll be happy with him, the vicious pirate*, he thought, grinding his teeth, knowing he was being unfair to Hornigold, who had no reputation for being vicious.

On the contrary, Hornigold was widely known for his restraint, and for taking only what he needed from the vessels he captured. He always gave prize ships back to his victims, unless it was needed by his company, along with the cargo his company could not sell. Hornigold was never cruel, he never killed except in battle, and he never attacked British ships. For these very reasons he'd been voted out of his captaincy on the *Adventure* in 1716. Two-thirds of his company had elected Sam Bellamy as captain instead, and the company had split. Hornigold and his quartermaster, Edward Teach, had been allowed to sail away in *Adventure* with the one-third of loyal pirates. What's more, as a leading pirate, Hornigold had always been respectful and kind to Greville, making sure the *Swan* and her people were not harmed.

By marrying Kath, Greville knew that Hornigold had saved her from being raped and brutalized by a ship's company of drunk men. It was an extraordinary thing for a pirate captain to do, and he should be grateful that Hornigold had saved Kath. And he *was*! But still, she was *his* Kath! *His* wench! He hammered the pillow with his fist, wishing it was Hornigold's pink face.

Greville fished in his pockets for his handkerchief. He

couldn't find it, but he did find the small blue velvet box with the diamond and ruby ring he had bought for Kath. He flung it violently across the room, and blew his nose on a corner of the sheet.

He thought of Miz Eva and the lovely whitewashed home she had made on top of the hill. Treacle, the settlement, *Kath*! Gone, all gone! It was more than he could bear, and tears squeezed from his tightly shut eyes. Why should he go on living?

It was twilight before Greville roused himself. His conscience stung him. He had wasted the whole afternoon in his room when he should have been down at the *Swan*, telling the others the news and taking on supplies for feeding and rebuilding the settlement. He jumped up and splashed water on his face, then cautiously opened his bedroom door. The coast was clear. There was no sight or sound of Kath or Hornigold. Quickly he crept down the stairs and out the side entrance of the inn, then down one alley after another until he arrived back at the waterfront. He would let the men do the shopping. He would sleep aboard tonight, and they could still leave on the morning tide.

*

Hornigold and Kath hired a horse and surrey and headed along the sandy bay track leading out to the eastern burial ground. Kath was dismayed at the ramshackle look of the town. The houses were shabby, made of rough planking, old sails and palmetto thatch, and built higgledy-piggledy along the track. Occasionally a householder had struggled to plant a garden, but mostly bush grew rampant wherever it pleased. Foul smelling heaps of refuse lay everywhere, picked over by packs of scrawny mongrels. Kath shook her head sadly when she thought how excited Shirley had been at the thought of coming to this place. She could see why the Stirrups had never brought her.

Soon sounds of revelry jolted her out of her thoughts. "That will be the lads tuning up," Hornigold said, a gleam in his eye. "Sounds like they're well into a keg."

"Ben, are you sure this is the best time to introduce me?" Kath asked hesitantly. "They sound very merry."

"We're here now, so we'd just as well stay. I know they're rowdy and loud, but they're all right. They're curious to see the woman who could make me settle down. If you still feel nervous after you meet them, I'll take you home."

"It's Captain Hornigold and his new bride! Hornigold!" a man bellowed, as Hornigold tied the horse to a silver buttonwood tree. Kath moved closer to Ben and took his arm as a group of men came towards them. The pirates were dirty, ragged and rough looking. Several had lost limbs, or carried disfiguring battle scars. One man had no ears and his nostrils had been slit.

"Ahoy there, mates!" Hornigold shouted genially. "Come and meet Mrs. Hornigold! She's the greatest treasure I've ever found!"

Kath stood up as straight and tall as she could, blushing and basking in Ben's praise. "Very pleased to meet you all," she said.

"She's the spitfire who shot Jenks?" someone asked. "Who'd think it to look at her?"

"No wonder Captain Hornigold forced her to sign Ship's Articles!" another quipped. "She can be his secret weapon."

A tall lean man of middle years stepped out of the crowd. He wore a black coat and waistcoat, with drab-colored knee breeches and a snowy white shirt. Silver flecked his black hair and streaked his temples, contrasting sharply with his walnut-tanned face. His long nose added to the impression he gave of commanding distinction.

"Mrs. Hornigold, may I present Captain Henry Jennings? Jennings, my wife, Kathryn."

"Your servant, Madam," Captain Jennings said, bowing over her hand. "It's a pleasure to meet you. You're already famous among the men, thanks to the tales from the *Bonnet's* crew." His dark eyes twinkled under heavy brows. "I suspect there's been some embroidery, y'know. Never mind. It will keep them on their best behavior with you, and that can only be to the good."

"Captain Hornigold," shouted a man from a small group sitting at a table under a woman's tongue tree. "The punch has been made this last hour. You'll have to hasten to catch up with us!"

"Just coming," Hornigold called. "That's Captain John Augur, m'dear," he told Kath. "He's a sly fox, not one of my particular confederates. However, come and meet him and the others. None of 'em are men you'd invite to tea."

Captain Jennings offered Kath his arm as they walked towards the table. She realized she was on the arms of two of the most infamous pirates in the world. "You can invite *me* to tea, my dear Mrs. Hornigold," he said, smiling down at her. "I should be very pleased to come."

Hornigold presented Kath to Captains John Cockram, Charles Vane, Yeates, and then to 'Calico Jack' Rackham, Captain Vane's quartermaster.

John Cockram was a burly man of about thirty, already balding and sporting a potbelly that he used as a rest for his drinking arm. He had a florid complexion, badly pockmarked, and pale blonde lashes rimming his light blue eyes. He wore a common blue and white checked shirt, with tarred wide-legged breeches. Cockram acknowledged Kath with a nod.

Captain Charles Vane was clearly a dandy. He wore a bright red brocade coat trimmed with black leather, with a black leather jerkin beneath, fastened by jeweled clips. Wavy chestnut hair hung loose to his shoulders, topped with a red brocade hat to match his coat. There was a jeweled brooch rakishly pinned to one side of his hat brim, with a white feather cockade. A small waxed mustache and goatee framed full red lips, set off by a square jaw and long red nose. His hazel eyes examined Kath appraisingly, as he rose to make his bow, waving a lacy handkerchief heavily scented with Bay Rum, a popular Jamaican perfume.

Captain Yeates was a small, dark man, taciturn, lithe and quick. He had sharp features and small black eyes that moved back and forth constantly, never missing anything. He looked shrewd and mean, but perhaps that was because of the livid scar that marred his face from left temple to his upper lip. In healing, the cut had given a cruel twist to his mouth. "How d'ye do," Yeates grunted on introduction.

John 'Calico Jack' Rackham – oh, Calico Jack! What a character he seemed. About twenty-seven years of age, with a short-trimmed red beard, a freckled countenance and a snub nose, he had a wide, generous mouth and lively greenish eyes. He wore a calico shirt and a calico vest – a different-patterned calico vest – no coat, and wide legged red seaman's breeches. Calico Jack had tied his head with a green calico handkerchief – yet another pattern – the ends of which fell over his left shoulder, and put a wide-brimmed straw hat over it. He wore one gold hoop in his right ear. When Hornigold called his name, he raised his glass of punch and tipped his head in Kath's direction, winked, took a deep pull from his glass and rapped it back on the table.

"Your most obedient, obliging servant, Madam," he said. "Call on me for anything at any time. And if ever Cap'n Hornigold forgets to be good to you, well, I only hope I'm in port!"

Kath gave him a radiant smile. "Thank you, Sir. I'll remember!" *A ladies' man*, she thought. *I hope Shirley never meets him.*

Calico Jack offered Kath a chair beside him, which she took. The men immediately started discussing the Act of Grace from the King. Governor Bennett of Bermuda had sent a sloop to New Providence with the news, which had arrived a few days before. Hornigold had met his confederates abuzz with it on his arrival, and found himself in good time for a general council.

"I'll definitely accept," Captain Jennings said. "As Governor Bennet was decent enough to send us tidings, I plan to give myself up in Bermuda. I'll take any men who want to go with me."

"Pish!" Captain Vane said. "Then what will you do? Plant onions and carrots? You have the rest of your life to live. What kind of life would that be, without the excitement of roving? Turnips will not buy you luxury and ease like good Spanish doubloons."

"I have enough of those put by me, Captain Vane, as have you, probably. There comes a time when a man yearns for peace and acceptance. It would be good to be normal again, able to sail into any port and shop in any store. I'd like to go back to England, or perhaps just stay on in Bermuda. It's warmer."

"And will they let you keep what you've plundered, Captain Jennings?" Captain Yeates interjected. "Ah, there's the rub, there's naught said about that point in the Act. Happen the King would like to get his greasy hands on our gold."

"Few of us have very much," Calico Jack put in. "I for one. Fast as I get a share, I spend it on some hussy. And most are like me. No, the King would get naught from the likes of us."

"I'll accept, and gladly," Hornigold said. "What say you, Cockram?"

"I haven't decided. There's time yet, I believe, and still rum to drink and a pipe to fill on the question. No need to be hasty."

The conversation went back and forth and Kath's mind strayed from the table. She was watching a buxom young woman who was flirting with a whole group of men. Calico Jack was aware of her presence, too.

"Who is she?" Kath whispered to Calico Jack.

"Anne Bonny," he replied. "She's a lass who arrived here last week from Carolina. With her husband!"

"Where is he? How can he let her run loose like this?" Kath asked.

"He has no say in the matter. Anne Bonny is a boisterous lass, with a mind of her own and a temper to match. And John Bonny is a fool."

Kath and Calico Jack watched a while longer, then Calico Jack took a last long swig of his punch and got up.

"Excuse me, gentlemen, Mrs. Hornigold," he said. "Duty calls."

Everyone expected him to walk into the bushes. Instead, he went straight over to Anne Bonny.

38

Anne Bonny watched Calico Jack approaching through the corner of her eyes. She tossed her head and ran her fingers through her wild mane of curly blonde hair, swinging it provocatively over one shoulder. Her low-cut bodice seemed bursting with bosom as she sucked in her stomach.

"Hullo, Mistress Anne Bonny," Calico Jack said, touching his hat, his audacious eyes caressing, his voice like velvet. "Is there room for one more swain at your feet?"

"That's not the best place for a man to be," Anne replied in her sultry voice. "I'm likely to trample him there."

"Don't think you'd walk over *me*. You'd trip and fall for me. I'd catch you so fast, woman, you'd never touch the ground."

"You think I'm that easy to catch?" she asked with a husky laugh, looking up at him through lowered lashes.

"Why don't you run and see?"

Anne took a sip of punch and looked at Calico Jack speculatively. Suddenly, she slammed down her tankard, picked up her skirts and took off running. Calico Jack sprinted after her. She was fast and he was tipsy, but he soon caught up with her. Then he dove for her legs and brought her down, the two of them rolling in the sand in a tangle of skirts and calico, shrieking laughter. A playful wave came in and wet them. They laughed all the harder, holding their sides as they scampered up the beach with their clothes sticking to them.

"See – you fell for me after all," Calico Jack said, gasping. Their eyes met and locked. "Don't think one roll in the sand means you've caught me, sailor," Anne said. "It'll take much more than that."

"Whatever it takes," Calico Jack said, nodding his head. "I'll do whatever it takes. But you are going to be *mine!*"

*

Captain Edward Teach, known to his confederates as Blackbeard, ate an enormous dinner at one of the waterfront taverns and washed it down with equally enormous quantities of punch. He rolled back to his large French Guineaman, the *Queen Anne's Revenge*, and fell heavily into his hammock to sleep it all off. He woke at five o'clock in the afternoon feeling thirsty and mean as a shark smelling blood. He stuck his spyglass out a porthole of the ship and saw the congregation of pirates ashore, including the captain of his consort, Major Stede Bonnet.

Blackbeard peered blearily into the square of polished metal that served him as a mirror and raked a comb through his greasy black locks, tying them at the nape of his neck with a bright red ribbon. No matter how thirsty, Blackbeard always took care of his beard, which bushed out from his cheekbones down to his waist. Now he combed it into eight sections, plaiting each with a different colored ribbon. He gave a tug to the hem of his navy blue cotton duck coat and strapped his two silk gun slings across his chest, adding his customary three brace of pistols. He looked in the mirror again and grunted with satisfaction. His large bloodshot eyes told him he was ready to meet his public.

Emerging on the main deck, he straightened to his full height of six feet three inches. His slim muscular build and boundless energy all contributed to his reputation as a Fury from Hell, a reputation that he carefully nurtured by frequent violent temper tantrums and the foulest language imaginable. Sometimes, when taking a prize, he wore lit, slow-burning hemp cords trailing from his hat, which wreathed him in acrid smoke. Nobody dared to cross him, he never had to fight or kill, and that was the way he wanted it. Now he bellowed hoarsely for someone to come and row him to shore.

Blackbeard swaggered up to the captains' table under the large spreading tree, grunted his salutation, poured himself a pint of punch and drank it in one draught. He blotted his mouth with his sleeve, poured another pint and drank that in two gulps. It was only then that he trusted himself to speak civilly.

"You all going to surrender?" he asked, pulling at his third pint of drink.

"We're thinking about it," Cockram said. "No need to be rash in deciding."

"*I'll* never surrender," Blackbeard spat. "What for? To be a lap dog to the gentry, pulling my forelock, bowing and scraping for two pence?

"Not me! I say we should fortify New Providence. We can put a fort at the eastern end of the harbor, lookout towers at the east and west ends of Nassau, and keep enough men here to man them. We could hold out against the Spanish, the French *and* the British Navy. Be the Pirates' Republic we've been bragging about all this time."

"So you think we should take on the whole civilized world, eh Teach?" Hornigold asked. Teach and Hornigold had sailed together as consorts ever since 1713, when they first went on the account. Hornigold had given Teach his first ship to captain, and Teach had been a founding member of Hornigold's Flying Gang in 1715, a group of pirates who took over New Providence. Now Teach was a pirate captain to be reckoned with.

Hornigold continued. "From this one little island, manned with a bunch of drunken scoundrels, we'll take on the British Navy? How long d'you s'pose we could hold out? A week?" Hornigold took a drink and wiped his mouth. "Jennings and I have definitely decided – we'll accept the Pardon."

Blackbeard swore volubly. "Have your guts turned to jelly?" he asked, his eyes narrowing. "Because you're rich, you think the King will accept you with open arms, sell you an estate and give you his daughter to wed? D'you think you will ever live down being a pirate?" He gave a ghastly smile and let out a few more choice words. "They call us the scum of the earth, the scourge of the sea. Now, I happen to like those titles. They're better than 'Lord This' and 'Sir That'."

Hornigold looked anxiously at Kath, who nodded in the direction of the horse and surrey. "Teach, in case you haven't noticed, we have a lady present. I'll thank you to contain yourself," Hornigold said.

"Damme, what's a lady doing here?" Blackbeard asked, swinging his huge head around and glaring at Kath.

"This lady is Mrs. Benjamin Hornigold. And she is here with her husband, who brought her to meet his friends," Hornigold said stiffly. "But you're right, Captain Teach, this is no place for a lady, so I'll excuse myself and take her home." He got up unsteadily. "Come, my Treasure..."

Kath rose hastily and took his arm. Hornigold staggered, and she held him steady. "Hornigold, don't go," Blackbeard said. "I meant no offense, man. Stay awhile and visit with your new wife. I've heard she's a wench of rare courage. For myself, I fancy more sport this evening than arguing with a bunch of sea captains. I'm off to see what other excitement I can find."

Hornigold sagged back into a chair. Kath did not know what to do. She wanted to get him back to the inn, but she did not want him to lose face in front of his confederates. She decided she would stay and perhaps he would sober up somewhat. This was a vain hope – Hornigold took another glass of punch. Kath bit her lip and looked away. What would she do if he got truly drunk? She looked back to see that Captain Jennings was observing her.

"It's all right, Mrs. Hornigold," he said quietly. "I'll see you're safe." He moved over to sit next to her, in the chair vacated by Calico Jack. She smiled at him gratefully, then looked away from the shore, towards the cemetery.

What she saw there made her sit up straight. Calico Jack and Anne Bonny were lying on the grass together, on top of a grave, deeply engaged with each other. Kath blushed and looked in another direction, where she saw several of the town whores socializing with the men, with one or two plying their trade under the trees.

Blackbeard had moved away to another table, where he was drinking with three of his cronies. A small man, probably a local shopkeeper, was passing on the road and had caught his eye.

"Come have a drink with us," Blackbeard bellowed, waving the man over.

"No, thank you," the man said pleasantly. "I have to go home."

Blackbeard swore. "Come and take a drink!"

The man was scared, but held his ground. "Please excuse me. I'm taking something home to cook for my children."

Blackbeard snatched a pistol from the sling across his stomach, cocked it and aimed at his unwilling guest. "Drink or be damned, man!" he roared. "Can't you be civil with visitors to your island?" He shot at the man's feet.

The shopkeeper leapt over. "That's better," Blackbeard said, passing him a full tankard. But the man's hands were shaking so that he spilled most of the punch. "See, you really needed a good drink," Blackbeard said, refilling the tankard. "Drink it down, man!" He filled it again twice before allowing the poor local to stagger away.

Hornigold was reaching for yet another glass of drink when Kath tugged softly at his sleeve. "Please take me home, Ben," she asked. "I'm tired, and you promised you'd take me if I got nervous. It's getting too wild for me." He looked at her in surprise. "Nervous, m'dear? Why? I'm here, aren't I? Perfectly safe!" His words were slurred and his face flushed.

"Hornigold, your wife is right," Captain Jennings said. "I'd like to leave myself. Will you give me a ride into town? I doubt any decisions will be made at this general council meeting tonight."

Kath and Jennings stood, and Ben reluctantly joined them. Jennings drove to the Nancy Lou Lilly, bade the couple good night, and left to return the horse and surrey to the stables. Kath helped Ben up to their room, dreading having to face one of the dragon innkeepers. Or worse still, Greville Knowles. They arrived safely, but Hornigold refused to stay.

"Must go back, got discussions afoot," Hornigold insisted. "Still early," he said, taking out his pocket watch and peering at it. "'S only coming up to seven. You're safe, home now. Won't be late. Don't wait up. Eat nice supper..." he mumbled and left, treading heavily down the stairs. A moment later the parlor door closed with a crash.

*

Kath took off her hat and sat on the side of the bed, rubbing her head and neck. Her muscles felt like stiff leather. There was a soft tap at the door. Now what?

"Mrs. Hornigold, are you within?" came a quavering voice.

"Yes, Miz Nancy. What is it?" Kath asked with a sinking feeling. *Ben made too much noise and she wants us to leave,* she thought.

"My sisters and I are about to eat supper in the kitchen. There's stewed fish. We thought you might like some with us. Are you hungry?"

"Oh, yes, thank you," she replied, relieved. "I'll be right out." She would be glad of some company tonight, as well. She did not want to be alone with her worries. She bit her lips and pinched her cheeks, then opened the door.

Miz Nancy was waiting with an oil lamp, the golden light gleaming off her kindly face and silver hair. "I'm glad you haven't eaten already," she said. "We sisters get weary of our own company. It will be such a treat to have you join us."

The kitchen was a separate stone building, twenty feet away from the main house. Miz Nancy opened the door and the smell of fresh baked bread billowed out. The food was delicious, and the three sisters were so hospitable that Kath soon found herself telling them her story. Of course they already knew most of it. There were no secrets in Nassau.

A knock on the kitchen door interrupted their cozy visit.

It was Obediah, Mate from the *Swan*.

"Captain Knowles sends his compliments and asks would you send his things, please Ma'am? On account we's leaving early in the morning and he won't be sleeping back here tonight."

"Come in, Obie," Miz Lilly said.

"Evening, ladies," Obie said as he came in, his straw hat in his hands. "Oh Hello, Miz Kath! Or I should say, Mrs. Hornigold!"

"Hello, Obie," Kath said, happy to see the rascal, although his Nancy Lou Lilly trick had cost her hours of needless worry.

"The whole town's talking about you," Obie continued. "Sounds like you gave them pirates a nasty dose of their own medicine. We're proud of you! And mighty glad none of us tried any tricks when *we* rescued you!"

Miz Nancy was still eating, but got up to go and get Greville's things. "You sit, Miz Nancy," Kath said. "I can pack Captain Knowles's things. We're like brother and sister, you know."

"Thank you, Mrs. Hornigold. He is in room 8 – the key's hanging on the board back of the front desk," she said, pointing to the main house.

"I'll just be a minute, Obie," Kath said.

"Fancy some stewed fish while you wait, Obie?" Miz Lou asked. "It's very tasty…"

*

It was a strange place, Kath reflected, where people were lionized for killing a man. But the memory of the shooting haunted her, was seldom far from her thoughts. Try as she would, Jenks's face refused to stay in the locked room with all her other unhappy memories.

Kath lit the lamp on the washstand in Greville's room and looked around. His clothes were neatly folded on a chair as usual, with his carpetbag lying crumpled on the floor beside them. Kath picked up the clothes and pressed them to her face, inhaling his scent, then put them into the bag. She

284

swallowed the hard lump in her throat and blinked rapidly, checking the drawers of the nightstand and bureau. When everything was packed, Kath took a last look around the room, holding the lamp high. She noticed a small blue box over in one corner. She picked it up, stroking the velvet case with her thumb. Overcome by curiosity, she opened it and gasped at the beautiful ring inside.

She took out the ring and examined it closely, up by the lamp. There was something engraved inside, in very fine writing. Squinting, she read "*Grev to Kath, 25 Dec. 1717.*" Her heart began its old, familiar plunge as the truth rushed in on her. He had been planning to ask her to marry him on Christmas Day – in three weeks – and this was to be her ring. He must have flung it into the corner after she told him she had married Hornigold.

Kath threw herself on the bed, burying her face in the pillow, the pillow that smelled so wonderfully of Greville. *I can't give way now*, she thought. *I have to give Obie the bag...* but she couldn't bear to part with the pillow, and she took it to her room, swapping it with one from her own bed. She raced down to the kitchen with the bag, quickly saying goodnight, pleading a long and tiring day, and a headache.

Upstairs again, she put on her nightdress. She took the ruby and diamond ring from its box, slipped it on the third finger of her left hand and admired it in the lamplight. She blew out the lamp and curled up in bed, hugging Greville's pillow – which seemed slightly damp, for some reason.

"Just this one night," she told herself, "...for this one and only time, I'm going to sleep with the man I truly love."

She fell asleep eventually, breathing in his scent.

39

Hornigold straggled in the next morning about eleven, very contrite, very rough looking and very sorry for himself.

"I'm sorry," he said. "Sometimes when I get drinking with the lads, I forget everything else. I'm sorry..."

"It's all right, Ben," Kath said sighing. "You are your own man, you can make your own choices. I won't have you feeling hen-pecked because we're married now. It takes time to change."

"That's good of you, Treasure. I'll not let it happen again. I know you must have worried about me. I'll try to do better next time."

"Did you eat?"

"Not yet. Is that coffee in the pot?" he asked, brightening and moving to the small table on their balcony. He poured himself a cup. She was concerned to see that his hands shook.

"I did get some business done yesterday," Hornigold said. "Jennings will leave for Bermuda in a few days with several others, to accept the King's Pardon. He'll buy a thirty-foot Bermuda sloop and arrange for someone to sail it back here for me. He knows exactly what I want, so I feel confident that it'll be right. She'll be named 'Songbird', after you."

"I thank you for the honor, husband," Kath said, genuinely pleased. "But didn't you say that Jennings wasn't a particular friend of yours? That he had stolen a sloop off you a couple of years ago and sailed her down to Jamaica?"

"Yes, he did, and I harbored ill-will towards him for some time. He had a privateer's license then, and thought he was a cut above the rest of us. But the tide soon turned, and he was declared a pirate. He had to run from Jamaica to avoid arrest, and has been living here in Nassau as a fugitive for more than a year. We've buried our differences, and there's mutual respect between us. I'm convinced he would not steal from me again."

"Have you had any further thoughts on where we shall live?" she asked, to change the subject and make him more at ease. She was sorry for Ben, he looked so woebegone. She recalled him saying that drinking brought relief from his awful memories. She hoped she would not be tempted to drink herself, to get rid of Jenks's ghost. "I mean, I know you don't feel comfortable here at Misses Nancy Lou Lilly. There must be a house to rent in Nassau?"

"Are you happy here, Treasure?" Ben asked.

"Yes, of course. I have never enjoyed such luxury."

"Well, I am thinking you might just as well stay here for a while. I must take *Bonnet* and the company over to Harbour Island for a couple of weeks, and I wouldn't want you living alone while I'm gone. Nassau is a rough place for a decent woman. But you can make inquiries for a house while I'm away. Ask Nancy Lou Lilly. They know everything," Ben said heading for the door.

"Please freshen up first," Kath snapped. "You can't go about looking like that."

"All right, Treasure," Hornigold said mildly. "You're right, of course. I'm a rough sea captain, used to the company of even rougher men. You must teach me. But I had a bath just yesterday..."

"I'll lay out some fresh things for you while you have a wash."

*

Hornigold was organizing things for his future life ashore with determination. Not only had he ordered his personal Bermuda sloop, he had also selected a building site on the ridge above and to the west of the crumbling Fort Nassau, not far from where the old Governor's house stood. They would have a house with fine views of Nassau harbor and the ocean to the west, so he could watch from his home as ships came and went.

Also planning to accept the Pardon was Nathaniel Saunders, the *Bonnet's* carpenter, and he would be in charge of the building along with several men he knew. Hornigold had bought three slaves to help with clearing the lot and cutting wood for the building. More wood could be shipped from Harbour Island and North Eleuthera, and Ben would order some during his upcoming visit.

Hornigold introduced Kath to Nathaniel Saunders, who agreed she should take an active part in the design of the house. He and his men were shipwrights, after all – a few shacks on the beach had been their only experience with house building so far, and this would be their first attempt at a proper home. They would be glad for her suggestions.

Before Hornigold left, he took Kath to meet his agent in Nassau, Richard Noland. Noland had sailed with Hornigold in the past, and had formerly been quartermaster to the late Sam Bellamy. He had decided to come on the beach for a while, and would be accepting the King's Pardon. Noland would advance Kath any money she needed while Ben was gone, and would also oversee and pay the builders.

*

Ben Hornigold left for Harbour Island the first week of December, and returned the third week of January. Upon leaving Harbour Island, his company had voted to have one last pirating foray against the Spanish, so they had sailed out into the ocean. Now they returned triumphant with two well-armed Dutch ships, which had sixty-six guns between them.

Hornigold had trouble sorting out his feelings. On the one hand he was extremely proud at what his company had accomplished, but on the other, he had already made his decision to give up piracy and go on the beach. Among his comrades he strutted, but with Kath he was deeply embarrassed.

He had promised to put piracy behind him, and here he was, with two magnificent prizes! Well, *now* he would come ashore.

Ben was back in time for the pirates' general council. They all met near the Eastern Cemetery, to thrash out just what to do about the King's Pardon. There was so much raucous shouting back and forth that nothing was decided.

Charles Vane had come to prominence while Hornigold had been away. He and his faction had actually written to the Jacobites in France, pledging their allegiance and support to James III, the Catholic Pretender to the British throne. Now things became very tense between the pirates, those hoping for redemption and resumption of a normal life through the King's Pardon, versus Vane's anti-pardon group, which grew in strength daily through the promise of legitimacy by becoming privateers to the Jacobite government.

Hornigold was in the thick of things, as usual, and Kath hardly saw him. She realized that he had been the de facto Governor of Nassau for several years, and needed to steer the pirates for their own good. He had sent the *Bonnet* to Jamaica with 80 men who agreed to accept the Pardon, and to ask Governor Heywood to send a warship to Nassau to quell the Jacobite treason.

No warship came from Jamaica, but on 23rd February a sixth rate frigate, *HMS Phoenix*, arrived in Nassau harbor from New York, Captain Vincent Pearse. He brought more copies of the King's Pardon and news that a Royal Governor had been appointed for the Bahamas. It was to be none other than the famous privateer, Woodes Rogers, circumnavigator of the world, taker of a hugely valuable Spanish treasure ship in the Pacific, and author of a best-selling book about his adventures.

HMS Phoenix would issue certificates of intent for any pirates wishing to take the Pardon, which would stand them in good stead until they could sign the genuine article before a properly appointed Royal Governor.

Here was more to occupy Ben Hornigold. More general councils, arguments pro and con. Finally Hornigold carried the day with his suggestion that they all take certificates from Captain Pearse, and wait until Governor Woodes Rogers arrived. This would buy them time to think further on the matter. Soon longboats queued up at *HMS Phoenix* with men requesting certificates, but this did not happen without more tantrums from Charles Vane, whose heady taste of rabble rousing leadership had made him more rabid than ever.

*

In the midst of all the mayhem, Kath stayed steadily on her own course, visiting the building site every few days, buying and stitching materials to make curtains, pillows and other comforts for her new home. As the house took shape, it developed the same feeling as a wooden ship, which pleased Ben to no end.

"Would you mind very much if I had my own room, Treasure?" Ben asked. "I could keep my charts, spyglasses, other instruments and tools in there, with my own desk, and perhaps a comfortable sofa for a nap. I could entertain my friends there, away from your sitting room." He thought for a moment, then said, "And you might like to have your own room, too, where you can keep your sewing things and have your friends in for tea and personal chats."

"That's a wonderful idea, Ben," Kath agreed, and Nathaniel Saunders made it so.

By the middle of March 1718, the Hornigolds were in their new home. Ben sold two of his male slaves, keeping one as a groom and man about the place. He bought two female slaves for Kath, to help with the cooking and cleaning. Ben was spoiling Kath in every way he could think. This was in part to make up for the weeks he had been gone sailing, and the weeks since his return, which had consumed his time with pirate politics.

He also wanted to make up for his drinking bouts. About every ten days he disappeared for a couple of days at a time. Kath knew he was aboard one or other of the ships in harbor or under a tavern table down on the waterfront. Each time the penitent returned Kath found it easier to forgive him. It ceased to matter very much. There was no need to feel embarrassed in a town where the whole populace habitually drank. She became used to his ways, and accepted them as part of her life.

In fact, though, their personal relationship had slipped over the four months of their marriage, to the point where they were rarely intimate anymore. Ben's drinking sapped both his physical performance and her desire for him. Kath was concentrating on home building and nesting materials, while Ben was constantly off with his pirates sorting something or another. Ben was no longer the focus of her life, although she was unfailingly polite and solicitous, scrupulously looking after his home and welfare.

As for Hornigold, he tried hard to adapt to life ashore. He tried to become interested in his new citrus orchard, or in growing vegetables, but he simply did not enjoy gardening. There were few books on the island, but he grew restless after an hour of reading anyway. He missed his seaman's life, the boat and the camaraderie of other men.

Early one morning soon after they moved into the house, a pretty sloop came gliding over the bar of Nassau harbor. Hornigold examined her with his spyglass. "*Songbird*," he read aloud, then let out a wild whoop. "*Songbird*! It's my little *Songbird*, at last! Come to the wharf with me, Treasure?" he asked excitedly. "She's a beauty, and I want to take her out straight away. You must come for my first sail in her!"

"Of course, Ben!" Kath said, delighted to see him sparkle again. She hoped the sloop would bring a new interest to his life and help to heal his wounded spirit. She understood his boredom, and felt guilty that she could not love him more, although she always sang to him when he seemed down. What he needed, what she needed, too, was a good Catholic priest to hear their confessions.

*

Hornigold took Kath to a small, palm-fringed island northeast of Nassau. He was almost ecstatic over the lively way the new *Songbird* responded. "She's as sweet as honey, as fine a sailboat as any I've handled!" was his verdict – praise indeed. He brought the sloop about in the lee of a sandbar and threw out the anchor.

Kath lay on the bow, enjoying the gentle rocking of the waves, while Ben saw to the sails and pottered about. She listened to the gurgling laughter of the tide under the hull of the sloop, and the waves swishing on the beach. She looked around her, appreciating the contrast of colors, the lapis and sapphire of the deep Atlantic, the clear turquoise, emerald and peridot green of the shallows, with sun diamonds dancing over all. The beach lay like a string of pearls beside the jade green of the bush beyond. She turned her face up to the sun, closing her eyes, seeing fiery, ruby-red behind her lids. *With jewels like these, why must there be pirates? Why must we rob and kill?* She thought. She understood now why Ben needed the sloop. It gave him peace and a freedom he could never have on land.

"Take off your skirts and come ashore with me, Treasure," Ben said, standing over her, offering his hand to help her up. "I have something to show you."

On shore, blue skinks and little red land crabs scampered rustling into dead leaves that lay everywhere underfoot as they walked. Ben carried a shovel and held the bushes back for Kath, threading their way deeper into the middle of the island. At last he squinted up at a tall coconut tree, took a bearing off it with his arm, and counted fifty long paces.

"Here," he said, stopping by a darling-plum tree.

"What's here?" Kath asked.

"Part of our wealth," he replied, "...although most of it is in a bank in Bermuda, in your name. I had Henry Jennings take it there for safekeeping." He grinned at her, his eyes alight with love. "You're a very rich woman, Kathryn 'Treasure' Hornigold. See how much I love you?"

Kath gaped at him, her jaw dropping open.

"Surprised?" he asked, as he plunged the shovel into the sand. "I've decided this is too inconvenient, way out here. I had Nathaniel Saunders build us a special cubbyhole in the house where we can keep it."

"But Nathaniel will know about it..." Kath said.

Ben gave her a level look. "Nathaniel won't steal from us, Kath, nor will he tell anyone else."

*

With frequent stops, they carried the heavy chest back to the beach, then slowly heaved it onto the *Songbird*. Hornigold brought out a picnic basket and they ate their dinner on shore, with their backs against coconut trees.

"Do you remember our other little island, Treasure?" he asked when they were finished.

"How could I ever forget?" she asked softly, moved by his tenderness and his trust in her.

"The name of this island is Sandy Cay on the charts, but I think we should call it '*Honeymoon Island*'," he said shyly, moving to sit beside her. "Can't we have another stab at it?" he asked. "It was so perfect, so wonderful in Exuma. I know I've let you down, with my drinking and all. But I truly love you. Please let's give it another try!"

"Yes, please! Lets..." Kath said, turning to him. "I love you too, Ben..."

But the rest of her words went unspoken, as his lips covered hers.

40

Around four o'clock the *Songbird* was in Salt Cay Channel, returning to enter the eastern end of Nassau harbor. Hornigold looked around to the southeast, then took up his spyglass.

"I think that's the *Swan*, Kath," Hornigold said, as soon as he saw the schooner bearing down towards them from the east. "Let's go to meet her!" He came about and scudded along, spilling the air from *Songbird's* sails when they were within hailing distance.

"Ahoy there," Hornigold shouted. "Ahoy, Captain Knowles!"

The *Swan* put her sails in irons. "Ahoy! What news?" Greville shouted back. All the crew stood on deck, wondering why this unknown sloop was hailing them.

"We came to welcome you," Ben shouted. "We're almost related, after all, though *Swans* don't sing like *Songbirds*..."

Kath waved at the men, then gasped. "*Shirley!*" she shrieked. "*Shirley Stirrup!*"

"*Miz Kath!*" Shirley's own shriek came back. Shirley was jumping up and down and waving both arms. "How did you know we were coming?"

"We didn't," Ben shouted. We just happened to be out. We'll see you at the wharf..."

"What a day for surprises," Kath said, her face glowing. "That girl, Shirley Stirrup, is my best friend, Ben. She must come and stay with us."

"Of course, Treasure. You've told me about her before. It would do you good to have another female about the house, and we have plenty of room."

"I'll ask her! And we must invite Captain Knowles for supper too, though I don't know just what we'll eat."

*

The *Songbird* had accompanied *Swan* outside of Hog Island, down to the western entrance of Nassau harbor and then to the wharf. Kath and Shirley had hugged, and danced, and kissed, both had gabbled at the same time to each other, and happy confusion had reigned for at least ten minutes.

Shirley was all excited to meet the infamous Captain Benjamin Hornigold.

"Captain Hornigold, I'm so delighted to meet you," Shirley had gushed, when Kath presented him. "I've heard so much about you, and wondered what you'd be like for so long! How did you come to rescue Miz Kath from the Spanish frigate? Where did you marry her? Oh, there's so much *I don't know!*" Her dark eyes were sparkling, positively snapping with curiosity.

"And is it true you shot a man and *killed* him?" she demanded, swiveling round to Kath. "...And that you rescued Captain Hornigold from certain death? Oh it's all so romantic, I can hardly *stand* it!" she exclaimed, bouncing on her heels. "And Obie's been filling me with all sorts of tales, I don't know what to believe, what not! Miz Kath, all the *best things* happen to you!"

Hornigold gazed at Shirley in amazement, like he was seeing an exotic new creature for the first time. Which indeed he was. Kath rocked with laughter.

"Oh Shirley, *Shirley!*" Kath exclaimed, hugging her again, and the two did another little jig of happiness. "How wonderful to have you here! Captain Hornigold says you must stay with us, so we have *all* the time in the world to explore my adventures. All the *best things*, as you call them, have been fearfully uncomfortable for me, I must say."

Kath's eyes shifted to Ben's face as she said that, and she quickly amended her statement. "Well, not all the things – one thing has not been uncomfortable..." Kath gave Ben a

295

radiant smile and winked, remembering their time together that afternoon. He winked back.

For one instant Kath was blissfully happy. Then she caught a glimpse of Greville watching them, his eyes full of pain, and her own joy evaporated.

"Why don't you get your things, Shirley?" Kath asked. "I must speak to Captain Knowles for a moment. Ben, will you help Shirley please?"

"Of course, Treasure," he replied, and offered Shirley his arm. Shirley gave him a melting look, took his arm and strutted back to the *Swan*.

"Captain Knowles, may I invite you to supper tonight?" Kath called as she walked towards him.

"Thank you, Mrs. Hornigold, but I'm already engaged this evening," he replied.

"I'm sorry, perhaps another time?" she asked, relieved that he would not be coming. Ben was bound to drink too much punch.

"Yes, another time," Greville replied.

Kath was beside him how. She put a hand on his arm. "Greville, I want you to know that I have the ring," she said quietly.

A muscle twitched in his jaw. "How do you come to have it?" he asked, his voice ragged. "I threw it away somewhere..."

"It was in your room at the Nancy Lou Lilly. I found it when I went to pack your things for Obie. I want you to know that I keep it with me always. That I treasure it, and wear it over my heart." Kath pulled a short piece of ribbon from her bodice. The ring was sewn onto one end, the other end was pinned to a tiny pocket inside the left side of her bodice. "If you want it back of course... but I thought at the time that it was meant to be my Christmas present."

Greville and Kath looked at each other, the truth of their love starkly revealed between them for the first time, without any doubt.

"No," he said slowly. "You keep it. It was, indeed, meant to be your Christmas present." He blinked rapidly. "It will comfort me to know where it is, Kath – Mrs. Hornigold. Though it will be cold comfort..."

*

"Shirley, how did you persuade your parents to let you come to Nassau?" Kath asked, as they sat around the table after supper. During the meal, the conversation had been about Kath and Captain Hornigold. Now Ben was out on the porch with his pipe and a glass of punch, leaving the women to themselves.

"I'll tell you the truth," Shirley replied, looking shame-faced. "...I lied."

"I thought so."

"When the *Swan* arrived with all the supplies – oh, we were so glad to see them! The crew told us how they knew about the raid. The stories about you ran around the settlement like a lump of lard in a hot frying pan.

"We had our stories too, because if you hadn't thrown your food and cook pots into the bushes, I don't know how we would have eaten.

Your fishing lines, too – all ours were burnt in the houses. We all slept in Miz Eva's house and kitchen, the only buildings not burnt, and ate your peas and grits for the first few days. We wouldn't have had food or shelter if not for your quick thinking. We were in such shock, we hardly knew what to do at first.

We found Miz Eva and Treacle, of course. We found her Bible, too, out behind the big fig tree. Miz Eva had told Granny Reena she wanted to be buried out by her God-talking rock, so Mr. Harding dug her grave there. We went to look for old Mr. Cartwright, to see if he would read from the Bible. We had forgotten all about him until then; but when we got to his house, it was burnt to the ground, with him in it.

"So we buried Miz Eva, and put Treacle in with her. They were never apart in life, Mr. Harding said, so we should keep 'em together in death." Shirley wiped her eyes.

"Granny Reena really minded Miz Eva going like that.

She says she's the oldest one now, and she's too young to be the oldest, only sixty!" Shirley rolled her eyes and giggled. "Sixty sure sounds old enough to me!"

"Very interesting, Shirley. And thank you for your compliments! Now, what did you tell your mother?" Kath asked again, trying not to smile.

Shirley sighed. "All right. After the *Swan* left for Jamaica, I told *her* that Captain Knowles told *me* that you told *him* that, if she could spare me for a few months, you'd be glad of the company, seeing as you were in with all them pirates and no decent women about you for company," Shirley gabbled. She caught her breath and smiled. "So you don't know how glad I was when you said I could stay with you and Captain Hornigold, because I didn't know what else I was going to do! And I didn't want to go back on the *Swan* with my daddy!

"Miz Kath, I just had to get out of Fortune Island! It was killing me, it was so dull, especially with you gone. That first month after the raid was so hard! And you were down here having all sorts of fun and good times! I thought..." Shirley wound down and trailed off. "I hope you're not angry with me about it," she muttered.

Kath smiled. "Angry? Oh no, Shirley! You're the *very best thing*, of all the best things that have happened to me since I left Fortune Island!"

Shirley's face lit up. "I told Momma that you'd need me to help sew your trousseau, and curtains and such for your house. Everybody in Fortune Island is so taken with you now, they'd give you anything!

"I was able to make clothes, too," Shirley continued, "from the cloth you gave me to save from the Spanish. Several people ran in the bushes with only their nightclothes on. Stupid sheep didn't even save their clothes! We had undressed Miz Eva, to wash her and make her ready, you know, so we decided to sew a shroud out of her bedcover, and gave her clothes to different women to use. Granny Reena said that's what Miz Eva would want, and we needed clothes so badly.

"Well, anyway, I sewed them some things. So Momma

was pleased with me and said I could come with my daddy when the *Swan* came back from Jamaica. So here I am!"

"I'm very glad to see you, Shirley," Kath said, looking at her fondly. "You only *thought* you were lying to your Momma. All that you told her was the truth! I've missed you very much – and we *do* have a lot of sewing to do!"

*

Shirley was up early the next morning. She went out back to the kitchen to help Jane and Susan fix breakfast. Her feet seemed to be on springs, she was so excited. She bounced from the kitchen into the house and back again, waiting impatiently for Kath and Ben to get up. Kath lay in bed listening to the patter of Shirley's little feet going back and forth, the back door banging behind her with increasing force each time.

"Shirley's up so early because she's desperate to see the town," she told Ben with a chuckle. "She doesn't quite dare to knock on our door, but she's making sure we're awake. I'll bet her head is full of fantasies about how the men in Nassau will look at her. We'd better get up, husband, and put her out of her misery."

"She's not one of those man-crazed wenches, is she?" Ben asked, swinging his feet to the floor.

"She's seventeen," Kath replied. "Do you remember what you were like at seventeen? No, probably not. Well, at her age, the world is a mystery, waiting to be discovered. And to discover *her*, God help the world."

Breakfast was soon over. Shirley did not think the slaves needed her in the kitchen anymore. Not to help with the dishes, anyway. Besides, she was wearing her best dress. Kath noticed that it was new. Shirley had made it from the finest piece of cloth in the bundle saved from the Spanish.

"You're going to be very disappointed with Nassau," Kath said. "I'm afraid it's a shabby, poor sort of place, with garbage heaps everywhere and bushes growing wild among the houses. Everything is dilapidated. People don't bother to fix things, because they think the Spanish or French may raid them at any moment. That's their excuse at any rate. I think they're more interested in having a good time."

"A good time sounds good," Shirley said brightly. "I don't care much for houses either!"

Kath gave her a sidelong glance. "Well, I'll ask Jacob to get the surrey ready and drive us in. I want to call at Mr. Taylor's for some more cloth, and I'll start introducing you around."

"You have your *own* horse and surrey?" Shirley didn't wait for an answer. She rushed from the room to check herself in the hall mirror again, then came skipping back into the dining room. "You and Captain Hornigold must have the largest house in Nassau," she said. "I've just looked down the hill, and from what I saw last night, yours is the best. Are you rich?"

"I suppose ours is the largest private house," Kath said slowly. "And yes, I believe we are rich. So you'll have to mind your p's and q's if you're going to stay with us. No running after sailors, or bloody, swearing pirates if you please, Miss."

"Captain Hornigold swears," Shirley said artlessly, "and he was quite bloody, from what I've heard. He threatened to murder the Chief Justice of New Providence two years ago. Made the poor man run with his family to South Carolina."

"That may be. But he's reformed, now, and we must help him break his bad habits. What will the new Governor think when he comes?" Kath asked, teasing her.

Shirley's head jerked around. "A new Governor? When?"

"Any day now. And he may have a good-looking son, or at least a whole company of soldiers. So mind your reputation, Shirley, or you won't be received by the best people."

"They won't want to know me anyway," Shirley said. "I'm only a 'free colored' to them. Little more than a slave."

She was quiet the whole way into town.

41

They had just come out of Mr. Taylor's dark shop when Kath sensed a change in Shirley, caused by something she saw over Kath's shoulder. Kath looked around and spied George Rounsivel ambling along the street.

"Here's someone you can meet, Shirley," Kath said, smiling. She should have known it would be a handsome man.

"He's a pirate, but he's not bloody and doesn't swear too much. He used to be in my husband's company on the *Bonnet*. In fact he was my guard when they first took me onto the *Bonnet* from the Spanish frigate, and I know him quite well. He's waiting for Governor Rogers to arrive to get his Pardon from the King." Kath paused. "Want me to introduce you?"

"Oh, yes, please!" Shirley replied, tugging at her bodice and smoothing her skirt. "Do I look all right?"

"As lovely as the dawn.

"Good morning, George," Kath called. "Come and meet my friend from Fortune Island..."

Soon the two young people were chattering away as they strolled along Bay Street, Shirley being very animated. George was describing the rigging of a brig tied at the wharf, a subject that clearly fascinated her. "A brig has two masts, see, fore and main, with square sails on both. See, it has no mizzenmast..." George ground on interminably, with Shirley's sparkling eyes encouraging him. "Now a *brigantine* has the same rigging, but it only has square sails on the foremast, see, that's how you can tell the difference..."

"Excuse me, George," Kath interrupted. "I must continue

my shopping. Will you entertain Shirley here for a moment while I get some sugar from Mrs. Albury?"

"Of course, Mrs. Hornigold. Perhaps I might buy her a cup of chocolate at the Mermaid's Tail, and you can meet us there?"

"Oh yes, please," Shirley replied, batting her lashes. "I'm dying of thirst!"

Kath turned away to hide her smile. Poor George was finished!

*

One morning in the middle of April, Ben came to find Kath in her sewing room. "Treasure, I've been thinking. I've been waiting for Governor Rogers to arrive, so I can exchange this certificate from *HMS Phoenix* for the Pardon from the King. But Governor Heywood of Jamaica took the trouble to send Holford and West to tell me about the Act of Grace. The least I can do to return his favor is surrender to him in Kingston, and thank him personally for what he did for me. Giving Benjamin Hornigold his pardon will look good on Heywood's reports to London, too.

"Also, there are a few more of my old company who've decided they'll take the Pardon, and I want to make sure they do. These people are like waves on the seashore, they come and go, their ideas and loyalties shift with the tide.

"Now you have Shirley here for company, this would be a good time for me to run down to Jamaica. It would only take a few weeks, six, maybe seven at the most."

"Of course, Ben! I know you're anxious to get the thing done, and you need a trip. When will you go? Will you take *Bonnet* or *Songbird*?"

"I'll take *Bonnet*. It may be the last time I sail in her. When Rogers comes, he may claim her in the name of the King. George says he'll wait for Rogers. Says he'll keep an eye on all my women for me – you, Shirley and *Songbird*. So I can leave with a clear mind."

"Yes, of course. I expect George would like to keep an eye on Shirley and *Songbird* particularly!" Kath said with a smile.

"He's very fond of them both! And I have my work cut out for me. I'll keep busy until you get back. When do you leave?"

"Tonight, if we can get the provisioning done. I want to be here when Governor Rogers arrives, so it'll be a quick trip."

"Is there anything I can do to help you get ready?"

Hornigold smiled down at her fondly. "No, my Treasure. I know all about provisioning a ship. Although I've never had to be so particular in the past. Usually if we needed anything, we could find and take what we wanted!" His eyes sparkled, and he leaned down and kissed Kath on the lips. "Goodbye, wife! I promise I won't run off a-pirating this time! I shall see you in a few weeks, by the middle of June at the very latest!"

*

Shirley had George enthralled. He would hang around the house as much as Kath let him, or as long as Shirley could tolerate his mooning adoration. His parents were wealthy people from Weymouth in Dorset, and had educated him until he was eleven, when he went as cabin boy on his uncle's privateering ship. George read anything printed that he could find, and was an intelligent young man. However, Shirley was intelligent, shrewd and *clever*, so she ran circles around George, tying him in knots.

George knew a lot about ships and pirate Ships' Articles, as well as rigging, careening, caulking, celestial navigation and maintaining a ship. Unfortunately, it was all he knew, and it was his only conversation. He tried to impress Shirley and teach it all to her, and she was losing interest by the time Hornigold returned from Jamaica.

But George was the best of the suitors in Nassau around her own age. Shirley began to dream about the new Governor's arrival – and with him, she hoped, many young sailors and a company of English soldiers.

*

True to his word, Ben Hornigold returned from Jamaica by the first week of June, the proud bearer of the King's Pardon for all his misdeeds.

The weeks drifted by. Shirley's antics amused Kath and Ben, helping to ease the tension that was growing in their marriage. Hornigold was struggling with his drinking, using any excuse to mix his favorite punch. He genuinely wanted to give it up, but the addiction had him by the throat and he could seldom go without a drink for more than a day or so. His maudlin guilt over his drinking was hard for Kath to bear.

Increasingly, she encouraged him to go into town and see his friends. It kept him out of her way, and he did not have to hide his liquor and pretend he was not drinking. He loved the *Songbird* and went sailing or fishing in her whenever the weather was right and he could find someone to go with him. Kath always encouraged George to go along and keep an eye on him. Ben seemed to drink less when he went sailing. The truth was that she did not know how else to help Ben. She was beginning to suspect that he was beyond help.

Nor could she help herself, as her own guilty feelings began to overwhelm her. Not only was she a thief and murderer, but she was encouraging her husband to drink himself to death. She was a married woman and had promised to love her husband, but she was in love with another man. She was almost glad of Ben's increasing sexual disinterest and physical incapacity, yet she felt guilty that she did not desire her husband.

There was yet another guilt – Kath no longer said her rosary, nor prayed, nor believed that God cared about her. She thought she was a heretic. She had asked Shirley what had happened to Miz Eva's Bible. Shirley thought it had been given to Captain Knowles as a memento of his Gammie.

Kath felt guilty about her promise to Miz Eva, too. It was Miz Eva's only request as she was about to die, and Kath had faithfully promised that she would read a chapter of the Bible every day. And here it was, she hadn't even tried to do this one simple thing!

Kath had another problem, too. Her specters refused

to stay locked away, now that her life was settling into easy domesticity. Mental pictures flashed across her mind at odd times when she was doing ordinary household tasks. She had nightmares, and would wake sweating and screaming. Jenks, sagging to his knees after she had shot him, coming for her on his knees, holding his bloody entrails out to her appealingly. Miz Eva and Treacle in their bloody death throes. And Duncan, waving to her from the cart on his way to the scaffold.

Her heart ached for Kevin, to know if he was dead or alive, for Maggie and her noisy brood, and for the cool green of Ireland. She ached for Greville.

There was yet another guilt. She felt guilty because, now that she had everything she had ever wanted in life – fine clothes, money, respect, a faithful husband who loved her, a fine house, her own carriage, household slaves even – she was not happy.

42

It was well after dinner, about 3 o'clock, on the afternoon of July 26th, 1718, and Kath, Shirley and Captain Hornigold were sitting on the porch, trying to stay cool in the shade of a large sapodilla tree. The two women were sewing and chattering as usual, while Ben was smoking his pipe and staring longingly out to sea. He picked up his spyglass and trained it on the western horizon, as he often did in idle moments.

"There's a ship coming in," he said.

"Think it's the Governor?" Shirley asked hopefully.

"Too soon to see who she is. With this light breeze, might be another half hour before I can say."

For the next forty minutes, Hornigold strode back and forth on the porch, checking the ship in his glass until at last it was clear – she was a British Navy frigate.

"It very likely is the Governor, Shirley," Ben said, brimming with excitement. "I must ride down to the harbor cove and tell the others. They can't see her from their vantage point." He disappeared into the house, bellowing for Jacob to saddle his horse.

"I wonder what the Governor will be like..." Shirley's eyes were shining.

"He's a very well-known man," Kath replied. "A distinguished privateer from Bristol, who made a fortune ten years ago by taking a Spanish treasure ship in the Pacific Ocean. He sailed around the world and rescued a man who was shipwrecked on a small island for years and years. He wrote a book about his adventures, which made him famous. The pirates here think he's a great man."

"I wonder how old he is... Probably a doddering old fogy by now."

"No, I believe he's about the same age as my husband."

"Well, that's pretty old," Shirley said morosely. Then her face brightened. "Maybe he'll have children my age, and they'll have parties and dances. And if there's a company of soldiers, they'll have to invite me, colored or not. There'll be nobody much else to ask, except those stuck-up Pritchard girls, who are too good for anybody."

"What will you do with poor old George?"

"Pish! He can look after himself," she replied, picking up the spyglass and squinting at the incoming ship. "She's a three-master, under full sail, with courses, topsails, top-gallants and royals," Shirley exclaimed. "Looks like she's gaff-rigged, with stay sails and a bowsprit. She has one, two, three... oh... seventeen gun ports this side. That means she has 34 cannon and probably chasers and swivels, too. She'll probably have a complement of at least a hundred and fifty men!"

"You've been spending too much time with George," Kath said, laughing. "You're beginning to sound just like him."

"I certainly know a lot about ships now," Shirley said, laughing too. "It puts me in good stead to talk with all the sailors coming in. Do you think there's a company of soldiers on that ship too?"

"We'll soon find out," Kath said, threading her needle. "Aren't a hundred and fifty sailors enough to choose from?"

Shirley gave a wicked grin and winked. "The more the merrier," she said. She looked through the glass again, sweeping the horizon. "There's another sail behind," she said excitedly. "There are *two* ships! We were so interested in the first one, we never even noticed the second."

"Are you sure? Let me see," Kath said, taking the glass. "You're right, Shirley. We'd better send Jacob down to let Captain Hornigold know."

"Let's wait a few minutes, until we can see what kind of ship she is."

Fifteen minutes of anxious peering later, Shirley announced that the second ship was a sloop.

*

The pirates were in a tumult over the news. Most had decided they would accept the King's Pardon, but many were still wavering. Captain Charles Vane led the undecided, along with Captain Yeates, his consort.

"I'm going to wait and see whether 'surrender' means giving up our prizes. I'll sink mine before I'll give it over to any Governor," Captain Vane declared hotly.

"Well, you don't have long to do it," Hornigold said cheerfully. "The man is within an hour or two of the harbor."

Captain Vane had Calico Jack, his quartermaster, call his company together. The word went out for anyone else who did not want to surrender to join the meeting.

"All right men, it's time for a definite decision. Any of you who want to accept the King's Pardon, leave now." A dozen men slunk away from the group.

"We need to hold a council and decide what to do. You all know my position. If the Governor says we must surrender our plunder in exchange for the King's Pardon, I plan to stand and fight. I'll not give up all we've worked for."

The men muttered, swore and discussed, drinking punch the while. Captain Vane was all for fighting the Governor's frigate. If they could sink it, they could carry on business as usual in Nassau. What right had the King of England – that fat Hanoverian King, anyway – to be here in the Bahamas? He couldn't even speak English! Now, if it had been the true, Catholic Jacobite King, James III. That would have been a different story. There was further discussion and mutterings.

"Here's what I think we should do then," Captain Vane said at last, anxious for a consensus. Time was moving on. "We'll send the Governor a letter asking whether we must give up our prizes. If he says, 'Yes', we can fight. If he says 'No', then we can accept the Pardon and see how it goes. What say you?"

"How will we get away if he decides to take our prizes? D'you expect him to bow and show us the door?" one of the men asked. "Don't forget, the Governor's got a frigate. He could blast us out of the water."

"We can fight him," Vane shouted vehemently. "We'll clear the brig for action and give him a taste of our guns. If it gets too hot for us, we can out-sail him, any day."

"Not in that fancy French brig, we can't," someone shouted back.

"You can come aboard the *Ranger*," Captain Yeates said. "We can go out the eastern end of the harbor. The frigate can't follow us, her keel's too deep. We can go up to Green Turtle Cay and regroup, take another prize for you to go aboard, and get on with business as usual. All in favor?"

There was general agreement to the plan.

"Right. Let's get the brig ready and take our gear aboard the *Ranger*. There's no time to lose."

*

Captain Whitney stood on the quarterdeck of *HMS Rose* and studied the shore through his glass. His elation at winning the race to New Providence with his sister frigate, the *HMS Milford*, was giving place to apprehension. Should he wait outside the harbor for the others, as Woodes Rogers had commanded him? He hated waiting. Besides, he did not take his orders from that upstart privateer. He would go in, and strike a little fear into the pirates on shore. Anyway, the *Shark* would soon join him. All reports had said the fort was useless, so they could pound Nassau into rubble from the ships if they had to. Look at it – it was just a mass of ramshackle huts made with sticks, canvas and palmetto. His mouth twisted down.

HMS Milford, and Woodes Rogers' own ships, the *Delicia*, *Willing Mind*, *Samuel*, and *Buck*, another sloop, would arrive within hours. The squadron of seven ships had called at Harbour Island, in the northwestern Bahamas, for news of pirate activities in New Providence. They had also hired pilots familiar with the waters. The *Rose* and *Milford* crews had placed friendly bets on who would arrive in New Providence's harbor first.

Now Hiram Russell, the Bahamian pilot, took over the helm from the *Rose's* coxswain and the frigate crossed the harbor bar. Captain Whitney noted that there were a good number of ships already at anchor, mostly sloops, up towards the eastern end of the harbor. There were two Dutch armed ships, and an exceptionally handsome French brig.

The anchor splashed down with a rattle of chains. Swarms of small boats came crowding around the frigate from the shore, bringing fresh produce for sale. Others had whores, sitting provocatively in the bows, enticing the sailors on deck. There were three skiffs full of young boys offering to dive for coins. Several local worthies also came out to welcome the new Governor, dressed in their Sunday clothes.

"Where is he, then?" one called from a rowboat.

"He's not aboard the *Rose*," a sailor shouted back. "He's coming on his own ship, with soldiers and farmers to settle here. There's another six ships arriving tonight!"

Excitement rippled through the people in the boats. There had never been such a large squadron here before, nor such a splendid chance to make money.

Captain Whitney stayed in his great cabin, thinking, only half hearing the hubbub going on outside. People at Harbour Island had already told him there were over a thousand pirates in New Providence, and also that Charles Vane would likely not surrender, but was planning to defend the town. Finally he pulled the bell rope, and asked his steward to send in Hiram Russell, the pilot.

*

An hour later, the *Shark* arrived and anchored west of the *Rose*, causing new excitement among the little boats.

Just after sunset, when all the boats had gone back in, Hiram Russell and two men lowered a longboat from the *Rose* and quietly rowed to the wharf. They got out and headed for the Mermaid's Tail Tavern. Suddenly six men appeared out of the shadows.

"Come with us, Russell," one growled. "Captain Vane wants a word with you."

Russell went for the pistol in his belt, but the tip of a knife nicked his wrist before he could draw it. "None of that," his captor said. "Come quiet like, man, we'll not harm you. The Captain just wants to talk. He has a word for your new Governor."

Inside, the Mermaid's Tail stank of tallow candles, unwashed bodies, tobacco and rum. The group of men walked past the bar and into the private parlor behind, where Captain Charles Vane sat with Captain Yeates. A bowl of punch, tankards, a pouch of tobacco, and a dozen clay pipes lay before them on the table.

Captain Vane looked up and smiled. "So it *was* you, Hiram Russell," he said. "I told Robert Deal it was you I saw at the helm this afternoon. You know Captain Yeates? Some punch and a pipe? Sit, man, sit! As you can see, you're expected. I knew you'd come ashore to see what was happening."

"Well then – what's happening, Cap'n Vane?" Russell asked, taking the proffered chair. "You planning to surrender tomorrow with the others?"

Vane swore. "You know better, Russell! But maybe I can be persuaded, if the new Governor is a sensible man. Rumor says it's Woodes Rogers, the famous privateer?"

"That's who it is," Russell replied, accepting a mug of punch and taking a swallow. He grimaced; the concoction was half rum, and burned his throat.

Captain Vane reclined in his chair, puffing on his pipe. "When you've had your drink, I want you to go back aboard that frigate and tell your Mr. Woodes Rogers the conditions I'll agree to surrender. Here's a letter for him from me. And I want his answer back in two hours."

*

"Who the devil does Vane think he is, dictating terms to a

Royal Governor? The sheer insolence of the man!" Captain Whitney fumed, pacing up and down his great cabin. "Did you tell him the Governor hasn't arrived yet?"

"I did, Sir," Russell replied. "Vane said it made no difference to him. You must accept his terms or he'll stand and fight. He expects to hear by ten o'clock tonight."

"I have no authority to parley with pirates! My mission is to accompany the Governor here, and insure his peaceful acceptance on the island. Vane will have to wait until the *Delicia* arrives." Captain Whitney laughed ruefully, shaking his head. "I admit he does not lack courage. Sending demands to a fully armed naval frigate. He'll stand and fight! Let him stew. If he tries any tricks, we'll blow him to pieces."

And stew Captain Charles Vane did, sitting in the smoky, evil-smelling little parlor of the Mermaid's Tail with Captain Yeates and Robert Deal, Yeates's quartermaster. There was a knock on the door, which opened immediately to admit a man panting and disheveled from running.

"Cap'n Vane," he gasped, "...the lookout says another frigate's beating back and forth outside the harbor bar, and there are two more ships coming in. Looks like an East Indiaman and another sloop. It's hard to tell in the dark."

"Just as Russell said," Vane said to Captain Yeates. "They won't reply to us – they're too grand to discuss terms with pirates. We'll be trapped in his harbor like cockroaches in a jar. A pox on 'em! Let's go! Where are the volunteers?"

"Already aboard the Frenchie..."

It was two in the morning before everything was ready and the brig was set up as a fire ship. The tide had begun to ebb, pulling water out of the harbor.

"Right, men," Captain Vane said to the four men left on board. "The sails are all set, and the tide will help take her down. Make sure she's headed directly for the *Rose* and burning well. Jeremiah will be alongside in the longboat, you have only to drop into it. You have plenty of time to get to shore. The fire will discharge the guns long before it reaches the gunpowder in the hold. Cut your cable as we leave."

"Aye, aye, Captain," the men chorused, clearly relishing their night's work.

*

Captain Whitney had placed the *Rose* on full alert until midnight, then told the crew they could stand down to their normal watch. The night had been so quiet he could hear the humidity dripping from the yardarms. Everything seemed normal. He yawned, stretched, and scratched beneath his wig. It had been a long and tiring day, with an even more tedious day still to come. Certain that the pirates would do nothing until dawn, Whitney went to his bunk and fell into a sweaty, uneasy sleep.

"Captain Whitney, Captain Whitney!" a voice insisted, amidst banging on the cabin door.

"Come in!" he replied, instantly alert.

"Please Sir, the brig is on fire..."

There was an ear-splitting crash of cannon at close quarters. Captain Whitney sprang to the door, to stare aghast at the spectacle. The French brig, her sails and rigging blazing, was bearing straight down towards them.

43

"Mr Yelverton, cut the cables," Captain Whitney barked to his First Lieutenant. "Order all hands on deck!"

"Aye, aye, Sir," he shouted, turning to relay the orders. Two men began hacking at the thick anchor ropes with hatchets. The boatswain's silver whistle piped and crew came boiling out of the forecastle, to scramble up the masts and along the yardarms, unfurling sails and pulling lines. The *Shark* was already under way, moving slowly towards the harbor bar and safety. Two more cannon thundered from the burning brig, the balls splashing down just short of *Rose*.

The heat and roar of the fire came down to them on the slight wind. "Mr. Yelverton, order boats and sweeps," Captain Whitney shouted. More crew scrambled, lowering longboats filled with men and long oars. They took lines from *Rose* and began towing her towards the bar, goaded on by the roar of more cannon. *Rose* slowly pulled away from the brig. As she crossed the bar to the ocean outside, the brig exploded, sending burning debris soaring into the sky. The French hulk sank with a resounding hiss.

*

Captain Woodes Rogers limped along the dew-wet quarterdeck of the *Delicia*, gnawing on a ship's biscuit that he softened by dunking into a tankard of coffee. His old battle wounds ached, and the warm, moist air made him gasp for breath. Sweat trickled down his back. His hair and face were soaked, and sweat collected on his upper lip. He wiped his face and neck yet again with his wet handkerchief and flapped it to make a little breeze. He had not felt dry since entering the tropics.

The demons of doubt were assailing him. They were always worst at this time of night, before daylight brought the reassurance of hope and possibilities. Should he have accepted this post? He had been glad enough to get away from Sarah, and their two noisy young children. He was especially glad to get away from Sarah!

He had chafed at the social round, the peaceful domesticity of his life in Queen Square, Bristol. His well-born, spoiled wife, always harping on about something, needling him about money. He had lost his looks and his sex appeal since his battles in the Pacific, where a Spanish musket ball had shot out his left jaw, and a wood splinter from a cannon ball hitting the deck of his ship had taken out his left heel. Sarah didn't relish being married to a disfigured man, who had lost half his teeth, fed on slops, drooled on occasion, and could only walk with a cane. The lawsuits against him, his subsequent bankruptcy, and stint in debtors' prison had not helped their relationship either. Woodes Rogers had never suffered fools gladly, but he was often in pain and this affected his temperament too.

Now it was wonderful to feel the deck of his own ship beneath his feet again, and the thought of something challenging to do for the King soothed his guilt at leaving his family in Bristol, parked conveniently with his widowed mother-in-law.

But had he undertaken more than he could handle? Captain Whitney had just left, after reporting the events of the night in the harbor. It had been a stormy meeting. The new Governor of the Bahamas had been furious.

"Did I not expressly say, Sir, that all the ships should meet and sail into the harbor together, to make an intimidating statement?" Rogers asked heatedly.

"Did you, Sir?" Whitney asked casually, flicking a thread off the sleeve of his uniform. "I remember no such order. Nor do you have the right to order me, Sir. You are not my superior officer in the British Navy."

"I did not order it, Sir," Rogers replied, almost spitting. "I commanded it as the representative of his Gracious Majesty, King George I. As such, I have the right to expect you to obey my requests!" Then the Governor had a shrewd idea. "How much did you stand to gain by beating *Milford* into Nassau harbor?"

"Fifty pounds, Sir," Whitney answered, jutting out his chin.

"I thought as much. You had a wager. So, Captain Whitney, you endangered your ship and my mission for the sake of fifty pounds! Rest assured the Admiralty shall hear of this."

The rest of the meeting had gone from bad to worse, the two men almost coming to blows. Now Captain Rogers rubbed the sunken scar on his left cheek. *I shall have trouble with that Captain Whitney*, he thought. *The man is too arrogant by half!*

Soon the sun struggled from its bed and a pearly tinge appeared on the horizon. When it was light enough, Rogers took his glass from his pocket and squinted at the shore and down the harbor. A large sloop, *Ranger*, was getting underway, heading east. She was hoisting her flag... black... the skull and crossbones. *Captain Charles Vane*, he thought. "Mr. Turnley, signal *Buck* to chase that sloop!" Rogers yelled to his second in command.

The signal flags broke from the *Delicia's* mast a moment later, and *Buck* responded immediately, entering the western end of the harbor under full sail. The *Ranger* ran out her guns and sent a broadside at *Buck*. The deafening roar reverberated over the water, echoing back from the hills ranged a mile from Nassau's shoreline.

Ranger tacked and headed quickly for the Eastern Narrows of Nassau harbor, with *Buck* in hot pursuit.

"Mr. Turnley, signal the others. Let's go in and anchor. We can see if there are any more hot-heads in there."

*

Most of the people in Nassau had been watching the harbor to see what Captain Vane would do, and they had not been disappointed. Now they put on their best clothes and went down to the waterfront to talk over the night's adventures. Shirley and Kath wore their prettiest summer dresses and tied matching ribbons in their caps. Hornigold could hardly contain his excitement. He kept whipping out his glass and examining the *Delicia's* decks for a sight of Captain Woodes Rogers.

A few small boats went out to the *Delicia* to welcome the Governor, but most people stayed ashore, waiting to see what would happen next. One man tried to take wagers over the *Buck* and the *Ranger*, but everyone wanted to back the *Ranger*.

Longboats filled with soldiers, sailors and the people who had come to settle in New Providence began rowing to shore, headed for the sandy cove hard by Fort Nassau. The whole town rushed down to the cove and lined the street leading to the fort. Finally Captain Rogers came ashore, and the people went wild with jubilation.

"Hurrah for King George!" they shouted, "Hurrah, hurrah…" and the pirates fired their muskets into the air.

Captain Woodes Rogers was a muscular man, lean and brown as a Portuguese, with a strong-looking face. He had been handsome before his disfiguring scar, which made the left side of his face cave in and gave his mouth a cynical twist. His eyes, though, were dark and intelligent, missing nothing. He was dressed in a dark green coat trimmed with gold braid, black knee breeches, white worsted stockings and black leather shoes with large silver buckles. Fine lace foamed at his throat and frothed down his chest and at his wrists. His ornamental sword hilt gleamed like gold. A full-bottomed white wig crowned all this glory. He had a pronounced limp and needed a cane, but he walked with a quick step nonetheless. No one could doubt his efficiency, character or strength of purpose.

All Nassau was on hand to meet the new Governor. Some 300 pirates formed an honor guard either side of the lane leading up to the ramshackle fort, shooting their muskets into the air in a running salute as Captain Woodes Rogers passed by, accompanied by Mr. Walker, the former justice, and Benjamin Hornigold, the former premier pirate.

The three men mounted the steps to the fort. Signaling for silence, the new Governor read his Royal Commission, appointing him as Governor of the Bahama Islands, followed by the Royal Proclamation of Pardon.

*

Shirley Stirrup hardly listened to the reading. It was in formal, complex language that soon lost her attention. She was more interested in the men who had come ashore, and her saucy dark eyes examined them, one by one. A quick glance was enough for some, but others needed closer attention, especially the younger ones. Then she saw him.

He was tall and loose-limbed, tanned, with sun-streaked hair. He stood at the end of a line of soldiers, holding his musket with easy grace and wearing his hat pushed a little too far back on his head, giving him a nonchalant air. He was staring out to sea when Shirley first saw him, but as she stared, he turned his head and looked straight at her. His eyes were blue, a pale surprise in his tanned face. One corner of his mouth curved up and he gave Shirley a deliberate wink. Her heart started pounding and she licked her lips. *He's the one*, she thought. *How can I meet him?*

The pirates swarmed around the new Governor after the ceremony, clamoring for Certificates of Pardon. "We'll get down to business tomorrow," Governor Rogers said. "I'd like to walk about today, to see the town and get to know people."

Still accompanied by Walker and Hornigold, Rogers set off at the head of a long procession, followed by most of the townspeople. His heart fell when he saw how dilapidated everything was. He could hardly pass in some streets for rubble and bushes. The sun beat down fiercely, and his woolen clothing clung wetly to his body. Flies exploded in clouds about him as he passed mounds of garbage, which lay everywhere. He put his silk handkerchief over his nose as he passed a dead dog lying bloated in the middle of an alley.

The problems were overwhelming. So this was the town of Nassau! This malodorous, steamy maze of huts and bushes. This was the capital of the Pirates' Republic! The new Governor asked questions and took notes, looking grim. Then he set up his temporary office in the private parlor at the Mermaid's Tail.

In the middle of the afternoon the *Buck* came back, alone. She had not caught the *Ranger* – Captain Vane and his pirates had sailed clean away.

*

Governor Rogers was up early the next day with renewed enthusiasm. He declared martial law and commissioned Mr. Richard Turnley as Chief Pilot, whose first job was to board every ship in the harbor and make inventories of their cargoes.

In the following two weeks, Rogers set up a Council of 12 men and appointed necessary town officials. He organized militia companies to clean the streets, build a garrison for the soldiers, repair the fort and guard the town. He got everybody working. Once the pirates had their Certificates of Pardon, Rogers appointed them to tasks like everybody else. Order and civilization could, and *would* be imposed on the town of Nassau.

*

One day Captain Benjamin Hornigold and Captain Thomas Cockram waited on the Governor at his office.

"Your Excellency, we can't do this land work," Hornigold said, holding his hat in his hands. "There's a shipload of us men who need to be on the sea. Captain Cockram and I have been considering how we can help you and help ourselves, too."

"How's that?"

"There's a rumor going around that Captain Vane's been threatening you. We hear he's promised to come here with shiploads of other pirates to burn your guard ship, for your impudence in chasing him instead of answering his letter."

The Governor shifted in his seat and looked down at his hands. This town was too small to keep anything secret. He looked back at the men. "That's so."

Captain Cockram spoke. "Hornigold and I reckon you have enough to think about, setting up the town and worrying about the Spanish. We were thinking how we could go after Captain Vane."

"You could commission us to do it," Hornigold said eagerly. "We could go after Vane, and anybody else who's lurking about out there. I know where Vane careens. He's probably up there in Green Turtle Cay, in Abaco. That's where he said he was going before you came. He was all provisioned and about to leave when you arrived and blockaded him into the harbor. Captain Cockram and I can get our lads and go aboard the *Bonnet*. She's the only ship I know that can out-sail the *Ranger*."

Governor Rogers fingered his scar for a moment. Could he trust these two rogues? Would they try to bring Vane in, or join up with him? It went against his grain to sit in Nassau and leave Vane roving free, especially after his insolent message. And he had to trust these men sometime, if only to show them that the King's Pardon was real. If he didn't give them suitable work to do, they'd fall back into their old ways. Besides, he understood their feelings. It was the call of the sea that had made him so restless at home. It was exactly why he found himself in Nassau now.

Rogers clapped his hands together. "Right, then men. A commission for catching pirates will be ready for you in the morning. If you can bring Vane in, that will rid us of another nuisance. How soon can you be ready?"

Hornigold and Cockram looked at each other and grinned. "Tomorrow afternoon," Hornigold said. "We can leave at two o'clock."

44

Kath and Shirley went down to the shore to see the *Bonnet* off.

Shirley was very cool with 'poor George' – as Kath always referred to him now. He tried to take Shirley's hand, but she shoved it into her pocket.

He asked for a kiss and bent over her, his puckered lips aiming for hers. Shirley turned her head at the last moment, and poor George had to make do with her velvety cheek.

"What's the matter with you, girl?" George asked, exasperated, and not for the first time. "You're so stand-offish here of late, a fellow doesn't know what to think."

"Think what you like, George. You can't go kissing me in public. I have to be careful of my reputation."

"What do you mean? Everybody knows you're my girl. I'll be asking you an important question when we get back, so plan to give me your answer."

Shirley was surprised. She had not been thinking of George as a husband since the first week they'd met, but she did want to be married, and no one else had come forward. She had glimpsed the good-looking soldier several times, but he paid her no mind. She'd found out his name was Christopher Clark, and that he was walking out with one of the Pritchard girls.

"I'll think about it, George," she said soberly.

"Please do. And don't be sashaying around town making eyes at any of them new fellows while I'm gone. I mean it, Shirley. You know I'll find out!"

"Listen to you! You sound like we're engaged already."

"We are, as far as I'm concerned."

"I haven't made any promises to anybody, so far as I know."

"Don't fool with me, girl."

"Why? What are you going to do?"

"Don't try me. I've fought before and I wouldn't hesitate to fight again for what's mine."

"Ooh – how exciting. You'd fight a duel for me, George? Like Captain Hornigold fought for Miz Kath?"

"You bet I would," he said, grabbing her to him. This time Shirley yielded, and held up her face for his kiss.

*

Kath and Shirley lingered along Bay Street, shopping. Mr. Taylor had sent word to Kath that he had some new fabrics for sale, brought by Governor Rogers on the *Delicia*. They went into Mr. Taylor's shop to find that Mrs. Pritchard and her three daughters had already been there.

"It's all right, Mrs. Hornigold," Mr. Taylor said. "You're my best customer. I kept a few bolts aside for you to see first, in the colors I thought might please you."

"Thank you, Mr. Taylor. That was thoughtful. I would have come straight away, only my husband has been commissioned by the Governor to go after Captain Vane, and we went to see him off first."

"I heard he was leaving today," he said, bringing four bolts of cloth from his back room and laying them on the counter in front of Kath. "The whole town's buzzing with the news. There are plenty of jealous mariners wishing they could go too. They'd rather have a good sea fight any day, than be cleaning up the town."

"Yes," Kath nodded "It's hard to exchange the freedom of a pirate ship for labor in this hot sun. It's the rainy season, too, and the mosquitoes are bad on shore."

"And now the fever's breaking out, everybody wants to get away," Taylor added.

"What? Fever here?"

"I hear a couple of the soldiers came down with it this morning. Won't be long before they've all caught it. Yellow Jack loves fresh blood. All these new people from England will get a dose. You had it yet, Mrs. Hornigold?"

"Yes. I nearly died from it when I first arrived. Captain Knowles's grandmother nursed me through it thank Heaven."

"You'll not catch it again, not Yellow Jack, at any rate. One of the other kind, though, that's something else."

"What other kinds are there?" Kath asked.

"Why, there's break-bone, typhoid, malaria... and others too. Anybody can catch them anytime, and we don't know what kind is going around yet. You ladies take my advice. Stay quietly at home as much as possible. No need to tempt fate."

Kath bought a dress length for herself, one for Shirley, and some blue brocade to make Hornigold a new coat. She fancied one she had seen Governor Rogers wearing and thought to copy it. While she was settling the bill, the youngest Pritchard girl came in.

"Hello, Miss Melinda," Shirley said.

"Miss Stirrup," Melinda replied with a nod.

"Which materials did you choose?" Shirley asked and the two girls went over to the counter with the bolts of cloth and started talking. The door opened and Miss Georgina Pritchard came in. She looked around and saw Melinda with Shirley, rushed over to them and grabbed Melinda's arm.

"Come away this instant," Georgina commanded loudly, pulling her away. "Or I'll have to tell Mother who you were talking to."

Melinda looked embarrassed, but followed Georgina meekly over to the other side of the shop.

Kath turned in surprise and saw Shirley's stricken face. "What do you mean by that remark, Miss Georgina?" Kath asked.

"I mean, Mrs. Hornigold – if it's any of your business – that we are not permitted to speak to colored people. Except if they're our slaves."

Kath's face blazed with heat. "You will speak to many

worse people in your lives than Miss Shirley Stirrup," she said haughtily. "Miss Stirrup is my ward and, as such, is totally respectable." Kath turned to Shirley and held out her arm. Shirley was glad to lean into it. She was feeling very small and shaky inside.

"Come, my dear," Kath said clearly, "...we shall not invite them to the dance we are giving for the Governor when Captain Hornigold returns."

Gathering their parcels, Kath and Shirley swept out of Mr. Thomas Taylor's shop.

*

On Bay Street again, the two women walked towards the Mermaid's Tail. "Let's go and get some hot chocolate," Kath suggested.

"All right," Shirley answered. "What dance are we giving for the Governor, Miz Kath?" But before Kath could reply, Shirley pointed to the wharf. "Oh look! Isn't that the *Swan* tying up?"

"Yes... it is. Let's go and see them. You'll want to see your father, and he probably has news from your momma. That'll cheer you up."

They went over to the schooner, waving to the men busy tidying the lines. Greville Knowles came out of his cabin and Kath felt the old rush of exhilaration at seeing him again. As soon as he noticed Kath and Shirley he came ashore, but there was no smile on his face.

"Hello, Captain Knowles," the women chorused. Greville touched his hat.

"Good afternoon," he said gravely. "Will you ladies come with me to the Mermaid's Tail? I have something important to tell you."

"Yes, of course," Kath said quickly. "We were just going there ourselves."
Greville took their parcels and the three walked towards the tavern.

"We're surprised to see you," Kath said. "You're not

usually here in August, are you?"

"No. We've been off our usual schedule ever since we were caught in the Charleston blockade."

"What blockade, Captain Knowles?" Shirley asked.

"Blackbeard had us all bottled up in Charleston harbor for several weeks. He was prowling outside the bar, taking all the ships coming in or out. He took hostages, then held the whole colony to ransom, demanding provisions and medicines. We couldn't venture out until the problem was solved, so we're later than usual."

"You're only just coming from Charleston?" Kath asked.

"No. On our way down we put in to Nassau for two days, only to off-load and provision, then left immediately for Fortune Island. The men were worried about their families, in case they were short of things. The *Swan* is the only vessel that calls there regularly, as you know."

Greville opened the door for Kath and Shirley, then pointed to a corner table. "We can be quiet there," he said.

After they ordered, Greville opened his mouth to speak but closed it again. His eyes were full of pain. Kath's scalp prickled. "What is it, Greville? What's the matter?"

Greville dropped his head into his hands. "I don't know how to tell you." He looked up, and there were tears in his eyes. "The settlement at Fortune Island is no more," he said, his voice breaking. "The Spanish came back..."

Shirley clapped her hands over her mouth, and Kath pulled her close.

"We arrived to find the whole place burned, dead bodies everywhere. They had been dead for some time. Then we noticed that all the dead were men," Greville continued. "No women or children. We were so shocked – and sick – we went back aboard the *Swan* to decide what to do. Of course, we had to bury the dead."

Shirley hid her face in Kath's shoulder. "What do you think happened?" Kath asked.

"We didn't know what to think," he said. "We were all numb. Then young Samuel Harding came in his skiff. He told us he'd been fishing that day, and saw the Spanish in the harbor when he was coming home. He hid in some mangroves. He says he heard everyone screaming. They plundered the settlement, took the women and children, the animals – and then burned everything else. Houses, fields – all gone. The only thing they left was the well. I suppose they plan to use it themselves from time to time.

"Samuel says it happened on the 26th July. He lived rough, eating conch, and hid out waiting for us to come. He says the ship was the same one that came before, the one that took you, Kath."

"The *Jacinta de Chavez*," she said softly. "Don Francisco de Cornego!"

"Yes," Greville nodded. He looked bleakly at Kath. "Taking revenge for what your husband did to them no doubt."

"What do you think happened to the women and children?" Shirley whispered.

"All taken away, to Cuba or Hispaniola. They'll probably be sold as slaves."

Shirley shrieked and fell forward on the table, sobbing. Kath held her close, rocking her, stroking her hair. "Oh thank God... thank God you were here with me, Shirley," Kath said with a tremor in her voice.

The waitress rushed over with their hot drinks and the story ran quickly around the tavern. Greville drank his coffee, his hand shaking as he lifted the mug. He stood up. "I must tell Governor Rogers about the raid," he said, heading for the parlor where the Governor still kept his office. "Wait here for me, Kath, and I'll see you home."

45

"You're *sure* you had Yellow Jack when you were little, Shirley?" Kath asked. "Mr. Taylor says that's what the soldiers have."

"Yes, Miz Kath, I'm sure it was Yellow Jack. You don't have to worry about me."

"Well, I was thinking we might volunteer to help nurse those men. Mr. Taylor says four more died this morning. That makes sixteen so far, and the barracks are full of the sick. Those who are well don't want to help in case they catch the fever, and the sick can't help themselves."

Shirley raised troubled eyes from her sewing. "If you think so, Miz Kath. It's a messy illness, though. A lot of cleaning up to do," she said, wrinkling her nose. "Can we take Jane, Susan and Jacob to help too?"

"No. I'm not sure if they've had it. Jacob says he has not, and Jane and Susan don't speak English well enough for me to ask. It's not fair to put them at risk."

"They're only slaves, Miz Kath," Shirley said, rolling her eyes.

Kath smiled and stroked Shirley's hair. "So are your momma and brothers now. You'd want their owner to protect them, wouldn't you?"

Shirley burst into tears and threw herself into Kath's arms. "But for the grace of God, Shirley, we might be slaves too." Kath held her close, rocking her. "I escaped slavery twice – once by a hurricane, and once by a pirate rescue. You would have been a slave by now, had you not come to Nassau when you did.

"Will you help me with these soldiers? I would be dead now, if not for Miz Eva. However hard it is, we owe it to the men, Shirley. We lived because others cared for us, and we need to pass it along."

Right after dinner, Kath and Shirley went down to the fort. Shirley's glum face brightened when she saw that the Officer in Charge was none other than Lieutenant Christopher Clark.

"God bless you, Mrs. Hornigold," he said when Kath had explained their mission. "Our fellows are in a sad way. A woman's touch would mean a lot to them. We're dying like dogs here."

"Perhaps others will volunteer too," Kath said. "Have the Pritchard ladies had this fever?"

Lieutenant Clark smiled ruefully. "I doubt this sort of thing would interest them. But I can ask. I'm to sup with them this evening."

*

It was hard work. Kath and Shirley went down to the barracks early every day and left late in the afternoon. Shirley soon overcame her initial distaste and worked tirelessly, singing as she went about her chores. She and Christopher Clark grew very close. He brought her mugs of hot coffee and took her walking on the fort walls for fresh air. The two managed to laugh and flirt in spite of the misery around them.

The Pritchard ladies never came to help, but several of the town whores did. Kath's two slave women made broth and bush medicine, just like Miz Eva, but there was no way of telling if it was effective. By the time the *Bonnet* returned from Abaco early in October, forty-eight men had died, and the epidemic showed no signs of slowing.

*

Captain Hornigold had anchored *Bonnet* off north Eleuthera after an exhilarating sail from Nassau that afternoon. They would leave at dawn for Harbour Island, visit Cockram's wife and see if there was further news of Charles Vane. The Harbour Islanders always knew everything.

"Aye, Cockram, this is the life for me," Hornigold said with a beaming smile. "I don't like piracy. I love my wife, and I'm grateful for the King's Pardon, but oh, I missed my sweet *Bonnet!*"

John Cockram knew just what he meant. "I married Eliza Thompson back in 1714," he said. "I love her, too, and I'll be glad to see her again. But, I wasn't married for three months before I was going stir-crazy, sitting down in the house, tending the garden and going fishing. It was no life for me." He took a sip of punch. "She understood. We're still good friends, but not like husband and wife any more. She set me free long ago."

"I went to sea as a cabin boy, when I was eight years old," Hornigold said. "Only saw home once after that. My wife's a good woman, and I hope we'll make it, but my heart still belongs to the sea – and a good bowl of punch!" He laughed, and poured himself another tankard. "We're lucky devils, you know? We've survived years of roving, we're straight with the King, and now we have a decent job, without the hard life in the Navy or the merchant service. I don't know which one is worse. The Navy, I suppose."

"I know which one is the best," Cockram replied. "Give me a good pirate ship any day. Tell you the truth, Hornigold, I don't know how long I can hang around, cleaning up garbage, building forts and such. Here we are, going after a man who had the guts to stand up to the lot of 'em and do what he likes. I feel like a traitor."

"Yes," Hornigold nodded thoughtfully. "I can understand that feeling, to a degree. But I hated all the blood and violence we sometimes had to use to get the goods." They were silent for a few minutes, listening to the slap of waves under the hull.

"Charles Vane, now," Hornigold continued. "He seems to love cruelty. Did you hear him bragging about what they did to those two Bermuda sloops in April? They hanged a man, cut him down just before he died, and told him he could live. Then one of those brutes hacked him across the collarbone with a cutlass. Nearly took the man's neck off. They thought that was great sport.

"Then on the next sloop they took, they tied a foremast man to the bowsprit, put lit matches to his eyes and a pistol muzzle into his mouth. That was to make him tell where the money was. Poor creature, what did he know about any money? He was just an ordinary seaman, who was unfortunate enough to come from Bermuda. Vane has it in for Bermudans."

Hornigold took a sip of punch and wiped his mouth with the back of his hand. "That kind of thing makes me ashamed. I'll go after Vane! He's a monster."

"If you're so squeamish about a little rough treatment, you'd better stay on the beach," Cockram replied. "I'll go after Vane with you, but I can't promise how long I can stick around New Providence with this fancy Government. A lot of the others feel the same way. We just don't like being tied down."

*

Governor Rogers was coming to realize the same thing. These people hated responsibility or work. They refused to worry about a Spanish invasion. The Spanish and French had sacked their homes, or other settlements in the Bahamas, thirty-four times over the past fifteen years, the reason they gave for living in shacks. When Rogers had his officers make surprise inspections of the militia, they found men drunk or asleep on duty, or not at their posts at all. Fines and punishments meant nothing to them.

The Governor racked his brain to think how he could encourage ambition in his citizens, but poverty was all they had ever known. They were perfectly contented with their shanties, with fish, turtles, conch, and a few potatoes from their fields. The Nassau folk yearned for the old pirate days, for wrecks to salvage, and idle hours in the taverns. One by one, the ex-pirates began to slip away.

Woodes Rogers thought Hornigold and Cockram might be the key to this problem. He should not expect mariners to be happy working on shore. After all, seamanship was all they knew. It was where their pride lay. He needed to find legitimate work for them to do on the ocean.

The Governor spent hours thinking about the problem before making his decision. He would outfit two vessels and send them trading with the French islands. The French colonials were always happy to have English products, and he had brought a good supply out with him on *Delicia*. That would employ some of the sailors, and return a profit to himself as well.

They could also become pirate hunters, like Hornigold and Cockram now, patrolling the Bahama Islands and flushing out any pirates in hiding. They could make money by bringing the pirates in for the rewards set out in the Royal Proclamation.

If only war would break out again! Those seamen who didn't fancy trading, could be commissioned as privateers, to prey on the Spanish. That would bring him a share of the profits, too, while satisfying their desire for adventure in a way that was harmless to British colonial shipping.

*

Now the Governor waited as impatiently for news of Hornigold and Cockram as for Vane. The *Bonnet* should have returned within a week. As the third week dragged by, Rogers kicked himself for being such a gullible fool. He should have known the knaves would return to their old habits. But Hornigold's face had been so eager, so honest! Surely his instincts had not been wrong?

A hearty rap at his office door snapped him out of his reverie. "Come," he called, and Captain Hornigold's affable face appeared around the door. The Governor sighed with relief. "Captain Hornigold! Back at last. I was beginning to give you up."

"Thought I'd run off with Captain Vane?" Hornigold teased, smiling. "Sorry we took so long. I've come to give our report, if you have the time."

"By all means. Sit down, man, I'm longing to hear what happened."

"Captin Cockram and I went first to Harbour Island, just as we said we would. The people there were very helpful. Cockram is married to a Harbour Island woman, you know, and he operated out of there when he went roving. I've spent a lot of time with them myself over the years.

"They told us Vane took a Barbados sloop at the end of July. He forced her crew to sign his Ship's Articles and put Captain Yeates and twenty-five hands in her.

"Two days later, they took a merchantman, rich with pieces-of-eight. She was a fair ship, so Captain Vane added her to his fleet. I believe he put his quartermaster aboard her, Calico Jack Rackham. Anyway, the three ships went to careen in Green Turtle Cay, Abaco. He'd want to fit out the merchantman, of course. Take out the decks, raise the gunwales, that sort of thing. And of course, they'd want to share out the booty. We reckoned they'd still be there. They would want to celebrate. There was likely a good supply of Barbados rum on board the sloop, too.

"We sailed up to the Cay and moored, then tried to find them in the ship's boat. That took time, but with three vessels to our one, we could only hope to take them by stealth, strike when the time was right.

"We found them and brought the *Bonnet* nearer, but not so near that they might see us. Of course if they did, we could always lie and say we'd run away too, though just how we were going to convince Vane of that I wasn't sure. Vane knew Cockram and I had always planned on taking the King's pardon.

"Anyhow, we kept watch on Vane from the land, and mighty uncomfortable it was! The sandflies and mosquitoes nearly sucked us dry. Captain Vane's a wily one. He worked one ship at a time, keeping the other two afloat and ready for action. Five days after we started watching he finished his work and sailed out.

"I'm sorry, Governor Rogers, but it would have been suicide to try and take him. We thought about trailing him, but he would have been able to see our sails out on the ocean, so we gave up and came home."

Rogers nodded thoughtfully. "Good work, Captain Hornigold. I can see how you wouldn't want to get involved with his three ships."

"No, Sir. We brought you one small prize, though. The *Wolf*, Captain Nicholas Woodall. You gave him permission to go turtling, but we caught him trading with Vane, bringing him supplies of food, ammunition, and news."

"Thank you, Captain Hornigold. They're down at the wharf?"

"Yes Sir. Captain Cockram is handling that now. He's turned them over to the Constable."

"Good. I'll go along shortly and see for myself. You have a reward coming your way, too, Hornigold, for bringing them in."

"Call on me anytime, Governor Rogers. You might want to keep us on patrol, so to speak, looking for those scurvy fellows. I'd be happy to do it. Captain Cockram too."

"Thank you, Captain Hornigold. I've been thinking of something like that myself. We'll talk more later."

46

As soon as he could get off the *Bonnet*, George Rounsivel rushed up West Hill Street to see Shirley.

"Miz Shirley ain't here," Jacob said. "She an' Miz Kath down by da fort. Dey looking after da sick soldier dem"

"Thanks, Jacob," George said, disappointed. He'd walked all this way, up that hill in the hot sun, and Shirley was down by the waterfront! He walked back down the hill, switching at the tallest weeds by the side of the road with a stick. He was quickly below the fort, and dripping with sweat.

George swiped his face with his forearm, leaving a dirty streak on his cheek and matted wet hairs on his arm. He squinted up at the fort and could hardly believe what he saw. There on the ramparts was Shirley, walking arm in arm with one of the soldiers. She was laughing and looking up at him adoringly.

George ground his teeth and balled his hands into fists. What a lovesick fool he was! Pining for more than three weeks, dreaming of how she would look... feel... smell – when he came home and took her in his arms. He'd ask her to marry him. She would say "Oh *Yes*, Georgie!" and look up at him, *just like she was looking at that soldier right now*!

Angry tears blinded him and he stubbed his bare foot on a rock. He grabbed his toe and hopped on the other foot, bellowing curses. When he could see straight, he realized that Shirley and her fancy-soldier-man were watching him, still laughing, only now it was at *him*. Everything exploded into a red haze.

"Shirley Stirrup, you get down here *this minute!*" George howled.

"What if I won't? You don't own me, George Rounsivel!" Shirley hollered back.

"If you don't come down, I'm coming up to get you!"

"I'd like to see you try," she called gaily. "Can we stop him coming up?" she asked Christopher.

"Let him come," Christopher answered, sticking out his chest and standing tall. "I'm here to protect you."

George leapt up the stairs like a goat, his adrenaline pumping. He was soon face to face with the pair of them. In his haste to see Shirley, he had not stopped to bathe or shave. He stank of sweaty, unwashed clothes, and his heaving chest, red face and wet, salt-rimed hair made him look like a wild beast. Lieutenant Christopher Clark definitely out-classed him, a fact that George realized immediately. Still, he had come looking for an answer to his question, and he would have it!

"I came for the answer I asked you to give me when I came back," George ground out between clenched teeth. "Have you decided? What'll it be?"

"What exactly was the question, George?" Shirley asked sweetly. "I don't remember you asking me any question."

George balled his fists. He was shaking. He felt as though someone had doused him with a bucket of cold water. Suddenly he knew what to do.

"If you don't remember the question, Shirley, that's my answer," he said, cold as steel. "Goodbye."

He wheeled around, ran down the stairs, and walked out of the fort without a backward glance.

*

"What did you say to George this morning, Shirley?" Captain Hornigold asked, as he cut into his lamb chop. "He came running back to the *Bonnet* for his things. Said he was shipping out with John Augur on the *Bachelor's Adventure*. They're going to Green Cay to find some stock animals."

Kath looked sharply at Shirley. "I thought you two were all but engaged."

"Well, we were talking about it." Shirley looked down at her plate.

"What happened?" Kath demanded. "Don't tell me you threw George over for that Lieutenant Clark! He won't marry you, my girl... and I don't think he's nearly as bright or as nice as George!"

"I know. Lieutenant Clark doesn't care for books." Shirley looked wistful. Then a mischievous smile tweaked the corners of her lips. "... But he's awfully good looking. Besides, we work together. Why shouldn't I drink my coffee with him?" she asked defensively. "George came running up to us out of the blue. He was wet and dirty and smelled as ripe as an outhouse. He wanted me to say I'd marry him, right in front of Lieutenant Clark! And looking like that! I know he was jealous, but George has no delicacy. He should know better."

"Zounds, girl!" Hornigold exclaimed. "George has been mooning over you this past month – the whole trip! He couldn't wait to see you, and all you can say is 'he has no delicacy'?" Hornigold shook his head. "I tried to stop him going with Augur, but he wouldn't listen. I don't trust that man. George has no business aboard his sloop."

"Maybe Jacob can take me down to the wharf?" Shirley asked hopefully.

"Too late, my lass," Hornigold answered. "*Bachelor's Adventure* sailed at noon. We'll just have to hope for the best. They should be back in a week."

A contrite Shirley went to bed that night. And the next morning brought her more worry, for when she and Kath went to the barracks, they found Lieutenant Christopher Clark in bed with fever.

*

Two weeks passed and the *Bachelor's Adventure* had not returned.

Hornigold tried not to let Shirley and Kath see how

concerned he was about the delay. They were under enough strain from their work at the barracks, which now looked more like a hospital. Scores of men were dying, including Lieutenant Christopher Clark, who had developed a severe case of the fever. The women almost lived by his side, but to no avail. One morning he gave up his struggle and slipped into eternity.

Shirley was holding his hand when he died. She was too tired to feel anything except relief that his suffering had ended. Kath saw her bleak face and rushed over. "Come my dear," she said gently, tugging Shirley to her feet. "It's time we took a break. Let's go home and ask my husband to take us sailing. It's a beautiful day. We need to get away from this place and remember that we're still alive."

Shirley's eyes were full of misery, but she said nothing, nor did she cry. Kath half-supported her as they walked up the hill to the house. What had she done? Shirley was so young! She should not have asked her to spend weeks – now months – tending the sick. *I was doing penance for killing Jenks, trying to fill my own empty heart*, Kath thought with a pang. *I should not have put this burden on her.*

"Where's Captain Hornigold, Jacob?" Kath asked when they got home.

"Da Gubnor send for him 'bout a hour ago," he said.

It was just as well. "Tell Jane to bring us limeade in Miz Shirley's room. Tell her to make it with some rum. Tell her to hurry."

Kath closed the shutters, undressed Shirley and put her to bed. Shirley was still speechless, still wore that suffering expression. How could she have pushed her so far without realizing that she needed rest? The men had died anyway. Eighty-six of them so far, and the epidemic still raged. Kath crawled in beside Shirley and cradled her in her arms. Soon Kath felt her trembling, and tears came at last.

"I want George," Shirley moaned. "Where's George? Why hasn't he come back yet?"

*

Governor Woodes Rogers looked pale and ill. He sat at his desk with his head propped in his left hand, writing with his right. He turned watery eyes on Hornigold when he entered the office.

"Good of you to come, Captain Hornigold," he said in a reedy voice. "This dreadful fever has me by the throat. I'm slowly getting over it, God be thanked!"

"Yes, Sir, I heard you were sick."

"It makes me even sicker to tell you my news," he said with a sigh. "The *Bachelor's Adventure*, Captain John Augur, left two weeks ago to search for stock animals on Green Cay. I had misgivings sending Augur, but he had surrendered the same way you did, and I thought to try him out. All you mariners need honest work."

The Governor leaned wearily back in his chair and let his arm drop to his lap. "I'm weak as a kitten. Ridiculous, with so much to be done..." He closed his eyes for a moment, then inhaled deeply and pulled himself together again. "This morning the *Lancaster* came in. She's a trading vessel out of Kingston. *Bachelor's Adventure* stopped her in the Exuma Cays, under the black flag. Augur came aboard, took her cargo, provisions, side arms – the usual booty.

"*Lancaster's* captain says Augur has fifteen men with him now, which means he's marooned part of his crew somewhere. They're probably at Green Cay. I'll send another vessel to search for them, but I want you and Cockram to find Augur. Find them, engage them, and bring them back! Blow them out of the water if you have to. I'm going to make an example of them." He slapped the top of his desk. "We won't tolerate piracy in these islands anymore!"

The Governor unrolled a chart and stabbed it with his index finger. "*Lancaster* was attacked here," he said. "There's no telling where Augur is now, of course, but perhaps they stopped to celebrate. The *Bonnet's* fast. You might still find them in the Exumas."

"We'll leave right away."

"Godspeed, Captain Hornigold. *Bring those scoundrels in!*"

"Thank you, Sir, I will." Hornigold touched his hat and left. He bounced back to the *Bonnet*, hardly able to suppress the smile that lit his face. This was the job for him – to go hunting a sloop, with the possibility of a fight! Two weeks ashore had been quite enough.

*

The *Bonnet* came back ten days later. As soon as she entered the harbor the townspeople crowded down on the wharf. The atmosphere was tense; the vessel docked almost in silence. A buzz of conversation broke out, but lapsed into silence again as the pirates came up on deck in irons. The *Bonnet's* crew was conscious of their place in the limelight, as they escorted their prisoners ashore and handed them over to the soldiers. Four of the prisoners stared at their feet, but the other six looked around, grinning and calling to their friends in the crowd.

Kath suggested that Shirley should stay at home, but she had insisted on coming to the wharf. Tears slid down her face as George shuffled past, looking thin and bedraggled. She cried out his name, and George glared angrily at her before hanging his head again.

Kath tightened her arm around Shirley's waist. "We can try to see him later," she said. "One good thing, we know everyone at the fort – and they owe us a big favor."

Captain Hornigold came over. "Hello, Treasure," he said, kissing Kath. "I have to see the Governor, then I'll come and tell you everything." He dropped his voice. "You go on home. Take care of Shirley. It doesn't look too good for George."

Kath nodded. "I'll see you later then..."

His face softened. "I missed you, Treasure..."

"Come, sweeting," Kath said, taking Shirley's arm. "Let's go bake some of those scones George likes so much. We can take him some stew and bread, too. The poor soul looks like he hasn't eaten in a week. We can send him food, even if they don't let us see him."

47

Two hours later, Shirley took her basket to the guardroom of Fort Nassau, where Sergeant Tom Evans was on duty. This was a piece of luck, as she had nursed Sergeant Evans through the fever.

"Sergeant Evans, I've brought some necessaries for George Rounsivel, one of the prisoners who was just brought in. Could I go in and see him?"

"I don't know, Miss Stirrup," he began, then stopped when he saw Shirley's disappointed face. He looked around. "I don't see what harm it could do. You've come on errands of mercy a hundred times before and nobody stopped you. Let me have a look in your basket first, though."

"Please take a scone for your tea," Shirley offered. "They're still warm."

"Thanks!" He put a scone in his coat pocket. "Is Rounsivel a relative?"

"No, Sir. We were keeping company, only we had a quarrel and he ran off to sea before we could patch things up..." Her eyes filled.

"I see. I'm so sorry! Well, everything looks all right. I'll take you in."

Sergeant Evans lit a lantern and led the way down a dank passage, stopping before a grilled iron door. "George Rounsivel, someone to see you," he called. He opened the grill and put Shirley's basket into the room, then locked it again. There was the sound of leg irons chinking and George materialized out of the gloom.

"I'll give you a few minutes..." the Sergeant said, and went back to his post.

"George, why did you fly off like that?" Shirley asked.

"You made me look like a fool. You broke my heart, Shirley."

"We're even, then, 'cause now you've broken mine."

"I'm sure your fancy Lieutenant will comfort you."

"Don't be stupid. He's dead now, anyway. He died of fever days ago."

"So it's back to dear old George," he said bitterly.

"Let's not fight," Shirley said softly. "We only have a few minutes. What happened, George? How come you went on the account again?"

"I didn't want to be marooned on Green Cay. Besides, I didn't see any reason to come back here."

"You know they'll probably hang you..."

"Probably."

Shirley snuffled and wiped her eyes with her sleeve. They were silent for a moment.

"Anyway, I brought you some stew and bread, and scones. Miz Kath sent you some soap and fresh clothes. Everything's in that basket."

"Why are you so sweet to me now? Fattening the pig to kill it?"

"Oooh, George, you're so stupid sometimes!" Shirley balled her fists, and stamped her foot. "Can't you see that I love you? Why don't you ask me your question now?"

"Humph," George grunted. "What's the point? I'll be dead in a couple weeks."

"Ask me anyway..."

There was an awkward pause. George cleared his throat. "Will you marry me?" he asked with a quaver in his voice.

"Yes, George, I will," Shirley replied firmly. "Now we just have to see if we can get you out of this mess!"

*

Hornigold was eating his stew with relish. "There's a lot to be said for having a wife and a well-ordered home. I look forward to the end of a trip nowadays."

Kath smiled her thanks for his compliment. "Tell me about your trip. It must have been exciting."

"It wasn't, as a matter of fact. Your old friend, Don Francisco de Cornego, did all the work for me."

"Don Francisco again! He must be prowling around these islands continually."

"Yes. Well, we found our men marooned on a cay. Augur told us a Spanish privateer had attacked them when they were on their way home from Green Cay. Of course he didn't mention that they went on the account again. He acted surprised when we clapped irons on them and sent them below."

Hornigold swallowed another mouthful. "I got the full story from George. It all started when Augur spied a trading schooner out of Jamaica. He knew she belonged to a rich merchant, and they thought chasing her would be more profitable than chasing animals in the hot sun. A few of Augur's crew didn't agree, so he imprisoned them and later marooned them at Green Cay.

"After that, they headed across to the Exuma Cays and took the *Lancaster*. Remember? She was the sloop that complained to the Governor, which is why we went out. Well, Augur was hardly finished with her before they spied another sail and went after it. By the time they realized they were chasing a Spanish frigate, it was too late. The Spaniard gave them a couple of broadsides, which sent *Bachelor's Adventure* to the bottom. She sank with several men, and the Spanish picked up the rest and left them ashore with a barrel of water. Three more of them died later, of their wounds, and we brought in the remaining ten. It's lucky George is still alive."

Kath frowned and began playing with her fingers. "How lucky can he be? Won't they hang him?"

Hornigold nodded soberly. "You know how I feel about that boy," he said with a catch to his voice. "He's the nearest thing I have to a son. I've done my best to protect him, keeping him out of the hottest action so he wouldn't be harmed.

It tore me apart to bring him in like that, all trussed up in chains." He sighed. "But I'm the King's man now, and I have to do my duty. George knew the penalty for what he was doing."

He took a sip of his ale and looked out the window at Nassau harbor, Hog Island and the dark Atlantic beyond. "I have to say this, too, Kath. It hurts that someone I've sheltered in my own home was the cause of him running off like that. You know I don't begrudge you Shirley's company, my dear, now I'm gone so much of the time. Sometimes I think she's too flighty, though, especially where men are concerned. You should talk to her about it."

Kath looked down at her hands again. "Yes, perhaps I've been too easy with her. She's the closest thing I have to a child now, too, Ben. You know what the English did to my boys. I guess I've been enjoying her high spirits and not looking at what they were doing to her character."

She reached out and took both Hornigold's hands. "You're right, I am at fault. But please don't blame Shirley for being young and silly. After all, a lovers' quarrel doesn't usually cause young men to go on the account. George chose to do that all by himself."

They were quiet for a moment. "You're right, of course," he said reflectively. "Shirley couldn't possibly have known George would dash off and do something so stupid. I can't blame her."

Hornigold took another swallow of ale and changed the subject to something less distressing. "Anyway, to get back to my story, it turned out that the Spaniard was Don Francisco de Cornego, on the *Jacinta de Chavez*. Amazing, isn't it? George says he's still mad as a wet hen from the treatment we gave him a year ago. He told them he was going to become the scourge of the Bahama Islands. Says he won't stop until there are no more pirates, no more English, and the islands belong to Spain again."

"I guess you're sorry you ever tangled with him," Kath said, frowning. "If you hadn't, all the people on Fortune

343

Island would still be alive, and he wouldn't be out looking to fight everyone else."

"We can't be sure of that. Anyway, how could I be sorry?" Hornigold kissed Kath's hand. "If I hadn't taken him as a prize I would never have found you. And to me you're the greatest treasure in the whole world."

Kath smiled fondly at him. "And I would have been a slave in some Spanish island. Thank you for rescuing me!"

She watched Ben as he finished his food. She loved him at times like this. He could be so sweet and gallant when he was sober. He was gone a lot, and nowadays when he was at home he didn't drink as often as before.

However, when Hornigold took out the punchbowl, as likely as not he would drink it to the dregs. His face would flame red and his eyes would narrow to squints. Sweat would trickle from his body and make him smell of stale rum and tobacco. He would get loud and abusive, shouting and swearing, throwing and kicking things, fighting unseen foes.

Then Shirley would lock herself in her room, the slaves would tiptoe about the house, and the two cats would slink off into the bush. Kath would sit in the living room, feeling as though a hundred butterflies were caught in the net of her stomach.

A single drunken rampage would undo weeks of her efforts to love him.

48

The trial date was set for 9th December, 1718. Kath and Shirley continued their daily nursing visits to the fort, so Shirley was able to see George every day and make him as comfortable as possible. The epidemic seemed to be ending at last, leaving ninety-eight soldiers dead, in addition to scores of victims in town, many among the new colonists Woodes Rogers had brought with him. Each day dragged, yet seemed to fly by, as the date of the trial approached.

"Can't you think of anything that might help you at the trial?" Shirley asked George for the tenth time. "Can't you say you were scared, that you only signed on because you thought you would starve, marooned at Green Cay?"

"No, Shirley," George said patiently. "How could I starve with all those sheep and goats pastured on the island? Anyway, Augur left the men with a fishing line and a bucket for water. They had a good knife and a tinderbox. Besides, we knew the Governor would send after us when we didn't come back. So that reason won't help me. Nor would saying that I went off in a fit of rage, which is the truth." George looked sick with worry. "There's no way out. I'll plead 'not guilty' like the others, but we have to face it. They're going to hang me."

"But you didn't kill anybody, George."

"You don't have to kill anybody. The penalty for piracy is hanging, and I'm a pirate. People hang for much less than that."

"Oh, George, there has to be something..." Shirley said, wringing her hands. She was growing thin, and was having problems keeping food down. She blamed herself for George's predicament.

At last the 9th December arrived. The Vice Admiralty Court convened in His Majesty's Guardroom at Fort Nassau, a stuffy, echoing, damp room, with sunlight struggling in through an iron-grilled window. Governor Woodes Rogers sat at the head of the table as President, with the Vice Admiralty Judge seated to his right. Six other commissioners also sat around the table, three civilians and three ship's captains. The Registrar sat off to one side at a small table of his own.

The Registrar was a scrawny, middle-aged man, wearing a black stuff robe. He wore white linen bands at his neck and a wispy gray wig, frizzled on each side, with a pigtail behind. He opened the proceedings by reading the Governor's commission for assembling the court under the recent Act of Grace, Proclamation for Suppression of the Pirates.

The accused sat in their fetters on benches at the other end of the room, with armed soldiers standing guard. One prisoner jiggled his heels up and down, another wagged his knees and others looked down at their hands, or off into space. The legal formalities meant nothing to them. At last came the charge, and the prisoners sat up straight.

The Registrar read off their names. 'You are charged with accepting the King's Pardon, then returning to your former evil ways of robbery and piracy. On October 26th you combined together at a desolate island called Green Cay to mutiny and steal the *Bachelor's Adventure* and *Lancaster*, their cargoes and tackle. You are further charged with marooning James Kerr, merchant, and others on Green Cay while you proceeded to the island of Exuma. How plead you? Are you guilty or not guilty?"

They all pleaded 'Not Guilty'. The Registrar called witnesses to give evidence – their former shipmates, and the crew of the *Lancaster*. Their evidence was damning, as was that of Captains Hornigold, Cockram, and the crew of the *Bonnet*.

The Court examined each prisoner individually and then

passed sentence. One man only was found not guilty – the boatswain from the Lancaster. The pirates had needed a boatswain on board *Bachelor's Adventure* and they had forced him. For all the others the Registrar pronounced sentence.

"George Rounsivel..."

George stood like a block of stone when his name was called. His stomach plunged and an icy prickling washed over his body.

"...George Rounsivel, you have been found guilty of the most heinous crime of piracy. It is the sentence of this court that you be held until ten o'clock on Friday, December 12th, when you will be taken to a place of execution and hanged by the neck until you are dead. And may God have mercy upon your soul."

His ears buzzed and the room swam. He gritted his teeth, mashed his lips together and clenched his fists, determined to take his sentence like a man. For three weeks he had been steeling himself for this moment, and now he felt almost relieved.

*

There was no room for the public inside the guardroom, so the population thronged around the fort waiting for word to trickle out. Kath and Shirley waited in the barracks, trying to keep their minds on their patients. At last Captain Hornigold's burly figure appeared in the barracks doorway. The pain in his eyes confirmed their awful fears.

"Oh no, no..." Shirley whimpered, her face crumpling as she sagged against Hornigold.

"Let's get her home," he said to Kath. "I told Jacob to be ready with the surrey."

They walked around to the back of the fort, where Jacob was waiting. Hornigold helped the women into the surrey and sat in the front beside Jacob, then turned to talk to them. "I have an appointment with the Governor tomorrow afternoon, and I want you women to come with me. He thinks I'm coming to claim the *Bonnet's* reward for bringing in the pirates. That's true; the lads are due their money. But I thought perhaps we might convince him to pardon George."

"You think there's a chance?" Shirley looked up into his face, hope flickering in her dark eyes.

"We can try."

"Don't waste your breath," Kath spat out, her face grotesque with venom. "You forget I tried that before with the English. I hate them! 'The criminal classes,' they call us. In their minds, we're no more than rats."

Hornigold tried to take her hand. "Now, Treasure..." he started. Kath wrenched her hand away from him.

"Don't 'now Treasure' me! They hanged my Duncan for killing a lamb, just like a farmer would destroy a rogue dog. Someone told me down at the barracks that you can be hanged for over 350 offenses in English law. He said they could sentence you to death for stealing anything worth more than one shilling, too. A shilling! That's what you pay for a quart of milk in this island!"

Hornigold reached for her hand again. "I know it's not fair – it's not even reasonable. But Governor Rogers is a different man than most. I've come to know him quite well, one way and another. I think it's worth a try."

Kath stared off into the bushes. "Try if you like," she said in a huff. "Just don't ask *me* to go groveling before any Royal Governor."

"I'll go," Shirley said plaintively. "I'd do anything for George!"

"And what kind of reception d'you think you'd get, Miss?" Kath demanded, her eyes glistening with angry tears. "You know how the precious English Pritchards treat you. D'you think Rogers will be any different from them? You're mulatto, so you're no more than slave material. Doesn't matter that you're free, intelligent and beautiful, and have feelings too."

Tears spilled down Shirley's cheeks. Jacob halted the horse at the front door and the three passengers alighted wordlessly. Shirley ran into the house, the door banging behind her. Hornigold took Kath's arm and hooked it through his own. "Come, my dear. I know you're upset. Let's eat something and have a rest. I'm not going until tomorrow. I only want you to think about it. Maybe you'll change your mind by then. You've never even met the Governor, have you?"

"No! And I never want to, either. I tell you, I hate the English!"

"But I'm English, and you don't hate *me*. George is English, and you don't hate *him*. You've been slaving over English soldiers at the barracks. You don't hate *them*...″

Kath's throat constricted. She put her hands up to her throbbing temples and rocked from side to side. "Leave me alone, Ben," she groaned. "I've had all I can take for one day!"

She ran to their room, threw herself across the bed and gave full vent to the sobs that wracked her body. She pounded her pillow – Greville's pillow – with her fists.

"Oh George, George! Oh my poor George! Oh God... Oh Blessed Virgin ... *Oh hell and damnation!*"

*

"Come in, Captain Hornigold," Governor Rogers invited when Hornigold stuck his head around his office door. "I'm just finishing my report for that wretched business yesterday. I've given you full credit for the part you played, my dear fellow. Here ... let me read part of what I've written to the Secretary of State.

> " *'I am glad of this new proof that Captain Hornigold has given the world to wipe off the infamous name he has hitherto been known by, though in the very acts of piracy he committed most people spoke well of his generosity.'*

"How does that please you, eh? A mention in dispatches quite different from those of your earlier years!"

Hornigold's ears grew pink. "Thank you, Your Excellency, it's very kind. I never expected anything like that. But I came to discuss another matter entirely."

"Indeed you did, and a very important one too! I calculate that the Crown owes the *Bonnet* two hundred and eighty pounds reward. Do you agree? The Bonnet is doing well out of catching pirates! You made good money bringing in Woodall and the *Wolf* last month, too."

"Yes, Sir. The crew is glad of the money..."

"But not you? Captain, what's wrong? You're not having regrets about betraying your former comrades, are you?"

"Not exactly, Sir. That is, only about one – young George Rounsivel." Hornigold looked down and fingered his hat. "That lad is like a son to me. He came on board as my cabin boy, back in the old privateering days when I sailed consort with Captain Henry Jennings. All these years, I've taken pains to teach him – good seamanship, courage – all the things my old captain in the Navy taught me as a lad." His mouth twitched and he swallowed, then he looked straight into the Governor's eyes. "Bringing him to you in fetters was the hardest thing I've ever done."

"I understand," the Governor nodded sympathetically. "Unfortunately, he was caught – you caught him yourself – with a sloop-full of seasoned pirates. And he could give no proof of his being forced to join them. We examined each man particularly on that point, hoping to spare as many as possible."

"I know, Sir," he said. "But the lad went off in a fit of jealousy after a lovers' quarrel..." Hornigold told George's story. "...So that's how he came to be with Augur and his company.

"My wife says the work at the barracks is difficult and depressing," Hornigold continued. "Miss Stirrup has volunteered every day under the most trying conditions. Instead of doing whatever young women normally do with their time, she nursed scores of dying men. Miss Stirrup is inconsolable now. All her hopes for happiness are as dead as many of the soldiers she tended these past twelve weeks."

Governor Rogers listened with troubled eyes. He sighed deeply. "You're asking me to pardon the boy, aren't you?" he said at last. "How can I do that, Captain Hornigold? One of my main purposes for being here is to suppress piracy. I must use whatever means I have to do the job. It's important that

I make an example of this company, so others will know that we will not tolerate piracy here. I can't show favoritism. I'm sure you, of all people, can understand that."

Hornigold grunted, and his eyes hardened as he looked away from the Governor. "I can see that there is no mercy in the law, even for those who deserve it. Oh, I don't mean mercy just for George, though his only real crime is that he was foolish and reckless. I suppose you and I have been the same many times, and not only in our youth.

"I mean mercy for Miss Stirrup, who has slaved over your sick soldiers, cleaning their vomit, carrying slops, changing sheets and washing fevered bodies. In doing so, she has shown far greater mercy than the law. And to men she doesn't know, who might not give her the time of day ordinarily, since she is a mulatto."

A muscle twitched in his jaw. "I mean mercy for Mrs. Hornigold, who has already lost two sons about George's age, to the vengeful arm of English law. My wife is an Irish woman, with good reasons to hate English soldiers. Despite her dislike for them as a group, she tended them because they were God's creatures and far from home, with no women of their own to look after them."

"I've heard of their work. The officers speak of them like angels..." Governor Rogers began. Hornigold waved his comment aside and attacked again.

"Could a young mulatto girl of no special distinction, and an ordinary Irish woman, transported for stealing – could they possibly be greater, more merciful than the Crown – than the King himself?

"I ask you to think on it, Governor Rogers," Hornigold pleaded. "That young man, George Rounsivel, is worth far more alive than he is dead. He is a clever, faithful, honest sort of fellow, the kind you don't often meet with. That he is a pirate is probably my fault – but it's also the fault of the world we live in. For who could want the life of an able-bodied seaman before the mast in the Navy or the merchant service? We both know its brutality, its lack of comfort, of the bad food and pay. The risks to life and limb."

Hornigold stopped at last, his breast heaving. The ticking of a brass clock on the corner shelf was the only noise for a full minute. Governor Rogers took a deep breath. "I had no idea you were such an orator, my dear Captain Hornigold." He gave a conciliating smile. "As you say, I must think on it." He shifted in his chair.

"Now, to the business at hand. Here is the two hundred and eighty pounds reward money. I know your crew will be waiting for it..."

*

Kath tossed all night and spent a miserable day, nursing her hatred for British Government officials and memories of her ill treatment at their hands in Ireland. She felt awful knowing that she was doing nothing to help George. But she loathed the thought of going before the English Governor to beg for his life. Her pride still refused to let her join Hornigold when he left after dinner for his appointment. He was bitterly disappointed in her, which shamed her even more.

Shirley stayed in her room, refusing to come out or to eat, or speak to anyone. Kath felt wretched when she remembered her own horrid words to the grieving girl. She sat on the porch with a piece of embroidery, but her thoughts were not on her stitches. Eventually she realized that, uncomfortable as it might be, she had to do whatever she could to save George. She sighed and decided she would go to see the Governor.

Later that same evening, Kath tapped on Shirley's door. No answer. She opened the door a crack and peeped in. Shirley was sitting in the middle of her bed. Her clothes were mashed, her hair stuck up in spikes, and her eyes were red and swollen.

"Shirley..." Kath said gently. Shirley looked at her, then hung her head.

"I'm sorry I lashed out at you last night," Kath apologized, coming into the room. "I feel almost as bad as you do about George, you know. I got angry with the wrong person. Forgive me?"

Shirley nodded. "Did Captain Hornigold go to see the Governor like he said he would?" Her voice was husky, slightly hoarse.

"Yes, he went at three o'clock."

"Has he come back? What time is it now?"

"Seven thirty. He's not back. He must have gone to the *Bonnet* to pay off the men. I guess they went to drink at the Wheel of Fortune."

"How could he not come back to tell us what the Governor said? He knows we're waiting to hear..."

"Yes, I'm sure he does. He probably hasn't come back because he has no good news. That means he's likely to get drunk. I'd prefer he stays in the tavern."

Kath sat on the bed, stroking Shirley's hair and back. "Can you eat a little something, sweeting? Jane has boiled fish in the kitchen. You haven't eaten since day before yesterday."

"No, thanks. I feel like there's a lump of something hard in my stomach."

Kath sighed. "Shirley, I've been thinking all this time about what we might possibly do for George. Would you come with me to see the Governor tomorrow?"

"You'll go to see him?"

"Yes. I think it might just help. I have an idea..."

49

The next morning Kath and Shirley went down to the Governor's office in their best summer dresses. Introductions were soon made and they were seated before his desk.

"Thank you for seeing us without an appointment, Your Excellency," Kath said with her most charming smile. "I know how busy you are."

"I'm glad to meet you both at last, Mrs. Hornigold," the Governor said warily. "My officers have told me much about you. We are grateful for your kindness to the many sick men at the fort." He took a deep breath and looked frankly at them, his eyes troubled. "I think I know your reason for coming to see me today. Is it about George Rounsivel? Your husband has already tackled me on that matter."

Kath blushed vividly. "Yes, Sir, it *is* about George. I don't know what my husband has said to you. We haven't discussed it. But we – Miss Stirrup and I – have a proposition to make regarding George, which I hope you'll let us explain."

The Governor was not surprised she did not know the details of his conversation with Hornigold. He'd seen him at the Wheel of Fortune late the night before, getting roaring drunk with his shipmates. He nodded for her to continue.

"You may know that I was shipwrecked in these islands and lived for a time at Fortune Island. That is where I met Miss Stirrup. Luckily she was visiting me when Don Francisco de Cornego took all her relatives and friends away, so she was spared." Kath smiled fondly at Shirley. "Well, while we were on Fortune Island, I ran a small school. Miss Stirrup was a monitor, helping me with the youngest children and teaching the older girls how to sew.

"It strikes me that there is no school here in Nassau, and there are many children running about with little to do. I've been thinking that what we really need here is a school."

The Governor's eyes brightened. "Yes, indeed we do, Mrs. Hornigold. Would you be interested in starting one?"

"Yes, Sir. Miss Stirrup and I could start a school... but we would need a man to help. We feel that the ideal man would be George Rounsivel. George is an intelligent young man, who comes from a wealthy family in England. He reads and writes very well. His arithmetic is also good. He knows all about sailing vessels, their building and rigging, and he loves children. He could teach the boys."

The Governor's eyes twitched between Kath and Shirley's faces as she talked. He was clearly interested in their idea. This encouraged Kath to go on.

"Sir, George's only problem is that he's not settled down. He's in love with Miss Stirrup. He got jealous when he came home from sea and saw her talking with a handsome officer on the ramparts. He would be fine if they were married and lived ashore together, with decent work to do."

"We would be married, Sir," Shirley said eagerly. "We're engaged, you see..."

Kath put a gentle hand on Shirley's knee, then continued. "So many young men have died over the past three months... won't you let one live? Won't you please think about our idea and pardon George? You can give him into our custody. My husband and I will gladly take responsibility for him."

The Governor held up the palm of his right hand. "Stop, Mrs. Hornigold, I beg you. I have promised to make an example of this company of pirates. My whole purpose for being here is to expel pirates and restore commerce. This is the very first occasion I am proving the King's authority by hanging pirates in this colony. If I show any lack of resolution, any wavering in my intent, these fellows will think me weak. They will not take me seriously in future. As much as I might wish to pardon George Rounsivel, I *cannot* do it!"

*

The whole town turned out to watch the hanging. People went down to the fort from early morning to secure a place with full view of the ramparts – and the stage built in the clearing below the walls, on the sea side, where nine gallows stood beneath a pole flying a black flag.

Some people waited in small boats anchored off from the beach. Security was tight. There were over a hundred soldiers and militiamen on guard on the ramparts, around the fort, and especially near the gallows.

Excited children ran about, chased by barking dogs and scolding mothers. Former pirates muttered together in small knots, torn between lust for a grisly spectacle and shame at doing nothing to save their doomed friends. Governor Rogers paced up and down in the Officers' Quarters in the fort, his hands clasped behind his back, from time to time peering out the window or checking his pocket watch.

Finally it was ten o'clock, and the rattle of a drum emerged from the guardhouse. Most of the nine pirates had taken special pains with their appearance. They had bathed, shaved and put on clean clothes.

George wore the new suit that Shirley had made for him. One man, Dennis McCarthy, had tied long blue ribbons at his neck, wrists, knees, and on his cap. His friend, Thomas Morris, wore long red ribbons in the same fashion. These two walked with a bounce in time with the drum, skipping up the stairs to the ramparts, where they bowed with a flourish to the crowd.

Dennis McCarthy walked to the edge of the wall and called out to the crowd. "I remember when there were many brave fellows on this island. They wouldn't have stood by and let me die like a dog!"

Another pirate treated the whole thing like a wonderful joke. He kept smiling and chuckling to himself. John Augur looked ashamed and penitent; he went unshaven and un-washed, and stood in the same dirty clothes he had worn when captured. Another man looked guilty and miserable, yet another was sullen and withdrawn. George did his best to hold up resolutely. He looked around at the crowd, seemingly in a daze, his eyes searching for Shirley. When his eyes met hers, he stared down at his hands.

The provost marshal read a couple of psalms and prayers, a few of the spectators joining in the responses. After the service, the guards loosed their prisoners' bonds and led them down a ladder to the bottom of the wall, outside the fort. There, another ladder led up to the stage, set on three large barrels with ropes tied around them. The crowd surged forward, straining against the linked arms of the soldiers.

Governor Rogers stepped forward, lifting his arms for silence. "You men have forty-five minutes to prepare your souls to meet your Maker. You can say anything you have to say for the last."

Dennis McCarthy sprang up the ladder to the stage, bowing cheerfully again to the crowd. He pulled off his shoes and kicked them onto the ground below. "I swore I'd never die in my shoes," he said, laughing. "Wear 'em who will!"

Thomas Morris raised his fists, his red ribbons waving gaily in the light breeze. "I could have been a much worse plague to these islands. Now, I wish I had been!"

"Can't we have one last drink?" another prisoner whined. "Let's have a round for us and these men here!" He waved grandly towards some bystanders.

"Don't you understand anything?" one of the penitents asked. "We're about to die! *Water* would be more suitable for us."

The Governor nodded to one of his men who ran off and came back a few minutes later with several bottles of claret. He poured a glass for each of the prisoners.

"I drink to the success of Governor Rogers and the Bahama Islands," John Augur proposed, bowing to the Governor. The others tipped their glasses and drank.

The men spent the rest of their allotted time in various ways, depending on their temperaments. The few penitents sang psalms, while the others shouted jokes and ribald comments to friends in the crowd. George stood to one side with his lips pressed together, looking out to sea, trying hard to stop trembling.

Shirley, Kath and Hornigold got as close to George as the guards would let them. "I love you, George," Shirley called, her tears and nose streaming. "I'll never love anyone else, as long as I live."

"I love you too, Shirley," George cried, looking longingly down at her. "With all my heart. I'm sorry, s-s-sorry..." his face crumpled, and he blotted his eyes with his forearm.

Kath twisted her handkerchief in her hands, while Hornigold fortified himself with nips from a bottle of brandy. "We'll never forget ye, lad," he said, his voice breaking.

Governor Rogers stood below the stage, not far from the Hornigolds, checking his pocket watch. Finally the time came and he motioned to the provost marshal. The crowd fell silent as the hooded hangman stepped forward, dressed in black. He climbed onto the stage and deftly tied a noose around each pirate's neck. His work done, he came back down the ladder and stood with his arms folded across his chest.

Woodes Rogers stood at attention, his scarred cheek twitching as the drummer beat a tattoo. The ropes from the barrels were hitched to three horses now, and their drivers stood watching for the Governor's signal, their whips raised.

The Governor took a deep breath and looked at the Hornigolds. Kath stared at him savagely, defiant yet still pleading. Hornigold stood with fists clenched by his sides, the empty bottle on the ground at his feet. Shirley looked steadfastly up at George, who was pale and sweating with his eyes tightly closed, lips clamped above his puckered chin. The Governor followed Shirley's gaze up to George.

He looked so young. Vulnerable and scared, so like his own eldest son, William, back in England, might turn out to be one day. His heart melted and Hornigold's question rang in his memory.

Could a young mulatto girl of no special distinction, and an ordinary Irish woman, transported for stealing – could they possibly be greater, more merciful than the Crown – than the King himself?

"Provost marshal!" the Governor barked. "Untie George Rounsivel and bring him to me. I shall exercise the King's prerogative of mercy in his case."

It took a moment to sink in, but then the crowd babbled excitedly. Several in the crowd shouted "God bless you, Governor." Kath and Shirley looked at each other open-mouthed, then shrieked and jumped up and down together. Hornigold's tears ran unchecked into his sandy beard. Anyone looking at Governor Rogers would have noticed his scarred face contorted with the effort of maintaining his dignity. The great man quickly brushed at his eyes and cleared his throat, as the provost marshal brought an unbelieving, shaking George to stand before him.

"George Rounsivel, in the name of King George, I hereby pardon you once again – and for the last time – for the crime of piracy." His face broke into its twisted smile and, taking George's hand, the Governor limped over to Shirley, Kath and Hornigold. "I release you into the care and custody of these three people. They have given their recognizance for your future good behavior as a citizen of this town. Miss Stirrup has pledged her life by promising to marry you, so see that you make her happy!"

As George and Shirley embraced, the Governor stepped back into the area kept clear by the guard, his face grimly determined. He nodded to the provost marshal. The drum rolled and the three horses jumped under the lash, plunging forward, pulling the barrels from beneath the stage.

Eight men swung by the neck into space, leaving one gallows empty beneath the listless black flag. Blue and red ribbons streamed from two of the dead bodies as they oscillated slowly in the air, pathetic defiance against the solid ramparts of the fort.

50

"Shirley, keep still!" Kath admonished through a mouthful of pins. "It'll only take a minute..." Kath was altering her Spanish dress to fit Shirley for her wedding. The rose pink color made Shirley's brown skin glow, and the skirt sprang out from her tiny waist in a burst of joy.

Shirley stroked the watered silk of the overskirt, then traced the flowers embroidered on the bodice with her index finger. She smiled at her reflection in the pier glass for the twentieth time.

"Oh, Miz Kath, I'm going to be *married*!" she said breathlessly, clasping her hands in delight.

Kath chuckled. "And you're going to be stuck with a pin. Keep still!"

"You don't know how often I've dreamed of this day. I've planned my bride dress a hundred times..."

Kath met her eyes in the mirror, her own eyes merry and soft with love. "I know, sweeting..."

"But in all my dreams, I've never imagined a dress as wonderful as this! I never knew they *made* cloth like this!"

"Umm. You look like a princess."

"*Thank you* for letting me wear it! Especially since the Governor's coming to our wedding. Oh, everything's perfect! I can hardly wait!" she bounced on her heels. "Ouch!"

"Well, I warned you..." Kath said through clenched lips, pins wiggling up and down as she spoke. She took them out of her mouth.

"It's like a dream, isn't it?" Kath looked at Shirley, wonder in her eyes. "One moment George had the hangman's noose around his neck, the next, the Governor's saying you can marry him. All this week I've pinched myself. I can hardly believe it!"

"You know, Miz Kath, the people on Fortune Island used to say you were a blessing," Shirley said thoughtfully. "And I used to get jealous. But not anymore. You are a blessing, especially to me. If not for you, I might have been married to Jonah Cartwright. I wouldn't be here at all. I'd be a slave in Cuba, or Hispaniola. Or dead! And if you had not made me help at the barracks, we couldn't have helped George. I wouldn't know how to sew, or read and write anything more than my name..."

Shirley swallowed and blinked rapidly. "I remember last March when I lied to Momma and came down here," she said with a catch in her voice. "You told me I was the *very best thing* that had happened to you. You remember that?"

"Uh huh. I still think that, sweeting."

"I'll always remember that. You should've been mad with me. You don't owe me anything. You could have turned me loose and let me go to the dogs in this wicked town. But you and Captain Hornigold treated me like I was white folks." Shirley turned and threw her arms around Kath, nuzzling her face in Kath's neck. "I love you! I'd do anything for you. Die even..."

"I love you too, Shirley," Kath said, holding her close. "You're the daughter I never had. I want you to be happy!" Kath pulled away and looked searchingly into her eyes. "You do love George, don't you? You're not just marrying him because everyone expects it now, and you want to be a married woman?"

"Yes, I do love him. I've thought a lot since George ran off with those pirates. He has his funny ways, just like I have mine. But I really do love him. I plan to be the best wife, the most faithful, hard working woman he could ever have. These past couple of months have made me grow up. I'm finished with my nonsense."

"Good!" Kath nodded, satisfied.

*

On Saturday, the 24th December, 1718 at 2 p.m. Shirley Stirrup became Mrs. George Rounsivel, at the little church on George Street. Everyone walked back to the Hornigold house for a reception on the flower-decked porch overlooking the sea. Governor Woodes Rogers put in an appearance for a short while and toasted the couple with a glass of punch, as did the local general store owner, Mr. Thomas Taylor.

A marked snobbery had begun to creep into Nassau since the Governor's arrival. Although everyone was poor, whites no longer mixed as freely with coloreds and blacks, and those who had never been pirates looked down on those who had. If certain ladies were distant to Kath when they met in town now, she realized that it was not because she was Irish, or a Roman Catholic. It was because she was married to a former pirate captain, and insisted on befriending a mulatto. This did not bother Kath. She was richer by far than the snobs, and made sure that she and Shirley were the best-dressed women in Nassau. She copied the fashion sketches from London as soon as Mr. Taylor displayed them in his store.

For the reception, Kath invited families who would not feel it was beneath them to attend the wedding of a mulatto and a pirate. George had asked the crew from the *Bonnet*. Shirley had invited her favorite soldiers and three "women of the town" whom she had come to know and like during the fever epidemic. They had hoped the *Swan* would come in time for the wedding, so Shirley's father, Hector, and the rest of the crew from Fortune Island could enjoy the fun, but *Swan* didn't arrive as it usually did.

Anyway, there were enough people to dance quadrilles and reels in the living room, played by the musicians from the barracks and off the various ships in port. And Kath made sure the buffet was the most lavish ever seen in Nassau. *Let those snobby English women hear about this*, was her thought. And she was sure they would hear of it. Shirley and George's wedding would be the talk of the town.

Benjamin Hornigold kept everyone well-oiled with drinks. He was officiating over an enormous punch bowl on the back porch, surrounded by his cronies.

"Cockram, what happened to Kennedy?" Hornigold asked. "And Welch? You said they would come, but they haven't."

"I don't know what happened to 'em," Cockram replied. "Maybe they went fishing. Kennedy was talking about going fishing yesterday. They were provisioning the sloop."

"*Fishing?*" Hornigold demanded. "Kennedy's no fisherman. And he'd never turn down free victuals and punch. Something's not right."

"Ach, don't think nothin' about that," Cockram replied. "They probably started early at the Wheel of Fortune and got too drunk to make it up the hill. It's Christmas Eve, after all."

"Let's drink to 'em," another sailor suggested, holding up his mug. Then someone raised a song and the others joined in, bellowing lustily.

At nine o'clock the newlyweds went proudly to Shirley's bedroom for the night, accompanied by ribald jokes and suggestions from the more experienced. They planned to leave the next morning on the *Songbird* for a two-week honeymoon. Most of the guests left after this, but Hornigold, red of eye and face, hearty in song, still drank with several of his friends out in the back yard.

Kath went to their bedroom and locked the door behind her. She unpinned her hair, kneaded her tight scalp and neck, undressed, then flopped on the bed and stared at the ceiling. The singing grated on her nerves. She plugged her ears with her fingers and lay there, boiling in her own blood.

Gritting her teeth, she grabbed Greville's pillow and punched it under her head. His scent had long disappeared, but she still used it to conjure up his face, his calm hazel eyes. Now she sought this comfort again, but it would not come. Oh, why hadn't the *Swan* come into port? In a way she was glad Greville was not here to see her husband at his worst, but she longed to see him again. Closing her eyes, she tried to conjure him up, but all that would come was a vision of Ben, sweating, flushed and very drunk. She squeezed her eyes shut and felt hot tears dribble down her temples into her hair. Was this all that life had to offer?

*

Hornigold's raucous bunch went down to the Wheel of Fortune at some point during the night, or at least that's what Kath assumed when she woke to find him gone. He never came home until the following Tuesday morning, looking much the worse for wear. He went to bed without saying a word.

Kath had given the slaves a three-day holiday, starting Christmas night, so the house was deathly quiet. She slept in Shirley's room and crept about, lonely and depressed. Hornigold finally emerged on Wednesday afternoon, hungry as a barracuda.

"I'm going down to the wharf," he said as he finished the large pan of ham, eggs and fried potatoes that Kath had fixed. "Cockram told me something at the wedding that makes me uneasy. I'll be back later, all right?"

Kath folded her arms and stared at the wall. "All right."

Hornigold dropped his eyes, then put his callused hand on her arm. "I know I've given you a miserable Christmas," he mumbled. "I'll try to make it up to you somehow. I'm not a very good husband, am I?"

"No," Kath admitted in a low voice. "I don't know if I can take much more of this, Ben. We have no life at all."

He sighed heavily. "I want to do better, Kath, I really do. I try. It's not your fault. It's the thirst. When that gets on me, I can't help myself!"

"It makes a different man of you, Ben. When you're drunk, you change from a tabby to a tiger. You holler and curse, and you get mean." She dropped her forehead into her hands. "I *hate* you when you drink."

Hornigold's eyes filled. "Oh, God, Kath what can I do? I don't want to be like this," he pleaded. "I love you, more than life itself. I want you to be proud of me. I don't want you to hate me. I know how disgusting I get when I drink, but I can't seem to help myself."

He leapt from his chair, almost overturning the dining table. "I've got to go to the wharf…" he said wildly, and rushed out the door.

*

The *Bonnet* was not in her customary berth. A scrawny gray cat wound round Hornigold's legs, mewing softly. He kicked it hard, swearing. He knew in his heart that Kennedy and Welch had gone back on the account, that they had stolen *Bonnet*. He remembered how the two of them had looked at the hanging, ashamed of their part in bringing the pirates to justice. He thought back to a conversation he'd had with Kennedy, too, when they had gone after Charles Vane. He'd had misgivings ever since, half expecting then that Kennedy might blow their cover while they watched Vane's careened ships, and go to join Vane's company.

They had been hatching this plan all week, he thought, snatching his hat from his head. It had been the perfect time to provision. Everyone was buying more groceries than usual, with Christmas coming. Nobody would think anything if Kennedy or Welch had done the same. And Kennedy had spread that story about going fishing over Christmas. Ben himself hadn't had time to go aboard *Bonnet*, nor been around the taverns to hear any news. He'd been too busy provisioning the *Songbird* for George and Shirley, and seeing to arrangements for the wedding. Hornigold flailed a dock piling with his hat, then jammed it back on his head.

Kennedy and Welch knew him so well! They had counted on his being drunk for several days after the wedding, giving them time for a clean getaway. They would not make the same mistake as John Augur, and hang around the Bahama Islands. Hornigold cursed foully. He hurled himself against a large barrel left on the wharf, sending it splashing into the sea. He lost his balance and nearly fell overboard himself. Clenching his jaw and balling up his fists, he strode into the Wheel of Fortune.

*

Early on Thursday morning Hornigold went down to the Mermaid's Tail for breakfast. He sat at the table by the front door.

"Kennedy's stolen the *Bonnet* and gone back on the account," he burst out as soon as Governor Rogers came through the door.

"You're sure?"

"Sure as I'm standing here. Kennedy and Welch left on the day of the wedding, Christmas Eve, telling people they were going fishing. They didn't tell *me* that story, though. I know they're no fishermen. Besides, nobody goes fishing over Christmas. That's when decent sailors try to be in port."

"Maybe they went to Eleuthera to their families?"

"No. Kennedy doesn't live with his wife, and Welch has no family here. They've gone on the account, I tell you. Can I get a crew and go after them?"

By now they had reached the Governor's office. Woodes Rogers dropped into his chair. "What boat would you use? They have *Bonnet*, and she's the fastest sloop we had, besides *Buck*. I suppose you've heard about *Buck*?" He cocked an eyebrow.

"No. What happened? I've been out of circulation, with the wedding to organize."

"A Welshman named Howell Davis has her." He sighed. "I brought expensive European goods with me in *Delicia*, to trade with the French and Spanish islands. Well, I fitted out *Buck* and *Mumvil Trader* and they left six weeks ago, loaded with these goods." He stared out the window, his knuckles whitening as he gripped the arms of his chair. He turned back to Hornigold, grim-faced.

"Seems Davis sailed on *Buck*. He organized a mutiny during the voyage, killed *Buck's* captain, and he and his men took *Buck* during the night. Then they surprised *Mumvil Trader* and persuaded most of her crew to join them in *Buck*.

They stripped *Mumvil* and gave her to the men who wouldn't join them. *Mumvil* has only just managed to get back." The Governor closed his eyes for a moment and his mouth twisted in a bitter line. "So believe me, Captain Hornigold, when I say that I know how you feel. At least you haven't lost a fortune in merchandise."

Rogers leaned forward with both elbows on his desk, looking intently at Hornigold. "You can pardon a man. You can give him honorable work, pay a decent wage and do your best for him. You can trust him, hoping that your trust will make him trustworthy in return. You can beggar yourself. But no matter what you do, you cannot save a man who doesn't want to be saved.

"There's nothing we can do about Kennedy and Welch. They're halfway to Carolina by now, or the Bay of Honduras. You may as well face it. If they haven't gone fishing, you'll never see the *Bonnet* again."

51

Hornigold talked to the captain of the harbor guard ship, and read the entry in the ship's log for 24th December. 'Spoke *Bonnet* at 3 p.m. going night fishing.'

He went down to the wharf every day hoping for news of the *Bonnet*, but none of the boats coming in had seen her. Dispirited, he would go home to sit on the back porch, scan the horizon with his spyglass and sip punch.

Hornigold was sitting on a wooden box outside the Wheel of Fortune when the *Songbird* sailed into the harbor. He walked onto the wharf to meet her.

"Ahoy, George and Shirley," he called. George threw him a rope. "You took your time about coming back."

"You said we could have her for two weeks," George replied.

"That was up yesterday."

"The wind died a couple of days ago. We're only a day late. That's not so bad."

"It felt like you were never coming back." Hornigold tied the rope around a piling. "Kennedy and Welch went on the account again, in *Bonnet*. They left during your wedding, and I've been going crazy on this island ever since."

"On the account?" George asked, his mouth open. "You sure?"

Hornigold nodded. "Been gone fifteen days now. Told people they were going fishing. That's some fishing trip, especially for Kennedy. He doesn't know how to tie a hook to a line."

"And they took the *Bonnet*!" George said, still digesting the information.

Hornigold nodded and held out a hand to help Shirley onto the wharf.

"Ooh, the ground's moving," she said, holding onto his arm.

"That's your sea legs. You're used to the roll of the boat now. And I can't wait to feel it again. I'll take her out soon as you get straight. Blow the stench of this town from my nostrils."

"She's straight now, Captain Hornigold," Shirley said quickly. "She's all tidy below."

He sprang aboard the *Songbird*. "Any food left?"

"Yes, plenty," Shirley said. "You must've thought we were a couple of horses."

"I've heard that honeymoons give people powerful appetites," he said with a wicked grin. "Didn't want m'boy George to fall down on his duties from lack of sustenance." He gave George an exaggerated wink.

George's ears turned pink. He threw his canvas bag onto the wharf, then swung ashore. "You coming up to the house with us?" he asked.

"No. Tell Mrs. Hornigold I've gone for a sail."

"I'll go with you. Just let me take Shirley home." George could see that Hornigold had been drinking. "Why don't you come too, for some dinner?" he coaxed. "We can tell you all about our trip."

"No. It's not even noon yet. You said there was food aboard. I might stay a couple of days."

Georges face fell. "A couple of days? I can't go for that long. Shirley and I have to start keeping school."

"She's tied you, hands and feet, eh boy?"

George nodded, grinning. "It's better than being tied by the neck. I tried that, didn't like it at all!"

"I'll grant you that. Any rum left?"

George nodded again. "The keg you put on board. We didn't open it. You'll need some fresh water, though."

"I'll get some in Eleuthera."

"Pass me the bucket. I'll fill up for you," George said, his eyes concerned. "But I wish you'd wait. Don't go off by yourself."

Hornigold swore. "Ain't you been sailing this boat for two weeks by yourself? Look at that sky! Beautiful!" He untied the rope from the piling. "Take your bride home, Mr. School Teacher. I'll see you in a few days."

*

Hornigold was happy for the first time in weeks. He hummed a ditty the 'foremast men sang at the capstan and looked up at the sails, enjoying the soft southeast wind streaming in his face. He felt alive, like a man again. She might not be *Bonnet*, but *Songbird* was a lively little sloop, a real pleasure to sail.

Three hours later, the sky clouded over and grew dark on the horizon. The wind had moved into the south, then southwest, then west, and now blew from northwest. It was getting chilly, and he only wore a thin cotton shirt. Whitecaps began slamming into the hull. He put *Songbird* in irons and dropped sail. He went below, looking around the cabin for something to wrap around himself. His eyes settled on the rum keg.

He took out the bung and poured rum into a pewter tankard. Should he head for home? He didn't like the look of the weather, especially the clocking wind. Quickly he gulped his rum and went back on deck, grabbing the tiller firmly as the sloop bucked the waves. He saw a wall of rain rushing towards him across the sea, and heard the rattle of the halyard against the mast in the rising wind. There was no time to head back to New Providence.

Anxious, he looked around to get his bearings. Rose Island was a smudge on his right horizon. He could run over towards Rose Island, try to get through the channel to the south of it and anchor in the lee. Even that was fraught with danger. Could he make it through the reef that fringed its north side? He would have to try. He pushed the tiller and the sloop changed direction just as the squall hit.

Hornigold's teeth chattered. He moved off the transom and hunched down in the boat's cockpit, but it made no difference. It took all his strength to hold the tiller steady in the churning sea. He strained to see Rose Island, hoping he still headed in the right direction, but he could see nothing through the cold, stinging rain. He fumbled for the stern rope with his left hand, wrapped it around his body three times and tied it, leaving enough slack for him to move from port to starboard. Whatever happened, he would stay with the boat.

The rain lashed down for half an hour, flooding the cockpit with water, then stopped as suddenly as it had begun. It had seemed an eternity to Hornigold. The wind swung into the north, then rapidly into the northeast. A wave crashed against the *Songbird*, wrenching the tiller from Hornigold's grasp, hurling the sloop up, and then down the other side. Hornigold leaped for the tiller just as the boom broke free and swung across, smashing into his head.

The rainwater sloshing in the cockpit slowly turned bright red.

*

Four days later, there was a knock on Kath's door. She opened it to a stranger, in seaman's garb.

"Mrs. Hornigold? My name's Daniel Stilwell," he said, sticking out his hand.

"Come in, Mr. Stilwell. What is it?"

"Maybe we should sit down. I have some bad news."

Kath led the way into the parlor, her heart thumping. "It's about my husband, isn't it?"

Stilwell nodded. "We found him drifting out by Booby Rocks. We were coming in from Eleuthera yesterday when my son spotted the boat half sunk in the water. We went over to check on her. I said she was Captain Hornigold's Bermuda sloop right away. I'd seen her many times down at the wharf. Captain Hornigold used to live near us in Harbour Island a few years ago, so we knew him well."

"You only found the sloop? What of my husband?"

"He had tied himself to the stern of the boat. I reckon he got caught in that cold front that came through Monday afternoon. We had 50, 60-knot winds in Eleuthera, then it turned cold. Well, a good sailor would tie himself to the boat in case a wave washed him over or he slipped. He'd need to stay with the vessel."

"Did you bring him back? Where is he?"

"No, Ma'am. I'm sorry. He was in no fit state. It had been a couple of days, you see... I reckon it was the boom hit him in his head. The boom was swinging free when we found the sloop..." Mr. Stilwell took out a large red handkerchief and blew his nose. "We wrapped him in a jib sail, tied the anchor on, and gave him to the sea. We thought he would like that best, anyway. Captain Hornigold was never one for the land."

Kath nodded, her eyes filling. "No. You did the right thing, Mr. Stilwell."

"About the boat, Mrs. Hornigold..." Stilwell shifted uneasily. "We towed it in as salvage. I was going to the Vice-Admiralty Judge with it, but the Chief Pilot – you know, Mr. Turnley – he said you might like the chance to pay me instead."

Kath dropped her head in her hands for a moment, then looked blankly at Stilwell. "I can't think, Mr. Stilwell. It's such a shock. Can I let you know?"

"Yes, Ma'am. I'm staying at the Wheel of Fortune for a few days."

"How much would you want?"

Stilwell dropped his eyes. "Twenty-five pounds? She's a fine sloop...."

"That's a lot of money, Mr. Stilwell. I must think about it, and talk to George Rounsivel." Kath stood up, unsteadily. "You're sure it was Captain Hornigold? It couldn't have been someone else?"

"Yes, Ma'am," he said, nodding. "It was Captain Hornigold, in the *Songbird*. As I say, we knew him well. I'm sorry."

Kath closed the door behind Daniel Stilwell and went out on the back porch. She sat in Ben's favorite chair and looked out to sea, over the western entrance to Nassau harbor, beyond the black Atlantic to the horizon. Slowly she turned her eyes along the panorama of Hog Island, down to the eastern end of the harbor. It was hard to understand that Ben would never sit here again with his pipe and his bowl of punch, would never squint down his spyglass at white sails in the west, and wonder which ship was coming in. He was gone, passed into eternity.

Four days ago. And she'd had no inkling, no intuition that he no longer existed in the world.

Well, why should his spirit seek her out after death? She had never loved him as a wife should. Their marriage had come to mean an uneasy truce. She had done her duty, kept his home and seen to his comfort as far as she could, but there had been no intimacy. She had never surrendered her inner being to Benjamin Hornigold. Right from the start, she had stood outside of her body, as it were, watching herself from a distance. Perhaps that was the reason Ben drank. He had tried to reach a phantom, a wife who had never been there.

No. His death was not her fault. He had died in the ideal way for him, in his sloop, riding out a storm. If he could no longer enjoy the view from his house, he was also beyond his fits of boredom on land, beyond the soul-sickness that drove him to drink himself unconscious. He would no longer rant, and swear, and bellow songs; no longer wake to the horror of that accursed thirst again. She would hunt out her rosary and say some prayers for him. That's all she could do for him now.

Then her heart skipped a beat. She was free again, free to marry Greville. Kath checked the thought quickly. She must not think like that! Greville had never given her any encouragement to hope, before her marriage nor since. He had not even been to call on her, not once. She had probably imagined his interest that day she'd confronted him with the ring. Kath pulled the ribbon from her bodice and looked at the ruby and diamond ring again, read its inscription for the millionth time. Greville *had* loved her, had bought this ring for her. He'd intended to ask her to marry him, just a little over a year ago.

But that was then. Did he still love her now?

52

The New Year, 1719, wore on with more changes. Kath made herself a handsome mourning dress and wore it every day as a penance. But gradually she realized that she missed Ben, missed his humor and rough gallantry towards her. In short, she missed Ben when he was sober. As the weeks passed, however, so did the sharp memory of Ben when he was drunk.

George had bargained Mr. Stilwell down to fourteen pounds for the *Songbird.* He had reminded Stilwell of how Hornigold had rescued him from being hanged as a pirate a few years before, when Judge Walker was sending him for trial in Jamaica. Hornigold had intercepted the ship and freed Stilwell, taking him safely home to his family in Harbour Island. Hornigold had destroyed the Judge's careful paperwork, too, so no charge could subsequently be laid against Stilwell. Surely that was worth being reasonable with his widow now, over the redemption of *Songbird?*

George careened *Songbird* with a swarm of small boys to help, and used her to teach them how to sail. Occasionally Kath joined George and Shirley in an afternoon sail, and eventually she stopped feeling sad about Ben when she stepped aboard his boat.

She could not stop being sad about her love for Greville Knowles, however. He had not written, nor come to see her. He seemed to have dropped off the edge of the world. Where was he? What was he doing? Did he know about Hornigold's death? Was he involved with another woman by now, married even? Was he alive and safe?

Shirley and George started their school with a few children under the sapodilla tree in Kath's front yard, and Kath pitched in to help.

Governor Rogers was having a schoolroom built in town and appointed as Headmaster a Mr. Alexander, who had been a schoolteacher back in England. The new school was ready after Easter, when Shirley, George and their pupils all moved in. Kath spent most of her days alone after that. She spent the hot nights fretting for Greville, tossing with the frustration of not knowing where he was, and pining for him.

*

It was a stifling August day, with no wind. Kath went out on her shuttered front porch and flopped on a bench. Sunlight streamed in through the slats of the wooden louvres, making a geometric pattern on the floor. Damp tendrils of hair clung to her neck, perspiration trickled down her chest and made damp patches under her arms. She could hardly breathe. She waved a palmetto fan to and fro and tried to remember the cool green of Ireland, or a winter's snowy day.

Ireland seemed like a dream to her now. Did it really exist? What of Maggie and her children, of the friends she used to know – were they still alive? She had often wanted to write Maggie, but had no way of getting a letter to her. Should she think of going back to Ireland herself? She would have to wait four more years if she went, and pretend she had served her sentence. But what was there for her to go back to?

The sound of footsteps brought her out of her reverie. Someone was tramping in the dusty street beyond the front garden wall. She moved to peer out between the louvres. A tall man was slowly passing her house, with his head down and hands behind his back. Who could that be? *I hope he's not coming to see me*, she thought, but the man walked on by. A moment later he passed again, going in the opposite direction, then turned on his heel and passed a third time. Who was that? She squinted through the shutters again and caught her breath. It was *Greville Knowles*!

Kath threw open the porch door and jumped into the street in front of him.

"Surprise! What are you doing, walking up and down in front of my house, Captain Knowles? Are you trying to make a rut in the road?"

Greville started, and then his face broke into a joyous smile. "How long have you been watching me? You always manage to catch me off-guard!"

"Come in! It's too hot to be out today. Let's have some limeade... or a cup of tea. How are you? I was wondering if you were dead or alive, or if you had fallen off the earth!"

"I've been in Carolina, and Virginia; it was a long trip. I got back last night and just heard that Captain Hornigold had died. I was rehearsing my condolences, but now I've forgotten what I was going to say..." He looked intently into her eyes and took her hand. "How are you, my wench?" he asked tenderly. "Still in mourning, I see."

"Yes." She was dismayed at the quaver in her voice. "I thought that was the least I could do. Ben Hornigold was good to me."

"Do you miss him very much?" Now Greville's voice wavered, but Kath was too flustered to notice.

"Yes, I miss him. That is, I miss him somewhat... I miss the man he could have been. He drank heavily at times, you know..."

"My poor wench!" he exclaimed, alarmed. "He didn't hurt you, did he?"

"No, nothing like that."

Greville breathed a sigh of relief. "Thank God. If you only knew how often I've prayed that you'd be all right!"

She swayed slightly and his arms came up and caught her to him. "Oh Kath, Kath..." he said, his voice raw with emotion. "If you only knew..."

His heart pounded – or was it her own? "I *do* know, my love," she whispered. "I've longed for you so!"

His arms tightened, and her heart soared as she breathed in the woodsy smell of him, the scent she had searched for, with her nose buried in his pillow. Oh, it was delicious! One day she would tell him.

"I love you, Kath, I love you..." he breathed into her hair, kissing her forehead, her eyes, nose, and finally her lips.

When he lifted his head, his eyes were full of desire. "Please, my darling, never leave me. How I've suffered, these past twenty months!"

Kath leaned against him, almost swooning. He was trembling. "I'm weak at the knees," he said. "I've got to sit down."

They sat nestled together, with Kath on his lap. "I suppose I'm wicked to be so happy that another man is dead," Greville said. "I was at the Nancy Lou Lilly when Miz Nancy told me last night. I wanted to shout, and jig, and rush over to see you, but I thought better of it. The gossips would have had a field day. So I waited until a decent hour this morning to call. I was so excited at the thought of seeing you again, at the thought that you were *free!*"

He gave her a little squeeze. "I've been in agony, especially since that day on the wharf, when you showed me the ring and let me know your feelings. That you might have been mine, but for my stupid insecurities!" He stroked the curve of her cheek, and brushed her lips with his finger. "Do you still have it? The ring, I mean."

"Yes, it's right here, over my heart like I told you." Kath tugged on the ribbon and brought it out of her bodice.

"May I have it, please?"

"It's sewn on..."

"I have a knife."

He cut the ribbon, lifted her gently onto the bench beside him, and then kneeled before her. "Kath, will you marry me?"

"Yes! Oh yes!"

Solemnly he took her left hand and put the ring on her finger. "I know the date's wrong, but I don't want to waste another minute!"

"The date's fine!" she said, her face glowing. "My heart was always yours, but this is the date I knew that your heart was also mine!"

"It was yours from the moment I found you buried in the sand," he said, kissing her again.

"Can we marry at Christmas?" Greville asked. "Would that be too soon after Captain Hornigold's death?"

"It would be nearly a year. But can't we marry sooner?"

He sighed. "I wish we could – today! But I have to leave for Jamaica day after tomorrow, then go back to Charleston. I have some business to finish in Virginia, too. I want to resign as Captain of the *Swan*, perhaps sell my share in her. It will all take time. I have to find another captain. I've been thinking it through. I didn't sleep at all last night! We have so much to plan..."

Her eyes clouded. "Are you sure you want to come ashore, Greville? I wouldn't ask that of you. I saw what it did to Ben!"

"Yes, I'm sure. I want to be with you. I decided long ago that I'd give up the sea for a wife. It's too hard on a woman. I watched my mother suffer with my father away so much. Where would you like to live, my wench?"

"Anywhere you choose. Here, if you like. This house is very comfortable."

He dropped his eyes. "Yes, but it was Captain Hornigold's house. I can't give you such a nice one, Kath, but I'd like us to build our own house together. I don't want to take you to a dead husband's bed."

"Oh, we could have a new bed," she said, looking at him through the corner of her eyes. "But the one I have was hardly ever used."

"What do you mean?"

"Ours wasn't an intimate marriage. He was away a lot. I worked out that, of the fourteen months we were married, Ben was away seven months of it. And of the seven months we were together, Ben stayed on his sloop, or in a tavern, at least two months of that. Much of the remaining time, he was either involved in pirate politics, or discussions with the Governor, or whatever. And, as I told you, he drank a great deal.

Greville's smile lit up the shadowy porch. "Are you telling me...?"

Kath nodded. "I am the most neglected wife you are ever likely to meet!"

"Oh my poor wench!" he said laughing, and folding her in his arms. "And there I was, sweating blood, imagining the two of you together, trying desperately *not* to... when all along..." He stopped short, and gave her a smoldering look. "Remember that *I don't drink at all!*"

"I know," she said, and moistened her lips. "Can't we marry when you come back through from Jamaica? I could come with you to Charleston," she raced on. "We could have another couple of rooms built onto this house, too, while we're gone. It's not yet two years old, but if you don't like it..."

"I like it just fine! But I must find something to do, I must make money to keep you in the way you've become accustomed."

"Oh, don't worry about that!" Kath said lightly. "I am a very wealthy woman, with money here, and in a large account in Bermuda, in my own name! You will not have to work if you don't want to."

"I couldn't possibly live off your money. Or worse still, the ill-gotten money from your husband!"

"Greville, money is money. We have no idea who the money came from, so we are unable to pay it back. Money has no 'good or bad' to it, it's only how we use it that's good or bad. We can find a lot of good things to do with it. Will you accept that?"

"I'll have to think about it. But for the moment, it means I won't have to worry about where our next meal will come from!"

"Besides, Captain Knowles, I recall not having a thing to call my own, not even a piece of clothing, when you found me. You fed and clothed me, you gave me shelter, and your grandmother, the dearest thing in the world to you. Now it's my turn to give something back to you.

"We can work this out, Greville. What's yours will be mine, and what's mine, is already yours."

53

Kath got busy as soon as Greville left. They had decided to have a simple house wedding in October, when he came back from Jamaica.

As her wedding surprise for Greville, Kath hired men to build another spacious bedroom and a new mahogany bed. She altered the rose-pink Spanish dress again, copying a fashion illustration from London she had seen in Mr. Taylor's shop. Then Shirley helped her make cotton nightgowns, one for Kath and one for Greville, and new bed linen. Jacob, Jane and Susan cut grass and dried it in the sun on an old sail, to stuff into sacks of heavy cotton for a new mattress and pillows.

Kath threw off her mourning dress and sang as she worked. She stopped agonizing about her marriage to Ben and spent hours daydreaming about her future with Greville. She no longer worried about his being a well-to-do captain while she was a despised Irish Catholic convict. She was white and he was colored, which made her a cut above him in this society.

Kath was chagrined when she realized that, a year before, she would never have thought herself better than Greville simply because she was white. Nassau attitudes were rubbing off on her. She smiled ruefully to herself when she remembered how inadequate she felt when she had first met Captain Knowles. *And rightly so*, she thought.

Greville was educated, well-traveled, a fine sea captain and a successful man of business. He owned a share in the

Swan, and a house on Fortune Island. He was also handsome and charming, with gracious manners that belied his humble birth. She was only an indigent seamstress, and a convicted criminal as well. And a murderess as well! She had money now, but it had been gained through piracy and a dubious marriage to an alcoholic sea-robber. She could hardly take pride in that – but in this strange society, she had been lionized because she had killed a pirate! So many things were topsy-turvy.

It was not that she cared about race. She was marrying the man she adored, he loved her in return and that should be enough to ensure her happiness. However, there was a niggling feeling of discontent eating at her that she had not acknowledged before. Indeed, there had been no purpose in thinking about it before, when she was married to Ben. Now, though, as she stitched her bridal clothing, her mind kept returning to the problem like a tongue to a broken tooth. Greville was not a Roman Catholic.

She had asked Greville for Miz Eva's Bible and was at last fulfilling her promise to read a chapter each day. All through the past two years, though, things she had read for Miz Eva would pop into her mind. That book had changed the way she thought and acted, while she had been completely unaware. Of course Miz Eva knew this would happen; and since, on reflection, the change had been for the good, comforting her and bringing her hope, she was happy to renew the habit.

To Kath's astonishment, the Bible hardly mentioned the Blessed Mother, who seemed to be the crux of her own religion. She found nothing wrong with the teachings of the Protestant Bible, and accepted them as taught to her by Miz Eva. She also recalled that the evil Captain Vane and his company of degenerates had all claimed to be Catholic and vigorously supported the Catholic Pretender to the English throne. Being Catholic had not made them better people, by any means, and comparing the murderous Vane to a Greville Knowles! Well! There *was* no comparison.

Kath sighed. It seemed she could never escape religion.

It was the plague of her life. In Ireland, she had been persecuted for it. Here in this godless place no one seemed to care – except Greville. They had discussed the religious aspects of their union, and Greville had been adamant. He would continue to worship at the small Church of England chapel not far from her house, and hoped that she would join him.

Further, he wanted any children they might have to be Protestant.

How could she convert? To give up the One True Faith would damn her soul to hell. She winced inwardly as she thought of marrying a Protestant. Theirs would not be a marriage in the eyes of the true Church. She would be living in sin. It would be no better than her pirate marriage to Ben. She had to resign herself now to what had been unthinkable three years ago – and Greville had to, as well. They could not be married in church, since she was Catholic, which troubled him just as much as she minded marrying a Protestant.

Well, there was no Catholic church in these islands, no priest, no other Catholics even, certainly not that she would wish to associate with. If there had been, of course, she would still have married Greville. She was glad she did not have the choice. She hoped that the 'no choice' situation would speak for her at the Judgment Day, an argument she had already perfected to explain her marriage to Ben. At least Greville was not an *English* Protestant.

Nothing was perfect.

*

Greville spent an impatient three weeks sailing down to Jamaica. Providence was kind; the wind never died and no tropical storm held him up. He quickly off-loaded his cargo and took on freight at Kingston, then headed back to the Bahamas.

He could hardly believe his luck. At last, Kath was going to be his wife! She was the only woman he had ever hankered after. He looked around at his familiar cabin, his sturdy table and sea chest bolted to the floor. He would give it all up without a pang. He was weary of the constant traveling, the uncertainty of weather and cargoes, the delays and tedium that were inevitable in a sailor's life. He grinned at the thought of his new career: *Greville Knowles, Planter.* Would he keep the 'Captain" appellation? He thought not. After all, he had not been a captain in the English Navy, or the Army.

His eyes followed the foamy wake of the *Swan* without seeing it. He would be so proud, introducing Kath to his business associates in Charleston. "This is my wife, Katherine," he would say, and Kath would tip her head in that charming way she had, and shake their hands. He'd take her to Bermuda, and maybe Virginia, too, one day.

Greville shifted in his chair. He had not told Kath what his business in Virginia had been. He had not wanted to raise any false hopes. He had taken cargo to Williamsburg and, while there, had appointed a Mr. John Brendan, Solicitor, to locate Kevin O'Brien, indentured servant of about seventeen years of age.

This was the reason he had been so long away from his usual commercial run, and why he could not take Kath with him to Charleston after the wedding. He wanted to go back to Virginia and find out if Brendan had any news. Greville had left money with Brendan to buy the boy's indentures from his master, and see he was properly housed, fed and clothed afterwards. However, if the lad had been found, and he was at any distance from Williamsburg, Greville would have to go and do the business himself.

Aside from Williamsburg there were no large towns in Virginia. All the plantations were settled along riverbanks, with their own docks for transporting their goods. Business was done by letter, or at church or other social gatherings. Finding Kevin might mean difficult traveling over rough terrain, on riverboats and horseback, with no lodgings or comforts available. He did not want to put Kath through that, especially if in the end he was unsuccessful.

Greville smiled to himself as he imagined walking into Kath's home with her son. If he *were* successful, what an incredible wedding present that would be for Kath!

*

When Greville docked the *Swan* at the wharf, Kath was there to meet him. He swung off the schooner and caught her up in his arms. "Did you miss me, wench?"

"So much! I could hardly stand it another second!"

He looked into her eyes. "Let's get married tomorrow. Have you spoken to the Magistrate?"

Kath blushed prettily. "Yes. It's Mr. Taylor – you know him, the owner of the general store on Bay Street? We can go now and confirm it for tomorrow, if you like."

His arm tightened around her waist. "I like! Then let's go to Nancy Lou Lilly for some dinner. You can talk to the old girls while I have a good wash. Can we invite them?"

"Of course. I also want to ask Shirley and George, and your crew on the *Swan*."

"Perfect." Greville helped Kath into the surrey. "I'm only sorry Gammie isn't here. She'll be smiling down on us, no doubt. She was always after me to marry you."

"Why didn't you ask me at Fortune Island?"

"I don't know. One day soon we can talk about it. Let's not ruin our happiness now with regrets about yesterday. But I realize that, if I had married you, Hornigold would not have been able to marry you and save you from his pirate company. You might have been a slave in Cuba now. So it's just as well things turned out as they did."

"Mr. Taylor's shop, Jacob," Kath said, settling into the seat. "Then we'll go to the Nancy Lou Lilly."

"Yes'um," Jacob replied, and slapped the reins over the horse's back.

"Can you still stay for ten days after the wedding?" Kath asked Greville.

"Yes. The crew will careen the boat over on Hog Island." He bent his lips to her ear and whispered "...while I careen you."

Kath's face blazed. Greville chuckled and looked at her

384

tenderly. "I'm glad you can still blush, even after being married to a pirate."

*

Kath and Greville were married at two o'clock the following afternoon. Greville could not take his eyes off her, as she floated amongst their guests in her pink gown. Everyone toasted the bride and groom, but soon left, including Shirley and George.

Alone at last, Greville and Kath were strangely shy with each other. He poured wine and they took it out onto the back porch to watch the sun set. Without speaking they leaned on the railing and looked over the harbor, watching a fishing smack sailing across the bar. Then Greville put down his glass and reached for her, holding her close against his heart. Kath inhaled his tantalizing scent, expelling her breath with a sigh.

"I've waited for this moment all my life," he said with a catch in his voice. "Now it's here, I don't know what to say. It seems sacred, somehow."

Kath snuggled closer and lifted her face for his kiss. "It's been a long trip, Cap'n Grev," she said huskily. "Don't you think it's time you did that careening you promised? I can take off all these sails, get rid of the cargo, and present my weedy bottom for scraping and caulking..."

"Good idea, First Mate," he said. Sweeping her up in his arms, he headed towards the new bedroom.

*

Their days together sped by, with lazy mornings and tender passionate nights. They went on excursions in the afternoons, picnics in the *Songbird*, or rode out to the small, makeshift fort being built at the eastern end of the harbor. They talked about Miz Eva and Fortune Island. Kath told Greville about her experiences with the Spanish, the pirates, how she came to shoot Jenks, and her introduction to the pirate life. Greville told her about Charleston, Jamaica and Port Royal, and Bermuda. They discussed plans for the future and

385

decided to go to Bermuda in the spring, so Kath could claim the money Ben had sent there with Captain Jennings.

One day at the end of the week, Kath was strangely withdrawn. "Why can't I come with you when you go to Charleston?" she asked, pouting. "Other captains take their wives with them sometimes."

"I've told you already, my darling," Greville replied gently. "I wish you could come, but I have nowhere to stay in Charleston, except on board. It's too cramped for you, especially with the crew living there as well."

"Couldn't we take lodgings at a boarding house?"

"I suppose so, but I have a lot of business to do. I wouldn't have time to be with you. Don't forget, I'm going to try and sell my share in the *Swan*, I have to find a new captain and all sorts of things. I also have to go back to Virginia, and that trip may take another month or even more. Besides, sailing can be quite rough in November. I'll be back as soon as I can, I promise."

"I realize it's not practical, but I wish I could go with you," Kath said reluctantly. "We've wasted so much time already, I don't want to be separated from you for another minute of my life. I feel like I might never see you again."

"Nonsense, wench, I'll try to be back in January. Of course, this time we're spending here now means I definitely can't get back for Christmas, but I'll be back, never fear."

Reluctantly she let him leave without her. After waving him off from the wharf, Kath went home and sat on her back porch. She watched as his sails slowly disappeared into the northwest.

*

Kath, Shirley and George had a special dinner on the 24th December to celebrate their first anniversary.

"Miz Kath, your appetite is good today," Shirley said. "I thought you said you weren't feeling well. Didn't you say you were coming down with a stomach sickness?"

"Yes, I was. I was feeling terrible every morning..." Kath

trailed off with a gasp. So that was the problem. She giggled. "I'm fine, Shirley. Never been better." She would have wonderful news for Greville when he got back, and they would cancel their plans for Bermuda.

So Christmas came and went uneventfully, with Kath hoping that Greville would come home in time for the New Year, by some miracle. He did not come. And not during the whole month of January. As February wore on, Kath made herself a new dress and started making other garments, very tiny ones. She sat on the back porch staring out to sea, her eyes raking the horizon for a sail. Where was Greville? What could have happened?

One afternoon she watched a British Navy warship, *HMS Flamborough*, arrive and anchor in the harbor.

"She has twenty-four guns, Miz Kath," George said excitedly. "We're going to take *Songbird* out and sail around her. Do you want to come?"

"No thanks, George. You two run along."

"Maybe I can get one of her crew to let me go aboard. I'd love to see her inside."

"Don't you dare, George Rounsivel," Shirley said hotly. "Before you know it, they'll be pressing you into the Navy and I'll never see you again! You know how those naval ships are. They're always undermanned. They use up men faster than chickens peck corn, especially here where fresh men die off so fast. They'd love to show you her inside, all right."

George grinned sheepishly. "I guess you're right, Shirley. I'll be careful. But let's go look at her now."

The two young people left in their usual chattering clatter, leaving Kath to her troubled thoughts. England and Spain were at war again, ever since the beginning of the year. Could that be what had happened to Greville? Had a Spanish privateer sunk the *Swan*? Even worse, had he been pressed into the Royal Navy while strolling along the waterfront in Charleston?

54

Early on the morning of 24th February, 1720, Kath was sitting on the back porch sewing, checking the northwest from time to time with Ben's spyglass. When Greville came back, it would be through the Northwest Providence Channel, which was the direction most ships came from. Her heart was heavy as usual these days, and her head was full of dire thoughts. God was punishing her for marrying a Protestant. She would have to raise a child all alone in this harsh world.

Now she fully understood why Greville had said that loving a sailor was so hard on a woman. This waiting day after day, never knowing whether her beloved was safe, or even alive, was unbearable. If he ever came back to her, she would support him whole-heartedly in anything he chose to do ashore.

She squinted through her glass again and her heart beat faster. There was a sail. It was a long way off and hard to see on the misty horizon, but she was sure it was a sail! A surge of hope rushed through her. That sail might be the *Swan*, might just be Greville coming home! Twenty minutes later, she checked again. There was not just one sail, but several. It looked almost like when Governor Rogers arrived, all those ships. Soon she could make out twelve sails. This was not good. She had better alert the Governor.

"Jacob, put the horse to the surrey. And hurry!" Kath ordered and ran back indoors to freshen up. She took another look through the glass before leaving the house. There were indeed twelve sails. They were small, still at a good distance.

The Governor's Secretary looked up as Kath bustled into the Mermaid's Tail. "Good morning, Mrs. Hornigold. You're in a rush today! Is anything the matter?"

"Yes, Mr. Gohier. I need to see Governor Rogers immediately. Is he in?"

"Yes, but he's busy right now, Mrs. Hornigold. Can I make an appointment?"

"Mr. Gohier, I am no longer Mrs. Hornigold. I am now married to Captain Greville Knowles. An appointment will be too late. The Spanish are coming. I live on West Hill Street, with a full view of the ocean. There are twelve sails headed towards us, and I think the Governor should know about them, don't you?"

Mr. Gohier started up from his chair. "Wait right here, Mrs. Knowles..." He rapped on the Governor's door and went in without waiting. A moment later, the Governor and Sir William Fairfax burst from the office.

"Oh, it's you, Mrs. Hornigold. I thought Mr. Gohier said a Mrs. Knowles... You've seen twelve ships coming in?"

"Yes, Sir. They're still a good way off, but I thought it best to tell you. I *am* Mrs. Knowles now, by the way."

"Indeed! Thank you for your prompt action. It may save the whole town." Kath bobbed a curtsy and turned to leave.

Governor Rogers began barking orders. "Gohier, call the Council immediately. Get Wingate Gale from the *Delicia* and Captain Hildesley from the *Flamborough*. Tell 'em all to meet me at the fort. I'll get Lieutenant McManus from the Garrison and sound the alarm. Mrs. Knowles..."

Kath stopped at the door when she heard her name. "Mrs. Knowles, please go home and keep a look-out. If we cannot see the ships from the fort, we'll come to your house."

At home again, Kath rushed to the back porch. There were definitely twelve ships, larger now, but still several hours away. She trained her spyglass down onto the fort and saw soldiers swarming on the battlements. A group of men was standing on the lookout tower, with glasses raised to their eyes. By now they'll be able to see the ships, she thought. Then she broke into a sweat. What would she do if the Spanish invaded the Island? She was alone, unprotected, and lived in one of the nicest houses here. She would have to leave, run into the bush again and lose everything. And what of her unborn baby?

She continued to watch the fort and the on-coming ships. The *Delicia* and *HMS Flamborough* moved their positions in the harbor and ran out their guns, ready for action. Soldiers were busy around the cannon in the fort, too. She did a quick count of guns. There were fifty in Fort Nassau, thirty-four on *Delicia* and twenty-four on *Flamborough*, and the eastern battery had at least two. That made one hundred and ten large guns to protect Nassau that she knew about. Would it be enough? At the very least, they could give the Spanish a hot reception.

George and Shirley came in from their school. "Everyone's in an uproar down town," George said. "I've come to ask if I can take *Songbird* over to Harbour Island and Eleuthera, to alert them. Governor Rogers wants every able-bodied man to come to New Providence and help with defense. I doubt they'll leave their own homes and families unprotected, but that's what the Governor wants me to do. Is it all right?" His eyes shone with excitement.

"Of course, George," Kath replied. "Take Jacob to help you provision. Who's going with you?"

"Craddock and Inkley – you know, old shipmates from the *Bonnet*."

"Good. You'd better hurry. Did you see the ships coming in? Here, look..." she handed him the spyglass.

George whistled. "Looks like three frigates, a brigantine, and eight sloops-of-war! Let's see, that means they have about...1,300 men at least!" He calculated. "I'd better get going. Hope I can get back. Once the Spanish get here, they're likely to blockade the harbor. But *Songbird* can come in the eastern end."

Shirley threw herself into a chair as George ran off. "Men have all the fun," she said. "I wish I was a man..."

"They do," Kath agreed. "Life's very hard for women. Shirley, maybe we should pack some things, in case we have to run into the bush as we did on Fortune Island. Let's get our food and clothes ready..."

*

The Spanish fleet sailed right up to the mouth of the harbor, then anchored outside the bar, well out of range of cannon shot. Everyone was relieved that the Spanish were not going to enter the harbor – yet. However, about three o'clock in the afternoon, several of the sloops weighed anchor and headed east, behind Hog Island. Governor Rogers quickly mobilized sentries along the eastern foreshore and sent men to the eastern battery. He only had about 500 men, but at least they were soldiers, sailors or ex-pirates, men who hated the Spanish and were eager to fight.

It was an anxious day for everyone, and night brought an uneasy quiet, but no rest. Even the stray dogs seemed to feel the tension and ceased their infernal barking. In the thick dark of midnight, the townspeople heard gunfire from the east and quaked in their beds, wondering if the morning would find the dreaded Spanish at their doors. Just before dawn there was more firing, this time from the west.

People thronged Bay Street in the morning, eagerly listening to the heroes of the night. In the east, two sentries had enthusiastically peppered boatloads of the Spanish with musket fire, discouraging them from landing, while a group of bloodthirsty ex-pirates had repelled a detachment of Spanish soldiers in the west. Morale soared, and for once the Governor was glad that his citizens were seasoned fighters rather than town-builders.

The Spanish fleet lurked outside the harbor for weeks, prowling about the islands at will, keeping a blockade on Nassau but not daring to attack the town or bothering with small fishing boats. However, the people of Nassau never knew if or when the Spanish might strike. By now, they knew the name of the Spanish commander. He was their old enemy,

391

Don Francisco de Cornego, out of Havana, Cuba.

*

Kath had lurid nightmares of Don Francisco jumbled with Hornigold and Greville. She woke sweating, with Ben's drunken laughter and Don Francisco's accented voice ringing in her ears. She would lie awake wondering if Greville were dead or alive. Knowing what had actually happened to him would be a relief, even if he were dead, she thought. Eventually she would fall asleep again, only to have more nightmares.

George came back safely from his mission after four days, which made one thing less to worry about. With school suspended during the crisis, George happily did his best for the security of the town along with the other men. Shirley stopped complaining about being a woman when George was on night watch and had to patrol, come cold, rain, moon or dark. Then she was glad to be a woman and stay in her cozy bed.

Twenty days into the Spanish blockade, Kath was scanning the horizon from her back porch as usual. She doubted the *Swan* could enter the harbor anyway, even if she came. What would Don Francisco do?

Would he plunder the cargo, like a privateer, taking it as the spoils of war? Maybe he would take the whole ship and put the crew ashore.

There was a knock at the door.

"Jane, answer the door," Kath called, not stirring from her chair. She heard the door close, but Jane did not come to call her. *Probably some tradesman*, Kath thought, continuing her inspection of the horizon. Slowly, an uneasy feeling crept over her, as though she was being inspected herself. Kath lowered the glass and turned – to see Captain Greville Knowles leaning in the doorway, observing her with glowing eyes.

"Watching for me, my darling?" he asked.

With a cry, Kath threw herself into his arms and buried her face in his chest, laughing and crying at the same time. "Where did you come from? How did you get here? I was so worried..." she stammered, when at last she could speak. "I never saw you come, and I've been watching constantly, since – since *Christmas*!"

"I know, my wench. It all took far longer than I hoped." He leaned away, studying her face, brushing her hair back. "You look well – quite rosy – and plump! And here I was, thinking you'd be pining for me, off your food! That puts me in my place!"

Kath nestled back into his arms again, squeezing him tight. "I have been pining and off my food. I was quite sick for a while..." She looked up into his face. "Then I realized that I needed to eat, and more than usual. I'm feeding two, you see..."

Greville's puzzled look changed to astonishment. "You mean – you don't mean..."

Kath nodded. "We're going to have a baby!"

"Oh Kath! Kath, my wench," he said, holding her closer still. "What a wonderful surprise!"

Kath giggled. "I thought you might like it," she said with a joyous lilt in her voice. "But how did you sneak past the Spanish blockade? I've been watching every day, at all hours."

"We were passing through the Berries, small islands to the northwest," he said, waving his arm in that direction. "A sloop out of Harbour Island hailed us and told us about the blockade. They suggested we keep well away from the harbor and anchor in a bay to the west of town, where some of the Governor's settlers have plantations. Since the *Swan* has a new captain, they were able to drop us off, unload some cargo and continue on to Jamaica. We came into town along the west bay track."

Susan came out then, with a pot of coffee, some johnnycake and jam. "You must be hungry, Cap'n Grev," she said, her eyes bright with affection. The slave woman went back to the kitchen and Kath turned to the tray.

"That's strange," she said. "Susan's put out three cups."

"Oh – I'd almost forgotten," Greville said, his face lighting up. "I have a surprise for you too, my wench. I was so amazed at your news, I completely forgot my own. I've brought some-one home to see you."

Kath's face fell. "You brought company, Greville? When we haven't been together for so long?"

Greville smiled. "This is company you'll be glad to see, I'll wager. Besides, it's not company – it's family. Sit down and I'll bring him in. He's waiting on the front porch." Greville disappeared inside.

"Are you sitting down, Kath?" he called.

"Yes!"

"Close your eyes!"

"All right! They're closed! Hurry! I can't stand another surprise!"

She heard footsteps crossing the porch and felt an eddy of air against her face.

"Open your eyes, my darling," Greville said.

She opened them, and gasped. "Kevin! Kevin, my son…"

"Hello, Mam…"

There he stood, taller by six inches, in smart new clothes. She could hardly believe her eyes. In a flash, they were in each other's arms. "Where did you come from?" she asked Kevin, then turned to Greville. "How did you find him?"

Greville chuckled, pleased with himself. "It wasn't easy," he said. "It's taken fifteen months in all. That's what I've been doing up in Virginia. Looking for Kevin."

"I was in the wilderness, Mam," Kevin said. "Miles from the coast. Captain Knowles came and got me."

"When I went back in November, we had news of him at last," Greville said. "I had to go to find him, then buy his in-dentures from his master. That's why I couldn't take you on this last trip, my wench," he said tenderly. "It was rough trav-eling, with mules and packs, through forests and wild Indians. Not where I could safely take you – especially not in your del-icate condition, as it turns out. Although leaving you here in Nassau nearly broke me apart! Finding Kevin is my wedding present to you."

Their eyes met and a warm current of love surged between

them. This was the dream that had kept her alive during those awful, hard times, ever since that morning more than three years ago in Ireland, when her life had suddenly changed.

Change was inevitable, she knew, but whatever happened during the rest of her life, she would remember this one moment as perfect.

She had her own family at last. She had the husband of her heart, her son, the hope of a new baby, and Shirley and George. And it was enough.

Made in the USA
Middletown, DE
17 December 2023

45866756R00221